Jack London

John Griffith London (born John Griffith Chaney; January 12, 1876 – November 22, 1916) was an American novelist, journalist, and social activist. A pioneer in the world of commercial magazine fiction, he was one of the first writers to become a worldwide celebrity and earn a large fortune from writing. He was also an innovator in the genre that would later become known as science fiction. His most famous works include The Call of the Wild and White Fang, both set in the Klondike Gold Rush, as well as the short stories "To Build a Fire", "An Odyssey of the North", and "Love of Life". He also wrote about the South Pacific in stories such as "The Pearls of Parlay" and "The Heathen". London was part of the radical literary group "The Crowd" in San Francisco and a passionate advocate of unionization, socialism, and the rights of workers. He wrote several powerful works dealing with these topics, such as his dystopian novel The Iron Heel, his non-fiction exposé The People of the Abyss, and The War of the Classes. (Source: Wikipedia)

Literary works:

The Cruise of the Dazzler (1902)
A Daughter of the Snows (1902)
The Call of the Wild (1903)
The Kempton-Wace Letters (1903)
The Sea-Wolf (1904)
The Game (1905)
White Fang (1906)
Before Adam (1907)
The Iron Heel (1908)
Martin Eden (1909)
Burning Daylight (1910)
Adventure (1911)
The Scarlet Plague (1912)
A Son of the Sun (1912)
The Abysmal Brute (1913)
The Valley of the Moon (1913)

THE COLLECTED WORKS
OF
JACK LONDON
VOL. 04 (OF 25)

THE RED ONE
THE NIGHT-BORN

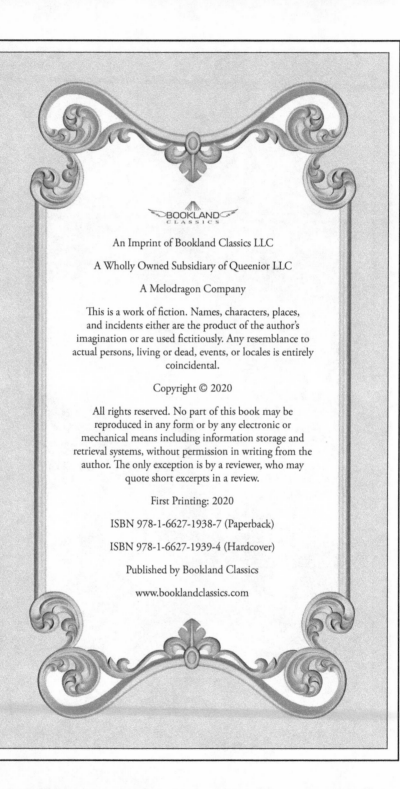

BOOKLAND
CLASSICS

An Imprint of Bookland Classics LLC

A Wholly Owned Subsidiary of Queenior LLC

A Melodragon Company

First Printing: 2020

ISBN 978-1-6627-1938-7 (Paperback)

ISBN 978-1-6627-1939-4 (Hardcover)

Published by Bookland Classics

www.booklandclassics.com

Contents

THE COLLECTED WORKS
OF
JACK LONDON
VOL. 04 (OF 25)

THE RED ONE

THE RED ONE

There it was! The abrupt liberation of sound! As he timed it with his watch, Bassett likened it to the trump of an archangel. Walls of cities, he meditated, might well fall down before so vast and compelling a summons. For the thousandth time vainly he tried to analyse the tone-quality of that enormous peal that dominated the land far into the strong-holds of the surrounding tribes. The mountain gorge which was its source rang to the rising tide of it until it brimmed over and flooded earth and sky and air. With the wantonness of a sick man's fancy, he likened it to the mighty cry of some Titan of the Elder World vexed with misery or wrath. Higher and higher it arose, challenging and demanding in such profounds of volume that it seemed intended for ears beyond the narrow confines of the solar system. There was in it, too, the clamour of protest in that there were no ears to hear and comprehend its utterance.

—Such the sick man's fancy. Still he strove to analyse the sound. Sonorous as thunder was it, mellow as a golden bell, thin and sweet as a thrummed taut cord of silver—no; it was none of these, nor a blend of these. There were no words nor semblances in his vocabulary and experience with which to describe the totality of that sound.

Time passed. Minutes merged into quarters of hours, and quarters of hours into half-hours, and still the sound persisted, ever changing from its initial vocal impulse yet never receiving fresh impulse—fading, dimming, dying as enormously as it had sprung into being. It became a confusion of troubled mutterings and babblings and colossal whisperings. Slowly it withdrew, sob by sob, into whatever great bosom had birthed it, until it whimpered deadly whispers of wrath and as equally seductive whispers of delight, striving still to be heard, to convey some cosmic secret, some understanding of infinite import and value. It dwindled to a ghost of sound that had lost its menace and promise, and became a thing that pulsed on in the sick man's consciousness for minutes after it had ceased. When he could hear it no longer, Bassett glanced at his watch. An hour had elapsed ere that archangel's trump had subsided into tonal nothingness.

Was this, then, *his* dark tower?—Bassett pondered, remembering his Browning and gazing at his skeleton-like and fever-wasted hands. And the fancy made him smile—of Childe Roland bearing a slug-horn to his lips with an arm as feeble as his was. Was it months, or years, he asked himself, since he first heard that mysterious call on the beach at Ringmanu? To save himself he could not tell. The long sickness had been most long. In conscious count of time he knew of months, many of them; but he had no way of estimating the long intervals of delirium and stupor. And how fared Captain Bateman of the blackbirder *Nari*? he wondered; and had Captain Bateman's drunken mate died of delirium tremens yet?

From which vain speculations, Bassett turned idly to review all that had occurred since that day on the beach of Ringmanu when he first heard the sound and plunged into the jungle after it. Sagawa had protested. He could see him yet, his queer little monkeyish face eloquent with fear, his back burdened with specimen cases, in his hands Bassett's butterfly net and naturalist's shot-gun, as he quavered, in Bêche-de-mer English: "Me fella too much fright along bush. Bad fella boy, too much stop'm along bush."

Bassett smiled sadly at the recollection. The little New Hanover boy had been frightened, but had proved faithful, following him without hesitancy into the bush in the quest after the source of the wonderful sound. No fire-hollowed tree-trunk, that, throbbing war through the jungle depths, had been Bassett's conclusion. Erroneous had been his next conclusion, namely, that the source or cause could not be more distant than an hour's walk, and that he would easily be back by mid-afternoon to be picked up by the *Nari's* whale-boat.

"That big fella noise no good, all the same devil-devil," Sagawa had adjudged. And Sagawa had been right. Had he not had his head hacked off within the day? Bassett shuddered. Without doubt Sagawa had been eaten as well by the "bad fella boys too much" that stopped along the bush. He could see him, as he had last seen him, stripped of the shot-gun and all the naturalist's gear of his master, lying on the narrow trail where he had been decapitated barely the moment before. Yes, within a minute the thing had happened. Within a minute, looking back, Bassett had seen him trudging patiently along under his burdens. Then Bassett's own trouble had come upon him. He looked at the cruelly healed stumps of the first and second fingers of his left hand, then rubbed them softly into the indentation in the back of his skull. Quick as had been the flash of the long handled tomahawk, he had been quick enough to duck away his head and partially to deflect the stroke with his up-flung hand. Two fingers and a hasty scalp-wound had been the price he paid for his life. With one barrel of his ten-gauge shot-gun he had blown the life out of the bushman who had so nearly got him; with the other barrel he had peppered the bushmen bending over Sagawa, and had the pleasure of knowing that the major portion of the charge had gone into the one who leaped away with Sagawa's head. Everything had occurred in a flash. Only himself, the slain bushman, and what remained of Sagawa, were in the narrow, wild-pig run of a path. From the dark jungle on either side came no rustle of movement or sound of life. And he had suffered distinct and dreadful shock. For the first time in his life he had killed a human being, and he knew nausea as he contemplated the mess of his handiwork.

Then had begun the chase. He retreated up the pig-run before his hunters, who were between him and the beach. How many there were, he could not guess. There might have been one, or a hundred, for aught he saw of them. That some of them took to the trees and travelled along through the jungle roof he was certain; but at the most he never glimpsed more than an occasional flitting of shadows. No bow-strings twanged that he could hear; but every little while, whence discharged he knew not, tiny arrows whispered past him or struck tree-boles and fluttered to the ground beside him. They were bone-tipped and feather shafted, and the feathers, torn from the breasts of humming-birds, iridesced like jewels.

Once—and now, after the long lapse of time, he chuckled gleefully at the recollection—he had detected a shadow above him that came to instant rest as he turned his gaze upward. He could make out nothing, but, deciding to chance it, had fired at it a heavy charge of number five shot. Squalling like

15

an infuriated cat, the shadow crashed down through tree-ferns and orchids and thudded upon the earth at his feet, and, still squalling its rage and pain, had sunk its human teeth into the ankle of his stout tramping boot. He, on the other hand, was not idle, and with his free foot had done what reduced the squalling to silence. So inured to savagery has Bassett since become, that he chuckled again with the glee of the recollection.

What a night had followed! Small wonder that he had accumulated such a virulence and variety of fevers, he thought, as he recalled that sleepless night of torment, when the throb of his wounds was as nothing compared with the myriad stings of the mosquitoes. There had been no escaping them, and he had not dared to light a fire. They had literally pumped his body full of poison, so that, with the coming of day, eyes swollen almost shut, he had stumbled blindly on, not caring much when his head should be hacked off and his carcass started on the way of Sagawa's to the cooking fire. Twenty-four hours had made a wreck of him—of mind as well as body. He had scarcely retained his wits at all, so maddened was he by the tremendous inoculation of poison he had received. Several times he fired his shot-gun with effect into the shadows that dogged him. Stinging day insects and gnats added to his torment, while his bloody wounds attracted hosts of loathsome flies that clung sluggishly to his flesh and had to be brushed off and crushed off.

Once, in that day, he heard again the wonderful sound, seemingly more distant, but rising imperiously above the nearer war-drums in the bush. Right there was where he had made his mistake. Thinking that he had passed beyond it and that, therefore, it was between him and the beach of Ringmanu, he had worked back toward it when in reality he was penetrating deeper and deeper into the mysterious heart of the unexplored island. That night, crawling in among the twisted roots of a banyan tree, he had slept from exhaustion while the mosquitoes had had their will of him.

Followed days and nights that were vague as nightmares in his memory. One clear vision he remembered was of suddenly finding himself in the midst of a bush village and watching the old men and children fleeing into the jungle. All had fled but one. From close at hand and above him, a whimpering as of some animal in pain and terror had startled him. And looking up he had seen her—a girl, or young woman rather, suspended by one arm in the cooking sun. Perhaps for days she had so hung. Her swollen, protruding tongue spoke as much. Still alive, she gazed at him with eyes of terror. Past help, he decided, as he noted the swellings of her legs which advertised that the joints had been crushed and the great bones broken. He resolved to shoot her, and there the vision terminated. He could not remember whether he had or not, any more than could he remember how he chanced to be in that village, or how he succeeded in getting away from it.

Many pictures, unrelated, came and went in Bassett's mind as he reviewed that period of his terrible wanderings. He remembered invading another village of a dozen houses and driving all before him with his shot-gun save, for one old man, too feeble to flee, who spat at him and whined and snarled as he dug open a ground-oven and from amid the hot stones dragged forth a roasted pig that steamed its essence deliciously through its green-leaf wrappings. It was at this place that a wantonness of savagery had seized upon him. Having feasted, ready to depart with a hind-quarter of the pig in his hand, he deliberately fired the grass thatch of a house with his burning glass.

But seared deepest of all in Bassett's brain, was the dank and noisome jungle. It actually stank with evil, and it was always twilight. Rarely did a shaft of sunlight penetrate its matted roof a hundred feet overhead. And beneath that roof was an aerial ooze of vegetation, a monstrous, parasitic dripping of decadent life-forms that rooted in death and lived on death. And through all this he drifted, ever pursued by the flitting shadows of the anthropophagi, themselves ghosts of evil that dared not face him in battle but that knew that, soon or late, they would feed on him. Bassett remembered that at the time, in lucid moments, he had likened himself to a wounded bull pursued by plains' coyotes too cowardly to battle with him for the meat of him, yet certain of the inevitable end of him when they would be full gorged. As the bull's horns and stamping hoofs kept off the coyotes, so his shot-gun kept off these Solomon Islanders, these twilight shades of bushmen of the island of Guadalcanal.

Came the day of the grass lands. Abruptly, as if cloven by the sword of God in the hand of God, the jungle terminated. The edge of it, perpendicular and as black as the infamy of it, was a hundred feet up and down. And, beginning at the edge of it, grew the grass—sweet, soft, tender, pasture grass that would have delighted the eyes and beasts of any husbandman and that extended, on and on, for leagues and leagues of velvet verdure, to the backbone of the great island, the towering mountain range flung up by some ancient earth-cataclysm, serrated and gullied but not yet erased by the erosive tropic rains. But the grass! He had crawled into it a dozen yards, buried his face in it, smelled it, and broken down in a fit of involuntary weeping.

And, while he wept, the wonderful sound had pealed forth—if by *peal*, he had often thought since, an adequate description could be given of the enunciation of so vast a sound melting sweet. Sweet it was, as no sound ever heard. Vast it was, of so mighty a resonance that it might have proceeded from some brazen-throated monster. And yet it called to him across that leagues-wide savannah, and was like a benediction to his long-suffering, pain racked spirit.

He remembered how he lay there in the grass, wet-cheeked but no longer sobbing, listening to the sound and wondering that he had been able to hear it on the beach of Ringmanu. Some freak of air pressures and air currents, he reflected, had made it possible for the sound to carry so far. Such conditions might not happen again in a thousand days or ten thousand days, but the one day it had happened had been the day he landed from the *Nari* for several hours' collecting. Especially had he been in quest of the famed jungle butterfly, a foot across from wing-tip to wing-tip, as velvet-dusky of lack of colour as was the gloom of the roof, of such lofty arboreal habits that it resorted only to the jungle roof and could be brought down only by a dose of shot. It was for this purpose that Sagawa had carried the ten-gauge shot-gun.

Two days and nights he had spent crawling across that belt of grass land. He had suffered much, but pursuit had ceased at the jungle-edge. And he would have died of thirst had not a heavy thunderstorm revived him on the second day.

And then had come Balatta. In the first shade, where the savannah yielded to the dense mountain jungle, he had collapsed to die. At first she had squealed with delight at sight of his helplessness, and was for beating his brain out with a stout forest branch. Perhaps it was his very utter helplessness that had appealed to her, and perhaps it was her human curiosity that made her refrain. At any rate, she had refrained, for he opened his eyes again under the impending blow, and saw her studying him intently. What especially struck her about him were his blue eyes and white skin. Coolly she had squatted on her hams, spat on his arm, and with her finger-tips scrubbed away the dirt of days and nights of muck and jungle that sullied the pristine whiteness of his skin.

And everything about her had struck him especially, although there was nothing conventional about her at all. He laughed weakly at the recollection, for she had been as innocent of garb as Eve before the fig-leaf adventure. Squat and lean at the same time, asymmetrically limbed, string-muscled as if with lengths of cordage, dirt-caked from infancy save for casual showers, she was as unbeautiful a prototype of woman as he, with a scientist's eye, had ever gazed upon. Her breasts advertised at the one time her maturity and youth; and, if by nothing else, her sex was advertised by the one article of finery with which she was adorned, namely a pig's tail, thrust though a hole in her left ear-lobe. So lately had the tail been severed, that its raw end still oozed blood that dried upon her shoulder like so much candle-droppings. And her face! A twisted and wizened complex of apish features, perforated by upturned, sky-open, Mongolian nostrils, by a mouth that sagged from a huge upper-lip and faded precipitately into a retreating chin, by peering querulous eyes that blinked as blink the eyes of denizens of monkey-cages.

Not even the water she brought him in a forest-leaf, and the ancient and half-putrid chunk of roast pig, could redeem in the slightest the grotesque hideousness of her. When he had eaten weakly for a space, he closed his eyes in order not to see her, although again and again she poked them open to peer at the blue of them. Then had come the sound. Nearer, much nearer, he knew it to be; and he knew equally well, despite the weary way he had come, that it was still many hours distant. The effect of it on her had been startling. She cringed under it, with averted face, moaning and chattering with fear. But after it had lived its full life of an hour, he closed his eyes and fell asleep with Balatta brushing the flies from him.

19

When he awoke it was night, and she was gone. But he was aware of renewed strength, and, by then too thoroughly inoculated by the mosquito poison to suffer further inflammation, he closed his eyes and slept an unbroken stretch till sun-up. A little later Balatta had returned, bringing with her a half-dozen women who, unbeautiful as they were, were patently not so unbeautiful as she. She evidenced by her conduct that she considered him her find, her property, and the pride she took in showing him off would have been ludicrous had his situation not been so desperate.

Later, after what had been to him a terrible journey of miles, when he collapsed in front of the devil-devil house in the shadow of the breadfruit tree, she had shown very lively ideas on the matter of retaining possession of him. Ngurn, whom Bassett was to know afterward as the devil-devil doctor, priest, or medicine man of the village, had wanted his head. Others of the grinning and chattering monkey-men, all as stark of clothes and bestial of appearance as Balatta, had wanted his body for the roasting oven. At that time he had not understood their language, if by *language* might be dignified the uncouth sounds they made to represent ideas. But Bassett had thoroughly understood the matter of debate, especially when the men pressed and prodded and felt of the flesh of him as if he were so much commodity in a butcher's stall.

Balatta had been losing the debate rapidly, when the accident happened. One of the men, curiously examining Bassett's shot-gun, managed to cock and pull a trigger. The recoil of the butt into the pit of the man's stomach had not been the most sanguinary result, for the charge of shot, at a distance of a yard, had blown the head of one of the debaters into nothingness.

Even Balatta joined the others in flight, and, ere they returned, his senses already reeling from the oncoming fever-attack, Bassett had regained possession of the gun. Whereupon, although his teeth chattered with the ague and his swimming eyes could scarcely see, he held on to his fading consciousness until he could intimidate the bushmen with the simple magics of compass, watch, burning glass, and matches. At the last, with due emphasis, of solemnity and awfulness, he had killed a young pig with his shot-gun and promptly fainted.

Bassett flexed his arm-muscles in quest of what possible strength might reside in such weakness, and dragged himself slowly and totteringly to his feet. He was shockingly emaciated; yet, during the various convalescences of the many months of his long sickness, he had never regained quite the same degree of strength as this time. What he feared was another relapse such as he had already frequently experienced. Without drugs, without even quinine, he had managed so far to live through a combination of the most pernicious and most malignant of malarial and black-water fevers. But could he continue to endure? Such was his everlasting query. For, like the genuine scientist he was, he would not be content to die until he had solved the secret of the sound.

Supported by a staff, he staggered the few steps to the devil-devil house where death and Ngurn reigned in gloom. Almost as infamously dark and evil-stinking as the jungle was the devil-devil house—in Bassett's opinion. Yet therein was usually to be found his favourite crony and gossip, Ngurn, always willing for a yarn or a discussion, the while he sat in the ashes of death and in a slow smoke shrewdly revolved curing human heads suspended from the rafters. For, through the months' interval of consciousness of his long sickness, Bassett had mastered the psychological simplicities and lingual difficulties of the language of the tribe of Ngurn and Balatta and Vngngn— the latter the addle-headed young chief who was ruled by Ngurn, and who, whispered intrigue had it, was the son of Ngurn.

"Will the Red One speak to-day?" Bassett asked, by this time so accustomed to the old man's gruesome occupation as to take even an interest in the progress of the smoke-curing.

With the eye of an expert Ngurn examined the particular head he was at work upon.

"It will be ten days before I can say 'finish,'" he said. "Never has any man fixed heads like these."

Bassett smiled inwardly at the old fellow's reluctance to talk with him of the Red One. It had always been so. Never, by any chance, had Ngurn or any other member of the weird tribe divulged the slightest hint of any physical characteristic of the Red One. Physical the Red One must be, to emit the wonderful sound, and though it was called the Red One, Bassett could not be sure that red represented the colour of it. Red enough were the deeds and powers of it, from what abstract clues he had gleaned. Not alone, had Ngurn informed him, was the Red One more bestial powerful than the neighbour tribal gods, ever athirst for the red blood of living human sacrifices, but the neighbour gods themselves were sacrificed and tormented before him. He was the god of a dozen allied villages similar to this one, which was the central and commanding village of the federation. By virtue of the Red One many alien villages had been devastated and even wiped out, the prisoners sacrificed to the Red One. This was true to-day, and it extended back into old history carried down by word of mouth through the generations. When he, Ngurn, had been a young man, the tribes beyond the grass lands had made a war raid. In the counter raid, Ngurn and his fighting folk had made many prisoners. Of children alone over five score living had been bled white before the Red One, and many, many more men and women.

The Thunderer was another of Ngurn's names for the mysterious deity. Also at times was he called The Loud Shouter, The God-Voiced, The Bird-Throated, The One with the Throat Sweet as the Throat of the Honey-Bird, The Sun Singer, and The Star-Born.

Why The Star-Born? In vain Bassett interrogated Ngurn. According to that old devil-devil doctor, the Red One had always been, just where he was at present, for ever singing and thundering his will over men. But Ngurn's father, wrapped in decaying grass-matting and hanging even then over their heads among the smoky rafters of the devil-devil house, had held otherwise. That departed wise one had believed that the Red One came from out of the starry night, else why—so his argument had run—had the old and forgotten ones passed his name down as the Star-Born? Bassett could not but recognize something cogent in such argument. But Ngurn affirmed the long years of his long life, wherein he had gazed upon many starry nights, yet never had he found a star on grass land or in jungle depth—and he had looked for them. True, he had beheld shooting stars (this in reply to Bassett's contention); but likewise had he beheld the phosphorescence of fungoid growths and rotten meat and fireflies on dark nights, and the flames of wood-fires and of blazing candle-nuts; yet what were flame and blaze and glow when they had flamed and blazed and glowed? Answer: memories, memories only, of things which had ceased to be, like memories of matings accomplished, of feasts forgotten, of desires that were the ghosts of desires, flaring, flaming, burning, yet unrealized in achievement of easement and satisfaction. Where was the appetite of yesterday? the roasted flesh of the wild pig the hunter's arrow failed to slay? the maid, unwed and dead ere the young man knew her?

A memory was not a star, was Ngurn's contention. How could a memory be a star? Further, after all his long life he still observed the starry night-sky unaltered. Never had he noted the absence of a single star from its accustomed place. Besides, stars were fire, and the Red One was not fire—which last involuntary betrayal told Bassett nothing.

"Will the Red One speak to-morrow?" he queried.

Ngurn shrugged his shoulders as who should say.

"And the day after?—and the day after that?" Bassett persisted.

"I would like to have the curing of your head," Ngurn changed the subject. "It is different from any other head. No devil-devil has a head like it. Besides, I would cure it well. I would take months and months. The moons would come and the moons would go, and the smoke would be very slow, and I should myself gather the materials for the curing smoke. The skin would not wrinkle. It would be as smooth as your skin now."

He stood up, and from the dim rafters, grimed with the smoking of countless heads, where day was no more than a gloom, took down a matting-wrapped parcel and began to open it.

"It is a head like yours," he said, "but it is poorly cured."

Bassett had pricked up his ears at the suggestion that it was a white man's head; for he had long since come to accept that these jungle-dwellers, in the midmost centre of the great island, had never had intercourse with white men. Certainly he had found them without the almost universal bêche-de-mer English of the west South Pacific. Nor had they knowledge of tobacco, nor of gunpowder. Their few precious knives, made from lengths of hoop-iron, and their few and more precious tomahawks from cheap trade hatchets, he had surmised they had captured in war from the bushmen of the jungle beyond the grass lands, and that they, in turn, had similarly gained them from the salt-water men who fringed the coral beaches of the shore and had contact with the occasional white men.

"The folk in the out beyond do not know how to cure heads," old Ngurn explained, as he drew forth from the filthy matting and placed in Bassett's hands an indubitable white man's head.

Ancient it was beyond question; white it was as the blond hair attested. He could have sworn it once belonged to an Englishman, and to an Englishman of long before by token of the heavy gold circlets still threaded in the withered ear-lobes.

"Now your head . . . " the devil-devil doctor began on his favourite topic.

"I'll tell you what," Bassett interrupted, struck by a new idea. "When I die I'll let you have my head to cure, if, first, you take me to look upon the Red One."

"I will have your head anyway when you are dead," Ngurn rejected the proposition. He added, with the brutal frankness of the savage: "Besides, you have not long to live. You are almost a dead man now. You will grow less strong. In not many months I shall have you here turning and turning in the smoke. It is pleasant, through the long afternoons, to turn the head of one you have known as well as I know you. And I shall talk to you and tell you the many secrets you want to know. Which will not matter, for you will be dead."

"Ngurn," Bassett threatened in sudden anger. "You know the Baby Thunder in the Iron that is mine." (This was in reference to his all-potent and all-awful shotgun.) "I can kill you any time, and then you will not get my head."

24

"Just the same, will Vngngn, or some one else of my folk get it," Ngurn complacently assured him. "And just the same will in the end turn devil-devil house in the smoke. The quicker you slay me with your Baby Thunder, the quicker will your head turn in the smoke."

And Bassett knew he was beaten in the discussion.

What was the Red One?—Bassett asked himself a thousand times in the succeeding week, while he seemed to grow stronger. What was the source of the wonderful sound? What was this Sun Singer, this Star-Born One, this mysterious deity, as bestial-conducted as the black and kinky-headed and monkey-like human beasts who worshipped it, and whose silver-sweet, bull-mouthed singing and commanding he had heard at the taboo distance for so long?

Ngurn had he failed to bribe with the inevitable curing of his head when he was dead. Vngngn, imbecile and chief that he was, was too imbecilic, too much under the sway of Ngurn, to be considered. Remained Balatta, who, from the time she found him and poked his blue eyes open to recrudescence of her grotesque female hideousness, had continued his adorer. Woman she was, and he had long known that the only way to win from her treason of her tribe was through the woman's heart of her.

Bassett was a fastidious man. He had never recovered from the initial horror caused by Balatta's female awfulness. Back in England, even at best the charm of woman, to him, had never been robust. Yet now, resolutely, as only a man can do who is capable of martyring himself for the cause of science, he proceeded to violate all the fineness and delicacy of his nature by making love to the unthinkably disgusting bushwoman.

He shuddered, but with averted face hid his grimaces and swallowed his gorge as he put his arm around her dirt-crusted shoulders and felt the contact of her rancid oily and kinky hair with his neck and chin. But he nearly screamed when she succumbed to that caress so at the very first of the courtship and mowed and gibbered and squealed little, queer, pig-like gurgly noises of delight. It was too much. And the next he did in the singular courtship was to take her down to the stream and give her a vigorous scrubbing.

From then on he devoted himself to her like a true swain as frequently and for as long at a time as his will could override his repugnance. But marriage, which she ardently suggested, with due observance of tribal custom, he balked at. Fortunately, taboo rule was strong in the tribe. Thus, Ngurn could never touch bone, or flesh, or hide of crocodile. This had been ordained at his birth. Vngngn was denied ever the touch of woman. Such pollution, did it chance to occur, could be purged only by the death of the offending female. It had happened once, since Bassett's arrival, when a girl of nine, running in play, stumbled and fell against the sacred chief. And the girl-child was seen no more. In whispers, Balatta told Bassett that she had been three days and nights in dying before the Red One. As for Balatta, the breadfruit was taboo to her. For which Bassett was thankful. The taboo might have been water.

For himself, he fabricated a special taboo. Only could he marry, he explained, when the Southern Cross rode highest in the sky. Knowing his astronomy, he thus gained a reprieve of nearly nine months; and he was confident that within that time he would either be dead or escaped to the coast with full knowledge of the Red One and of the source of the Red One's wonderful voice. At first he had fancied the Red One to be some colossal statue, like Memnon, rendered vocal under certain temperature conditions of sunlight. But when, after a war raid, a batch of prisoners was brought in and the sacrifice made at night, in the midst of rain, when the sun could play no part, the Red One had been more vocal than usual, Bassett discarded that hypothesis.

In company with Balatta, sometimes with men and parties of women, the freedom of the jungle was his for three quadrants of the compass. But the fourth quadrant, which contained the Red One's abiding place, was taboo. He made more thorough love to Balatta—also saw to it that she scrubbed herself more frequently. Eternal female she was, capable of any treason for the sake of love. And, though the sight of her was provocative of nausea and the contact of her provocative of despair, although he could not escape her awfulness in his dream-haunted nightmares of her, he nevertheless was aware of the cosmic verity of sex that animated her and that made her own life of less value than the happiness of her lover with whom she hoped to mate. Juliet or Balatta? Where was the intrinsic difference? The soft and tender product of ultra-civilization, or her bestial prototype of a hundred thousand years before her?—there was no difference.

Bassett was a scientist first, a humanist afterward. In the jungle-heart of Guadalcanal he put the affair to the test, as in the laboratory he would have put to the test any chemical reaction. He increased his feigned ardour for the bushwoman, at the same time increasing the imperiousness of his will of desire over her to be led to look upon the Red One face to face. It was the old story, he recognized, that the woman must pay, and it occurred when the two of them, one day, were catching the unclassified and unnamed little black fish, an inch long, half-eel and half-scaled, rotund with salmon-golden roe, that frequented the fresh water, and that were esteemed, raw and whole, fresh or putrid, a perfect delicacy. Prone in the muck of the decaying jungle-floor, Balatta threw herself, clutching his ankles with her hands kissing his feet and making slubbery noises that chilled his backbone up and down again. She begged him to kill her rather than exact this ultimate love-payment. She told him of the penalty of breaking the taboo of the Red One—a week of torture, living, the details of which she yammered out from her face in the mire until he realized that he was yet a tyro in knowledge of the frightfulness the human was capable of wreaking on the human.

Yet did Bassett insist on having his man's will satisfied, at the woman's risk, that he might solve the mystery of the Red One's singing, though she should die long and horribly and screaming. And Balatta, being mere woman, yielded. She led him into the forbidden quadrant. An abrupt mountain, shouldering in from the north to meet a similar intrusion from the south, tormented the stream in which they had fished into a deep and gloomy gorge. After a mile along the gorge, the way plunged sharply upward until they crossed a saddle of raw limestone which attracted his geologist's eye. Still climbing, although he paused often from sheer physical weakness, they scaled forest-clad heights until they emerged on a naked mesa or tableland. Bassett recognized the stuff of its composition as black volcanic sand, and knew that a pocket magnet could have captured a full load of the sharply angular grains he trod upon.

And then holding Balatta by the hand and leading her onward, he came to it—a tremendous pit, obviously artificial, in the heart of the plateau. Old history, the South Seas Sailing Directions, scores of remembered data and connotations swift and furious, surged through his brain. It was Mendana who had discovered the islands and named them Solomon's, believing that he had found that monarch's fabled mines. They had laughed at the old navigator's child-like credulity; and yet here stood himself, Bassett, on the rim of an excavation for all the world like the diamond pits of South Africa.

But no diamond this that he gazed down upon. Rather was it a pearl, with the depth of iridescence of a pearl; but of a size all pearls of earth and time, welded into one, could not have totalled; and of a colour undreamed of in any pearl, or of anything else, for that matter, for it was the colour of the Red One. And the Red One himself Bassett knew it to be on the instant. A perfect sphere, full two hundred feet in diameter, the top of it was a hundred feet below the level of the rim. He likened the colour quality of it to lacquer. Indeed, he took it to be some sort of lacquer, applied by man, but a lacquer too marvellously clever to have been manufactured by the bush-folk. Brighter than bright cherry-red, its richness of colour was as if it were red builded upon red. It glowed and iridesced in the sunlight as if gleaming up from underlay under underlay of red.

In vain Balatta strove to dissuade him from descending. She threw herself in the dirt; but, when he continued down the trail that spiralled the pit-wall, she followed, cringing and whimpering her terror. That the red sphere had been dug out as a precious thing, was patent. Considering the paucity of members of the federated twelve villages and their primitive tools and methods, Bassett knew that the toil of a myriad generations could scarcely have made that enormous excavation.

He found the pit bottom carpeted with human bones, among which, battered and defaced, lay village gods of wood and stone. Some, covered with obscene totemic figures and designs, were carved from solid tree trunks forty or fifty feet in length. He noted the absence of the shark and turtle gods, so common among the shore villages, and was amazed at the constant recurrence of the helmet motive. What did these jungle savages of the dark heart of Guadalcanal know of helmets? Had Mendana's men-at-arms worn helmets and penetrated here centuries before? And if not, then whence had the bush-folk caught the motive?

Advancing over the litter of gods and bones, Balatta whimpering at his heels, Bassett entered the shadow of the Red One and passed on under its gigantic overhang until he touched it with his finger-tips. No lacquer that. Nor was the surface smooth as it should have been in the case of lacquer. On the contrary, it was corrugated and pitted, with here and there patches that showed signs of heat and fusing. Also, the substance of it was metal, though unlike any metal, or combination of metals, he had ever known. As for the colour itself, he decided it to be no application. It was the intrinsic colour of the metal itself.

He moved his finger-tips, which up to that had merely rested, along the surface, and felt the whole gigantic sphere quicken and live and respond. It was incredible! So light a touch on so vast a mass! Yet did it quiver under the finger-tip caress in rhythmic vibrations that became whisperings and rustlings and mutterings of sound—but of sound so different; so elusively thin that it was shimmeringly sibilant; so mellow that it was maddening sweet, piping like an elfin horn, which last was just what Bassett decided would be like a peal from some bell of the gods reaching earthward from across space.

He looked at Balatta with swift questioning; but the voice of the Red One he had evoked had flung her face downward and moaning among the bones. He returned to contemplation of the prodigy. Hollow it was, and of no metal known on earth, was his conclusion. It was right-named by the ones of old-time as the Star-Born. Only from the stars could it have come, and no thing of chance was it. It was a creation of artifice and mind. Such perfection of form, such hollowness that it certainly possessed, could not be the result of mere fortuitousness. A child of intelligences, remote and unguessable, working corporally in metals, it indubitably was. He stared at it in amaze, his brain a racing wild-fire of hypotheses to account for this far-journeyer who had adventured the night of space, threaded the stars, and now rose before him and above him, exhumed by patient anthropophagi, pitted and lacquered by its fiery bath in two atmospheres.

But was the colour a lacquer of heat upon some familiar metal? Or was it an intrinsic quality of the metal itself? He thrust in the blue-point of his pocket-knife to test the constitution of the stuff. Instantly the entire sphere burst into a mighty whispering, sharp with protest, almost twanging goldenly, if a whisper could possibly be considered to twang, rising higher, sinking deeper, the two extremes of the registry of sound threatening to complete the circle and coalesce into the bull-mouthed thundering he had so often heard beyond the taboo distance.

Forgetful of safety, of his own life itself, entranced by the wonder of the unthinkable and unguessable thing, he raised his knife to strike heavily from a long stroke, but was prevented by Balatta. She upreared on her own knees in an agony of terror, clasping his knees and supplicating him to desist. In the intensity of her desire to impress him, she put her forearm between her teeth and sank them to the bone.

He scarcely observed her act, although he yielded automatically to his gentler instincts and withheld the knife-hack. To him, human life had dwarfed to microscopic proportions before this colossal portent of higher life from within the distances of the sidereal universe. As had she been a dog, he kicked the ugly little bushwoman to her feet and compelled her to start with him on an encirclement of the base. Part way around, he encountered horrors. Even, among the others, did he recognize the sun-shrivelled remnant of the nine-years girl who had accidentally broken Chief Vngngn's personality taboo. And, among what was left of these that had passed, he encountered what was left of one who had not yet passed. Truly had the bush-folk named themselves into the name of the Red One, seeing in him their own image which they strove to placate and please with such red offerings.

Farther around, always treading the bones and images of humans and gods that constituted the floor of this ancient charnel-house of sacrifice, he came upon the device by which the Red One was made to send his call singing thunderingly across the jungle-belts and grass-lands to the far beach of Ringmanu. Simple and primitive was it as was the Red One's consummate artifice. A great king-post, half a hundred feet in length, seasoned by centuries of superstitious care, carven into dynasties of gods, each superimposed, each helmeted, each seated in the open mouth of a crocodile, was slung by ropes, twisted of climbing vegetable parasites, from the apex of a tripod of three great forest trunks, themselves carved into grinning and grotesque adumbrations of man's modern concepts of art and god. From the striker king-post, were suspended ropes of climbers to which men could apply their strength and direction. Like a battering ram, this king-post could be driven end-onward against the mighty red-iridescent sphere.

Here was where Ngurn officiated and functioned religiously for himself and the twelve tribes under him. Bassett laughed aloud, almost with madness, at the thought of this wonderful messenger, winged with intelligence across space, to fall into a bushman stronghold and be worshipped by ape-like, man-eating and head-hunting savages. It was as if God's World had fallen into the muck mire of the abyss underlying the bottom of hell; as if Jehovah's Commandments had been presented on carved stone to the monkeys of the monkey cage at the Zoo; as if the Sermon on the Mount had been preached in a roaring bedlam of lunatics.

The slow weeks passed. The nights, by election, Bassett spent on the ashen floor of the devil-devil house, beneath the ever-swinging, slow-curing heads. His reason for this was that it was taboo to the lesser sex of woman, and therefore, a refuge for him from Balatta, who grew more persecutingly and perilously loverly as the Southern Cross rode higher in the sky and marked the imminence of her nuptials. His days Bassett spent in a hammock swung under the shade of the great breadfruit tree before the devil-devil house. There were breaks in this programme, when, in the comas of his devastating fever-attacks, he lay for days and nights in the house of heads. Ever he struggled to combat the fever, to live, to continue to live, to grow strong and stronger against the day when he would be strong enough to dare the grass-lands and the belted jungle beyond, and win to the beach, and to some labour-recruiting, black-birding ketch or schooner, and on to civilization and the men of civilization, to whom he could give news of the message from other worlds that lay, darkly worshipped by beastmen, in the black heart of Guadalcanal's midmost centre.

31

On the other nights, lying late under the breadfruit tree, Bassett spent long hours watching the slow setting of the western stars beyond the black wall of jungle where it had been thrust back by the clearing for the village. Possessed of more than a cursory knowledge of astronomy, he took a sick man's pleasure in speculating as to the dwellers on the unseen worlds of those incredibly remote suns, to haunt whose houses of light, life came forth, a shy visitant, from the rayless crypts of matter. He could no more apprehend limits to time than bounds to space. No subversive radium speculations had shaken his steady scientific faith in the conservation of energy and the indestructibility of matter. Always and forever must there have been stars. And surely, in that cosmic ferment, all must be comparatively alike, comparatively of the same substance, or substances, save for the freaks of the ferment. All must obey, or compose, the same laws that ran without infraction through the entire experience of man. Therefore, he argued and agreed, must worlds and life be appanages to all the suns as they were appanages to the particular of his own solar system.

Even as he lay here, under the breadfruit tree, an intelligence that stared across the starry gulfs, so must all the universe be exposed to the ceaseless scrutiny of innumerable eyes, like his, though grantedly different, with behind them, by the same token, intelligences that questioned and sought the meaning and the construction of the whole. So reasoning, he felt his soul go forth in kinship with that august company, that multitude whose gaze was forever upon the arras of infinity.

Who were they, what were they, those far distant and superior ones who had bridged the sky with their gigantic, red-iridescent, heaven-singing message? Surely, and long since, had they, too, trod the path on which man had so recently, by the calendar of the cosmos, set his feet. And to be able to send a message across the pit of space, surely they had reached those heights to which man, in tears and travail and bloody sweat, in darkness and confusion of many counsels, was so slowly struggling. And what were they on their heights? Had they won Brotherhood? Or had they learned that the law of love imposed the penalty of weakness and decay? Was strife, life? Was the rule of all the universe the pitiless rule of natural selection? And, and most immediately and poignantly, were their far conclusions, their long-won wisdoms, shut even then in the huge, metallic heart of the Red One, waiting for the first earth-man to read? Of one thing he was certain: No drop of red dew shaken from the lion-mane of some sun in torment, was the sounding sphere. It was of design, not chance, and it contained the speech and wisdom of the stars.

What engines and elements and mastered forces, what lore and mysteries and destiny-controls, might be there! Undoubtedly, since so much could be enclosed in so little a thing as the foundation stone of a public building, this enormous sphere should contain vast histories, profounds of research achieved beyond man's wildest guesses, laws and formulæ that, easily mastered, would make man's life on earth, individual and collective, spring up from its present mire to inconceivable heights of purity and power. It was Time's greatest gift to blindfold, insatiable, and sky-aspiring man. And to him, Bassett, had been vouchsafed the lordly fortune to be the first to receive this message from man's interstellar kin!

No white man, much less no outland man of the other bush-tribes, had gazed upon the Red One and lived. Such the law expounded by Ngurn to Bassett. There was such a thing as blood brotherhood. Bassett, in return, had often argued in the past. But Ngurn had stated solemnly no. Even the blood brotherhood was outside the favour of the Red One. Only a man born within the tribe could look upon the Red One and live. But now, his guilty secret known only to Balatta, whose fear of immolation before the Red One fast-sealed her lips, the situation was different. What he had to do was to recover from the abominable fevers that weakened him, and gain to civilization. Then would he lead an expedition back, and, although the entire population of Guadalcanal he destroyed, extract from the heart of the Red One the message of the world from other worlds.

But Bassett's relapses grew more frequent, his brief convalescences less and less vigorous, his periods of coma longer, until he came to know, beyond the last promptings of the optimism inherent in so tremendous a constitution as his own, that he would never live to cross the grass lands, perforate the perilous coast jungle, and reach the sea. He faded as the Southern Cross rose higher in the sky, till even Balatta knew that he would be dead ere the nuptial date determined by his taboo. Ngurn made pilgrimage personally and gathered the smoke materials for the curing of Bassett's head, and to him made proud announcement and exhibition of the artistic perfectness of his intention when Bassett should be dead. As for himself, Bassett was not shocked. Too long and too deeply had life ebbed down in him to bite him with fear of its impending extinction. He continued to persist, alternating periods of unconsciousness with periods of semi-consciousness, dreamy and unreal, in which he idly wondered whether he had ever truly beheld the Red One or whether it was a nightmare fancy of delirium.

Came the day when all mists and cob-webs dissolved, when he found his brain clear as a bell, and took just appraisement of his body's weakness. Neither hand nor foot could he lift. So little control of his body did he have, that he was scarcely aware of possessing one. Lightly indeed his flesh sat upon his soul, and his soul, in its briefness of clarity, knew by its very clarity that the black of cessation was near. He knew the end was close; knew that in all truth he had with his eyes beheld the Red One, the messenger between the worlds; knew that he would never live to carry that message to the world—that message, for aught to the contrary, which might already have waited man's hearing in the heart of Guadalcanal for ten thousand years. And Bassett stirred with resolve, calling Ngurn to him, out under the shade of the breadfruit tree, and with the old devil-devil doctor discussing the terms and arrangements of his last life effort, his final adventure in the quick of the flesh.

"I know the law, O Ngurn," he concluded the matter. "Whoso is not of the folk may not look upon the Red One and live. I shall not live anyway. Your young men shall carry me before the face of the Red One, and I shall look upon him, and hear his voice, and thereupon die, under your hand, O Ngurn. Thus will the three things be satisfied: the law, my desire, and your quicker possession of my head for which all your preparations wait."

To which Ngurn consented, adding:

"It is better so. A sick man who cannot get well is foolish to live on for so little a while. Also is it better for the living that he should go. You have

34

been much in the way of late. Not but what it was good for me to talk to such a wise one. But for moons of days we have held little talk. Instead, you have taken up room in the house of heads, making noises like a dying pig, or talking much and loudly in your own language which I do not understand. This has been a confusion to me, for I like to think on the great things of the light and dark as I turn the heads in the smoke. Your much noise has thus been a disturbance to the long-learning and hatching of the final wisdom that will be mine before I die. As for you, upon whom the dark has already brooded, it is well that you die now. And I promise you, in the long days to come when I turn your head in the smoke, no man of the tribe shall come in to disturb us. And I will tell you many secrets, for I am an old man and very wise, and I shall be adding wisdom to wisdom as I turn your head in the smoke."

So a litter was made, and, borne on the shoulders of half a dozen of the men, Bassett departed on the last little adventure that was to cap the total adventure, for him, of living. With a body of which he was scarcely aware, for even the pain had been exhausted out of it, and with a bright clear brain that accommodated him to a quiet ecstasy of sheer lucidness of thought, he lay back on the lurching litter and watched the fading of the passing world, beholding for the last time the breadfruit tree before the devil-devil house, the dim day beneath the matted jungle roof, the gloomy gorge between the shouldering mountains, the saddle of raw limestone, and the mesa of black volcanic sand.

Down the spiral path of the pit they bore him, encircling the sheening, glowing Red One that seemed ever imminent to iridesce from colour and light into sweet singing and thunder. And over bones and logs of immolated men and gods they bore him, past the horrors of other immolated ones that yet lived, to the three-king-post tripod and the huge king-post striker.

Here Bassett, helped by Ngurn and Balatta, weakly sat up, swaying weakly from the hips, and with clear, unfaltering, all-seeing eyes gazed upon the Red One.

"Once, O Ngurn," he said, not taking his eyes from the sheening, vibrating surface whereon and wherein all the shades of cherry-red played unceasingly, ever a-quiver to change into sound, to become silken rustlings, silvery whisperings, golden thrummings of cords, velvet pipings of elfland, mellow distances of thunderings.

"I wait," Ngurn prompted after a long pause, the long-handled tomahawk unassumingly ready in his hand.

"Once, O Ngurn," Bassett repeated, "let the Red One speak so that I may see it speak as well as hear it. Then strike, thus, when I raise my hand; for, when I raise my hand, I shall drop my head forward and make place for the stroke at the base of my neck. But, O Ngurn, I, who am about to pass out of the light of day for ever, would like to pass with the wonder-voice of the Red One singing greatly in my ears."

"And I promise you that never will a head be so well cured as yours," Ngurn assured him, at the same time signalling the tribesmen to man the propelling ropes suspended from the king-post striker. "Your head shall be my greatest piece of work in the curing of heads."

Bassett smiled quietly to the old one's conceit, as the great carved log, drawn back through two-score feet of space, was released. The next moment he was lost in ecstasy at the abrupt and thunderous liberation of sound. But such thunder! Mellow it was with preciousness of all sounding metals. Archangels spoke in it; it was magnificently beautiful before all other sounds; it was invested with the intelligence of supermen of planets of other suns; it was the voice of God, seducing and commanding to be heard. And—the everlasting miracle of that interstellar metal! Bassett, with his own eyes, saw colour and colours transform into sound till the whole visible surface of the vast sphere was a-crawl and titillant and vaporous with what he could not tell was colour or was sound. In that moment the interstices of matter were his, and the interfusings and intermating transfusings of matter and force.

Time passed. At the last Bassett was brought back from his ecstasy by an impatient movement of Ngurn. He had quite forgotten the old devil-devil one. A quick flash of fancy brought a husky chuckle into Bassett's throat. His shot-gun lay beside him in the litter. All he had to do, muzzle to head, was to press the trigger and blow his head into nothingness.

But why cheat him? was Bassett's next thought. Head-hunting, cannibal beast of a human that was as much ape as human, nevertheless Old Ngurn had, according to his lights, played squarer than square. Ngurn was in himself a forerunner of ethics and contract, of consideration, and gentleness in man. No, Bassett decided; it would be a ghastly pity and an act of dishonour to cheat the old fellow at the last. His head was Ngurn's, and Ngurn's head to cure it would be.

And Bassett, raising his hand in signal, bending forward his head as agreed so as to expose cleanly the articulation to his taut spinal cord, forgot Balatta, who was merely a woman, a woman merely and only and undesired. He knew, without seeing, when the razor-edged hatchet rose in the air behind him. And for that instant, ere the end, there fell upon Bassett the shadows of the Unknown, a sense of impending marvel of the rending of walls before the imaginable. Almost, when he knew the blow had started and just ere the edge of steel bit the flesh and nerves it seemed that he gazed upon the serene face of the Medusa, Truth—And, simultaneous with the bite of the steel on the onrush of the dark, in a flashing instant of fancy, he saw the vision of his head turning slowly, always turning, in the devil-devil house beside the breadfruit tree.

THE END

Waikiki, Honolulu,

May 22, 1916.

THE HUSSY

There are some stories that have to be true—the sort that cannot be fabricated by a ready fiction-reckoner. And by the same token there are some men with stories to tell who cannot be doubted. Such a man was Julian Jones. Although I doubt if the average reader of this will believe the story Julian Jones told me. Nevertheless I believe it. So thoroughly am I convinced of its verity that I am willing, nay, eager, to invest capital in the enterprise and embark personally on the adventure to a far land.

It was in the Australian Building at the Panama Pacific Exposition that I met him. I was standing before an exhibit of facsimiles of the record nuggets which had been discovered in the goldfields of the Antipodes. Knobbed, misshapen and massive, it was as difficult to believe that they were not real gold as it was to believe the accompanying statistics of their weights and values.

"That's what those kangaroo-hunters call a nugget," boomed over my shoulder directly at the largest of the specimens.

I turned and looked up into the dim blue eyes of Julian Jones. I looked up, for he stood something like six feet four inches in height. His hair, a wispy, sandy yellow, seemed as dimmed and faded as his eyes. It may have been the sun which had washed out his colouring; at least his face bore the evidence of a prodigious and ardent sun-burn which had long since faded to yellow. As his eyes turned from the exhibit and focussed on mine I noted a queer look in them as of one who vainly tries to recall some fact of supreme importance.

"What's the matter with it as a nugget?" I demanded.

The remote, indwelling expression went out of his eyes as he boomed

"Why, its size."

"It does seem large," I admitted. "But there's no doubt it's authentic. The Australian Government would scarcely dare—"

"Large!" he interrupted, with a sniff and a sneer.

"Largest ever discovered—" I started on.

"Ever discovered!" His dim eyes smouldered hotly as he proceeded. "Do you think that every lump of gold ever discovered has got into the newspapers and encyclopedias?"

"Well," I replied judicially, "if there's one that hasn't, I don't see how we're to know about it. If a really big nugget, or nugget-finder, elects to blush unseen—"

"But it didn't," he broke in quickly. "I saw it with my own eyes, and, besides, I'm too tanned to blush anyway. I'm a railroad man and I've been in the tropics a lot. Why, I used to be the colour of mahogany—real old mahogany, and have been taken for a blue-eyed Spaniard more than once—"

It was my turn to interrupt, and I did.

"Was that nugget bigger than those in there, Mr.—er—?"

"Jones, Julian Jones is my name."

He dug into an inner pocket and produced an envelope addressed to such a person, care of General Delivery, San Francisco; and I, in turn, presented him with my card.

"Pleased to know you, sir," he said, extending his hand, his voice booming as if accustomed to loud noises or wide spaces. "Of course I've heard of you, seen your picture in the papers, and all that, and, though I say it that shouldn't, I want to say that I didn't care a rap about those articles you wrote on Mexico. You're wrong, all wrong. You make the mistake of all Gringos in thinking a Mexican is a white man. He ain't. None of them ain't— Greasers, Spiggoties, Latin-Americans and all the rest of the cattle. Why, sir, they don't think like we think, or reason, or act. Even their multiplication table is different. You think seven times seven is forty-nine; but not them. They work it out different. And white isn't white to them, either. Let me give you an example. Buying coffee retail for house-keeping in one-pound or ten-pound lots—"

"How big was that nugget you referred to?" I queried firmly. "As big as the biggest of those?"

"Bigger," he said quietly. "Bigger than the whole blamed exhibit of them put together, and then some." He paused and regarded me with a steadfast gaze. "I don't see no reason why I shouldn't go into the matter with you. You've got a reputation a man ought to be able to trust, and I've read you've done some tall skylarking yourself in out-of-the-way places. I've been browsing around with an eye open for some one to go in with me on the proposition."

"You can trust me," I said.

And here I am, blazing out into print with the whole story just as he told it to me as we sat on a bench by the lagoon before the Palace of Fine Arts with the cries of the sea gulls in our ears. Well, he should have kept his appointment with me. But I anticipate.

As we started to leave the building and hunt for a seat, a small woman, possibly thirty years of age, with a washed-out complexion of the farmer's wife sort, darted up to him in a bird-like way, for all the world like the darting veering gulls over our heads and fastened herself to his arm with the accuracy and dispatch and inevitableness of a piece of machinery.

"There you go!" she shrilled. "A-trottin' right off and never givin' me a thought."

I was formally introduced to her. It was patent that she had never heard of me, and she surveyed me bleakly with shrewd black eyes, set close together and as beady and restless as a bird's.

"You ain't goin' to tell him about that hussy?" she complained.

"Well, now, Sarah, this is business, you see," he argued plaintively. "I've been lookin' for a likely man this long while, and now that he's shown up it seems to me I got a right to give him the hang of what happened."

The small woman made no reply, but set her thin lips in a needle-like line. She gazed straight before her at the Tower of Jewels with so austere an expression that no glint of refracted sunlight could soften it. We proceeded slowly to the lagoon, managed to obtain an unoccupied seat, and sat down with mutual sighs of relief as we released our weights from our tortured sightseeing feet.

"One does get so mortal weary," asserted the small woman, almost defiantly.

Two swans waddled up from the mirroring water and investigated us. When their suspicions of our niggardliness or lack of peanuts had been confirmed, Jones half-turned his back on his life-partner and gave me his story.

"Ever been in Ecuador? Then take my advice—and don't. Though I take that back, for you and me might be hitting it for there together if you can rustle up the faith in me and the backbone in yourself for the trip. Well, anyway, it ain't so many years ago that I came ambling in there on a rusty, foul-bottomed, tramp collier from Australia, forty-three days from land to land. Seven knots was her speed when everything favoured, and we'd had a two weeks' gale to the north'ard of New Zealand, and broke our engines down for two days off Pitcairn Island.

"I was no sailor on her. I'm a locomotive engineer. But I'd made friends with the skipper at Newcastle an' come along as his guest for as far as Guayaquil. You see, I'd heard wages was 'way up on the American railroad runnin' from that place over the Andes to Quito. Now Guayaquil—"

"Is a fever-hole," I interpolated.

Julian Jones nodded.

"Thomas Nast died there of it within a month after he landed.—He was our great American cartoonist," I added.

"Don't know him," Julian Jones said shortly. "But I do know he wasn't the first to pass out by a long shot. Why, look you the way I found it. The pilot grounds is sixty miles down the river. 'How's the fever?' said I to the pilot who came aboard in the early morning. 'See that Hamburg barque,'

41

said he, pointing to a sizable ship at anchor. 'Captain and fourteen men dead of it already, and the cook and two men dying right now, and they're the last left of her.'

"And by jinks he told the truth. And right then they were dying forty a day in Guayaquil of Yellow Jack. But that was nothing, as I was to find out. Bubonic plague and small-pox were raging, while dysentery and pneumonia were reducing the population, and the railroad was raging worst of all. I mean that. For them that insisted in riding on it, it was more dangerous than all the other diseases put together.

"When we dropped anchor off Guayaquil half a dozen skippers from other steamers came on board to warn our skipper not to let any of his crew or officers go ashore except the ones he wanted to lose. A launch came off for me from Duran, which is on the other side of the river and is the terminal of the railroad. And it brought off a man that soared up the gangway three jumps at a time he was that eager to get aboard. When he hit the deck he hadn't time to speak to any of us. He just leaned out over the rail and shook his fist at Duran and shouted: 'I beat you to it! I beat you to it!'

"'Who'd you beat to it, friend?' I asked. 'The railroad,' he said, as he unbuckled the straps and took off a big '44 Colt's automatic from where he wore it handy on his left side under his coat, 'I staved as long as I agreed— three months—and it didn't get me. I was a conductor.'

"And that was the railroad I was to work for. All of which was nothing to what he told me in the next few minutes. The road ran from sea level at Duran up to twelve thousand feet on Chimborazo and down to ten thousand at Quito on the other side the range. And it was so dangerous that the trains didn't run nights. The through passengers had to get off and sleep in the towns at night while the train waited for daylight. And each train carried a guard of Ecuadoriano soldiers which was the most dangerous of all. They were supposed to protect the train crews, but whenever trouble started they unlimbered their rifles and joined the mob. You see, whenever a train wreck occurred, the first cry of the spiggoties was 'Kill the Gringos!' They always did that, and proceeded to kill the train crew and whatever chance Gringo passengers that'd escaped being killed in the accident. Which is their kind of arithmetic, which I told you a while back as being different from ours.

"Shucks! Before the day was out I was to find out for myself that that ex-conductor wasn't lying. It was over at Duran. I was to take my run on the first division out to Quito, for which place I was to start next morning—only one through train running every twenty-four hours. It was the afternoon of my first day, along about four o'clock, when the boilers of the *Governor Hancock* exploded and she sank in sixty feet of water alongside the dock. She was the big ferry boat that carried the railroad passengers across the river to Guayaquil. It was a bad accident, but it was the cause of worse that followed. By half-past four, big trainloads began to arrive. It was a feast day and they'd run an excursion up country but of Guayaquil, and this was the crowd coming back.

"And the crowd—there was five thousand of them—wanted to get ferried across, and the ferry was at the bottom of the river, which wasn't our fault. But by the Spiggoty arithmetic, it was. 'Kill the Gringos!' shouts one of them. And right there the beans were spilled. Most of us got away by the skin of our teeth. I raced on the heels of the Master Mechanic, carrying one of his babies for him, for the locomotives that was just pulling out. You see, way down there away from everywhere they just got to save their locomotives in times of trouble, because, without them, a railroad can't be run. Half a dozen American wives and as many children were crouching on the cab floors along with the rest of us when we pulled out; and the Ecuadoriano soldiers, who should have been protecting our lives and property, turned loose with their rifles and must have given us all of a thousand rounds before we got out of range.

"We camped up country and didn't come back to clean up until next day. It was some cleaning. Every flat-car, box-car, coach, asthmatic switch engine, and even hand-car that mob of Spiggoties had shoved off the dock into sixty feet of water on top of the *Governor Hancock*. They'd burnt the round house, set fire to the coal bunkers, and made a scandal of the repair shops. Oh, yes, and there were three of our fellows they'd got that we had to bury mighty quick. It's hot weather all the time down there."

Julian Jones came to a full pause and over his shoulder studied the straight-before-her gaze and forbidding expression of his wife's face.

"I ain't forgotten the nugget," he assured me.

"Nor the hussy," the little woman snapped, apparently at the mud-hens paddling on the surface of the lagoon.

"I've been travelling toward the nugget right along—"

"There was never no reason for you to stay in that dangerous country," his wife snapped in on him.

"Now, Sarah," he appealed. "I was working for you right along." And to me he explained: "The risk was big, but so was the pay. Some months I earned as high as five hundred gold. And here was Sarah waiting for me back in Nebraska—"

"An' us engaged two years," she complained to the Tower of Jewels.

"—What of the strike, and me being blacklisted, and getting typhoid down in Australia, and everything," he went on. "And luck was with me on that railroad. Why, I saw fellows fresh from the States pass out, some of them not a week on their first run. If the diseases and the railroad didn't get them, then it was the Spiggoties got them. But it just wasn't my fate, even that time I rode my engine down to the bottom of a forty-foot washout. I lost my fireman; and the conductor and the Superintendent of Rolling Stock (who happened to be running down to Duran to meet his bride) had their heads knifed off by the Spiggoties and paraded around on poles. But I lay snug as a bug under a couple of feet of tender coal, and they thought I'd headed for tall timber—lay there a day and a night till the excitement cooled down. Yes, I was lucky. The worst that happened to me was I caught a cold once, and another time had a carbuncle. But the other fellows! They died like flies, what of Yellow Jack, pneumonia, the Spiggoties, and the railroad. The trouble was I didn't have much chance to pal with them. No sooner'd I get some intimate with one of them he'd up and die—all but a fireman named Andrews, and he went loco for keeps.

"I made good on my job from the first, and lived in Quito in a 'dobe house with whacking big Spanish tiles on the roof that I'd rented. And I never had much trouble with the Spiggoties, what of letting them sneak free rides in the tender or on the cowcatcher. Me throw them off? Never! I took notice, when Jack Harris put off a bunch of them, that I attended his funeral *muy pronto*—"

"Speak English," the little woman beside him snapped.

"Sarah just can't bear to tolerate me speaking Spanish," he apologized. "It gets so on her nerves that I promised not to. Well, as I was saying, the goose hung high and everything was going hunky-dory, and I was piling up my wages to come north to Nebraska and marry Sarah, when I run on to Vahna—"

"The hussy!" Sarah hissed.

"Now, Sarah," her towering giant of a husband begged, "I just got to mention her or I can't tell about the nugget.—It was one night when I was taking a locomotive—no train—down to Amato, about thirty miles from Quito. Seth Manners was my fireman. I was breaking him in to engineer for himself, and I was letting him run the locomotive while I sat up in his seat meditating about Sarah here. I'd just got a letter from her, begging as usual for me to come home and hinting as usual about the dangers of an unmarried man like me running around loose in a country full of senoritas and fandangos. Lord! If she could only a-seen them. Positive frights, that's what they are, their faces painted white as corpses and their lips red as—as some of the train wrecks I've helped clean up.

"It was a lovely April night, not a breath of wind, and a tremendous big moon shining right over the top of Chimborazo.—Some mountain that. The railroad skirted it twelve thousand feet above sea level, and the top of it ten thousand feet higher than that.

"Mebbe I was drowsing, with Seth running the engine; but he slammed on the brakes so sudden hard that I darn near went through the cab window.

"'What the—' I started to yell, and 'Holy hell,' Seth says, as both of us looked at what was on the track. And I agreed with Seth entirely in his remark. It was an Indian girl—and take it from me, Indians ain't Spiggoties by any manner of means. Seth had managed to fetch a stop within twenty feet of her, and us bowling down hill at that! But the girl. She—"

I saw the form of Mrs. Julian Jones stiffen, although she kept her gaze fixed balefully upon two mud-hens that were prowling along the lagoon shallows below us. "The hussy!" she hissed, once and implacably. Jones had stopped at the sound, but went on immediately.

"She was a tall girl, slim and slender, you know the kind, with black hair, remarkably long hanging, down loose behind her, as she stood there no more afraid than nothing, her arms spread out to stop the engine. She was wearing a slimpsy sort of garment wrapped around her that wasn't cloth but ocelot skins, soft and dappled, and silky. It was all she had on—"

"The hussy!" breathed Mrs. Jones.

But Mr. Jones went on, making believe that he was unaware of the interruption.

"'Hell of a way to stop a locomotive,' I complained at Seth, as I climbed down on to the right of way. I walked past our engine and up to the girl, and what do you think? Her eyes were shut tight. She was trembling that violent that you would see it by the moonlight. And she was barefoot, too.

"'What's the row?' I said, none too gentle. She gave a start, seemed to come out of her trance, and opened her eyes. Say! They were big and black and beautiful. Believe me, she was some looker—"

"The hussy!" At which hiss the two mud-hens veered away a few feet. But Jones was getting himself in hand, and didn't even blink.

"'What are you stopping this locomotive for?' I demanded in Spanish. Nary an answer. She stared at me, then at the snorting engine and then burst into tears, which you'll admit is uncommon behaviour for an Indian woman.

"'If you try to get rides that way,' I slung at her in Spiggoty Spanish (which they tell me is some different from regular Spanish), 'you'll be taking one smeared all over our cowcatcher and headlight, and it'll be up to my fireman to scrape you off.'

"My Spiggoty Spanish wasn't much to brag on, but I could see she understood, though she only shook her head and wouldn't speak. But great Moses, she was some looker—"

I glanced apprehensively at Mrs. Jones, who must have caught me out of the tail of her eye, for she muttered: "If she hadn't been do you think he'd a-taken her into his house to live?"

"Now hold on, Sarah," he protested. "That ain't fair. Besides, I'm telling this.—Next thing, Seth yells at me, 'Goin' to stay here all night?'

"'Come on,' I said to the girl, 'and climb on board. But next time you want a ride don't flag a locomotive between stations.' She followed along; but when I got to the step and turned to give her a lift-up, she wasn't there. I went forward again. Not a sign of her. Above and below was sheer cliff, and the track stretched ahead a hundred yards clear and empty. And then I spotted her, crouched down right against the cowcatcher, that close I'd almost stepped on her. If we'd started up, we'd have run over her in a second. It was all so nonsensical, I never could make out her actions. Maybe she was trying to suicide. I grabbed her by the wrist and jerked her none too gentle to her feet. And she came along all right. Women do know when a man means business."

I glanced from this Goliath to his little, bird-eyed spouse, and wondered if he had ever tried to mean business with her.

"Seth kicked at first, but I boosted her into the cab and made her sit up beside me—"

"And I suppose Seth was busy running the engine," Mrs. Jones observed.

"I was breaking him in, wasn't I?" Mr. Jones protested. "So we made the run into Amato. She'd never opened her mouth once, and no sooner'd the engine stopped than she'd jumped to the ground and was gone. Just like that. Not a thank you kindly. Nothing.

"But next morning when we came to pull out for Quito with a dozen flat cars loaded with rails, there she was in the cab waiting for us; and in the daylight I could see how much better a looker she was than the night before.

"'Huh! she's adopted you,' Seth grins. And it looked like it. She just stood there and looked at me—at us—like a loving hound dog that you love, that you've caught with a string of sausages inside of him, and that just knows you ain't going to lift a hand to him. 'Go chase yourself!' I told her *pronto*." (Mrs. Jones her proximity noticeable with a wince at the Spanish word.) "You see, Sarah, I'd no use for her, even at the start."

Mrs. Jones stiffened. Her lips moved soundlessly, but I knew to what syllables.

"And what made it hardest was Seth jeering at me. 'You can't shake her that way,' he said. 'You saved her life—' 'I didn't,' I said sharply; 'it was you.' 'But she thinks you did, which is the same thing,' he came back at me. 'And now she belongs to you. Custom of the country, as you ought to know.'"

"Heathenish," said Mrs. Jones, and though her steady gaze was set upon the Tower of Jewels I knew she was making no reference to its architecture.

"'She's come to do light housekeeping for you,' Seth grinned. I let him rave, though afterwards I kept him throwing in the coal too fast to work his mouth very much. Why, say, when I got to the spot where I picked her up, and stopped the train for her to get off, she just flopped down on her knees, got a hammerlock with her arms around my knees, and cried all over my shoes. What was I to do?"

With no perceptible movement that I was aware of, Mrs. Jones advertised her certitude of knowledge of what *she* would have done.

"And the moment we pulled into Quito, she did what she'd done before—vanished. Sarah never believes me when I say how relieved I felt to be quit of her. But it was not to be. I got to my 'dobe house and managed a cracking fine dinner my cook had ready for me. She was mostly Spiggoty and half Indian, and her name was Paloma.—Now, Sarah, haven't I told you she was older'n a grandmother, and looked more like a buzzard than a dove? Why, I couldn't bear to eat with her around where I could look at her. But she did make things comfortable, and she was some economical when it came to marketing.

"That afternoon, after a big long siesta, what'd I find in the kitchen, just as much at home as if she belonged there, but that blamed Indian girl. And old Paloma was squatting at the girl's feet and rubbing the girl's knees and legs like for rheumatism, which I knew the girl didn't have from the way I'd sized up the walk of her, and keeping time to the rubbing with a funny sort of gibberish chant. And I let loose right there and then. As Sarah knows, I never could a-bear women around the house—young, unmarried women, I mean. But it was no go! Old Paloma sided with the girl, and said if the girl went she went, too. Also, she called me more kinds of a fool than the English language has accommodation for. You'd like the Spanish lingo, Sarah, for expressing yourself in such ways, and you'd have liked old Paloma, too. She was a good woman, though she didn't have any teeth and her face could kill a strong man's appetite in the cradle.

"I gave in. I had to. Except for the excuse that she needed Vahna's help around the house (which she didn't at all), old Paloma never said why she stuck up for the girl. Anyway, Vahna was a quiet thing, never in the way. And she never gadded. Just sat in-doors jabbering with Paloma and helping with the chores. But I wasn't long in getting on to that she was afraid of something. She would look up, that anxious it hurt, whenever anybody called, like some of the boys to have a gas or a game of pedro. I tried to worm it out of Paloma what was worrying the girl, but all the old woman did was to look solemn and shake her head like all the devils in hell was liable to precipitate a visit on us.

"And then one day Vahna had a visitor. I'd just come in from a run and was passing the time of day with her—I had to be polite, even if she had butted in on me and come to live in my house for keeps—when I saw a queer expression come into her eyes. In the doorway stood an Indian boy. He looked like her, but was younger and slimmer. She took him into the kitchen and they must have had a great palaver, for he didn't leave until after dark. Inside the week he came back, but I missed him. When I got home, Paloma put a fat nugget of gold into my hand, which Vahna had sent him for. The blamed thing weighed all of two pounds and was worth more than five hundred dollars. She explained that Vahna wanted me to take it to pay for her keep. And I had to take it to keep peace in the house.

"Then, after a long time, came another visitor. We were sitting before the fire—"

"Him and the hussy," quoth Mrs. Jones.

"And Paloma," he added quickly.

"Him and his cook and his light housekeeper sitting by the fire," she amended.

"Oh, I admit Vahna did like me a whole heap," he asserted recklessly, then modified with a pang of caution: "A heap more than was good for her, seeing that I had no inclination her way.

"Well, as I was saying, she had another visitor. He was a lean, tall, white-headed old Indian, with a beak on him like an eagle. He walked right in without knocking. Vahna gave a little cry that was half like a yelp and half like a gasp, and flumped down on her knees before me, pleading to me with deer's eyes and to him with the eyes of a deer about to be killed that don't want to be killed. Then, for a minute that seemed as long as a life-time, she and the old fellow glared at each other. Paloma was the first to talk, in his own lingo, for he talked back to her. But great Moses, if he wasn't the high and mighty one! Paloma's old knees were shaking, and she cringed to him like a hound dog. And all this in my own house! I'd have thrown him out on his neck, only he was so old.

"If the things he said to Vahna were as terrible as the way he looked! Say! He just spit words at her! But Paloma kept whimpering and butting in, till something she said got across, because his face relaxed. He condescended to give me the once over and fired some question at Vahna. She hung her head, and looked foolish, and blushed, and then replied with a single word and a shake of the head. And with that he just naturally turned on his heel and beat it. I guess she'd said 'No.'

"For some time after that Vahna used to fluster up whenever she saw me. Then she took to the kitchen for a spell. But after a long time she began hanging around the big room again. She was still mighty shy, but she'd keep on following me about with those big eyes of hers—"

"The hussy!" I heard plainly. But Julian Jones and I were pretty well used to it by this time.

"I don't mind saying that I was getting some interested myself—oh, not in the way Sarah never lets up letting me know she thinks. That two-pound nugget was what had me going. If Vahna'd put me wise to where it came from, I could say good-bye to railroading and hit the high places for Nebraska and Sarah.

"And then the beans were spilled . . . by accident. Come a letter from Wisconsin. My Aunt Eliza 'd died and up and left me her big farm. I let out a whoop when I read it; but I could have canned my joy, for I was jobbed out of it by the courts and lawyers afterward—not a cent to me, and I'm still paying 'm in instalments.

"But I didn't know, then; and I prepared to pull back to God's country. Paloma got sore, and Vahna got the weeps. 'Don't go! Don't go!' That was her song. But I gave notice on my job, and wrote a letter to Sarah here—didn't I, Sarah?

"That night, sitting by the fire like at a funeral, Vahna really loosened up for the first time.

"'Don't go,' she says to me, with old Paloma nodding agreement with her. 'I'll show you where my brother got the nugget, if you don't go.' 'Too late,' said I. And I told her why.

"And told her about me waiting for you back in Nebraska," Mrs. Jones observed in cold, passionless tones.

"Now, Sarah, why should I hurt a poor Indian girl's feelings? Of course I didn't.

"Well, she and Paloma talked Indian some more, and then Vahna says: 'If you stay, I'll show you the biggest nugget that is the father of all other nuggets.' 'How big?' I asked. 'As big as me?' She laughed. 'Bigger than you,' she says, 'much, much bigger.' 'They don't grow that way,' I said. But she said she'd seen it and Paloma backed her up. Why, to listen to them you'd have

51

thought there was millions in that one nugget. Paloma 'd never seen it herself, but she'd heard about it. A secret of the tribe which she couldn't share, being only half Indian herself."

Julian Jones paused and heaved a sigh.

"And they kept on insisting until I fell for—"

"The hussy," said Mrs. Jones, pert as a bird, at the ready instant.

"'No; for the nugget. What of Aunt Eliza's farm I was rich enough to quit railroading, but not rich enough to turn my back on big money—and I just couldn't help believing them two women. Gee! I could be another Vanderbilt, or J. P. Morgan. That's the way I thought; and I started in to pump Vahna. But she wouldn't give down. 'You come along with me,' she says. 'We can be back here in a couple of weeks with all the gold the both of us can carry.' 'We'll take a burro, or a pack-train of burros,' was my suggestion. But nothing doing. And Paloma agreed with her. It was too dangerous. The Indians would catch us.

"The two of us pulled out when the nights were moonlight. We travelled only at night, and laid up in the days. Vahna wouldn't let me light a fire, and I missed my coffee something fierce. We got up in the real high mountains of the main Andes, where the snow on one pass gave us some trouble; but the girl knew the trails, and, though we didn't waste any time, we were a full week getting there. I know the general trend of our travel, because I carried a pocket compass; and the general trend is all I need to get there again, because of that peak. There's no mistaking it. There ain't another peak like it in the world. Now, I'm not telling you its particular shape, but when you and I head out for it from Quito I'll take you straight to it.

"It's no easy thing to climb, and the person doesn't live that can climb it at night. We had to take the daylight to it, and didn't reach the top till after sunset. Why, I could take hours and hours telling you about that last climb, which I won't. The top was flat as a billiard table, about a quarter of an acre in size, and was almost clean of snow. Vahna told me that the great winds that usually blew, kept the snow off of it.

"We were winded, and I got mountain sickness so bad that I had to stretch out for a spell. Then, when the moon come up, I took a prowl around. It didn't take long, and I didn't catch a sight or a smell of anything that looked like gold. And when I asked Vahna, she only laughed and clapped her hands. Meantime my mountain sickness tuned up something fierce, and I sat down on a big rock to wait for it to ease down.

"'Come on, now,' I said, when I felt better. 'Stop your fooling and tell me where that nugget is.' 'It's nearer to you right now than I'll ever get,' she answered, her big eyes going sudden wistful. 'All you Gringos are alike. Gold is the love of your heart, and women don't count much.'

"I didn't say anything. That was no time to tell her about Sarah here. But Vahna seemed to shake off her depressed feelings, and began to laugh and tease again. 'How do you like it?' she asked. 'Like what?' 'The nugget you're sitting on.'

"I jumped up as though it was a red-hot stove. And all it was was a rock. I felt nay heart sink. Either she had gone clean loco or this was her idea of a joke. Wrong on both counts. She gave me the hatchet and told me to take a hack at the boulder, which I did, again and again, for yellow spots sprang up from under every blow. By the great Moses! it was gold! The whole blamed boulder!"

Jones rose suddenly to his full height and flung out his long arms, his face turned to the southern skies. The movement shot panic into the heart of a swan that had drawn nearer with amiably predatory designs. Its consequent abrupt retreat collided it with a stout old lady, who squealed and dropped her bag of peanuts. Jones sat down and resumed.

"Gold, I tell you, solid gold and that pure and soft that I chopped chips out of it. It had been coated with some sort of rain-proof paint or lacquer made out of asphalt or something. No wonder I'd taken it for a rock. It was ten feet long, all of five feet through, and tapering to both ends like an egg. Here. Take a look at this."

From his pocket he drew and opened a leather case, from which he took an object wrapped in tissue-paper. Unwrapping it, he dropped into my hand a chip of pure soft gold, the size of a ten-dollar gold-piece. I could make out the greyish substance on one side with which it had been painted.

"I chopped that from one end of the thing," Jones went on, replacing the chip in its paper and leather case. "And lucky I put it in my pocket. For right at my back came one loud word—more like a croak than a word, in my way of thinking. And there was that lean old fellow with the eagle beak that had dropped in on us one night. And there was about thirty Indians with him—all slim young fellows.

"Vahna'd flopped down and begun whimpering, but I told her, 'Get up and make friends with them for me.' 'No, no,' she cried. 'This is death. Good-bye, *amigo*—'"

Here Mrs. Jones winced, and her husband abruptly checked the particular flow of his narrative.

"'Then get up and fight along with me,' I said to her. And she did. She was some hellion, there on the top of the world, clawing and scratching tooth and nail—a regular she cat. And I wasn't idle, though all I had was that hatchet and my long arms. But they were too many for me, and there was no place for me to put my back against a wall. When I come to, minutes after they'd cracked me on the head—here, feel this."

Removing his hat, Julian Jones guided my finger tips through his thatch of sandy hair until they sank into an indentation. It was fully three inches long, and went into the bone itself of the skull.

"When I come to, there was Vahna spread-eagled on top of the nugget, and the old fellow with a beak jabbering away solemnly as if going through some sort of religious exercises. In his hand he had a stone knife—you know, a thin, sharp sliver of some obsidian-like stuff same as they make arrow-heads out of. I couldn't lift a hand, being held down, and being too weak besides. And—well, anyway, that stone knife did for her, and me they didn't even do the honour of killing there on top their sacred peak. They chucked me off of it like so much carrion.

"And the buzzards didn't get me either. I can see the moonlight yet, shining on all those peaks of snow, as I went down. Why, sir, it was a five-hundred-foot fall, only I didn't make it. I went into a big snow-drift in a crevice. And when I come to (hours after I know, for it was full day when I next saw the sun), I found myself in a regular snow-cave or tunnel caused by the water from the melting snow running along the ledge. In fact, the stone above actually overhung just beyond where I first landed. A few feet more to the side, either way, and I'd almost be going yet. It was a straight miracle, that's what it was.

"But I paid for it. It was two years and over before I knew what happened. All I knew was that I was Julian Jones and that I'd been blacklisted in the big strike, and that I was married to Sarah here. I mean that. I didn't know anything in between, and when Sarah tried to talk about it, it gave me pains in the head. I mean my head was queer, and I knew it was queer.

"And then, sitting on the porch of her father's farmhouse back in Nebraska one moonlight evening, Sarah came out and put that gold chip into my hand. Seems she'd just found it in the torn lining of the trunk I'd brought back from Ecuador—I who for two years didn't even know I'd been to Ecuador, or Australia, or anything! Well, I just sat there looking at the chip in the moonlight, and turning it over and over and figuring what it was and where it'd come from, when all of a sudden there was a snap inside my head as if something had broken, and then I could see Vahna spread-eagled on that big nugget and the old fellow with the beak waving the stone knife, and . . . and everything. That is, everything that had happened from the time I first left Nebraska to when I crawled to the daylight out of the snow after they had chucked me off the mountain-top. But everything that'd happened after that I'd clean forgotten. When Sarah said I was her husband, I wouldn't listen to her. Took all her family and the preacher that'd married us to convince me.

"Later on I wrote to Seth Manners. The railroad hadn't killed him yet, and he pieced out a lot for me. I'll show you his letters. I've got them at the hotel. One day, he said, making his regular run, I crawled out on to the track. I didn't stand upright, I just crawled. He took me for a calf, or a big dog, at first. I wasn't anything human, he said, and I didn't know him or anything.

As near as I can make out, it was ten days after the mountain-top to the time Seth picked me up. What I ate I don't know. Maybe I didn't eat. Then it was doctors at Quito, and Paloma nursing me (she must have packed that gold chip in my trunk), until they found out I was a man without a mind, and the railroad sent me back to Nebraska. At any rate, that's what Seth writes me. Of myself, I don't know. But Sarah here knows. She corresponded with the railroad before they shipped me and all that."

Mrs. Jones nodded affirmation of his words, sighed and evidenced unmistakable signs of eagerness to go.

"I ain't been able to work since," her husband continued. "And I ain't been able to figure out how to get back that big nugget. Sarah's got money of her own, and she won't let go a penny—"

"He won't get down to *that* country no more!" she broke forth.

"But, Sarah, Vahna's dead—you know that," Julian Jones protested.

"I don't know anything about anything," she answered decisively, "except that *that* country is no place for a married man."

Her lips snapped together, and she fixed an unseeing stare across to where the afternoon sun was beginning to glow into sunset. I gazed for a moment at her face, white, plump, tiny, and implacable, and gave her up.

"How do you account for such a mass of gold being there?" I queried of Julian Jones. "A solid-gold meteor that fell out of the sky?"

"Not for a moment." He shook his head. " It was carried there by the Indians."

"Up a mountain like that—and such enormous weight and size!" I objected.

"Just as easy," he smiled. "I used to be stumped by that proposition myself, after I got my memory back. Now how in Sam Hill—' I used to begin, and then spend hours figuring at it. And then when I got the answer

I felt downright idiotic, it was that easy." He paused, then announced: "They didn't."

"But you just—said they did."

"They did and they didn't," was his enigmatic reply. "Of course they never carried that monster nugget up there. What they did was to carry up its contents."

He waited until he saw enlightenment dawn in my face.

"And then of course melted all the gold, or welded it, or smelted it, all into one piece. You know the first Spaniards down there, under a leader named Pizarro, were a gang of robbers and cut-throats. They went through the country like the hoof-and-mouth disease, and killed the Indians off like cattle. You see, the Indians had lots of gold. Well, what the Spaniards didn't get, the surviving Indians hid away in that one big chunk on top the mountain, and it's been waiting there ever since for me—and for you, if you want to go in on it."

And here, by the Lagoon of the Palace of Fine Arts, ended my acquaintance with Julian Jones. On my agreeing to finance the adventure, he promised to call on me at my hotel next morning with the letters of Seth Manners and the railroad, and conclude arrangements. But he did not call. That evening I telephoned his hotel and was informed by the clerk that Mr. Julian Jones and wife had departed in the early afternoon, with their baggage.

Can Mrs. Jones have rushed him back and hidden him away in Nebraska? I remember that as we said good-bye, there was that in her smile that recalled the vulpine complacency of Mona Lisa, the Wise.

THE END

Kohala, Hawaii,

May 5, 1916.

LIKE ARGUS OF THE ANCIENT TIMES

It was the summer of 1897, and there was trouble in the Tarwater family. Grandfather Tarwater, after remaining properly subdued and crushed for a quiet decade, had broken out again. This time it was the Klondike fever. His first and one unvarying symptom of such attacks was song. One chant only he raised, though he remembered no more than the first stanza and but three lines of that. And the family knew his feet were itching and his brain was tingling with the old madness, when he lifted his hoarse-cracked voice, now falsetto-cracked, in:

Like Argus of the ancient times,

We leave this modern Greece,

Tum-tum, tum-tum, tum, tum, tum-tum,

To shear the Golden Fleece.

Ten years earlier he had lifted the chant, sung to the air of the "Doxology," when afflicted with the fever to go gold-mining in Patagonia. The multitudinous family had sat upon him, but had had a hard time doing it. When all else had failed to shake his resolution, they had applied lawyers to him, with the threat of getting out guardianship papers and of confining him in the state asylum for the insane—which was reasonable for a man who had, a quarter of a century before, speculated away all but ten meagre acres of a California principality, and who had displayed no better business acumen ever since.

The application of lawyers to John Tarwater was like the application of a mustard plaster. For, in his judgment, they were the gentry, more than any other, who had skinned him out of the broad Tarwater acres. So, at the time of his Patagonian fever, the very thought of so drastic a remedy was sufficient to cure him. He quickly demonstrated he was not crazy by shaking the fever from him and agreeing not to go to Patagonia.

Next, he demonstrated how crazy he really was, by deeding over to his family, unsolicited, the ten acres on Tarwater Flat, the house, barn, outbuildings, and water-rights. Also did he turn over the eight hundred dollars in bank that was the long-saved salvage of his wrecked fortune. But for this the family found no cause for committal to the asylum, since such committal would necessarily invalidate what he had done.

"Grandfather is sure peeved," said Mary, his oldest daughter, herself a grandmother, when her father quit smoking.

All he had retained for himself was a span of old horses, a mountain buckboard, and his one room in the crowded house. Further, having affirmed that he would be beholden to none of them, he got the contract to carry the United States mail, twice a week, from Kelterville up over Tarwater Mountain to Old Almaden—which was a sporadically worked quick-silver mine in the upland cattle country. With his old horses it took all his time to make the two weekly round trips. And for ten years, rain or shine, he had never missed a trip. Nor had he failed once to pay his week's board into Mary's hand. This board he had insisted on, in the convalescence from his Patagonian fever, and he had paid it strictly, though he had given up tobacco in order to be able to do it.

"Huh!" he confided to the ruined water wheel of the old Tarwater Mill, which he had built from the standing timber and which had ground wheat for the first settlers. "Huh! They'll never put me in the poor farm so long as I support myself. And without a penny to my name it ain't likely any lawyer fellows'll come snoopin' around after me."

And yet, precisely because of these highly rational acts, it was held that John Tarwater was mildly crazy!

The first time he had lifted the chant of "Like Argus of the Ancient Times," had been in 1849, when, twenty-two years' of age, violently attacked by the Californian fever, he had sold two hundred and forty Michigan acres, forty of it cleared, for the price of four yoke of oxen, and a wagon, and had started across the Plains.

"And we turned off at Fort Hall, where the Oregon emigration went north'ard, and swung south for Californy," was his way of concluding the narrative of that arduous journey. "And Bill Ping and me used to rope grizzlies out of the underbrush of Cache Slough in the Sacramento Valley."

Years of freighting and mining had followed, and, with a stake gleaned from the Merced placers, he satisfied the land-hunger of his race and time by settling in Sonoma County.

During the ten years of carrying the mail across Tarwater Township, up Tarwater Valley, and over Tarwater Mountain, most all of which land had once been his, he had spent his time dreaming of winning back that land before he died. And now, his huge gaunt form more erect than it had been for years, with a glinting of blue fires in his small and close-set eyes, he was lifting his ancient chant again.

"There he goes now—listen to him," said William Tarwater.

"Nobody at home," laughed Harris Topping, day labourer, husband of Annie Tarwater, and father of her nine children.

The kitchen door opened to admit the old man, returning from feeding his horses. The song had ceased from his lips; but Mary was irritable from a burnt hand and a grandchild whose stomach refused to digest properly diluted cows' milk.

"Now there ain't no use you carryin' on that way, father," she tackled him. "The time's past for you to cut and run for a place like the Klondike, and singing won't buy you nothing."

"Just the same," he answered quietly. "I bet I could go to that Klondike place and pick up enough gold to buy back the Tarwater lands."

"Old fool!" Annie contributed.

"You couldn't buy them back for less'n three hundred thousand and then some," was William's effort at squelching him.

"Then I could pick up three hundred thousand, and then some, if I was only there," the old man retorted placidly.

"Thank God you can't walk there, or you'd be startin', I know," Mary cried. "Ocean travel costs money."

"I used to have money," her father said humbly.

"Well, you ain't got any now—so forget it," William advised. "Them times is past, like roping bear with Bill Ping. There ain't no more bear."

"Just the same—"

But Mary cut him off. Seizing the day's paper from the kitchen table, she flourished it savagely under her aged progenitor's nose.

"What do those Klondikers say? There it is in cold print. Only the young and robust can stand the Klondike. It's worse than the north pole. And they've left their dead a-plenty there themselves. Look at their pictures. You're forty years older 'n the oldest of them."

John Tarwater did look, but his eyes strayed to other photographs on the highly sensational front page.

"And look at the photys of them nuggets they brought down," he said. "I know gold. Didn't I gopher twenty thousand outa the Merced? And wouldn't it a-ben a hundred thousand if that cloudburst hadn't busted my wing-dam? Now if I was only in the Klondike—"

"Crazy as a loon," William sneered in open aside to the rest.

"A nice way to talk to your father," Old Man Tarwater censured mildly. "My father'd have walloped the tar out of me with a single-tree if I'd spoke to him that way."

"But you *are* crazy, father—" William began.

"Reckon you're right, son. And that's where my father wasn't crazy. He'd a-done it."

"The old man's been reading some of them magazine articles about men who succeeded after forty," Annie jibed.

"And why not, daughter?" he asked. "And why can't a man succeed after he's seventy? I was only seventy this year. And mebbe I could succeed if only I could get to the Klondike—"

"Which you ain't going to get to," Mary shut him off.

"Oh, well, then," he sighed, "seein's I ain't, I might just as well go to bed."

He stood up, tall, gaunt, great-boned and gnarled, a splendid ruin of a man. His ragged hair and whiskers were not grey but snowy white, as were the tufts of hair that stood out on the backs of his huge bony fingers. He moved toward the door, opened it, sighed, and paused with a backward look.

"Just the same," he murmured plaintively, "the bottoms of my feet is itching something terrible."

Long before the family stirred next morning, his horses fed and harnessed by lantern light, breakfast cooked and eaten by lamp fight, Old Man Tarwater was off and away down Tarwater Valley on the road to Kelterville. Two things were unusual about this usual trip which he had made a thousand and forty times since taking the mail contract. He did not drive to Kelterville, but turned off on the main road south to Santa Rosa. Even more remarkable than this was the paper-wrapped parcel between his feet. It contained his one decent black suit, which Mary had been long reluctant to see him wear any more, not because it was shabby, but because, as he guessed what was at the back of her mind, it was decent enough to bury him in.

And at Santa Rosa, in a second-hand clothes shop, he sold the suit outright for two dollars and a half. From the same obliging shopman he received four dollars for the wedding ring of his long-dead wife. The span of horses and the wagon he disposed of for seventy-five dollars, although twenty-five was all he received down in cash. Chancing to meet Alton Granger on the street, to whom never before had he mentioned the ten dollars loaned him in '74, he reminded Alton Granger of the little affair, and was promptly paid. Also, of all unbelievable men to be in funds, he so found the town drunkard for whom he had bought many a drink in the old and palmy days. And from him John Tarwater borrowed a dollar. Finally, he took the afternoon train to San Francisco.

A dozen days later, carrying a half-empty canvas sack of blankets and old clothes, he landed on the beach of Dyea in the thick of the great Klondike Rush. The beach was screaming bedlam. Ten thousand tons of outfit lay heaped and scattered, and twice ten thousand men struggled with it and clamoured about it. Freight, by Indian-back, over Chilcoot to Lake Linderman, had jumped from sixteen to thirty cents a pound, which latter was a rate of six hundred dollars a ton. And the sub-arctic winter gloomed near at hand. All knew it, and all knew that of the twenty thousand of them very few would get across the passes, leaving the rest to winter and wait for the late spring thaw.

Such the beach old John Tarwater stepped upon; and straight across the beach and up the trail toward Chilcoot he headed, cackling his ancient chant, a very Grandfather Argus himself, with no outfit worry in the world, for he did not possess any outfit. That night he slept on the flats, five miles above Dyea, at the head of canoe navigation. Here the Dyea River became a rushing mountain torrent, plunging out of a dark canyon from the glaciers that fed it far above.

And here, early next morning, he beheld a little man weighing no more than a hundred, staggering along a foot-log under all of a hundred pounds of flour strapped on his back. Also, he beheld the little man stumble off the log and fall face-downward in a quiet eddy where the water was two feet deep and proceed quietly to drown. It was no desire of his to take death so easily, but the flour on his back weighed as much as he and would not let him up.

"Thank you, old man," he said to Tarwater, when the latter had dragged him up into the air and ashore.

While he unlaced his shoes and ran the water out, they had further talk. Next, he fished out a ten-dollar gold-piece and offered it to his rescuer.

Old Tarwater shook his head and shivered, for the ice-water had wet him to his knees.

"But I reckon I wouldn't object to settin' down to a friendly meal with you."

"Ain't had breakfast?" the little man, who was past forty and who had said his name was Anson, queried with a glance frankly curious.

"Nary bite," John Tarwater answered.

"Where's your outfit? Ahead?"

"Nary outfit."

"Expect to buy your grub on the Inside?"

"Nary a dollar to buy it with, friend. Which ain't so important as a warm bite of breakfast right now."

In Anson's camp, a quarter of a mile on, Tarwater found a slender, red-whiskered young man of thirty cursing over a fire of wet willow wood. Introduced as Charles, he transferred his scowl and wrath to Tarwater, who, genially oblivious, devoted himself to the fire, took advantage of the chill morning breeze to create a draught which the other had left stupidly blocked by stones, and soon developed less smoke and more flame. The third member of the party, Bill Wilson, or Big Bill as they called him, came in with a hundred-and-forty-pound pack; and what Tarwater esteemed to be a very rotten breakfast was dished out by Charles. The mush was half cooked and mostly burnt, the bacon was charred carbon, and the coffee was unspeakable.

Immediately the meal was wolfed down the three partners took their empty pack-straps and headed down trail to where the remainder of their outfit lay at the last camp a mile away. And old Tarwater became busy. He washed the dishes, foraged dry wood, mended a broken pack-strap, put an edge on the butcher-knife and camp-axe, and repacked the picks and shovels into a more carryable parcel.

What had impressed him during the brief breakfast was the sort of awe in which Anson and Big Bill stood of Charles. Once, during the morning, while Anson took a breathing spell after bringing in another hundred-pound pack, Tarwater delicately hinted his impression.

"You see, it's this way," Anson said. "We've divided our leadership. We've got specialities. Now I'm a carpenter. When we get to Lake Linderman, and the trees are chopped and whipsawed into planks, I'll boss the building of the boat. Big Bill is a logger and miner. So he'll boss getting out the logs and all mining operations. Most of our outfit's ahead. We went broke paying the Indians to pack that much of it to the top of Chilcoot. Our last partner is up there with it, moving it along by himself down the other side. His name's Liverpool, and he's a sailor. So, when the boat's built, he's the boss of the outfit to navigate the lakes and rapids to Klondike."

"And Charles—this Mr. Crayton—what might his speciality be?" Tarwater asked.

"He's the business man. When it comes to business and organization he's boss."

"Hum," Tarwater pondered. "Very lucky to get such a bunch of specialities into one outfit."

"More than luck," Anson agreed. "It was all accident, too. Each of us started alone. We met on the steamer coming up from San Francisco, and formed the party.—Well, I got to be goin'. Charles is liable to get kicking because I ain't packin' my share' just the same, you can't expect a hundred-pound man to pack as much as a hundred-and-sixty-pounder."

"Stick around and cook us something for dinner," Charles, on his next load in and noting the effects of the old man's handiness, told Tarwater.

And Tarwater cooked a dinner that was a dinner, washed the dishes, had real pork and beans for supper, and bread baked in a frying-pan that was so delectable that the three partners nearly foundered themselves on it. Supper dishes washed, he cut shavings and kindling for a quick and certain breakfast fire, showed Anson a trick with foot-gear that was invaluable to any hiker, sang his "Like Argus of the Ancient Times," and told them of the great emigration across the Plains in Forty-nine.

"My goodness, the first cheerful and hearty-like camp since we hit the beach," Big Bill remarked as he knocked out his pipe and began pulling off his shoes for bed.

"Kind of made things easy, boys, eh?" Tarwater queried genially.

All nodded. "Well, then, I got a proposition, boys. You can take it or leave it, but just listen kindly to it. You're in a hurry to get in before the freeze-up. Half the time is wasted over the cooking by one of you that he might be puttin' in packin' outfit. If I do the cookin' for you, you all'll get on that much faster. Also, the cookin' 'll be better, and that'll make you pack better. And I can pack quite a bit myself in between times, quite a bit, yes, sir, quite a bit."

Big Bill and Anson were just beginning to nod their heads in agreement, when Charles stopped them.

"What do you expect of us in return?" he demanded of the old man.

"Oh, I leave it up to the boys."

"That ain't business," Charles reprimanded sharply. "You made the proposition. Now finish it."

"Well, it's this way—"

"You expect us to feed you all winter, eh?" Charles interrupted.

"No, siree, I don't. All I reckon is a passage to Klondike in your boat would be mighty square of you."

"You haven't an ounce of grub, old man. You'll starve to death when you get there."

"I've been feedin' some long time pretty successful," Old Tarwater replied, a whimsical light in his eyes. "I'm seventy, and ain't starved to death never yet."

"Will you sign a paper to the effect that you shift for yourself as soon as you get to Dawson?" the business one demanded.

"Oh, sure," was the response.

Again Charles checked his two partners' expressions of satisfaction with the arrangement.

"One other thing, old man. We're a party of four, and we all have a vote on questions like this. Young Liverpool is ahead with the main outfit. He's got a say so, and he isn't here to say it."

"What kind of a party might he be?" Tarwater inquired.

"He's a rough-neck sailor, and he's got a quick, bad temper."

"Some turbulent," Anson contributed.

"And the way he can cuss is simply God-awful," Big Bill testified.

"But he's square," Big Bill added.

Anson nodded heartily to this appraisal.

"Well, boys," Tarwater summed up, "I set out for Californy and I got there. And I'm going to get to Klondike. Ain't a thing can stop me, ain't a thing. I'm going to get three hundred thousand outa the ground, too. Ain't a thing can stop me, ain't a thing, because I just naturally need the money. I don't mind a bad temper so long's the boy is square. I'll take my chance, an' I'll work along with you till we catch up with him. Then, if he says no to the proposition, I reckon I'll lose. But somehow I just can't see 'm sayin' no, because that'd mean too close up to freeze-up and too late for me to find another chance like this. And, as I'm sure going to get to Klondike, it's just plumb impossible for him to say no."

Old John Tarwater became a striking figure on a trail unusually replete with striking figures. With thousands of men, each back-tripping half a ton of outfit, retracing every mile of the trail twenty times, all came to know him and to hail him as "Father Christmas." And, as he worked, ever he raised his chant with his age-falsetto voice. None of the three men he had joined could complain about his work. True, his joints were stiff—he admitted to a trifle of rheumatism. He moved slowly, and seemed to creak and crackle when he moved; but he kept on moving. Last into the blankets at night, he was first out in the morning, so that the other three had hot coffee before their one before-breakfast pack. And, between breakfast and dinner and between dinner and supper, he always managed to back-trip for several packs himself.

Sixty pounds was the limit of his burden, however. He could manage seventy-five, but he could not keep it up. Once, he tried ninety, but collapsed on the trail and was seriously shaky for a couple of days afterward.

Work! On a trail where hard-working men learned for the first time what work was, no man worked harder in proportion to his strength than Old Tarwater. Driven desperately on by the near-thrust of winter, and lured madly on by the dream of gold, they worked to their last ounce of strength and fell by the way. Others, when failure made certain, blew out their brains. Some went mad, and still others, under the irk of the man-destroying strain, broke partnerships and dissolved life-time friendships with fellows just as good as themselves and just as strained and mad.

Work! Old Tarwater could shame them all, despite his creaking and crackling and the nasty hacking cough he had developed. Early and late, on trail or in camp beside the trail he was ever in evidence, ever busy at something, ever responsive to the hail of "Father Christmas." Weary back-trippers would rest their packs on a log or rock alongside of where he rested his, and would say: "Sing us that song of yourn, dad, about Forty-Nine." And, when he had wheezingly complied, they would arise under their loads, remark that it was real heartening, and hit the forward trail again.

"If ever a man worked his passage and earned it," Big Bill confided to his two partners, "that man's our old Skeezicks."

"You bet," Anson confirmed. "He's a valuable addition to the party, and I, for one, ain't at all disagreeable to the notion of making him a regular partner—"

"None of that!" Charles Crayton cut in. "When we get to Dawson we're quit of him—that's the agreement. We'd only have to bury him if we let him stay on with us. Besides, there's going to be a famine, and every ounce of grub'll count. Remember, we're feeding him out of our own supply all the way in. And if we run short in the pinch next year, you'll know the reason. Steamboats can't get up grub to Dawson till the middle of June, and that's nine months away."

"Well, you put as much money and outfit in as the rest of us," Big Bill conceded, "and you've a say according."

"And I'm going to have my say," Charles asserted with increasing irritability. "And it's lucky for you with your fool sentiments that you've got somebody to think ahead for you, else you'd all starve to death. I tell you that famine's coming. I've been studying the situation. Flour will be two dollars a pound, or ten, and no sellers. You mark my words."

Across the rubble-covered flats, up the dark canyon to Sheep Camp, past the over-hanging and ever-threatening glaciers to the Scales, and from the Scales up the steep pitches of ice-scoured rock where packers climbed with hands and feet, Old Tarwater camp-cooked and packed and sang. He blew across Chilcoot Pass, above timberline, in the first swirl of autumn snow. Those below, without firewood, on the bitter rim of Crater Lake, heard from the driving obscurity above them a weird voice chanting:

"Like Argus of the ancient times,

We leave this modern Greece,

Tum-tum, tum-tum, tum, tum, tum-tum,

To shear the Golden Fleece."

And out of the snow flurries they saw appear a tall, gaunt form, with whiskers of flying white that blended with the storm, bending under a sixty-pound pack of camp dunnage.

"Father Christmas!" was the hail. And then: "Three rousing cheers for Father Christmas!"

Two miles beyond Crater Lake lay Happy Camp—so named because here was found the uppermost fringe of the timber line, where men might warm themselves by fire again. Scarcely could it be called timber, for it was a dwarf rock-spruce that never raised its loftiest branches higher than a foot above the moss, and that twisted and grovelled like a pig-vegetable under the moss. Here, on the trail leading into Happy Camp, in the first sunshine of half a dozen days, Old Tarwater rested his pack against a huge boulder and caught his breath. Around this boulder the trail passed, laden men toiling slowly forward and men with empty pack-straps limping rapidly back for fresh loads. Twice Old Tarwater essayed to rise and go on, and each time, warned by his shakiness, sank back to recover more strength. From around the boulder he heard voices in greeting, recognized Charles Crayton's voice, and realized that at last they had met up with Young Liverpool. Quickly, Charles plunged into business, and Tarwater heard with great distinctness every word of Charles' unflattering description of him and the proposition to give him passage to Dawson.

"A dam fool proposition," was Liverpool's judgment, when Charles had concluded. "An old granddad of seventy! If he's on his last legs, why in hell did you hook up with him? If there's going to be a famine, and it looks like it, we need every ounce of grub for ourselves. We only out-fitted for four, not five."

"It's all right," Tarwater heard Charles assuring the other. "Don't get excited. The old codger agreed to leave the final decision to you when we caught up with you. All you've got to do is put your foot down and say no."

"You mean it's up to me to turn the old one down, after your encouraging him and taking advantage of his work clear from Dyea here?"

"It's a hard trail, Liverpool, and only the men that are hard will get through," Charles strove to palliate.

"And I'm to do the dirty work?" Liverpool complained, while Tarwater's heart sank.

"That's just about the size of it," Charles said. "You've got the deciding."

Then old Tarwater's heart uprose again as the air was rent by a cyclone of profanity, from the midst of which crackled sentences like:—"Dirty skunks! . . . See you in hell first! . . . My mind's made up! . . . Hell's fire and corruption! . . . The old codger goes down the Yukon with us, stack on that, my hearty!

70

. . . Hard? You don't know what hard is unless I show you! . . . I'll bust the whole outfit to hell and gone if any of you try to side-track him! . . . Just try to side-track him, that is all, and you'll think the Day of Judgment and all God's blastingness has hit the camp in one chunk!"

Such was the invigoratingness of Liverpool's flow of speech that, quite without consciousness of effort, the old man arose easily under his load and strode on toward Happy Camp.

From Happy Camp to Long Lake, from Long Lake to Deep Lake, and from Deep Lake up over the enormous hog-back and down to Linderman, the man-killing race against winter kept on. Men broke their hearts and backs and wept beside the trail in sheer exhaustion. But winter never faltered. The fall gales blew, and amid bitter soaking rains and ever-increasing snow flurries, Tarwater and the party to which he was attached piled the last of their outfit on the beach.

There was no rest. Across the lake, a mile above a roaring torrent, they located a patch of spruce and built their saw-pit. Here, by hand, with an inadequate whipsaw, they sawed the spruce-trunks into lumber. They worked night and day. Thrice, on the night-shift, underneath in the saw-pit, Old Tarwater fainted. By day he cooked as well, and, in the betweenwhiles, helped Anson in the building of the boat beside the torrent as the green planks came down.

The days grew shorter. The wind shifted into the north and blew unending gales. In the mornings the weary men crawled from their blankets and in their socks thawed out their frozen shoes by the fire Tarwater always had burning for them. Ever arose the increasing tale of famine on the Inside. The last grub steamboats up from Bering Sea were stalled by low water at the beginning of the Yukon Flats hundreds of miles north of Dawson. In fact, they lay at the old Hudson Bay Company's post at Fort Yukon inside the Arctic Circle. Flour in Dawson was up to two dollars a pound, but no one would sell. Bonanza and Eldorado Kings, with money to burn, were leaving for the Outside because they could buy no grub. Miners' Committees were confiscating all grub and putting the population on strict rations. A man who held out an ounce of grub was shot like a dog. A score had been so executed already.

And, under a strain which had broken so many younger men, Old Tarwater began to break. His cough had become terrible, and had not his exhausted comrades slept like the dead, he would have kept them awake nights. Also, he began to take chills, so that he dressed up to go to bed. When he had finished so dressing, not a rag of garment remained in his clothes bag. All he possessed was on his back and swathed around his gaunt old form.

"Gee!" said Big Bill. "If he puts all he's got on now, when it ain't lower than twenty above, what'll he do later on when it goes down to fifty and sixty below?"

They lined the rough-made boat down the mountain torrent, nearly losing it a dozen times, and rowed across the south end of Lake Linderman in the thick of a fall blizzard. Next morning they planned to load and start, squarely into the teeth of the north, on their perilous traverse of half a thousand miles of lakes and rapids and box canyons. But before he went to bed that night, Young Liverpool was out over the camp. He returned to find his whole party asleep. Rousing Tarwater, he talked with him in low tones.

"Listen, dad," he said.—"You've got a passage in our boat, and if ever a man earned a passage you have. But you know yourself you're pretty well along in years, and your health right now ain't exciting. If you go on with us you'll croak surer'n hell.—Now wait till I finish, dad. The price for a passage has jumped to five hundred dollars. I've been throwing my feet and I've hustled a passenger. He's an official of the Alaska Commercial and just has to get in. He's bid up to six hundred to go with me in our boat. Now the passage is yours. You sell it to him, poke the six hundred into your jeans, and pull South for California while the goin's good. You can be in Dyea in two days, and in California in a week more. What d'ye say?"

Tarwater coughed and shivered for a space, ere he could get freedom of breath for speech.

"Son," he said, "I just want to tell you one thing. I drove my four yoke of oxen across the Plains in Forty-nine and lost nary a one. I drove them plumb to Californy, and I freighted with them afterward out of Sutter's Fort to American Bar. Now I'm going to Klondike. Ain't nothing can stop me, ain't nothing at all. I'm going to ride that boat, with you at the steering sweep, clean to Klondike, and I'm going to shake three hundred thousand out of the moss-roots. That being so, it's contrary to reason and common sense for me to sell out my passage. But I thank you kindly, son, I thank you kindly."

The young sailor shot out his hand impulsively and gripped the old man's.

"By God, dad!" he cried. "You're sure going to go then. You're the real stuff." He looked with undisguised contempt across the sleepers to where Charles Crayton snored in his red beard. "They don't seem to make your kind any more, dad."

Into the north they fought their way, although old-timers, coming out, shook their heads and prophesied they would be frozen in on the lakes. That the freeze-up might come any day was patent, and delays of safety were no longer considered. For this reason, Liverpool decided to shoot the rapid stream connecting Linderman to Lake Bennett with the fully loaded boat. It was the custom to line the empty boats down and to portage the cargoes across. Even then many empty boats had been wrecked. But the time was past for such precaution.

"Climb out, dad," Liverpool commanded as he prepared to swing from the bank and enter the rapids.

Old Tarwater shook his white head.

"I'm sticking to the outfit," he declared. "It's the only way to get through. You see, son, I'm going to Klondike. If I stick by the boat, then the boat just naturally goes to Klondike, too. If I get out, then most likely you'll lose the boat."

"Well, there's no use in overloading," Charles announced, springing abruptly out on the bank as the boat cast off.

"Next time you wait for my orders!" Liverpool shouted ashore as the current gripped the boat. "And there won't be any more walking around rapids and losing time waiting to pick you up!"

What took them ten minutes by river, took Charles half an hour by land, and while they waited for him at the head of Lake Bennett they passed the time of day with several dilapidated old-timers on their way out. The famine news was graver than ever. The North-west Mounted Police, stationed at the foot of Lake Marsh where the gold-rushers entered Canadian territory, were refusing to let a man past who did not carry with him seven hundred pounds of grub. In Dawson City a thousand men, with dog-teams, were waiting the freeze-up to come out over the ice. The trading companies could not fill their grub-contracts, and partners were cutting the cards to see which should go and which should stay and work the claims.

"That settles it," Charles announced, when he learned of the action of the mounted police on the boundary. "Old Man, you might as well start back now."

"Climb aboard!" Liverpool commanded. "We're going to Klondike, and old dad is going along."

A shift of gale to the south gave them a fair wind down Lake Bennett, before which they ran under a huge sail made by Liverpool. The heavy weight of outfit gave such ballast that he cracked on as a daring sailor should when moments counted. A shift of four points into the south-west, coming just at the right time as they entered upon Caribou Crossing, drove them down that connecting link to lakes Tagish and Marsh. In stormy sunset and twilight— they made the dangerous crossing of Great Windy Arm, wherein they beheld two other boat-loads of gold-rushers capsize and drown.

Charles was for beaching for the night, but Liverpool held on, steering down Tagish by the sound of the surf on the shoals and by the occasional shore-fires that advertised wrecked or timid argonauts. At four in the morning, he aroused Charles. Old Tarwater, shiveringly awake, heard Liverpool order Crayton aft beside him at the steering-sweep, and also heard the one-sided conversation.

"Just listen, friend Charles, and keep your own mouth shut," Liverpool began. "I want you to get one thing into your head and keep it there: *old dad's going by the police. Understand? He's going by.* When they examine our outfit, old dad's got a fifth share in it, savvee? That'll put us all 'way under what we ought to have, but we can bluff it through. Now get this, and get it hard: *there ain't going to be any fall-down on this bluff—*"

"If you think I'd give away on the old codger—" Charles began indignantly.

"You thought that," Liverpool checked him, "because I never mentioned any such thing. Now—get me and get me hard: I don't care what you've been thinking. It's what you're going to think. We'll make the police post some time this afternoon, and we've got to get ready to pull the bluff without a hitch, and a word to the wise is plenty."

"If you think I've got it in my mind—" Charles began again.

"Look here," Liverpool shut him off. "I don't know what's in your mind. I don't want to know. I want you to know what's in my mind. If there's any slip-up, if old dad gets turned back by the police, I'm going to pick out the first quiet bit of landscape and take you ashore on it. And then I'm going to beat you up to the Queen's taste. Get me, and get me hard. It ain't going to be any half-way beating, but a real, two-legged, two-fisted, he-man beating. I don't expect I'll kill you, but I'll come damn near to half-killing you."

"But what can I do?" Charles almost whimpered.

"Just one thing," was Liverpool's final word. "You just pray. You pray so hard that old dad gets by the police that he does get by. That's all. Go back to your blankets."

Before they gained Lake Le Barge, the land was sheeted with snow that would not melt for half a year. Nor could they lay their boat at will against the bank, for the rim-ice was already forming. Inside the mouth of the river, just ere it entered Lake Le Barge, they found a hundred storm-bound boats of the argonauts. Out of the north, across the full sweep of the great lake, blew an unending snow gale. Three mornings they put out and fought it and

75

the cresting seas it drove that turned to ice as they fell in-board. While the others broke their hearts at the oars, Old Tarwater managed to keep up just sufficient circulation to survive by chopping ice and throwing it overboard.

Each day for three days, beaten to helplessness, they turned tail on the battle and ran back into the sheltering river. By the fourth day, the hundred boats had increased to three hundred, and the two thousand argonauts on board knew that the great gale heralded the freeze-up of Le Barge. Beyond, the rapid rivers would continue to run for days, but unless they got beyond, and immediately, they were doomed to be frozen in for six months to come.

"This day we go through," Liverpool announced. "We turn back for nothing. And those of us that dies at the oars will live again and go on pulling."

And they went through, winning half the length of the lake by nightfall and pulling on through all the night hours as the wind went down, falling asleep at the oars and being rapped awake by Liverpool, toiling on through an age-long nightmare while the stars came out and the surface of the lake turned to the unruffledness of a sheet of paper and froze skin-ice that tinkled like broken glass as their oar-blades shattered it.

As day broke clear and cold, they entered the river, with behind them a sea of ice. Liverpool examined his aged passenger and found him helpless and almost gone. When he rounded the boat to against the rim-ice to build a fire and warm up Tarwater inside and out, Charles protested against such loss of time.

"This ain't business, so don't you come horning in," Liverpool informed him. "I'm running the boat trip. So you just climb out and chop firewood, and plenty of it. I'll take care of dad. You, Anson, make a fire on the bank. And you, Bill, set up the Yukon stove in the boat. Old dad ain't as young as the rest of us, and for the rest of this voyage he's going to have a fire on board to sit by."

All of which came to pass; and the boat, in the grip of the current, like a river steamer with smoke rising from the two joints of stove-pipe, grounded on shoals, hung up on split currents, and charged rapids and canyons, as it drove deeper into the Northland winter. The Big and Little Salmon rivers were throwing mush-ice into the main river as they passed, and, below the riffles, anchor-ice arose from the river bottom and coated the surface with crystal scum. Night and day the rim-ice grew, till, in quiet places, it extended out a hundred yards from shore. And Old Tarwater, with all his clothes on, sat by the stove and kept the fire going. Night and day, not daring to stop for fear of the imminent freeze-up, they dared to run, an increasing mushiness of ice running with them.

"What ho, old hearty?" Liverpool would call out at times.

"Cheer O," Old Tarwater had learned to respond.

"What can I ever do for you, son, in payment?" Tarwater, stoking the fire, would sometimes ask Liverpool, beating now one released hand and now the other as he fought for circulation where he steered in the freezing stern-sheets.

"Just break out that regular song of yours, old Forty-Niner," was the invariable reply.

And Tarwater would lift his voice in the cackling chant, as he lifted it at the end, when the boat swung in through driving cake-ice and moored to the Dawson City bank, and all waterfront Dawson pricked its ears to hear the triumphant pæan:

Like Argus of the ancient times,

We leave this modern Greece,

Tum-tum, tum-tum, tum, tum, tum-tum,

To shear the Golden Fleece,

Charles did it, but he did it so discreetly that none of his party, least of all the sailor, ever learned of it. He saw two great open barges being filled up with

77

men, and, on inquiry, learned that these were grubless ones being rounded up and sent down the Yukon by the Committee of Safety. The barges were to be towed by the last little steamboat in Dawson, and the hope was that Fort Yukon, where lay the stranded steamboats, would be gained before the river froze. At any rate, no matter what happened to them, Dawson would be relieved of their grub-consuming presence. So to the Committee of Safety Charles went, privily to drop a flea in its ear concerning Tarwater's grubless, moneyless, and aged condition. Tarwater was one of the last gathered in, and when Young Liverpool returned to the boat, from the bank he saw the barges in a run of cake-ice, disappearing around the bend below Moose-hide Mountain.

Running in cake-ice all the way, and several times escaping jams in the Yukon Flats, the barges made their hundreds of miles of progress farther into the north and froze up cheek by jowl with the grub-fleet. Here, inside the Arctic Circle, Old Tarwater settled down to pass the long winter. Several hours' work a day, chopping firewood for the steamboat companies, sufficed to keep him in food. For the rest of the time there was nothing to do but hibernate in his log cabin.

Warmth, rest, and plenty to eat, cured his hacking cough and put him in as good physical condition as was possible for his advanced years. But, even before Christmas, the lack of fresh vegetables caused scurvy to break out, and disappointed adventurer after disappointed adventurer took to his bunk in abject surrender to this culminating misfortune. Not so Tarwater. Even before the first symptoms appeared on him, he was putting into practice his one prescription, namely, exercise. From the junk of the old trading post he resurrected a number of rusty traps, and from one of the steamboat captains he borrowed a rifle.

Thus equipped, he ceased from wood-chopping, and began to make more than a mere living. Nor was he downhearted when the scurvy broke out on his own body. Ever he ran his trap-lines and sang his ancient chant. Nor could the pessimist shake his surety of the three hundred thousand of Alaskan gold he as going to shake out of the moss-roots.

"But this ain't gold-country," they told him.

"Gold is where you find it, son, as I should know who was mining before you was born, 'way back in Forty-Nine," was his reply. "What was Bonanza Creek but a moose-pasture? No miner'd look at it; yet they washed five-hundred-dollar pans and took out fifty million dollars. Eldorado was just as bad. For all you know, right under this here cabin, or right over the next hill, is millions just waiting for a lucky one like me to come and shake it out."

At the end of January came his disaster. Some powerful animal that he decided was a bob-cat, managing to get caught in one of his smaller traps, dragged it away. A heavy snow-fall put a stop midway to his pursuit, losing the trail for him and losing himself. There were but several hours of daylight each day between the twenty hours of intervening darkness, and his efforts in the grey light and continually falling snow succeeded only in losing him more thoroughly. Fortunately, when winter snow falls in the Northland the thermometer invariably rises; so, instead of the customary forty and fifty and even sixty degrees below zero, the temperature remained fifteen below. Also, he was warmly clad and had a full matchbox. Further to mitigate his predicament, on the fifth day he killed a wounded moose that weighed over half a ton. Making his camp beside it on a spruce-bottom, he was prepared to last out the winter, unless a searching party found him or his scurvy grew worse.

But at the end of two weeks there had been no sign of search, while his scurvy had undeniably grown worse. Against his fire, banked from outer cold by a shelter-wall of spruce-boughs, he crouched long hours in sleep and long hours in waking. But the waking hours grew less, becoming semi-waking or half-dreaming hours as the process of hibernation worked their way with him. Slowly the sparkle point of consciousness and identity that was John Tarwater sank, deeper and deeper, into the profounds of his being that had been compounded ere man was man, and while he was becoming man, when he, first of all animals, regarded himself with an introspective eye and laid the beginnings of morality in foundations of nightmare peopled by the monsters of his own ethic-thwarted desires.

Like a man in fever, waking to intervals of consciousness, so Old Tarwater awoke, cooked his moose-meat, and fed the fire; but more and more time he spent in his torpor, unaware of what was day-dream and what was sleep-dream in the content of his unconsciousness. And here, in the unforgetable crypts of man's unwritten history, unthinkable and unrealizable, like passages of nightmare or impossible adventures of lunacy, he encountered the monsters created of man's first morality that ever since have vexed him into the spinning of fantasies to elude them or do battle with them.

In short, weighted by his seventy years, in the vast and silent loneliness of the North, Old Tarwater, as in the delirium of drug or anæsthetic, recovered within himself, the infantile mind of the child-man of the early world. It was in the dusk of Death's fluttery wings that Tarwater thus crouched, and, like his remote forebear, the child-man, went to myth-making, and sun-heroizing, himself hero-maker and the hero in quest of the immemorable treasure difficult of attainment.

Either must he attain the treasure—for so ran the inexorable logic of the shadow-land of the unconscious—or else sink into the all-devouring sea, the blackness eater of the light that swallowed to extinction the sun each night . . . the sun that arose ever in rebirth next morning in the east, and that had become to man man's first symbol of immortality through rebirth. All this, in the deeps of his unconsciousness (the shadowy western land of descending light), was the near dusk of Death down into which he slowly ebbed.

But how to escape this monster of the dark that from within him slowly swallowed him? Too deep-sunk was he to dream of escape or feel the prod of desire to escape. For him reality had ceased. Nor from within the darkened chamber of himself could reality recrudesce. His years were too heavy upon him, the debility of disease and the lethargy and torpor of the silence and the cold were too profound. Only from without could reality impact upon him and reawake within him an awareness of reality. Otherwise he would ooze down through the shadow-realm of the unconscious into the all-darkness of extinction.

But it came, the smash of reality from without, crashing upon his ear drums in a loud, explosive snort. For twenty days, in a temperature that had never risen above fifty below, no breath of wind had blown movement, no slightest sound had broken the silence. Like the smoker on the opium couch refocusing his eyes from the spacious walls of dream to the narrow confines of the mean little room, so Old Tarwater stared vague-eyed before him across his dying fire, at a huge moose that stared at him in startlement, dragging a wounded leg, manifesting all signs of extreme exhaustion; it, too, had been straying blindly in the shadow-land, and had wakened to reality only just ere it stepped into Tarwater's fire.

He feebly slipped the large fur mitten lined with thickness of wool from his right hand. Upon trial he found the trigger finger too numb for movement. Carefully, slowly, through long minutes, he worked the bare hand inside his blankets, up under his fur *parka*, through the chest openings of his shirts, and into the slightly warm hollow of his left arm-pit. Long minutes passed ere the finger could move, when, with equal slowness of caution, he gathered his rifle to his shoulder and drew bead upon the great animal across the fire.

At the shot, of the two shadow-wanderers, the one reeled downward to the dark and the other reeled upward to the light, swaying drunkenly on his scurvy-ravaged legs, shivering with nervousness and cold, rubbing swimming eyes with shaking fingers, and staring at the real world all about him that had returned to him with such sickening suddenness. He shook himself together, and realized that for long, how long he did not know, he had bedded in the arms of Death. He spat, with definite intention, heard the spittle crackle in the frost, and judged it must be below and far below sixty below. In truth, that day at Fort Yukon, the spirit thermometer registered seventy-five degrees below zero, which, since freezing-point is thirty-two above, was equivalent to one hundred and seven degrees of frost.

Slowly Tarwater's brain reasoned to action. Here, in the vast alone, dwelt Death. Here had come two wounded moose. With the clearing of the sky after the great cold came on, he had located his bearings, and he knew that both wounded moose had trailed to him from the east. Therefore, in the east, were men—whites or Indians he could not tell, but at any rate men who might stand by him in his need and help moor him to reality above the sea of dark.

He moved slowly, but he moved in reality, girding himself with rifle, ammunition, matches, and a pack of twenty pounds of moose-meat. Then, an Argus rejuvenated, albeit lame of both legs and tottery, he turned his back on the perilous west and limped into the sun-arising, re-birthing east. . . .

Days later—how many days later he was never to know—dreaming dreams and seeing visions, cackling his old gold-chant of Forty-Nine, like one drowning and swimming feebly to keep his consciousness above the engulfing dark, he came out upon the snow-slope to a canyon and saw below smoke rising and men who ceased from work to gaze at him. He tottered down the hill to them, still singing; and when he ceased from lack of breath they called him variously: Santa Claus, Old Christmas, Whiskers, the Last of the Mohicans, and Father Christmas. And when he stood among them he stood very still, without speech, while great tears welled out of his eyes. He cried silently, a long time, till, as if suddenly bethinking himself, he sat down in the snow with much creaking and crackling of his joints, and from this low vantage point toppled sidewise and fainted calmly and easily away.

In less than a week Old Tarwater was up and limping about the housework of the cabin, cooking and dish-washing for the five men of the creek. Genuine sourdoughs (pioneers) they were, tough and hard-bitten, who had been buried so deeply inside the Circle that they did not know there was a Klondike Strike. The news he brought them was their first word of it. They lived on an almost straight-meat diet of moose, caribou, and smoked salmon, eked out with wild berries and somewhat succulent wild roots they had stocked up with in the summer. They had forgotten the taste of coffee, made fire with a burning glass, carried live fire-sticks with them wherever they travelled, and in their pipes smoked dry leaves that bit the tongue and were pungent to the nostrils.

Three years before, they had prospected from the head-reaches of the Koyokuk northward and clear across to the mouth of the Mackenzie on the Arctic Ocean. Here, on the whaleships, they had beheld their last white men and equipped themselves with the last white man's grub, consisting principally of salt and smoking tobacco. Striking south and west on the long traverse to the junction of the Yukon and Porcupine at Fort Yukon, they had found gold on this creek and remained over to work the ground.

They hailed the advent of Tarwater with joy, never tired of listening to his tales of Forty-Nine, and rechristened him Old Hero. Also, with tea made from spruce needles, with concoctions brewed from the inner willow bark, and with sour and bitter roots and bulbs from the ground, they dosed his scurvy out of him, so that he ceased limping and began to lay on flesh over his bony framework. Further, they saw no reason at all why he should not gather a rich treasure of gold from the ground.

"Don't know about all of three hundred thousand," they told him one morning, at breakfast, ere they departed to their work, "but how'd a hundred thousand do, Old Hero? That's what we figure a claim is worth, the ground being badly spotted, and we've already staked your location notices."

"Well, boys," Old Tarwater answered, "and thanking you kindly, all I can say is that a hundred thousand will do nicely, and very nicely, for a starter. Of course, I ain't goin' to stop till I get the full three hundred thousand. That's what I come into the country for."

They laughed and applauded his ambition and reckoned they'd have to hunt a richer creek for him. And Old Hero reckoned that as the spring came on and he grew spryer, he'd have to get out and do a little snooping around himself.

"For all anybody knows," he said, pointing to a hillside across the creek bottom, "the moss under the snow there may be plumb rooted in nugget gold."

He said no more, but as the sun rose higher and the days grew longer and warmer, he gazed often across the creek at the definite bench-formation half way up the hill. And, one day, when the thaw was in full swing, he crossed the stream and climbed to the bench. Exposed patches of ground had already thawed an inch deep. On one such patch he stopped, gathered a bunch of moss in his big gnarled hands, and ripped it out by the roots. The sun smouldered on dully glistening yellow. He shook the handful of moss, and coarse nuggets, like gravel, fell to the ground. It was the Golden Fleece ready for the shearing.

Not entirely unremembered in Alaskan annals is the summer stampede of 1898 from Fort Yukon to the bench diggings of Tarwater Hill. And when Tarwater sold his holdings to the Bowdie interests for a sheer half-million and faced for California, he rode a mule over a new-cut trail, with convenient road houses along the way, clear to the steamboat landing at Fort Yukon.

At the first meal on the ocean-going steamship out of St. Michaels, a waiter, greyish-haired, pain-ravaged of face, scurvy-twisted of body, served him. Old Tarwater was compelled to look him over twice in order to make certain he was Charles Crayton.

"Got it bad, eh, son?" Tarwater queried.

"Just my luck," the other complained, after recognition and greeting. "Only one of the party that the scurvy attacked. I've been through hell. The other three are all at work and healthy, getting grub-stake to prospect up White River this winter. Anson's earning twenty-five a day at carpentering, Liverpool getting twenty logging for the saw-mill, and Big Bill's getting forty a day as chief sawyer. I tried my best, and if it hadn't been for scurvy . . ."

"Sure, son, you done your best, which ain't much, you being naturally irritable and hard from too much business. Now I'll tell you what. You ain't fit to work crippled up this way. I'll pay your passage with the captain in kind remembrance of the voyage you gave me, and you can lay up and take it easy the rest of the trip. And what are your circumstances when you land at San Francisco?"

Charles Crayton shrugged his shoulders.

"Tell you what," Tarwater continued. "There's work on the ranch for you till you can start business again."

"I could manage your business for you—" Charles began eagerly.

"No, siree," Tarwater declared emphatically. "But there's always post-holes to dig, and cordwood to chop, and the climate's fine . . . "

Tarwater arrived home a true prodigal grandfather for whom the fatted calf was killed and ready. But first, ere he sat down at table, he must stroll out and around. And sons and daughters of his flesh and of the law needs must go with him fulsomely eating out of the gnarled old hand that had half a million to disburse. He led the way, and no opinion he slyly uttered was preposterous or impossible enough to draw dissent from his following. Pausing by the ruined water wheel which he had built from the standing timber, his face beamed as he gazed across the stretches of Tarwater Valley, and on and up the far heights to the summit of Tarwater Mountain—now all his again.

A thought came to him that made him avert his face and blow his nose in order to hide the twinkle in his eyes. Still attended by the entire family, he strolled on to the dilapidated barn. He picked up an age-weathered single-tree from the ground.

"William," he said. "Remember that little conversation we had just before I started to Klondike? Sure, William, you remember. You told me I was crazy. And I said my father'd have walloped the tar out of me with a single-tree if I'd spoke to him that way."

"Aw, but that was only foolin'," William temporized.

William was a grizzled man of forty-five, and his wife and grown sons stood in the group, curiously watching Grandfather Tarwater take off his coat and hand it to Mary to hold.

"William—come here," he commanded imperatively.

No matter how reluctantly, William came.

"Just a taste, William, son, of what my father give me often enough," Old Tarwater crooned, as he laid on his son's back and shoulders with the single-tree. "Observe, I ain't hitting you on the head. My father had a gosh-wollickin' temper and never drew the line at heads when he went after tar.—Don't jerk your elbows back that way! You're likely to get a crack on one by accident. And just tell me one thing, William, son: is there nary notion in your head that I'm crazy?"

"No!" William yelped out in pain, as he danced about. "You ain't crazy, father of course you ain't crazy!"

"You said it," Old Tarwater remarked sententiously, tossing the singletree aside and starting to struggle into his coat. "Now let's all go in and eat."

THE END.

Glen Ellen, California,

September 14, 1916.

THE PRINCESS

A fire burned cheerfully in the jungle camp, and beside the fire lolled a cheerful-seeming though horrible-appearing man. This was a hobo jungle, pitched in a thin strip of woods that lay between a railroad embankment and the bank of a river. But no hobo was the man. So deep-sunk was he in the social abyss that a proper hobo would not sit by the same fire with him. A gay-cat, who is an ignorant new-comer on the "Road," might sit with such as he, but only long enough to learn better. Even low down bindle-stiffs and stew-bums, after a once-over, would have passed this man by. A genuine hobo, a couple of punks, or a bunch of tender-yeared road-kids might have gone through his rags for any stray pennies or nickels and kicked him out into the darkness. Even an alki-stiff would have reckoned himself immeasurably superior.

For this man was that hybrid of tramp-land, an alki-stiff that has degenerated into a stew-bum, with so little self-respect that he will never "boil-up," and with so little pride that he will eat out of a garbage can. He was truly horrible-appearing. He might have been sixty years of age; he might have been ninety. His garments might have been discarded by a rag-picker. Beside him, an unrolled bundle showed itself as consisting of a ragged overcoat and containing an empty and smoke-blackened tomato can, an empty and battered condensed milk can, some dog-meat partly wrapped in brown paper and evidently begged from some butcher-shop, a carrot that had been run over in the street by a wagon-wheel, three greenish-cankered and decayed potatoes, and a sugar-bun with a mouthful bitten from it and rescued from the gutter, as was made patent by the gutter-filth that still encrusted it.

A prodigious growth of whiskers, greyish-dirty and untrimmed for years, sprouted from his face. This hirsute growth should have been white, but the season was summer and it had not been exposed to a rain-shower for some time. What was visible of the face looked as if at some period it had stopped a hand-grenade. The nose was so variously malformed in its healed brokenness that there was no bridge, while one nostril, the size of a pea, opened downward, and the other, the size of a robin's egg, tilted upward to the sky. One eye, of normal size, dim-brown and misty, bulged to the verge of popping out, and as if from senility wept copiously and continuously. The other eye, scarcely larger than a squirrel's and as uncannily bright, twisted up obliquely into the hairy scar of a bone-crushed eyebrow. And he had but one arm.

Yet was he cheerful. On his face, in mild degree, was depicted sensuous pleasure as he lethargically scratched his ribs with his one hand. He pawed over his food-scraps, debated, then drew a twelve-ounce druggist bottle from his inside coat-pocket. The bottle was full of a colourless liquid, the contemplation of which made his little eye burn brighter and quickened his movements. Picking up the tomato can, he arose, went down the short path to the river, and returned with the can filled with not-nice river water. In the condensed milk can he mixed one part of water with two parts of fluid from the bottle. This colourless fluid was druggist's alcohol, and as such is known in tramp-land as "alki."

Slow footsteps, coming down the side of the railroad embankment, alarmed him ere he could drink. Placing the can carefully upon the ground between his legs, he covered it with his hat and waited anxiously whatever impended.

Out of the darkness emerged a man as filthy ragged as he. The new-comer, who might have been fifty, and might have been sixty, was grotesquely fat. He bulged everywhere. He was composed of bulges. His bulbous nose was the size and shape of a turnip. His eyelids bulged and his blue eyes bulged in competition with them. In many places the seams of his garments had parted across the bulges of body. His calves grew into his feet, for the broken elastic sides of his Congress gaiters were swelled full with the fat of him. One arm only he sported, from the shoulder of which was suspended a small and tattered bundle with the mud caked dry on the outer covering from the last place he had pitched his doss. He advanced with tentative caution, made sure of the harmlessness of the man beside the fire, and joined him.

"Hello, grandpa," the new-comer greeted, then paused to stare at the other's flaring, sky-open nostril. "Say, Whiskers, how'd ye keep the night dew out of that nose o' yourn?"

Whiskers growled an incoherence deep in his throat and spat into the fire in token that he was not pleased by the question.

"For the love of Mike," the fat man chuckled, "if you got caught out in a rainstorm without an umbrella you'd sure drown, wouldn't you?"

"Can it, Fatty, can it," Whiskers muttered wearily. "They ain't nothin' new in that line of chatter. Even the bulls hand it out to me."

"But you can still drink, I hope"; Fatty at the same time mollified and invited, with his one hand deftly pulling the slip-knots that fastened his bundle.

From within the bundle he brought to light a twelve-ounce bottle of alki. Footsteps coming down the embankment alarmed him, and he hid the bottle under his hat on the ground between his legs.

But the next comer proved to be not merely one of their own ilk, but likewise to have only one arm. So forbidding of aspect was he that greetings consisted of no more than grunts. Huge-boned, tall, gaunt to cadaverousness, his face a dirty death's head, he was as repellent a nightmare of old age as ever Doré imagined. His toothless, thin-lipped mouth was a cruel and bitter slash under a great curved nose that almost met the chin and that was like a buzzard's beak. His one hand, lean and crooked, was a talon. The beady grey eyes, unblinking and unwavering, were bitter as death, as bleak as absolute zero and as merciless. His presence was a chill, and Whiskers and Fatty instinctively drew together for protection against the unguessed threat of him. Watching his chance, privily, Whiskers snuggled a chunk of rock several pounds in weigh close to his hand if need for action should arise. Fatty duplicated the performance.

Then both sat licking their lips, guiltily embarrassed, while the unblinking eyes of the terrible one bored into them, now into one, now into another, and then down at the rock-chunks of their preparedness.

"Huh!" sneered the terrible one, with such dreadfulness of menace as to cause Whiskers and Fatty involuntarily to close their hands down on their cave-man's weapons.

"Huh!" the other repeated, reaching his one talon into his side coat pocket with swift definiteness. "A hell of a chance you two cheap bums 'd have with me."

The talon emerged, clutching ready for action a six-pound iron quoit.

"We ain't lookin' for trouble, Slim," Fatty quavered.

"Who in hell are you to call me 'Slim'?" came the snarling answer.

"Me? I'm just Fatty, an' seein' 's I never seen you before—"

"An' I suppose that's Whiskers, there, with the gay an' festive lamp tan-going into his eyebrow an' the God-forgive-us nose joy-riding all over his mug?"

"It'll do, it'll do," Whiskers muttered uncomfortably. "One monica's as good as another, I find, at my time of life. And everybody hands it out to me anyway. And I need an umbrella when it rains to keep from getting drowned, an' all the rest of it."

"I ain't used to company—don't like it," Slim growled. "So if you guys want to stick around, mind your step, that's all, mind your step."

He fished from his pocket a cigar stump, self-evidently shot from the gutter, and prepared to put it in his mouth to chew. Then he changed his mind, glared at his companions savagely, and unrolled his bundle. Appeared in his hand a druggist's bottle of alki.

"Well," he snarled, "I suppose I gotta give you cheap skates a drink when I ain't got more'n enough for a good petrification for myself."

Almost a softening flicker of light was imminent in his withered face as he beheld the others proudly lift their hats and exhibit their own supplies.

"Here's some water for the mixin's," Whiskers said, proffering his tomato-can of river slush. "Stockyards just above," he added apologetically. "But they say—"

"Huh!" Slim snapped short, mixing the drink. "I've drunk worse'n stockyards in my time."

Yet when all was ready, cans of alki in their solitary hands, the three things that had once been men hesitated, as if of old habit, and next betrayed shame as if at self-exposure.

Whiskers was the first to brazen it.

"I've sat in at many a finer drinking," he bragged.

"With the pewter," Slim sneered.

"With the silver," Whiskers corrected.

Slim turned a scorching eye-interrogation on Fatty.

Fatty nodded.

"Beneath the salt," said Slim.

"Above it," came Fatty's correction. "I was born above it, and I've never travelled second class. First or steerage, but no intermediate in mine."

"Yourself?" Whiskers queried of Slim.

"In broken glass to the Queen, God bless her," Slim answered, solemnly, without snarl or sneer.

"In the pantry?" Fatty insinuated.

Simultaneously Slim reached for his quoit, and Whiskers and Fatty for their rocks.

"Now don't let's get feverish," Fatty said, dropping his own weapon. "We aren't scum. We're gentlemen. Let's drink like gentlemen."

"Let it be a real drinking," Whiskers approved.

"Let's get petrified," Slim agreed. "Many a distillery's flowed under the bridge since we were gentlemen; but let's forget the long road we've travelled since, and hit our doss in the good old fashion in which every gentleman went to bed when we were young."

91

"My father done it—did it," Fatty concurred and corrected, as old recollections exploded long-sealed brain-cells of connotation and correct usage.

The other two nodded a descent from similar fathers, and elevated their tin cans of alcohol.

By the time each had finished his own bottle and from his rags fished forth a second one, their brains were well-mellowed and a-glow, although they had not got around to telling their real names. But their English had improved. They spoke it correctly, while the argo of tramp-land ceased from their lips.

"It's my constitution," Whiskers was explaining. "Very few men could go through what I have and live to tell the tale. And I never took any care of myself. If what the moralists and the physiologists say were true, I'd have been dead long ago. And it's the same with you two. Look at us, at our advanced years, carousing as the young ones don't dare, sleeping out in the open on the ground, never sheltered from frost nor rain nor storm, never afraid of pneumonia or rheumatism that would put half the young ones on their backs in hospital."

He broke off to mix another drink, and Fatty took up the tale.

"And we've had our fun," he boasted, "and speaking of sweethearts and all," he cribbed from Kipling, "'We've rogued and we've ranged—'"

"'In our time,'" Slim completed the crib for him.

"I should say so, I should say so," Fatty confirmed. "And been loved by princesses—at least I have."

"Go on and tell us about it," Whiskers urged. "The night's young, and why shouldn't we remember back to the roofs of kings?"

Nothing loth, Fatty cleared his throat for the recital and cast about in his mind for the best way to begin.

"It must be known that I came of good family. Percival Delaney, let us say, yes, let us say Percival Delaney, was not unknown at Oxford once upon a time—not for scholarship, I am frank to admit; but the gay young dogs of that day, if any be yet alive, would remember him—"

"My people came over with the Conqueror," Whiskers interrupted, extending his hand to Fatty's in acknowledgment of the introduction.

"What name?" Fatty queried. "I did not seem quite to catch it."

"Delarouse, Chauncey Delarouse. The name will serve as well as any."

Both completed the handshake and glanced to Slim.

"Oh, well, while we're about it . . . " Fatty urged.

"Bruce Cadogan Cavendish," Slim growled morosely. "Go on, Percival, with your princesses and the roofs of kings."

"Oh, I was a rare young devil," Percival obliged, "after I played ducks and drakes at home and sported out over the world. And I was some figure of a man before I lost my shape—polo, steeple-chasing, boxing. I won medals at buckjumping in Australia, and I held more than several swimming records from the quarter of a mile up. Women turned their heads to look when I went by. The women! God bless them!"

And Fatty, alias Percival Delaney, a grotesque of manhood, put his bulgy hand to his puffed lips and kissed audibly into the starry vault of the sky.

"And the Princess!" he resumed, with another kiss to the stars. "She was as fine a figure of a woman as I was a man, as high-spirited and courageous, as reckless and dare-devilish. Lord, Lord, in the water she was a mermaid, a sea-goddess. And when it came to blood, beside her I was parvenu. Her royal line traced back into the mists of antiquity.

"She was not a daughter of a fair-skinned folk. Tawny golden was she, with golden-brown eyes, and her hair that fell to her knees was blue-black and straight, with just the curly tendrilly tendency that gives to woman's hair its charm. Oh, there were no kinks in it, any more than were there kinks in the hair of her entire genealogy. For she was Polynesian, glowing, golden, lovely and lovable, royal Polynesian."

Again he paused to kiss his hand to the memory of her, and Slim, alias Bruce Cadogan Cavendish, took advantage to interject:

"Huh! Maybe you didn't shine in scholarship, but at least you gleaned a vocabulary out of Oxford."

"And in the South Seas garnered a better vocabulary from the lexicon of Love," Percival was quick on the uptake.

"It was the island of Talofa," he went on, "meaning love, the Isle of Love, and it was her island. Her father, the king, an old man, sat on his mats with paralysed knees and drank squareface gin all day and most of the night, out of grief, sheer grief. She, my princess, was the only issue, her brother having been lost in their double canoe in a hurricane while coming up from a voyage to Samoa. And among the Polynesians the royal women have equal right with the men to rule. In fact, they trace their genealogies always by the female line."

To this both Chauncey Delarouse and Bruce Cadogan Cavendish nodded prompt affirmation.

"Ah," said Percival, "I perceive you both know the South Seas, wherefore, without undue expenditure of verbiage on my part, I am assured that you will appreciate the charm of my princess, the Princess Tui-nui of Talofa, the Princess of the Isle of Love."

He kissed his hand to her, sipped from his condensed milk can a man-size drink of druggist's alcohol, and to her again kissed her hand.

"But she was coy, and ever she fluttered near to me but never near enough. When my arm went out to her to girdle her, presto, she was not there. I knew, as never before, nor since, the thousand dear and delightful anguishes of love frustrated but ever resilient and beckoned on by the very goddess of love."

"Some vocabulary," Bruce Cadogan Cavendish muttered in aside to Chauncey Delarouse. But Percival Delaney was not to be deterred. He kissed his pudgy hand aloft into the night and held warmly on.

"No fond agonies of rapture deferred that were not lavished upon me by my dear Princess, herself ever a luring delight of promise flitting just beyond my reach. Every sweet lover's inferno unguessed of by Dante she led me through. Ah! Those swooning tropic nights, under our palm trees, the distant surf a langourous murmur as from some vast sea shell of mystery, when she, my Princess, all but melted to my yearning, and with her laughter, that was as silver strings by buds and blossoms smitten, all but made lunacy of my lover's ardency.

"It was by my wrestling with the champions of Talofa that I first interested her. It was by my prowess at swimming that I awoke her. And it was by a certain swimming deed that I won from her more than coquettish smiles and shy timidities of feigned retreat.

"We were squidding that day, out on the reef—you know how, undoubtedly, diving down the face of the wall of the reef, five fathoms, ten fathoms, any depth within reason, and shoving our squid-sticks into the likely holes and crannies of the coral where squid might be lairing. With the squid-stick, bluntly sharp at both ends, perhaps a foot long, and held crosswise in the hand, the trick was to gouge any lazying squid until he closed his tentacles around fist, stick and arm.—Then you had him, and came to the surface with him, and hit him in the head which is in the centre of him, and peeled him off into the waiting canoe. . . . And to think I used to do that!"

Percival Delaney paused a moment, a glimmer of awe on his rotund face, as he contemplated the mighty picture of his youth.

"Why, I've pulled out a squid with tentacles eight feet long, and done it under fifty feet of water. I could stay down four minutes. I've gone down, with a coral-rock to sink me, in a hundred and ten feet to clear a fouled anchor. And I could back-dive with a once-over and go in feet-first from eighty feet above the surface—"

"Quit it, delete it, cease it," Chauncey Delarouse admonished testily. "Tell of the Princess. That's what makes old blood leap again. Almost can I see her. Was she wonderful?"

Percival Delaney kissed unutterable affirmation.

"I have said she was a mermaid. She was. I know she swam thirty-six hours before being rescued, after her schooner was capsized in a double-squall. I have seen her do ninety feet and bring up pearl shell in each hand. She was wonderful. As a woman she was ravishing, sublime. I have said she was a sea-goddess. She was. Oh, for a Phidias or a Praxiteles to have made the wonder of her body immortal!

"And that day, out for squid on the reef, I was almost sick for her. Mad—I know I was mad for her. We would step over the side from the big canoe, and swim down, side by side, into the delicious depths of cool and colour, and she would look at me, as we swam, and with her eyes tantalize me to further madness. And at last, down, far down, I lost myself and reached for her. She eluded me like the mermaid she was, and I saw the laughter on her face as she fled. She fled deeper, and I knew I had her for I was between her and the surface; but in the muck coral sand of the bottom she made a churning with her squid stick. It was the old trick to escape a shark. And she worked it on me, rolling the water so that I could not see her. And when I came up, she was there ahead of me, clinging to the side of the canoe and laughing.

"Almost I would not be denied. But not for nothing was she a princess. She rested her hand on my arm and compelled me to listen. We should play a game, she said, enter into a competition for which should get the more squid, the biggest squid, and the smallest squid. Since the wagers were kisses, you can well imagine I went down on the first next dive with soul aflame.

"I got no squid. Never again in all my life have I dived for squid. Perhaps we were five fathoms down and exploring the face of the reefwall for lurking places of our prey, when it happened. I had found a likely lair and just proved it empty, when I felt or sensed the nearness of something inimical. I turned. There it was, alongside of me, and no mere fish-shark. Fully a dozen feet in length, with the unmistakable phosphorescent cat's eye gleaming like a drowning star, I knew it for what it was, a tiger shark.

"Not ten feet to the right, probing a coral fissure with her squid stick, was the Princess, and the tiger shark was heading directly for her. My totality of thought was precipitated to consciousness in a single all-embracing flash. The man-eater must be deflected from her, and what was I, except a mad lover who would gladly fight and die, or more gladly fight and live, for his beloved? Remember, she was the woman wonderful, and I was aflame for her.

"Knowing fully the peril of my act, I thrust the blunt-sharp end of my squid-stick into the side of the shark, much as one would attract a passing acquaintance with a thumb-nudge in the ribs. And the man-eater turned on me. You know the South Seas, and you know that the tiger shark, like the bald-face grizzly of Alaska, never gives trail. The combat, fathoms deep under the sea, was on—if by combat may be named such a one-sided struggle.

"The Princess unaware, caught her squid and rose to the surface. The man-eater rushed me. I fended him off with both hands on his nose above his thousand-toothed open mouth, so that he backed me against the sharp coral. The scars are there to this day. Whenever I tried to rise, he rushed me, and I could not remain down there indefinitely without air. Whenever he rushed me, I fended him off with my hands on his nose. And I would have escaped unharmed, except for the slip of my right hand. Into his mouth it went to the elbow. His jaws closed, just below the elbow. You know how a shark's teeth are. Once in they cannot be released. They must go through to complete the bite, but they cannot go through heavy bone. So, from just below the elbow he stripped the bone clean to the articulation of the wrist-joint, where his teeth met and my good right hand became his for an appetizer.

"But while he was doing this, I drove the thumb of my left hand, to the hilt into his eye-orifice and popped out his eye. This did not stop him. The meat had maddened him. He pursued the gushing stump of my wrist. Half a dozen times I fended with my intact arm. Then he got the poor mangled arm again, closed down, and stripped the meat off the bone from the shoulder down to the elbow-joint, where his teeth met and he was free of his second mouthful of me. But, at the same time, with my good arm, I thumbed out his remaining eye."

Percival Delaney shrugged his shoulders, ere he resumed.

"From above, those in the canoe had beheld the entire happening and were loud in praise of my deed. To this day they still sing the song of me, and tell the tale of me. And the Princess." His pause was brief but significant. "The Princess married me. . . . Oh, well-a-day and lack-a-day, the whirligig of time and fortune, the topsyturviness of luck, the wooden shoe going up and the polished heel descending a French gunboat, a conquered island kingdom of Oceania, to-day ruled over by a peasant-born, unlettered, colonial gendarme, and . . . "

He completed the sentence and the tale by burying his face in the down-tilted mouth of the condensed milk can and by gurgling the corrosive drink down his throat in thirsty gulps.

After an appropriate pause, Chauncey Delarouse, otherwise Whiskers, took up the tale.

"Far be it from me to boast of no matter what place of birth I have descended from to sit here by this fire with such as . . . as chance along. I may say, however, that I, too, was once a considerable figure of a man. I may add that it was horses, plus parents too indulgent, that exiled me out over the world. I may still wonder to query: 'Are Dover's cliffs still white?'"

"Huh!" Bruce Cadogan Cavendish sneered. "Next you'll be asking: 'How fares the old Lord Warden?'"

"And I took every liberty, and vainly, with a constitution that was iron," Whiskers hurried on. "Here I am with my three score and ten behind me, and back on that long road have I buried many a youngster that was as rare and devilish as I, but who could not stand the pace. I knew the worst too young. And now I know the worst too old. But there was a time, alas all too short, when I knew, the best.

"I, too, kiss my hand to the Princess of my heart. She was truly a princess, Polynesian, a thousand miles and more away to the eastward and the south from Delaney's Isle of Love. The natives of all around that part of the South Seas called it the Jolly Island. Their own name, the name of the people who dwelt thereon, translates delicately and justly into 'The Island of Tranquil Laughter.' On the chart you will find the erroneous name given to it by the old navigators to be Manatomana. The seafaring gentry the round ocean around called it the Adamless Eden. And the missionaries for a time called it God's Witness—so great had been their success at converting the inhabitants. As for me, it was, and ever shall be, Paradise.

"It was *my* Paradise, for it was there my Princess lived. John Asibeli Tungi was king. He was full-blooded native, descended out of the oldest and highest chief-stock that traced back to Manua which was the primeval sea home of the race. Also was he known as John the Apostate. He lived a long life and apostasized frequently. First converted by the Catholics, he threw down the idols, broke the tabus, cleaned out the native priests, executed a few of the recalcitrant ones, and sent all his subjects to church.

"Next he fell for the traders, who developed in him a champagne thirst, and he shipped off the Catholic priests to New Zealand. The great majority of his subjects always followed his lead, and, having no religion at all, ensued the time of the Great Licentiousness, when by all South Seas missionaries his island, in sermons, was spoken of as Babylon.

"But the traders ruined his digestion with too much champagne, and after several years he fell for the Gospel according to the Methodists, sent his people to church, and cleaned up the beach and the trading crowd so spick and span that he would not permit them to smoke a pipe out of doors on Sunday, and, fined one of the chief traders one hundred gold sovereigns for washing his schooner's decks on the Sabbath morn.

"That was the time of the Blue Laws, but perhaps it was too rigorous for King John. Off he packed the Methodists, one fine day, exiled several hundred of his people to Samoa for sticking to Methodism, and, of all things, invented a religion of his own, with himself the figure-head of worship. In this he was aided and abetted by a renegade Fijian. This lasted five years. Maybe he grew tired of being God, or maybe it was because the Fijian decamped with the six thousand pounds in the royal treasury; but at any rate the Second Reformed Wesleyans got him, and his entire kingdom went Wesleyan. The pioneer Wesleyan missionary he actually made prime minister, and what he did to the trading crowd was a caution. Why, in the end, King John's kingdom was blacklisted and boycotted by the traders till the revenues diminished to zero, the people went bankrupt, and King John couldn't borrow a shilling from his most powerful chief.

"By this time he was getting old, and philosophic, and tolerant, and spiritually atavistic. He fired out the Second Reformed Wesleyans, called back the exiles from Samoa, invited in the traders, held a general love-feast, took the lid off, proclaimed religious liberty and high tariff, and as for himself went back to the worship of his ancestors, dug up the idols, reinstated a few octogenarian priests, and observed the tabus. All of which was lovely for the traders, and prosperity reigned. Of course, most of his subjects followed him back into heathen worship. Yet quite a sprinkling of Catholics, Methodists and Wesleyans remained true to their beliefs and managed to maintain a few squalid, one-horse churches. But King John didn't mind, any more than did he the high times of the traders along the beach. Everything went, so long as the taxes were paid. Even when his wife, Queen Mamare, elected to become a Baptist, and invited in a little, weazened, sweet-spirited, club-footed Baptist missionary, King John did not object. All he insisted on was that these wandering religions should be self-supporting and not feed a pennyworth's out of the royal coffers.

"And now the threads of my recital draw together in the paragon of female exquisiteness—my Princess."

Whiskers paused, placed carefully on the ground his half-full condensed milk can with which he had been absently toying, and kissed the fingers of his one hand audibly aloft.

"She was the daughter of Queen Mamare. She was the woman wonderful. Unlike the Diana type of Polynesian, she was almost ethereal.

She *was* ethereal, sublimated by purity, as shy and modest as a violet, as fragile-slender as a lily, and her eyes, luminous and shrinking tender, were as asphodels on the sward of heaven. She was all flower, and fire, and dew. Hers was the sweetness of the mountain rose, the gentleness of the dove. And she was all of good as well as all of beauty, devout in her belief in her mother's worship, which was the worship introduced by Ebenezer Naismith, the Baptist missionary. But make no mistake. She was no mere sweet spirit ripe for the bosom of Abraham. All of exquisite deliciousness of woman was she. She was woman, all woman, to the last sensitive quivering atom of her—

"And I? I was a wastrel of the beach. The wildest was not so wild as I, the keenest not so keen, of all that wild, keen trading crowd. It was esteemed I played the stiffest hand of poker. I was the only living man, white, brown, or black, who dared run the Kuni-kuni Passage in the dark. And on a black night I have done it under reefs in a gale of wind. Well, anyway, I had a bad reputation on a beach where there were no good reputations. I was reckless, dangerous, stopped at nothing in fight or frolic; and the trading captains used to bring boiler-sheeted prodigies from the vilest holes of the South Pacific to try and drink me under the table. I remember one, a calcined Scotchman from the New Hebrides. It was a great drinking. He died of it, and we laded him aboard ship, pickled in a cask of trade rum, and sent him back to his own place. A sample, a fair sample, of the antic tricks we cut up on the beach of Manatomana.

"And of all unthinkable things, what did I up and do, one day, but look upon the Princess to find her good and to fall in love with her. It was the real thing. I was as mad as a March hare, and after that I got only madder. I reformed. Think of that! Think of what a slip of a woman can do to a busy, roving man!—By the Lord Harry, it's true. I reformed. I went to church. Hear me! I became converted. I cleared my soul before God and kept my hands—I had two then—off the ribald crew of the beach when it laughed at this, my latest antic, and wanted to know what was my game.

"I tell you I reformed, and gave myself in passion and sincerity to a religious experience that has made me tolerant of all religion ever since. I discharged my best captain for immorality. So did I my cook, and a better never boiled water in Manatomana. For the same reason I discharged my chief clerk. And for the first time in the history of trading my schooners to the westward carried Bibles in their stock. I built a little anchorite bungalow up town on a mango-lined street squarely alongside the little house occupied by Ebenezer Naismith. And I made him my pal and comrade, and found him a veritable honey pot of sweetnesses and goodnesses. And he was a man, through and through a man. And he died long after like a man, which I would like to tell you about, were the tale of it not so deservedly long.

"It was the Princess, more than the missionary, who was responsible for my expressing my faith in works, and especially in that crowning work, the New Church, Our Church, the Queen-mother's church.

"'Our poor church,' she said to me, one night after prayer-meeting. I had been converted only a fortnight. 'It is so small its congregation can never grow. And the roof leaks. And King John, my hard-hearted father, will not contribute a penny. Yet he has a big balance in the treasury. And Manatomana is not poor. Much money is made and squandered, I know. I hear the gossip of the wild ways of the beach. Less than a month ago you lost more in one night, gambling at cards, than the cost of the upkeep of our poor church for a year.'

"And I told her it was true, but that it was before I had seen the light. (I'd had an infernal run of bad luck.) I told her I had not tasted liquor since, nor turned a card. I told her that the roof would be repaired at once, by Christian carpenters selected by her from the congregation. But she was filled with the thought of a great revival that Ebenezer Naismith could preach—she was a dear saint—and she spoke of a great church, saying:

"'You are rich. You have many schooners, and traders in far islands, and I have heard of a great contract you have signed to recruit labour for the German plantations of Upolu. They say, next to Sweitzer, you are the richest trader here. I should love to see some use of all this money placed to the glory of God. It would be a noble thing to do, and I should be proud to know the man who would do it.'

"I told her that Ebenezer Naismith would preach the revival, and that I would build a church great enough in which to house it.

"'As big as the Catholic church?' she asked.

"This was the ruined cathedral, built at the time when the entire population was converted, and it was a large order; but I was afire with love, and I told her that the church I would build would be even bigger.

"'But it will take money,' I explained. 'And it takes time to make money.'

"'You have much,' she said. 'Some say you have more money than my father, the King.

"'I have more credit,' I explained. 'But you do not understand money. It takes money to have credit. So, with the money I have, and the credit I have, I will work to make more money and credit, and the church shall be built.'

"Work! I was a surprise to myself. It is an amazement, the amount of time a man finds on his hands after he's given up carousing, and gambling, and all the time-eating diversions of the beach. And I didn't waste a second of all my new-found time. Instead I worked it overtime. I did the work of half a dozen men. I became a driver. My captains made faster runs than ever and earned bigger bonuses, as did my supercargoes, who saw to it that my schooners did not loaf and dawdle along the way. And I saw to it that my supercargoes did see to it.

"And good! By the Lord Harry I was so good it hurt. My conscience got so expansive and fine-strung it lamed me across the shoulders to carry it around with me. Why, I even went back over my accounts and paid Sweitzer fifty quid I'd jiggered him out of in a deal in Fiji three years before. And I compounded the interest as well.

"Work! I planted sugar cane—the first commercial planting on Manatomana. I ran in cargoes of kinky-heads from Malaita, which is in the Solomons, till I had twelve hundred of the blackbirds putting in cane. And I sent a schooner clear to Hawaii to bring back a dismantled sugar mill and a German who said he knew the field-end of cane. And he did, and he charged me three hundred dollars screw a month, and I took hold of the mill-end. I installed the mill myself, with the help of several mechanics I brought up from Queensland.

103

"Of course there was a rival. His name was Motomoe. He was the very highest chief blood next to King John's. He was full native, a strapping, handsome man, with a glowering way of showing his dislikes. He certainly glowered at me when I began hanging around the palace. He went back in my history and circulated the blackest tales about me. The worst of it was that most of them were true. He even made a voyage to Apia to find things out—as if he couldn't find a plenty right there on the beach of Manatomana! And he sneered at my failing for religion, and at my going to prayer-meeting, and, most of all, at my sugar-planting. He challenged me to fight, and I kept off of him. He threatened me, and I learned in the nick of time of his plan to have me knocked on the head. You see, he wanted the Princess just as much as I did, and I wanted her more.

"She used to play the piano. So did I, once. But I never let her know after I'd heard her play the first time. And she thought her playing *was* wonderful, the dear, fond girl! You know the sort, the mechanical one-two-three tum-tum-tum school-girl stuff. And now I'll tell you something funnier. Her playing was wonderful to me. The gates of heaven opened to me when she played. I can see myself now, worn out and dog-tired after the long day, lying on the mats of the palace veranda and gazing upon her at the piano, myself in a perfect idiocy of bliss. Why, this idea she had of her fine playing was the one flaw in her deliciousness of perfection, and I loved her for it. It kind of brought her within my human reach. Why, when she played her one-two-three, tum-tum-tum, I was in the seventh heaven of bliss. My weariness fell from me. I loved her, and my love for her was clean as flame, clean as my love for God. And do you know, into my fond lover's fancy continually intruded the thought that God in most ways must look like her.

"—That's right, Bruce Cadogan Cavendish, sneer as you like. But I tell you that's love that I've been describing. That's all. It's love. It's the realest, purest, finest thing that can happen to a man. And I know what I'm talking about. It happened to me."

Whiskers, his beady squirrel's eye glittering from out his ruined eyebrow like a live coal in a jungle ambush, broke off long enough to down a sedative draught from his condensed milk can and to mix another.

104

"The cane," he resumed, wiping his prodigious mat of face hair with the back of his hand. "It matured in sixteen months in that climate, and I was ready, just ready and no more, with the mill for the grinding. Naturally, it did not all mature at once, but I had planted in such succession that I could grind for nine months steadily, while more was being planted and the ratoons were springing up.

"I had my troubles the first several days. If it wasn't one thing the matter with the mill, it was another. On the fourth day, Ferguson, my engineer, had to shut down several hours in order to remedy his own troubles. I was bothered by the feeder. After having the niggers (who had been feeding the cane) pour cream of lime on the rollers to keep everything sweet, I sent them out to join the cane-cutting squads. So I was all alone at that end, just as Ferguson started up the mill, just as I discovered what was the matter with the feed-rollers, and just as Motomoe strolled up.

"He stood there, in Norfolk jacket, pigskin puttees, and all the rest of the fashionable get-up out of a bandbox, sneering at me covered with filth and grease to the eyebrows and looking like a navvy. And, the rollers now white from the lime, I'd just seen what was wrong. The rollers were not in plumb. One side crushed the cane well, but the other side was too open. I shoved my fingers in on that side. The big, toothed cogs on the rollers did not touch my fingers. And yet, suddenly, they did. With the grip of ten thousand devils, my finger-tips were caught, drawn in, and pulped to—well, just pulp. And, like a slick of cane, I had started on my way. There was no stopping me. Ten thousand horses could not have pulled me back. There was nothing to stop me. Hand, arm, shoulder, head, and chest, down to the toes of me, I was doomed to feed through.

"It did hurt. It hurt so much it did not hurt me at all. Quite detached, almost may I say, I looked on my hand being ground up, knuckle by knuckle, joint by joint, the back of the hand, the wrist, the forearm, all in order slowly and inevitably feeding in. O engineer hoist by thine own petard! O sugar-maker crushed by thine own cane-crusher!

"Motomoe sprang forward involuntarily, and the sneer was chased from his face by an expression of solicitude. Then the beauty of the situation dawned on him, and he chuckled and grinned. No, I didn't expect anything of him. Hadn't he tried to knock me on the head? What could he do anyway? He didn't know anything about engines.

"I yelled at the top of my lungs to Ferguson to shut off the engine, but the roar of the machinery drowned my voice. And there I stood, up to the elbow and feeding right on in. Yes, it did hurt. There were some astonishing twinges when special nerves were shredded and dragged out by the roots. But I remember that I was surprised at the time that it did not hurt worse.

"Motomoe made a movement that attracted my attention. At the same time he growled out loud, as if he hated himself, 'I'm a fool.' What he had done was to pick up a cane-knife—you know the kind, as big as a machete and as heavy. And I was grateful to him in advance for putting me out of my misery. There wasn't any sense in slowly feeding in till my head was crushed, and already my arm was pulped half way from elbow to shoulder, and the pulping was going right on. So I was grateful, as I bent my head to the blow.

"'Get your head out of the way, you idiot!' he barked at me.

"And then I understood and obeyed. I was a big man, and he took two hacks to do it; but he hacked my arm off just outside the shoulder and dragged me back and laid me down on the cane.

"Yes, the sugar paid—enormously; and I built for the Princess the church of her saintly dream, and . . . she married me."

He partly assuaged his thirst, and uttered his final word.

"Alackaday! Shuttlecock and battle-dore. And this at, the end of it all, lined with boilerplate that even alcohol will not corrode and that only alcohol will tickle. Yet have I lived, and I kiss my hand to the dear dust of my Princess long asleep in the great mausoleum of King John that looks across the Vale of Manona to the alien flag that floats over the bungalow of the British Government House. . . ."

Fatty pledged him sympathetically, and sympathetically drank out of his own small can. Bruce Cadogan Cavendish glared into the fire with implacable bitterness. He was a man who preferred to drink by himself. Across the thin lips that composed the cruel slash of his mouth played twitches of mockery that caught Fatty's eye. And Fatty, making sure first that his rock-chunk was within reach, challenged.

"Well, how about yourself, Bruce Cadogan Cavendish? It's your turn."

The other lifted bleak eyes that bored into Fatty's until he physically betrayed uncomfortableness.

"I've lived a hard life," Slim grated harshly. "What do I know about love passages?"

"No man of your build and make-up could have escaped them," Fatty wheedled.

"And what of it?" Slim snarled. "It's no reason for a gentleman to boast of amorous triumphs."

"Oh, go on, be a good fellow," Fatty urged. "The night's still young. We've still some drink left. Delarouse and I have contributed our share. It isn't often that three real ones like us get together for a telling. Surely you've got at least one adventure in love you aren't ashamed to tell about—"

Bruce Cadogan Cavendish pulled forth his iron quoit and seemed to debate whether or not he should brain the other. He sighed, and put back the quoit.

"Very well, if you will have it," he surrendered with manifest reluctance. "Like you two, I have had a remarkable constitution. And right now, speaking of armour-plate lining, I could drink the both of you down when you were at your prime. Like you two, my beginnings were far distant and different. That I am marked with the hall-mark of gentlehood there is no discussion . . . unless either of you care to discuss the matter now . . . "

His one hand slipped into his pocket and clutched the quoit. Neither of his auditors spoke nor betrayed any awareness of his menace.

"It occurred a thousand miles to the westward of Manatomana, on the island of Tagalag," he continued abruptly, with an air of saturnine disappointment in that there had been no discussion. "But first I must tell you of how I got to Tagalag. For reasons I shall not mention, by paths of descent I shall not describe, in the crown of my manhood and the prime of my devilishness in which Oxford renegades and racing younger sons had nothing on me, I found myself master and owner of a schooner so well known that she shall remain historically nameless. I was running blackbird labour from the west South Pacific and the Coral Sea to the plantations of Hawaii and the nitrate mines of Chili—"

"It was you who cleaned out the entire population of—" Fatty exploded, ere he could check his speech.

The one hand of Bruce Cadogan Cavendish flashed pocketward and flashed back with the quoit balanced ripe for business.

"Proceed," Fatty sighed. "I . . . I have quite forgotten what I was going to say."

"Beastly funny country over that way," the narrator drawled with perfect casualness. "You've read this Sea Wolf stuff—"

"You weren't the Sea Wolf," Whiskers broke in with involuntary positiveness.

"No, sir," was the snarling answer. "The Sea Wolf's dead, isn't he? And I'm still alive, aren't I?"

"Of course, of course," Whiskers conceded. "He suffocated head-first in the mud off a wharf in Victoria a couple of years back."

"As I was saying—and I don't like interruptions," Bruce Cadogan Cavendish proceeded, "it's a beastly funny country over that way. I was at Taki-Tiki, a low island that politically belongs to the Solomons, but that geologically doesn't at all, for the Solomons are high islands. Ethnographically it belongs to Polynesia, Melanesia, and Micronesia, because all the breeds of the South Pacific have gravitated to it by canoe-drift and intricately, degeneratively, and amazingly interbred. The scum of the scrapings of the bottom of the human pit, biologically speaking, resides in Taka-Tiki. And I know the bottom and whereof I speak.

"It was a beastly funny time of it I had, diving out shell, fishing beche-de-mer, trading hoop-iron and hatchets for copra and ivory-nuts, running niggers and all the rest of it. Why, even in Fiji the Lotu was having a hard time of it and the chiefs still eating long-pig. To the westward it was fierce—funny little black kinky-heads, man-eaters the last Jack of them, and the jackpot fat and spilling over with wealth—"

"Jack-pots?" Fatty queried. At sight of an irritable movement, he added: "You see, I never got over to the West like Delarouse and you."

"They're all head-hunters. Heads are valuable, especially a white man's head. They decorate the canoe-houses and devil-devil houses with them. Each village runs a jack-pot, and everybody antes. Whoever brings in a white man's head takes the pot. If there aren't openers for a long time, the pot grows to tremendous proportions. Beastly funny, isn't it?

"I know. Didn't a Holland mate die on me of blackwater? And didn't I win a pot myself? It was this way. We were lying at Lango-lui at the time. I never let on, and arranged the affair with Johnny, my boat-steerer. He was a kinky-head himself from Port Moresby. He cut the dead mate's head off and sneaked ashore in the night, while I whanged away with my rifle as if I were trying to get him. He opened the pot with the mate's head, and got it, too. Of course, next day I sent in a landing boat, with two covering boats, and fetched him off with the loot."

"How big was the pot?" Whiskers asked. "I heard of a pot at Orla worth eighty quid."

"To commence with," Slim answered, "there were forty fat pigs, each worth a fathom of prime shell-money, and shell-money worth a quid a fathom. That was two hundred dollars right there. There were ninety-eight fathoms of shell-money, which is pretty close to five hundred in itself. And there were twenty-two gold sovereigns. I split it four ways: one-fourth to

Johnny, one-fourth to the ship, one-fourth to me as owner, and one-fourth to me as skipper. Johnny never complained. He'd never had so much wealth all at one time in his life. Besides, I gave him a couple of the mate's old shirts. And I fancy the mate's head is still there decorating the canoe-house."

"Not exactly Christian burial of a Christian," Whiskers observed.

"But a lucrative burial," Slim retorted. "I had to feed the rest of the mate over-side to the sharks for nothing. Think of feeding an eight-hundred-dollar head along with it. It would have been criminal waste and stark lunacy.

"Well, anyway, it was all beastly funny, over there to the westward. And, without telling you the scrape I got into at Taki-Tiki, except that I sailed away with two hundred kinky-heads for Queensland labour, and for my manner of collecting them had two British ships of war combing the Pacific for me, I changed my course and ran to the westward thinking to dispose of the lot to the Spanish plantations on Bangar.

"Typhoon season. We caught it. The *Merry Mist* was my schooner's name, and I had thought she was stoutly built until she hit that typhoon. I never saw such seas. They pounded that stout craft to pieces, literally so. The sticks were jerked out of her, deckhouses splintered to match-wood, rails ripped off, and, after the worst had passed, the covering boards began to go. We just managed to repair what was left of one boat and keep the schooner afloat only till the sea went down barely enough to get away. And we outfitted that boat in a hurry. The carpenter and I were the last, and we had to jump for it as he went down. There were only four of us—"

"Lost all the niggers?" Whiskers inquired.

"Some of them swam for some time," Slim replied. "But I don't fancy they made the land. We were ten days' in doing it. And we had a spanking breeze most of the way. And what do you think we had in the boat with us? Cases of square-face gin and cases of dynamite. Funny, wasn't it? Well, it got funnier later on. Oh, there was a small beaker of water, a little salt horse, and some salt-water-soaked sea biscuit—enough to keep us alive to Tagalag.

"Now Tagalag is the disappointingest island I've ever beheld. It shows up out of the sea so as you can make its fall twenty miles off. It is a volcano cone thrust up out of deep sea, with a segment of the crater wall broken out. This gives sea entrance to the crater itself, and makes a fine sheltered harbour. And that's all. Nothing lives there. The outside and the inside of the crater are too steep. At one place, inside, is a patch of about a thousand coconut palms. And that's all, as I said, saving a few insects. No four-legged thing, even a rat, inhabits the place. And it's funny, most awful funny, with all those coconuts, not even a coconut crab. The only meat-food living was schools of mullet in the harbour—fattest, finest, biggest mullet I ever laid eyes on.

"And the four of us landed on the little beach and set up housekeeping among the coconuts with a larder full of dynamite and square-face. Why don't you laugh? It's funny, I tell you. Try it some time.—Holland gin and straight coconut diet. I've never been able to look a confectioner's window in the face since. Now I'm not strong on religion like Chauncey Delarouse there, but I have some primitive ideas; and my concept of hell is an illimitable coconut plantation, stocked with cases of square-face and populated by ship-wrecked mariners. Funny? It must make the devil scream.

"You know, straight coconut is what the agriculturists call an unbalanced ration. It certainly unbalanced our digestions. We got so that whenever hunger took an extra bite at us, we took another drink of gin. After a couple of weeks of it, Olaf, a squarehead sailor, got an idea. It came when he was full of gin, and we, being in the same fix, just watched him shove a cap and short fuse into a stick of dynamite and stroll down toward the boat.

"It dawned on me that he was going to shoot fish if there were any about; but the sun was beastly hot, and I just reclined there and hoped he'd have luck.

"About half an hour after he disappeared we heard the explosion. But he didn't come back. We waited till the cool of sunset, and down on the beach found what had become of him. The boat was there all right, grounded by the prevailing breeze, but there was no Olaf. He would never have to eat coconut again. We went back, shakier than ever, and cracked another square-face.

"The next day the cook announced that he would rather take his chance with dynamite than continue trying to exist on coconut, and that, though he didn't know anything about dynamite, he knew a sight too much about coconut. So we bit the detonator down for him, shoved in a fuse, and picked him a good fire-stick, while he jolted up with a couple more stiff ones of gin.

"It was the same programme as the day before. After a while we heard the explosion and at twilight went down to the boat, from which we scraped enough of the cook for a funeral.

"The carpenter and I stuck it out two days more, then we drew straws for it and it was his turn. We parted with harsh words; for he wanted to take a square-face along to refresh himself by the way, while I was set against running any chance of wasting the gin. Besides, he had more than he could carry then, and he wobbled and staggered as he walked.

"Same thing, only there was a whole lot of him left for me to bury, because he'd prepared only half a stick. I managed to last it out till next day, when, after duly fortifying myself, I got sufficient courage to tackle the dynamite. I used only a third of a stick—you know, short fuse, with the end split so as to hold the head of a safety match. That's where I mended my predecessors' methods. Not using the match-head, they'd too-long fuses. Therefore, when they spotted a school of mullet; and lighted the fuse, they had to hold the dynamite till the fuse burned short before they threw it. If they threw it too soon, it wouldn't go off the instant it hit the water, while the splash of it would frighten the mullet away. Funny stuff dynamite. At any rate, I still maintain mine was the safer method.

"I picked up a school of mullet before I'd been rowing five minutes. Fine big fat ones they were, and I could smell them over the fire. When I stood up, fire-stick in one hand, dynamite stick in the other, my knees were knocking together. Maybe it was the gin, or the anxiousness, or the weakness and the hunger, and maybe it was the result of all of them, but at any rate I was all of a shake. Twice I failed to touch the fire-stick to the dynamite. Then I did, heard the match-head splutter, and let her go.

"Now I don't know what happened to the others, but I know what I did. I got turned about. Did you ever stem a strawberry and throw the strawberry away and pop the stem into your mouth? That's what I did. I threw the fire-stick into the water after the mullet and held on to the dynamite. And my arm went off with the stick when it went off. . . . "

Slim investigated the tomato-can for water to mix himself a drink, but found it empty. He stood up.

"Heigh ho," he yawned, and started down the path to the river.

In several minutes he was back. He mixed the due quantity of river slush with the alcohol, took a long, solitary drink, and stared with bitter moodiness into the fire.

"Yes, but . . . " Fatty suggested. "What happened then?"

"Oh," sad Slim. "Then the princess married me, of course."

"But you were the only person left, and there wasn't any princess . . . " Whiskers cried out abruptly, and then let his voice trail away to embarrassed silence.

Slim stared unblinkingly into the fire.

Percival Delaney and Chauncey Delarouse looked at each other. Quietly, in solemn silence, each with his one arm aided the one arm of the other in rolling and tying his bundle. And in silence, bundles slung on shoulders, they went away out of the circle of firelight. Not until they reached the top of the railroad embankment did they speak.

"No gentleman would have done it," said Whiskers.

"No gentleman would have done it," Fatty agreed.

THE END

Glen Ellen, California,

September 26, 1916.

THE NIGHT-BORN

THE NIGHT-BORN

It was in the old Alta-Inyo Club—a warm night for San Francisco—and through the open windows, hushed and far, came the brawl of the streets. The talk had led on from the Graft Prosecution and the latest signs that the town was to be run wide open, down through all the grotesque sordidness and rottenness of man-hate and man-meanness, until the name of O'Brien was mentioned—O'Brien, the promising young pugilist who had been killed in the prize-ring the night before. At once the air had seemed to freshen. O'Brien had been a clean-living young man with ideals. He neither drank, smoked, nor swore, and his had been the body of a beautiful young god. He had even carried his prayer-book to the ringside. They found it in his coat pocket in the dressing-room... afterward.

Here was Youth, clean and wholesome, unsullied—the thing of glory and wonder for men to conjure with..... after it has been lost to them and they have turned middle-aged. And so well did we conjure, that Romance came and for an hour led us far from the man-city and its snarling roar. Bardwell, in a way, started it by quoting from Thoreau; but it was old Trefethan, bald-headed and dewlapped, who took up the quotation and for the hour to come was romance incarnate. At first we wondered how many Scotches he had consumed since dinner, but very soon all that was forgotten.

"It was in 1898—I was thirty-five then," he said. "Yes, I know you are adding it up. You're right. I'm forty-seven now; look ten years more; and the doctors say—damn the doctors anyway!"

He lifted the long glass to his lips and sipped it slowly to soothe away his irritation.

"But I was young... once. I was young twelve years ago, and I had hair on top of my head, and my stomach was lean as a runner's, and the longest day was none too long for me. I was a husky back there in '98. You remember me, Milner. You knew me then. Wasn't I a pretty good bit of all right?"

Milner nodded and agreed. Like Trefethan, he was another mining engineer who had cleaned up a fortune in the Klondike.

"You certainly were, old man," Milner said. "I'll never forget when you cleaned out those lumberjacks in the M. & M. that night that little newspaper man started the row. Slavin was in the country at the time,"—this to us—"and his manager wanted to get up a match with Trefethan."

"Well, look at me now," Trefethan commanded angrily. "That's what the Goldstead did to me—God knows how many millions, but nothing left in my soul..... nor in my veins. The good red blood is gone. I am a jellyfish, a huge, gross mass of oscillating protoplasm, a—a..."

But language failed him, and he drew solace from the long glass.

"Women looked at me then; and turned their heads to look a second time. Strange that I never married. But the girl. That's what I started to tell you about. I met her a thousand miles from anywhere, and then some. And she quoted to me those very words of Thoreau that Bardwell quoted a moment ago—the ones about the day-born gods and the night-born."

"It was after I had made my locations on Goldstead—and didn't know what a treasure-pot that that trip creek was going to prove—that I made that trip east over the Rockies, angling across to the Great Up North there the Rockies are something more than a back-bone. They are a boundary, a dividing line, a wall impregnable and unscalable. There is no intercourse across them, though, on occasion, from the early days, wandering trappers have crossed them, though more were lost by the way than ever came through. And that was precisely why I tackled the job. It was a traverse any man would be proud to make. I am prouder of it right now than anything else I have ever done.

"It is an unknown land. Great stretches of it have never been explored. There are big valleys there where the white man has never set foot, and Indian tribes as primitive as ten thousand years... almost, for they have had some contact with the whites. Parties of them come out once in a while to trade, and that is all. Even the Hudson Bay Company failed to find them and farm them.

"And now the girl. I was coming up a stream—you'd call it a river in California—uncharted—and unnamed. It was a noble valley, now shut in by high canyon walls, and again opening out into beautiful stretches, wide and long, with pasture shoulder-high in the bottoms, meadows dotted with flowers, and with clumps of timberspruce—virgin and magnificent. The dogs were packing on their backs, and were sore-footed and played out; while I was looking for any bunch of Indians to get sleds and drivers from and go on with the first snow. It was late fall, but the way those flowers persisted surprised me. I was supposed to be in sub-arctic America, and high up among the buttresses of the Rockies, and yet there was that everlasting spread of flowers. Some day the white settlers will be in there and growing wheat down all that valley.

"And then I lifted a smoke, and heard the barking of the dogs—Indian dogs—and came into camp. There must have been five hundred of them, proper Indians at that, and I could see by the jerking-frames that the fall hunting had been good. And then I met her—Lucy. That was her name. Sign language—that was all we could talk with, till they led me to a big fly—you know, half a tent, open on the one side where a campfire burned. It was all of moose-skins, this fly—moose-skins, smoke-cured, hand-rubbed, and golden-brown. Under it everything was neat and orderly as no Indian camp ever was. The bed was laid on fresh spruce boughs. There were furs galore, and on top of all was a robe of swanskins—white swan-skins—I have never seen anything like that robe. And on top of it, sitting cross-legged, was Lucy. She was nut-brown. I have called her a girl. But she was not. She was a woman, a nut-brown woman, an Amazon, a full-blooded, full-bodied woman, and royal ripe. And her eyes were blue.

"That's what took me off my feet—her eyes—blue, not China blue, but deep blue, like the sea and sky all melted into one, and very wise. More than that, they had laughter in them—warm laughter, sun-warm and human, very human, and... shall I say feminine? They were. They were a woman's eyes, a proper woman's eyes. You know what that means. Can I say more? Also, in those blue eyes were, at the same time, a wild unrest, a wistful yearning, and a repose, an absolute repose, a sort of all-wise and philosophical calm."

Trefethan broke off abruptly.

"You fellows think I am screwed. I'm not. This is only my fifth since dinner. I am dead sober. I am solemn. I sit here now side by side with my sacred youth. It is not I—'old' Trefethan—that talks; it is my youth, and it is my youth that says those were the most wonderful eyes I have ever seen—so very calm, so very restless; so very wise, so very curious; so very old, so very young; so satisfied and yet yearning so wistfully. Boys, I can't describe them. When I have told you about her, you may know better for yourselves."

"She did not stand up. But she put out her hand."

"'Stranger,' she said, 'I'm real glad to see you.'

"I leave it to you—that sharp, frontier, Western tang of speech. Picture my sensations. It was a woman, a white woman, but that tang! It was amazing that it should be a white woman, here, beyond the last boundary of the world—but the tang. I tell you, it hurt. It was like the stab of a flatted note. And yet, let me tell you, that woman was a poet. You shall see."

"She dismissed the Indians. And, by Jove, they went. They took her orders and followed her blind. She was hi-yu skookam chief. She told the bucks to make a camp for me and to take care of my dogs. And they did, too. And they knew enough not to get away with as much as a moccasin-lace of my outfit. She was a regular She-Who-Must-Be-Obeyed, and I want to tell you it chilled me to the marrow, sent those little thrills Marathoning up and down my spinal column, meeting a white woman out there at the head of a tribe of savages a thousand miles the other side of No Man's Land.

"'Stranger,' she said, 'I reckon you're sure the first white that ever set foot in this valley. Set down an' talk a spell, and then we'll have a bite to eat. Which way might you be comin'?'

"There it was, that tang again. But from now to the end of the yarn I want you to forget it. I tell you I forgot it, sitting there on the edge of that swan-skin robe and listening and looking at the most wonderful woman that ever stepped out of the pages of Thoreau or of any other man's book.

"I stayed on there a week. It was on her invitation. She promised to fit me out with dogs and sleds and with Indians that would put me across the best pass of the Rockies in five hundred miles. Her fly was pitched apart from the others, on the high bank by the river, and a couple of Indian girls did her cooking for her and the camp work. And so we talked and talked, while the first snow fell and continued to fall and make a surface for my sleds. And this was her story.

"She was frontier-born, of poor settlers, and you know what that means—work, work, always work, work in plenty and without end.

"'I never seen the glory of the world,' she said. 'I had no time. I knew it was right out there, anywhere, all around the cabin, but there was always the bread to set, the scrubbin' and the washin' and the work that was never done. I used to be plumb sick at times, jes' to get out into it all, especially in the spring when the songs of the birds drove me most clean crazy. I wanted to run out through the long pasture grass, wetting my legs with the dew of it, and to climb the rail fence, and keep on through the timber and up and up over the divide so as to get a look around. Oh, I had all kinds of hankerings—to follow up the canyon beds and slosh around from pool to pool, making friends with the water-dogs and the speckly trout; to peep on the sly and watch the squirrels and rabbits and small furry things and see what they was doing and learn the secrets of their ways. Seemed to me, if I had time, I could crawl among the flowers, and, if I was good and quiet, catch them whispering with themselves, telling all kinds of wise things that mere humans never know.'"

Trefethan paused to see that his glass had been refilled.

"Another time she said: 'I wanted to run nights like a wild thing, just to run through the moonshine and under the stars, to run white and naked in the darkness that I knew must feel like cool velvet, and to run and run and keep on running. One evening, plumb tuckered out—it had been a dreadful hard hot day, and the bread wouldn't raise and the churning had gone wrong, and I was all irritated and jerky—well, that evening I made mention to dad of this wanting to run of mine. He looked at me curious-some and a bit scared. And then he gave me two pills to take. Said to go to bed and get a good sleep and I'd be all hunky-dory in the morning. So I never mentioned my hankerings to him, or any one any more.'

"The mountain home broke up—starved out, I imagine—and the family came to Seattle to live. There she worked in a factory—long hours, you know, and all the rest, deadly work. And after a year of that she became waitress in a cheap restaurant—hash-slinger, she called it. She said to me once, 'Romance I guess was what I wanted. But there wan't no romance floating around in dishpans and washtubs, or in factories and hash-joints.'

"When she was eighteen she married—a man who was going up to Juneau to start a restaurant. He had a few dollars saved, and appeared prosperous. She didn't love him—she was emphatic about that, but she was all tired out, and she wanted to get away from the unending drudgery. Besides, Juneau was in Alaska, and her yearning took the form of a desire to see that wonderland. But little she saw of it. He started the restaurant, a little cheap one, and she quickly learned what he had married her for..... to save paying wages. She came pretty close to running the joint and doing all the work from waiting to dishwashing. She cooked most of the time as well. And she had four years of it.

"Can't you picture her, this wild woods creature, quick with every old primitive instinct, yearning for the free open, and mowed up in a vile little hash-joint and toiling and moiling for four mortal years?

"'There was no meaning in anything,' she said. 'What was it all about! Why was I born! Was that all the meaning of life—just to work and work and be always tired!—to go to bed tired and to wake up tired, with every day like every other day unless it was harder?' She had heard talk of immortal life from the gospel sharps, she said, but she could not reckon that what she was doin' was a likely preparation for her immortality.

"But she still had her dreams, though more rarely. She had read a few books—what, it is pretty hard to imagine, Seaside Library novels most likely; yet they had been food for fancy. 'Sometimes,' she said, 'when I was that dizzy from the heat of the cooking that if I didn't take a breath of fresh air I'd faint, I'd stick my head out of the kitchen window, and close my eyes and see most wonderful things. All of a sudden I'd be traveling down a country road, and everything clean and quiet, no dust, no dirt; just streams ripplin' down sweet meadows, and lambs playing, breezes blowing the breath of flowers, and soft sunshine over everything; and lovely cows lazying knee-deep in quiet pools, and young girls bathing in a curve of stream all white and slim and natural—and I'd know I was in Arcady. I'd read about that country once, in a book. And maybe knights, all flashing in the sun, would come riding around a bend in the road, or a lady on a milk-white mare, and in the distance I could see the towers of a castle rising, or I just knew, on the next turn, that I'd come upon some palace, all white and airy and fairy-like, with fountains playing, and flowers all over everything, and peacocks on the lawn..... and then I'd open my eyes, and the heat of the cooking range would strike on me, and I'd hear Jake sayin'—he was my husband—I'd hear Jake sayin', "Why ain't you served them beans? Think I can wait here all day!" Romance!—I reckon the nearest I ever come to it was when a drunken Armenian cook got the snakes and tried to cut my throat with a potato knife and I got my arm burned on the stove before I could lay him out with the potato stomper.

"'I wanted easy ways, and lovely things, and Romance and all that; but it just seemed I had no luck nohow and was only and expressly born for cooking and dishwashing. There was a wild crowd in Juneau them days, but I looked at the other women, and their way of life didn't excite me. I reckon I wanted to be clean. I don't know why; I just wanted to, I guess; and I reckoned I might as well die dishwashing as die their way.'"

Trefethan halted in his tale for a moment, completing to himself some thread of thought.

"And this is the woman I met up there in the Arctic, running a tribe of wild Indians and a few thousand square miles of hunting territory. And it happened, simply enough, though, for that matter, she might have lived and died among the pots and pans. But 'Came the whisper, came the vision.' That was all she needed, and she got it.

"'I woke up one day,' she said. 'Just happened on it in a scrap of newspaper. I remember every word of it, and I can give it to you.' And then she quoted Thoreau's Cry of the Human:

125

"'The young pines springing up, in the corn field from year to year are to me a refreshing fact. We talk of civilizing the Indian, but that is not the name for his improvement. By the wary independence and aloofness of his dim forest life he preserves his intercourse with his native gods and is admitted from time to time to a rare and peculiar society with nature. He has glances of starry recognition, to which our saloons are strangers. The steady illumination of his qenius, dim only because distant, is like the faint but satisfying light of the stars compared with the dazzling but ineffectual and short-lived blaze of candles. The Society Islanders had their day-born gods, but they were not supposed to be of equal antiquity with the..... night-born gods.'

"That's what she did, repeated it word for word, and I forgot the tang, for it was solemn, a declaration of religion—pagan, if you will; and clothed in the living garmenture of herself.

"'And the rest of it was torn away,' she added, a great emptiness in her voice. 'It was only a scrap of newspaper. But that Thoreau was a wise man. I wish I knew more about him.' She stopped a moment, and I swear her face was ineffably holy as she said, 'I could have made him a good wife.'

"And then she went on. 'I knew right away, as soon as I read that, what was the matter with me. I was a night-born. I, who had lived all my life with the day-born, was a night-born. That was why I had never been satisfied with cooking and dishwashing; that was why I had hankered to run naked in the moonlight. And I knew that this dirty little Juneau hash-joint was no place for me. And right there and then I said, "I quit." I packed up my few rags of clothes, and started. Jake saw me and tried to stop me.

"'What you doing?" he says.

"'Divorcin' you and me,' I says. 'I'm headin' for tall timber and where I belong.'"

"'No you don't,' he says, reaching for me to stop me. 'The cooking has got on your head. You listen to me talk before you up and do anything brash.'

"But I pulled a gun-a little Colt's forty-four—and says, 'This does my talkin' for me.'

"And I left."

Trefethan emptied his glass and called for another.

"Boys, do you know what that girl did? She was twenty-two. She had spent her life over the dish-pan and she knew no more about the world than I do of the fourth dimension, or the fifth. All roads led to her desire. No; she didn't head for the dance-halls. On the Alaskan Pan-handle it is preferable to travel by water. She went down to the beach. An Indian canoe was starting for Dyea—you know the kind, carved out of a single tree, narrow and deep and sixty feet long. She gave them a couple of dollars and got on board.

"'Romance?' she told me. 'It was Romance from the jump. There were three families altogether in that canoe, and that crowded there wasn't room to turn around, with dogs and Indian babies sprawling over everything, and everybody dipping a paddle and making that canoe go.' And all around the great solemn mountains, and tangled drifts of clouds and sunshine. And oh, the silence! the great wonderful silence! And, once, the smoke of a hunter's camp, away off in the distance, trailing among the trees. It was like a picnic, a grand picnic, and I could see my dreams coming true, and I was ready for something to happen 'most any time. And it did.

"'And that first camp, on the island! And the boys spearing fish in the mouth of the creek, and the big deer one of the bucks shot just around the point. And there were flowers everywhere, and in back from the beach the grass was thick and lush and neck-high. And some of the girls went through this with me, and we climbed the hillside behind and picked berries and roots that tasted sour and were good to eat. And we came upon a big bear in the berries making his supper, and he said "Oof!" and ran away as scared as we were. And then the camp, and the camp smoke, and the smell of fresh venison cooking. It was beautiful. I was with the night-born at last, and I knew that was where I belonged. And for the first time in my life, it seemed to me, I went to bed happy that night, looking out under a corner of the canvas at the stars cut off black by a big shoulder of mountain, and listening to the night-noises, and knowing that the same thing would go on next day and forever and ever, for I wasn't going back. And I never did go back.'

"'Romance! I got it next day. We had to cross a big arm of the ocean—twelve or fifteen miles, at least; and it came on to blow when we were in the middle. That night I was along on shore, with one wolf-dog, and I was the only one left alive.'

"Picture it yourself," Trefethan broke off to say. "The canoe was wrecked and lost, and everybody pounded to death on the rocks except her. She went ashore hanging on to a dog's tail, escaping the rocks and washing up on a tiny beach, the only one in miles.

"'Lucky for me it was the mainland,' she said. 'So I headed right away back, through the woods and over the mountains and straight on anywhere. Seemed I was looking for something and knew I'd find it. I wasn't afraid. I was night-born, and the big timber couldn't kill me. And on the second day I found it. I came upon a small clearing and a tumbledown cabin. Nobody had been there for years and years. The roof had fallen in. Rotted blankets lay in the bunks, and pots and pans were on the stove. But that was not the most curious thing. Outside, along the edge of the trees, you can't guess what I found. The skeletons of eight horses, each tied to a tree. They had starved to death, I reckon, and left only little piles of bones scattered some here and there. And each horse had had a load on its back. There the loads lay, in among the bones—painted canvas sacks, and inside moosehide sacks, and inside the moosehide sacks—what do you think?'"

She stopped, reached under a corner of the bed among the spruce boughs, and pulled out a leather sack. She untied the mouth and ran out into my hand as pretty a stream of gold as I have ever seen—coarse gold, placer gold, some large dust, but mostly nuggets, and it was so fresh and rough that it scarcely showed signs of water-wash.

"'You say you're a mining engineer,' she said, 'and you know this country. Can you name a pay-creek that has the color of that gold!'

"I couldn't! There wasn't a trace of silver. It was almost pure, and I told her so.

"'You bet,' she said. 'I sell that for nineteen dollars an ounce. You can't get over seventeen for Eldorado gold, and Minook gold don't fetch quite eighteen. Well, that was what I found among the bones—eight horse-loads of it, one hundred and fifty pounds to the load.'

"'A quarter of a million dollars!' I cried out.

"'That's what I reckoned it roughly,' she answered. 'Talk about Romance! And me a slaving the way I had all the years, when as soon as I ventured out, inside three days, this was what happened. And what became of the men that mined all that gold? Often and often I wonder about it. They left their horses, loaded and tied, and just disappeared off the face of the earth, leaving neither hide nor hair behind them. I never heard tell of them. Nobody knows anything about them. Well, being the night-born, I reckon I was their rightful heir.'"

Trefethan stopped to light a cigar.

"Do you know what that girl did? She cached the gold, saving out thirty pounds, which she carried back to the coast. Then she signaled a passing canoe, made her way to Pat Healy's trading post at Dyea, outfitted, and went over Chilcoot Pass. That was in '88—eight years before the Klondike strike, and the Yukon was a howling wilderness. She was afraid of the bucks, but she took two young squaws with her, crossed the lakes, and went down the river and to all the early camps on the Lower Yukon. She wandered several years over that country and then on in to where I met her. Liked the looks of it, she said, seeing, in her own words, 'a big bull caribou knee-deep in purple iris on the valley-bottom.' She hooked up with the Indians, doctored them, gained their confidence, and gradually took them in charge. She had only left that country once, and then, with a bunch of the young bucks, she went over Chilcoot, cleaned up her gold-cache, and brought it back with her.

"'And here I be, stranger,' she concluded her yarn, 'and here's the most precious thing I own.'

"She pulled out a little pouch of buckskin, worn on her neck like a locket, and opened it. And inside, wrapped in oiled silk, yellowed with age and worn and thumbed, was the original scrap of newspaper containing the quotation from Thoreau.

"'And are you happy... satisfied?' I asked her. 'With a quarter of a million you wouldn't have to work down in the States. You must miss a lot.'

"'Not much,' she answered. 'I wouldn't swop places with any woman down in the States. These are my people; this is where I belong. But there are times—and in her eyes smoldered up that hungry yearning I've mentioned—'there are times when I wish most awful bad for that Thoreau man to happen along.'

"'Why?' I asked.

"'So as I could marry him. I do get mighty lonesome at spells. I'm just a woman—a real woman. I've heard tell of the other kind of women that gallivanted off like me and did queer things—the sort that become soldiers in armies, and sailors on ships. But those women are queer themselves. They're more like men than women; they look like men and they don't have ordinary women's needs. They don't want love, nor little children in their arms and around their knees. I'm not that sort. I leave it to you, stranger. Do I look like a man?'

"She didn't. She was a woman, a beautiful, nut-brown woman, with a sturdy, health-rounded woman's body and with wonderful deep-blue woman's eyes.

"'Ain't I woman?' she demanded. 'I am. I'm 'most all woman, and then some. And the funny thing is, though I'm night-born in everything else, I'm not when it comes to mating. I reckon that kind likes its own kind best. That's the way it is with me, anyway, and has been all these years.'

"'You mean to tell me—' I began.

"'Never,' she said, and her eyes looked into mine with the straightness of truth. 'I had one husband, only—him I call the Ox; and I reckon he's still down in Juneau running the hash-joint. Look him up, if you ever get back, and you'll find he's rightly named.'

"And look him up I did, two years afterward. He was all she said—solid and stolid, the Ox—shuffling around and waiting on the tables.

"'You need a wife to help you,' I said.

"'I had one once,' was his answer.

"'Widower?'

"'Yep. She went loco. She always said the heat of the cooking would get her, and it did. Pulled a gun on me one day and ran away with some Siwashes in a canoe. Caught a blow up the coast and all hands drowned.'"

Trefethan devoted himself to his glass and remained silent.

"But the girl?" Milner reminded him.

"You left your story just as it was getting interesting, tender. Did it?"

"It did," Trefethan replied. "As she said herself, she was savage in everything except mating, and then she wanted her own kind. She was very nice about it, but she was straight to the point. She wanted to marry me.

"'Stranger,' she said, 'I want you bad. You like this sort of life or you wouldn't be here trying to cross the Rockies in fall weather. It's a likely spot. You'll find few likelier. Why not settle down! I'll make you a good wife.'

"And then it was up to me. And she waited. I don't mind confessing that I was sorely tempted. I was half in love with her as it was. You know I have never married. And I don't mind adding, looking back over my life, that she is the only woman that ever affected me that way. But it was too preposterous, the whole thing, and I lied like a gentleman. I told her I was already married.

"'Is your wife waiting for you?' she asked.

"I said yes.

"'And she loves you?'

"I said yes.

"And that was all. She never pressed her point... except once, and then she showed a bit of fire.

"'All I've got to do,' she said, 'is to give the word, and you don't get away from here. If I give the word, you stay on… But I ain't going to give it. I wouldn't want you if you didn't want to be wanted… and if you didn't want me.'

"She went ahead and outfitted me and started me on my way.

"'It's a darned shame, stranger,' she said, at parting. 'I like your looks, and I like you. If you ever change your mind, come back.'

"Now there was one thing I wanted to do, and that was to kiss her good-bye, but I didn't know how to go about it nor how she would take it.—I tell you I was half in love with her. But she settled it herself.

"'Kiss me,' she said. 'Just something to go on and remember.'

"And we kissed, there in the snow, in that valley by the Rockies, and I left her standing by the trail and went on after my dogs. I was six weeks in crossing over the pass and coming down to the first post on Great Slave Lake."

The brawl of the streets came up to us like a distant surf. A steward, moving noiselessly, brought fresh siphons. And in the silence Trefethan's voice fell like a funeral bell:

"It would have been better had I stayed. Look at me."

We saw his grizzled mustache, the bald spot on his head, the puff-sacks under his eyes, the sagging cheeks, the heavy dewlap, the general tiredness and staleness and fatness, all the collapse and ruin of a man who had once been strong but who had lived too easily and too well.

"It's not too late, old man," Bardwell said, almost in a whisper.

"By God! I wish I weren't a coward!" was Trefethan's answering cry. "I could go back to her. She's there, now. I could shape up and live many a long year… with her… up there. To remain here is to commit suicide. But I am an old man—forty-seven—look at me. The trouble is," he lifted his glass and glanced at it, "the trouble is that suicide of this sort is so easy. I am soft and tender. The thought of the long day's travel with the dogs appalls me; the thought of the keen frost in the morning and of the frozen sled-lashings frightens me—"

Automatically the glass was creeping toward his lips. With a swift surge of anger he made as if to crash it down upon the floor. Next came hesitancy and second thought. The glass moved upward to his lips and paused. He laughed harshly and bitterly, but his words were solemn:

"Well, here's to the Night-Born. She WAS a wonder."

THE MADNESS OF JOHN HARNED

I

TELL this for a fact. It happened in the bull-ring at Quito. I sat in the box with John Harned, and with Maria Valenzuela, and with Luis Cervallos. I saw it happen. I saw it all from first to last. I was on the steamer Ecuadore from Panama to Guayaquil. Maria Valenzuela is my cousin. I have known her always. She is very beautiful. I am a Spaniard—an Ecuadoriano, true, but I am descended from Pedro Patino, who was one of Pizarro's captains. They were brave men. They were heroes. Did not Pizarro lead three hundred and fifty Spanish cavaliers and four thousand Indians into the far Cordilleras in search of treasure? And did not all the four thousand Indians and three hundred of the brave cavaliers die on that vain quest? But Pedro Patino did not die. He it was that lived to found the family of the Patino. I am Ecuadoriano, true, but I am Spanish. I am Manuel de Jesus Patino. I own many haciendas, and ten thousand Indians are my slaves, though the law says they are free men who work by freedom of contract. The law is a funny thing. We Ecuadorianos laugh at it. It is our law. We make it for ourselves. I am Manuel de Jesus Patino. Remember that name. It will be written some day in history. There are revolutions in Ecuador. We call them elections. It is a good joke is it not?—what you call a pun?

John Harned was an American. I met him first at the Tivoli hotel in Panama. He had much money—this I have heard. He was going to Lima, but he met Maria Valenzuela in the Tivoli hotel. Maria Valenzuela is my cousin, and she is beautiful. It is true, she is the most beautiful woman in Ecuador. But also is she most beautiful in every country—in Paris, in Madrid, in New York, in Vienna. Always do all men look at her, and John Harned looked long at her at Panama. He loved her, that I know for a fact. She was Ecuadoriano, true—but she was of all countries; she was of all the world. She spoke many languages. She sang—ah! like an artiste. Her smile—wonderful, divine. Her eyes—ah! have I not seen men look in her eyes? They were what you English call amazing. They were promises of paradise. Men drowned themselves in her eyes.

Maria Valenzuela was rich—richer than I, who am accounted very rich in Ecuador. But John Harned did not care for her money. He had a heart—a funny heart. He was a fool. He did not go to Lima. He left the steamer at Guayaquil and followed her to Quito. She was coming home from Europe and other places. I do not see what she found in him, but she liked him. This I know for a fact, else he would not have followed her to Quito. She asked him to come. Well do I remember the occasion. She said:

"Come to Quito and I will show you the bullfight—brave, clever, magnificent!"

But he said: "I go to Lima, not Quito. Such is my passage engaged on the steamer."

"You travel for pleasure—no?" said Maria Valenzuela; and she looked at him as only Maria Valenzuela could look, her eyes warm with the promise.

And he came. No; he did not come for the bull-fight. He came because of what he had seen in her eyes. Women like Maria Valenzuela are born once in a hundred years. They are of no country and no time. They are what you call goddesses. Men fall down at their feet. They play with men and run them through their pretty fingers like sand. Cleopatra was such a woman they say; and so was Circe. She turned men into swine. Ha! ha! It is true—no?

It all came about because Maria Valenzuela said:

"You English people are—what shall I say?—savage—no? You prize-fight. Two men each hit the other with their fists till their eyes are blinded and their noses are broken. Hideous! And the other men who look on cry out loudly and are made glad. It is barbarous—no?"

"But they are men," said John Harned; "and they prize-fight out of desire. No one makes them prize-fight. They do it because they desire it more than anything else in the world."

Maria Valenzuela—there was scorn in her smile as she said: "They kill each other often—is it not so? I have read it in the papers."

"But the bull," said John Harned.

"The bull is killed many times in the bull-fight, and the bull does not come into the the ring out of desire. It is not fair to the bull. He is compelled to fight. But the man in the prize-fight—no; he is not compelled."

"He is the more brute therefore," said Maria Valenzuela.

"He is savage. He is primitive. He is animal. He strikes with his paws like a bear from a cave, and he is ferocious. But the bull-fight—ah! You have not seen the bullfight—no? The toreador is clever. He must have skill. He is modern. He is romantic. He is only a man, soft and tender, and he faces the wild bull in conflict. And he kills with a sword, a slender sword, with one thrust, so, to the heart of the great beast. It is delicious. It makes the heart beat to behold—the small man, the great beast, the wide level sand, the thousands that look on without breath; the great beast rushes to the attack, the small man stands like a statue; he does not move, he is unafraid, and in his hand is the slender sword flashing like silver in the sun; nearer and nearer rushes the great beast with its sharp horns, the man does not move, and then—so—the sword flashes, the thrust is made, to the heart, to the hilt, the bull falls to the sand and is dead, and the man is unhurt. It is brave. It is magnificent! Ah!—I could love the toreador. But the man of the prize-fight—he is the brute, the human beast, the savage primitive, the maniac that receives many blows in his stupid face and rejoices. Come to Quito and I will show you the brave sport of men, the toreador and the bull."

But John Harned did not go to Quito for the bull-fight. He went because of Maria Valenzuela. He was a large man, more broad of shoulder than we Ecuadorianos, more tall, more heavy of limb and bone. True, he was larger of his own race. His eyes were blue, though I have seen them gray, and, sometimes, like cold steel. His features were large, too—not delicate like ours, and his jaw was very strong to look at. Also, his face was smooth-shaven like a priest's. Why should a man feel shame for the hair on his face? Did not God put it there? Yes, I believe in God—I am not a pagan like many of you English. God is good. He made me an Ecuadoriano with ten thousand slaves. And when I die I shall go to God. Yes, the priests are right.

But John Harned. He was a quiet man. He talked always in a low voice, and he never moved his hands when he talked. One would have thought his heart was a piece of ice; yet did he have a streak of warm in his blood, for he followed Maria Valenzuela to Quito. Also, and for all that he talked low without moving his hands, he was an animal, as you shall see—the beast primitive, the stupid, ferocious savage of the long ago that dressed in wild skins and lived in the caves along with the bears and wolves.

Luis Cervallos is my friend, the best of Ecuadorianos. He owns three cacao plantations at Naranjito and Chobo. At Milagro is his big sugar plantation. He has large haciendas at Ambato and Latacunga, and down the coast is he interested in oil-wells. Also has he spent much money in planting rubber along the Guayas. He is modern, like the Yankee; and, like the Yankee, full of business. He has much money, but it is in many ventures, and ever he needs more money for new ventures and for the old ones. He has been everywhere and seen everything. When he was a very young man he was in the Yankee military academy what you call West Point. There was trouble. He was made to resign. He does not like Americans. But he did like Maria Valenzuela, who was of his own country. Also, he needed her money for his ventures and for his gold mine in Eastern Ecuador where the painted Indians live. I was his friend. It was my desire that he should marry Maria Valenzuela. Further, much of my money had I invested in his ventures, more so in his gold mine which was very rich but which first required the expense of much money before it would yield forth its riches. If Luis Cervallos married Maria Valenzuela I should have more money very immediately.

But John Harned followed Maria Valenzuela to Quito, and it was quickly clear to us—to Luis Cervallos and me that she looked upon John Harned with great kindness. It is said that a woman will have her will, but this is a case not in point, for Maria Valenzuela did not have her will—at least not with John Harned. Perhaps it would all have happened as it did, even if Luis Cervallos and I had not sat in the box that day at the bull-ring in Quito. But this I know: we DID sit in the box that day. And I shall tell you what happened.

The four of us were in the one box, guests of Luis Cervallos. I was next to the Presidente's box. On the other side was the box of General Jose Eliceo Salazar. With him were Joaquin Endara and Urcisino Castillo, both generals, and Colonel Jacinto Fierro and Captain Baltazar de Echeverria. Only Luis Cervallos had the position and the influence to get that box next to the Presidente. I know for a fact that the Presidente himself expressed the desire to the management that Luis Cervallos should have that box.

The band finished playing the national hymn of Ecuador. The procession of the toreadors was over. The Presidente nodded to begin. The bugles blew, and the bull dashed in—you know the way, excited, bewildered, the darts in its shoulder burning like fire, itself seeking madly whatever enemy to destroy. The toreadors hid behind their shelters and waited. Suddenly they appeared forth, the capadores, five of them, from every side, their colored capes flinging wide. The bull paused at sight of such a generosity of enemies, unable in his own mind to know which to attack. Then advanced one of the capadors alone to meet the bull. The bull was very angry. With its fore-legs it pawed the sand of the arena till the dust rose all about it. Then it charged, with lowered head, straight for the lone capador.

It is always of interest, the first charge of the first bull. After a time it is natural that one should grow tired, trifle, that the keenness should lose its edge. But that first charge of the first bull! John Harned was seeing it for the first time, and he could not escape the excitement—the sight of the man, armed only with a piece of cloth, and of the bull rushing upon him across the sand with sharp horns, widespreading.

"See!" cried Maria Valenzuela. "Is it not superb?"

John Harned nodded, but did not look at her. His eyes were sparkling, and they were only for the bull-ring. The capador stepped to the side, with a twirl of the cape eluding the bull and spreading the cape on his own shoulders.

"What do you think?" asked Maria Venzuela. "Is it not a—what-you-call—sporting proposition—no?"

"It is certainly," said John Harned. "It is very clever."

She clapped her hands with delight. They were little hands. The audience applauded. The bull turned and came back. Again the capadore eluded him, throwing the cape on his shoulders, and again the audience applauded. Three times did this happen. The capadore was very excellent. Then he retired, and the other capadore played with the bull. After that they placed the banderillos in the bull, in the shoulders, on each side of the back-bone, two at a time. Then stepped forward Ordonez, the chief matador, with the long sword and the scarlet cape. The bugles blew for the death. He is not so good as Matestini. Still he is good, and with one thrust he drove the sword to the heart, and the bull doubled his legs under him and lay down and died. It was a pretty thrust, clean and sure; and there was much applause, and many of the common people threw their hats into the ring. Maria Valenzuela clapped her hands with the rest, and John Harned, whose cold heart was not touched by the event, looked at her with curiosity.

"You like it?" he asked.

"Always," she said, still clapping her hands.

"From a little girl," said Luis Cervallos. "I remember her first fight. She was four years old. She sat with her mother, and just like now she clapped her hands. She is a proper Spanish woman.

"You have seen it," said Maria Valenzuela to John Harned, as they fastened the mules to the dead bull and dragged it out. "You have seen the bull-fight and you like it—no? What do you think?

"I think the bull had no chance," he said. "The bull was doomed from the first. The issue was not in doubt. Every one knew, before the bull entered the ring, that it was to die. To be a sporting proposition, the issue must be in doubt. It was one stupid bull who had never fought a man against five wise men who had fought many bulls. It would be possibly a little bit fair if it were one man against one bull."

"Or one man against five bulls," said Maria Valenzuela; and we all laughed, and Luis Ceryallos laughed loudest.

139

"Yes," said John Harned, "against five bulls, and the man, like the bulls, never in the bull ring before—a man like yourself, Senor Crevallos."

"Yet we Spanish like the bull-fight," said Luis Cervallos; and I swear the devil was whispering then in his ear, telling him to do that which I shall relate.

"Then must it be a cultivated taste," John Harned made answer. "We kill bulls by the thousand every day in Chicago, yet no one cares to pay admittance to see."

"That is butchery," said I; "but this—ah, this is an art. It is delicate. It is fine. It is rare."

"Not always," said Luis Cervallos. "I have seen clumsy matadors, and I tell you it is not nice."

He shuddered, and his face betrayed such what-you-call disgust, that I knew, then, that the devil was whispering and that he was beginning to play a part.

"Senor Harned may be right," said Luis Cervallos. "It may not be fair to the bull. For is it not known to all of us that for twenty-four hours the bull is given no water, and that immediately before the fight he is permitted to drink his fill?"

"And he comes into the ring heavy with water?" said John Harned quickly; and I saw that his eyes were very gray and very sharp and very cold.

"It is necessary for the sport," said Luis Cervallos. "Would you have the bull so strong that he would kill the toreadors?"

"I would that he had a fighting chance," said John Harned, facing the ring to see the second bull come in.

It was not a good bull. It was frightened. It ran around the ring in search of a way to get out. The capadors stepped forth and flared their capes, but he refused to charge upon them.

"It is a stupid bull," said Maria Valenzuela.

"I beg pardon," said John Harned; "but it would seem to me a wise bull. He knows he must not fight man. See! He smells death there in the ring."

True. The bull, pausing where the last one had died, was smelling the wet sand and snorting. Again he ran around the ring, with raised head, looking at the faces of the thousands that hissed him, that threw orange-peel at him and called him names. But the smell of blood decided him, and he charged a capador, so without warning that the man just escaped. He dropped his cape and dodged into the shelter. The bull struck the wall of the ring with a crash. And John Harned said, in a quiet voice, as though he talked to himself:

"I will give one thousand sucres to the lazar-house of Quito if a bull kills a man this day."

"You like bulls?" said Maria Valenzuela with a smile.

"I like such men less," said John Harned. "A toreador is not a brave man. He surely cannot be a brave man. See, the bull's tongue is already out. He is tired and he has not yet begun."

"It is the water," said Luis Cervallos.

"Yes, it is the water," said John Harned. "Would it not be safer to hamstring the bull before he comes on?"

Maria Valenzuela was made angry by this sneer in John Harned's words. But Luis Cervallos smiled so that only I could see him, and then it broke upon my mind surely the game he was playing. He and I were to be banderilleros. The big American bull was there in the box with us. We were to stick the darts in him till he became angry, and then there might be no marriage with Maria Valenzuela. It was a good sport. And the spirit of bull-fighters was in our blood.

The bull was now angry and excited. The capadors had great game with him. He was very quick, and sometimes he turned with such sharpness that his hind legs lost their footing and he plowed the sand with his quarter. But he charged always the flung capes and committed no harm.

"He has no chance," said John Harned. "He is fighting wind."

141

"He thinks the cape is his enemy," explained Maria Valenzuela. "See how cleverly the capador deceives him."

"It is his nature to be deceived," said John Harned. "Wherefore he is doomed to fight wind. The toreadors know it, you know it, I know it—we all know from the first that he will fight wind. He only does not know it. It is his stupid beast-nature. He has no chance."

"It is very simple," said Luis Cervallos. "The bull shuts his eyes when he charges. Therefore—"

"The man steps, out of the way and the bull rushes by," Harned interrupted.

"Yes," said Luis Cervallos; "that is it. The bull shuts his eyes, and the man knows it."

"But cows do not shut their eyes," said John Harned. "I know a cow at home that is a Jersey and gives milk, that would whip the whole gang of them."

"But the toreadors do not fight cows," said I.

"They are afraid to fight cows," said John Harned.

"Yes," said Luis Cervallos, "they are afraid to fight cows. There would be no sport in killing toreadors."

"There would be some sport," said John Harned, "if a toreador were killed once in a while. When I become an old man, and mayhap a cripple, and should I need to make a living and be unable to do hard work, then would I become a bull-fighter. It is a light vocation for elderly gentlemen and pensioners."

"But see!" said Maria Valenzuela, as the bull charged bravely and the capador eluded it with a fling of his cape. "It requires skill so to avoid the beast."

"True," said John Harned. "But believe me, it requires a thousand times more skill to avoid the many and quick punches of a prize-fighter who keeps his eyes open and strikes with intelligence. Furthermore, this bull does not want to fight. Behold, he runs away."

It was not a good bull, for again it ran around the ring, seeking to find a way out.

"Yet these bulls are sometimes the most dangerous," said Luis Cervallos. "It can never be known what they will do next. They are wise. They are half cow. The bull-fighters never like them.—See! He has turned!"

Once again, baffled and made angry by the walls of the ring that would not let him out, the bull was attacking his enemies valiantly.

"His tongue is hanging out," said John Harned. "First, they fill him with water. Then they tire him out, one man and then another, persuading him to exhaust himself by fighting wind. While some tire him, others rest. But the bull they never let rest. Afterward, when he is quite tired and no longer quick, the matador sticks the sword into him."

The time had now come for the banderillos. Three times one of the fighters endeavored to place the darts, and three times did he fail. He but stung the bull and maddened it. The banderillos must go in, you know, two at a time, into the shoulders, on each side the backbone and close to it. If but one be placed, it is a failure. The crowd hissed and called for Ordonez. And then Ordonez did a great thing. Four times he stood forth, and four times, at the first attempt, he stuck in the banderillos, so that eight of them, well placed, stood out of the back of the bull at one time. The crowd went mad, and a rain of hats and money fell on the sand of the ring.

And just then the bull charged unexpectedly one of the capadors. The man slipped and lost his head. The bull caught him—fortunately, between his wide horns. And while the audience watched, breathless and silent, John Harned stood up and yelled with gladness. Alone, in that hush of all of us, John Harned yelled. And he yelled for the bull. As you see yourself, John Harned wanted the man killed. His was a brutal heart. This bad conduct made those angry that sat in the box of General Salazar, and they cried out against John Harned. And Urcisino Castillo told him to his face that he was a dog of a Gringo and other things. Only it was in Spanish, and John Harned did not understand. He stood and yelled, perhaps for the time of ten seconds, when the bull was enticed into charging the other capadors and the man arose unhurt.

"The bull has no chance," John Harned said with sadness as he sat down. "The man was uninjured. They fooled the bull away from him." Then he turned to Maria Valenzuela and said: "I beg your pardon. I was excited."

She smiled and in reproof tapped his arm with her fan.

"It is your first bull-fight," she said. "After you have seen more you will not cry for the death of the man. You Americans, you see, are more brutal than we. It is because of your prize-fighting. We come only to see the bull killed."

"But I would the bull had some chance," he answered. "Doubtless, in time, I shall cease to be annoyed by the men who take advantage of the bull."

The bugles blew for the death of the bull. Ordonez stood forth with the sword and the scarlet cloth. But the bull had changed again, and did not want to fight. Ordonez stamped his foot in the sand, and cried out, and waved the scarlet cloth. Then the bull charged, but without heart. There was no weight to the charge. It was a poor thrust. The sword struck a bone and bent. Ordonez took a fresh sword. The bull, again stung to fight, charged once more. Five times Ordonez essayed the thrust, and each time the sword went but part way in or struck bone. The sixth time, the sword went in to the hilt. But it was a bad thrust. The sword missed the heart and stuck out half a yard through the ribs on the opposite side. The audience hissed the matador. I glanced at John Harned. He sat silent, without movement; but I could see his teeth were set, and his hands were clenched tight on the railing of the box.

All fight was now out of the bull, and, though it was no vital thrust, he trotted lamely what of the sword that stuck through him, in one side and out the other. He ran away from the matador and the capadors, and circled the edge of the ring, looking up at the many faces.

"He is saying: 'For God's sake let me out of this; I don't want to fight,'" said John Harned.

That was all. He said no more, but sat and watched, though sometimes he looked sideways at Maria Valenzuela to see how she took it. She was angry with the matador. He was awkward, and she had desired a clever exhibition.

The bull was now very tired, and weak from loss of blood, though far from dying. He walked slowly around the wall of the ring, seeking a way out. He would not charge. He had had enough. But he must be killed. There is a place, in the neck of a bull behind the horns, where the cord of the spine is unprotected and where a short stab will immediately kill. Ordonez stepped in front of the bull and lowered his scarlet cloth to the ground. The bull would not charge. He stood still and smelled the cloth, lowering his head to do so. Ordonez stabbed between the horns at the spot in the neck. The bull jerked his head up. The stab had missed. Then the bull watched the sword. When Ordonez moved the cloth on the ground, the bull forgot the sword and lowered his head to smell the cloth. Again Ordonez stabbed, and again he failed. He tried many times. It was stupid. And John Harned said nothing. At last a stab went home, and the bull fell to the sand, dead immediately, and the mules were made fast and he was dragged out.

"The Gringos say it is a cruel sport—no?" said Luis Cervallos. "That it is not humane. That it is bad for the bull. No?"

"No," said John Harned. "The bull does not count for much. It is bad for those that look on. It is degrading to those that look on. It teaches them to delight in animal suffering. It is cowardly for five men to fight one stupid bull. Therefore those that look on learn to be cowards. The bull dies, but those that look on live and the lesson is learned. The bravery of men is not nourished by scenes of cowardice."

Maria Valenzuela said nothing. Neither did she look at him. But she heard every word and her cheeks were white with anger. She looked out across the ring and fanned herself, but I saw that her hand trembled. Nor did John Harned look at her. He went on as though she were not there. He, too, was angry, coldly angry.

"It is the cowardly sport of a cowardly people," he said.

"Ah," said Luis Cervallos softly, "you think you understand us."

"I understand now the Spanish Inquisition," said John Harned. "It must have been more delightful than bull-fighting."

Luis Cervallos smiled but said nothing. He glanced at Maria Valenzuela, and knew that the bull-fight in the box was won. Never would she have further to do with the Gringo who spoke such words. But neither Luis Cervallos nor I was prepared for the outcome of the day. I fear we do not understand the Gringos. How were we to know that John Harned, who was so coldly angry, should go suddenly mad! But mad he did go, as you shall see. The bull did not count for much—he said so himself. Then why should the horse count for so much? That I cannot understand. The mind of John Harned lacked logic. That is the only explanation.

"It is not usual to have horses in the bull-ring at Quito," said Luis Cervallos, looking up from the program. "In Spain they always have them. But to-day, by special permission we shall have them. When the next bull comes on there will be horses and picadors-you know, the men who carry lances and ride the horses."

"The bull is doomed from the first," said John Harned. "Are the horses then likewise doomed!"

"They are blindfolded so that they may not see the bull," said Luis Cervallos. "I have seen many horses killed. It is a brave sight."

"I have seen the bull slaughtered," said John Harned "I will now see the horse slaughtered, so that I may understand more fully the fine points of this noble sport."

"They are old horses," said Luis Cervallos, "that are not good for anything else."

"I see," said John Harned.

The third bull came on, and soon against it were both capadors and picadors. One picador took his stand directly below us. I agree, it was a thin and aged horse he rode, a bag of bones covered with mangy hide.

146

"It is a marvel that the poor brute can hold up the weight of the rider," said John Harned. "And now that the horse fights the bull, what weapons has it?"

"The horse does not fight the bull," said Luis Cervallos.

"Oh," said John Harned, "then is the horse there to be gored? That must be why it is blindfolded, so that it shall not see the bull coming to gore it."

"Not quite so," said I. "The lance of the picador is to keep the bull from goring the horse."

"Then are horses rarely gored?" asked John Harned.

"No," said Luis Cervallos. "I have seen, at Seville, eighteen horses killed in one day, and the people clamored for more horses."

"Were they blindfolded like this horse?" asked John Harned.

"Yes," said Luis Cervallos.

After that we talked no more, but watched the fight. And John Harned was going mad all the time, and we did not know. The bull refused to charge the horse. And the horse stood still, and because it could not see it did not know that the capadors were trying to make the bull charge upon it. The capadors teased the bull their capes, and when it charged them they ran toward the horse and into their shelters. At last the bull was angry, and it saw the horse before it.

"The horse does not know, the horse does not know," John Harned whispered to himself, unaware that he voiced his thought aloud.

The bull charged, and of course the horse knew nothing till the picador failed and the horse found himself impaled on the bull's horns from beneath. The bull was magnificently strong. The sight of its strength was splendid to see. It lifted the horse clear into the air; and as the horse fell to its side on on the ground the picador landed on his feet and escaped, while the capadors lured the bull away. The horse was emptied of its essential organs. Yet did it rise to its feet screaming. It was the scream of the horse that did it, that made John Harned completely mad; for he, too, started to rise to his feet, I heard him curse low and deep. He never took his eyes from the horse, which, screaming, strove to run, but fell down instead and rolled on its back so that all its four legs were kicking in the air. Then the bull charged it and gored it again and again until it was dead.

John Harned was now on his feet. His eyes were no longer cold like steel. They were blue flames. He looked at Maria Valenzuela, and she looked at him, and in his face was a great loathing. The moment of his madness was upon him. Everybody was looking, now that the horse was dead; and John Harned was a large man and easy to be seen.

"Sit down," said Luis Cervallos, "or you will make a fool of yourself."

John Harned replied nothing. He struck out his fist. He smote Luis Cervallos in the face so that he fell like a dead man across the chairs and did not rise again. He saw nothing of what followed. But I saw much. Urcisino Castillo, leaning forward from the next box, with his cane struck John Harned full across the face. And John Harned smote him with his fist so that in falling he overthrew General Salazar. John Harned was now in what-you-call Berserker rage—no? The beast primitive in him was loose and roaring—the beast primitive of the holes and caves of the long ago.

"You came for a bull-fight," I heard him say, "And by God I'll show you a man-fight!"

It was a fight. The soldiers guarding the Presidente's box leaped across, but from one of them he took a rifle and beat them on their heads with it. From the other box Colonel Jacinto Fierro was shooting at him with a revolver. The first shot killed a soldier. This I know for a fact. I saw it. But the second shot struck John Harned in the side. Whereupon he swore, and with a lunge drove the bayonet of his rifle into Colonel Jacinto Fierro's body. It was horrible to behold. The Americans and the English are a brutal race. They sneer at our bull-fighting, yet do they delight in the shedding of blood. More men were killed that day because of John Harned than were ever killed in all the history of the bull-ring of Quito, yes, and of Guayaquil and all Ecuador.

It was the scream of the horse that did it, yet why did not John Harned go mad when the bull was killed? A beast is a beast, be it bull or horse. John Harned was mad. There is no other explanation. He was blood-mad, a beast himself. I leave it to your judgment. Which is worse—the goring of the horse by the bull, or the goring of Colonel Jacinto Fierro by the bayonet in the hands of John Harned! And John Harned gored others with that bayonet. He was full of devils. He fought with many bullets in him, and he was hard to kill. And Maria Valenzuela was a brave woman. Unlike the other women, she did not cry out nor faint. She sat still in her box, gazing out across the bull-ring. Her face was white and she fanned herself, but she never looked around.

From all sides came the soldiers and officers and the common people bravely to subdue the mad Gringo. It is true—the cry went up from the crowd to kill all the Gringos. It is an old cry in Latin-American countries, what of the dislike for the Gringos and their uncouth ways. It is true, the cry went up. But the brave Ecuadorianos killed only John Harned, and first he killed seven of them. Besides, there were many hurt. I have seen many bull-fights, but never have I seen anything so abominable as the scene in the boxes when the fight was over. It was like a field of battle. The dead lay around everywhere, while the wounded sobbed and groaned and some of them died. One man, whom John Harned had thrust through the belly with the bayonet, clutched at himself with both his hands and screamed. I tell you for a fact it was more terrible than the screaming of a thousand horses.

No, Maria Valenzuela did not marry Luis Cervallos. I am sorry for that. He was my friend, and much of my money was invested in his ventures. It was five weeks before the surgeons took the bandages from his face. And there is a scar there to this day, on the cheek, under the eye. Yet John Harned struck him but once and struck him only with his naked fist. Maria Valenzuela is in Austria now. It is said she is to marry an Arch-Duke or some high nobleman. I do not know. I think she liked John Harned before he followed her to Quito to see the bull-fight. But why the horse? That is what I desire to know. Why should he watch the bull and say that it did not count, and then go immediately and most horribly mad because a horse screamed? There is no understanding the Gringos. They are barbarians.

WHEN THE WORLD WAS YOUNG

HE was a very quiet, self-possessed sort of man, sitting a moment on top of the wall to sound the damp darkness for warnings of the dangers it might conceal. But the plummet of his hearing brought nothing to him save the moaning of wind through invisible trees and the rustling of leaves on swaying branches. A heavy fog drifted and drove before the wind, and though he could not see this fog, the wet of it blew upon his face, and the wall on which he sat was wet.

Without noise he had climbed to the top of the wall from the outside, and without noise he dropped to the ground on the inside. From his pocket he drew an electric night-stick, but he did not use it. Dark as the way was, he was not anxious for light. Carrying the night-stick in his hand, his finger on the button, he advanced through the darkness. The ground was velvety and springy to his feet, being carpeted with dead pine-needles and leaves and mold which evidently had been undisturbed for years. Leaves and branches brushed against his body, but so dark was it that he could not avoid them. Soon he walked with his hand stretched out gropingly before him, and more than once the hand fetched up against the solid trunks of massive trees. All about him he knew were these trees; he sensed the loom of them everywhere; and he experienced a strange feeling of microscopic smallness in the midst of great bulks leaning toward him to crush him. Beyond, he knew, was the house, and he expected to find some trail or winding path that would lead easily to it.

Once, he found himself trapped. On every side he groped against trees and branches, or blundered into thickets of underbrush, until there seemed no way out. Then he turned on his light, circumspectly, directing its rays to the ground at his feet. Slowly and carefully he moved it about him, the white brightness showing in sharp detail all the obstacles to his progress. He saw, an opening between huge-trunked trees, and advanced through it, putting out the light and treading on dry footing as yet protected from the drip of the fog by the dense foliage overhead. His sense of direction was good, and he knew he was going toward the house.

And then the thing happened—the thing unthinkable and unexpected. His descending foot came down upon something that was soft and alive, and that arose with a snort under the weight of his body. He sprang clear, and crouched for another spring, anywhere, tense and expectant, keyed for the onslaught of the unknown. He waited a moment, wondering what manner of animal it was that had arisen from under his foot and that now made no sound nor movement and that must be crouching and waiting just as tensely and expectantly as he. The strain became unbearable. Holding the night-stick before him, he pressed the button, saw, and screamed aloud in terror. He was prepared for anything, from a frightened calf or fawn to a belligerent lion, but he was not prepared for what he saw. In that instant his tiny searchlight, sharp and white, had shown him what a thousand years would not enable him to forget—a man, huge and blond, yellow-haired and yellow-bearded, naked except for soft-tanned moccasins and what seemed a goat-skin about his middle. Arms and legs were bare, as were his shoulders and most of his chest. The skin was smooth and hairless, but browned by sun and wind, while under it heavy muscles were knotted like fat snakes. Still, this alone, unexpected as it well was, was not what had made the man scream out. What had caused his terror was the unspeakable ferocity of the face, the wild-animal glare of the blue eyes scarcely dazzled by the light, the pine-needles matted and clinging in the beard and hair, and the whole formidable body crouched and in the act of springing at him. Practically in the instant he saw all this, and while his scream still rang, the thing leaped, he flung his night-stick full at it, and threw himself to the ground. He felt its feet and shins strike against his ribs, and he bounded up and away while the thing itself hurled onward in a heavy crashing fall into the underbrush.

As the noise of the fall ceased, the man stopped and on hands and knees waited. He could hear the thing moving about, searching for him, and he was afraid to advertise his location by attempting further flight. He knew that inevitably he would crackle the underbrush and be pursued. Once he drew out his revolver, then changed his mind. He had recovered his composure and hoped to get away without noise. Several times he heard the thing beating up the thickets for him, and there were moments when it, too, remained still and listened. This gave an idea to the man. One of his hands was resting on a chunk of dead wood. Carefully, first feeling about him in the darkness to know that the full swing of his arm was clear, he raised the chunk of wood and threw it. It was not a large piece, and it went far, landing noisily in a bush. He heard the thing bound into the bush, and at the same time himself crawled steadily away. And on hands and knees, slowly and cautiously, he crawled on, till his knees were wet on the soggy mold, When he listened he heard naught but the moaning wind and the drip-drip of the fog from the branches. Never abating his caution, he stood erect and went on to the stone wall, over which he climbed and dropped down to the road outside.

Feeling his way in a clump of bushes, he drew out a bicycle and prepared to mount. He was in the act of driving the gear around with his foot for the purpose of getting the opposite pedal in position, when he heard the thud of a heavy body that landed lightly and evidently on its feet. He did not wait for more, but ran, with hands on the handles of his bicycle, until he was able to vault astride the saddle, catch the pedals, and start a spurt. Behind he could hear the quick thud-thud of feet on the dust of the road, but he drew away from it and lost it. Unfortunately, he had started away from the direction of town and was heading higher up into the hills. He knew that on this particular road there were no cross roads. The only way back was past that terror, and he could not steel himself to face it. At the end of half an hour, finding himself on an ever increasing grade, he dismounted. For still greater safety, leaving the wheel by the roadside, he climbed through a fence into what he decided was a hillside pasture, spread a newspaper on the ground, and sat down.

"Gosh!" he said aloud, mopping the sweat and fog from his face.

And "Gosh!" he said once again, while rolling a cigarette and as he pondered the problem of getting back.

But he made no attempt to go back. He was resolved not to face that road in the dark, and with head bowed on knees, he dozed, waiting for daylight.

How long afterward he did not know, he was awakened by the yapping bark of a young coyote. As he looked about and located it on the brow of the hill behind him, he noted the change that had come over the face of the night. The fog was gone; the stars and moon were out; even the wind had died down. It had transformed into a balmy California summer night. He tried to doze again, but the yap of the coyote disturbed him. Half asleep, he heard a wild and eery chant. Looking about him, he noticed that the coyote had ceased its noise and was running away along the crest of the hill, and behind it, in full pursuit, no longer chanting, ran the naked creature he had encountered in the garden. It was a young coyote, and it was being overtaken when the chase passed from view. The man trembled as with a chill as he started to his feet, clambered over the fence, and mounted his wheel. But it was his chance and he knew it. The terror was no longer between him and Mill Valley.

He sped at a breakneck rate down the hill, but in the turn at the bottom, in the deep shadows, he encountered a chuck-hole and pitched headlong over the handle bar.

"It's sure not my night," he muttered, as he examined the broken fork of the machine.

Shouldering the useless wheel, he trudged on. In time he came to the stone wall, and, half disbelieving his experience, he sought in the road for tracks, and found them—moccasin tracks, large ones, deep-bitten into the dust at the toes. It was while bending over them, examining, that again he heard the eery chant. He had seen the thing pursue the coyote, and he knew he had no chance on a straight run. He did not attempt it, contenting himself with hiding in the shadows on the off side of the road.

And again he saw the thing that was like a naked man, running swiftly and lightly and singing as it ran. Opposite him it paused, and his heart stood still. But instead of coming toward his hiding-place, it leaped into the air, caught the branch of a roadside tree, and swung swiftly upward, from limb to limb, like an ape. It swung across the wall, and a dozen feet above the top, into the branches of another tree, and dropped out of sight to the ground. The man waited a few wondering minutes, then started on.

II

Dave Slotter leaned belligerently against the desk that barred the way to the private office of James Ward, senior partner of the firm of Ward, Knowles & Co. Dave was angry. Every one in the outer office had looked him over suspiciously, and the man who faced him was excessively suspicious.

"You just tell Mr. Ward it's important," he urged.

"I tell you he is dictating and cannot be disturbed," was the answer. "Come to-morrow."

"To-morrow will be too late. You just trot along and tell Mr. Ward it's a matter of life and death."

The secretary hesitated and Dave seized the advantage.

"You just tell him I was across the bay in Mill Valley last night, and that I want to put him wise to something."

"What name?" was the query.

"Never mind the name. He don't know me."

When Dave was shown into the private office, he was still in the belligerent frame of mind, but when he saw a large fair man whirl in a revolving chair from dictating to a stenographer to face him, Dave's demeanor abruptly changed. He did not know why it changed, and he was secretly angry with himself.

"You are Mr. Ward?" Dave asked with a fatuousness that still further irritated him. He had never intended it at all.

"Yes," came the answer.

"And who are you?"

"Harry Bancroft," Dave lied. "You don't know me, and my name don't matter."

"You sent in word that you were in Mill Valley last night?"

"You live there, don't you?" Dave countered, looking suspiciously at the stenographer.

"Yes. What do you mean to see me about? I am very busy."

"I'd like to see you alone, sir."

Mr. Ward gave him a quick, penetrating look, hesitated, then made up his mind.

"That will do for a few minutes, Miss Potter."

The girl arose, gathered her notes together, and passed out. Dave looked at Mr. James Ward wonderingly, until that gentleman broke his train of inchoate thought.

"Well?"

"I was over in Mill Valley last night," Dave began confusedly.

"I've heard that before. What do you want?"

And Dave proceeded in the face of a growing conviction that was unbelievable. "I was at your house, or in the grounds, I mean."

"What were you doing there?"

"I came to break in," Dave answered in all frankness.

"I heard you lived all alone with a Chinaman for cook, and it looked good to me. Only I didn't break in. Something happened that prevented. That's why I'm here. I come to warn you. I found a wild man loose in your grounds—a regular devil. He could pull a guy like me to pieces. He gave me the run of my life. He don't wear any clothes to speak of, he climbs trees like a monkey, and he runs like a deer. I saw him chasing a coyote, and the last I saw of it, by God, he was gaining on it."

Dave paused and looked for the effect that would follow his words. But no effect came. James Ward was quietly curious, and that was all.

155

"Very remarkable, very remarkable," he murmured. "A wild man, you say. Why have you come to tell me?"

"To warn you of your danger. I'm something of a hard proposition myself, but I don't believe in killing people... that is, unnecessarily. I realized that you was in danger. I thought I'd warn you. Honest, that's the game. Of course, if you wanted to give me anything for my trouble, I'd take it. That was in my mind, too. But I don't care whether you give me anything or not. I've warned you any way, and done my duty."

Mr. Ward meditated and drummed on the surface of his desk. Dave noticed they were large, powerful hands, withal well-cared for despite their dark sunburn. Also, he noted what had already caught his eye before—a tiny strip of flesh-colored courtplaster on the forehead over one eye. And still the thought that forced itself into his mind was unbelievable.

Mr. Ward took a wallet from his inside coat pocket, drew out a greenback, and passed it to Dave, who noted as he pocketed it that it was for twenty dollars.

"Thank you," said Mr. Ward, indicating that the interview was at an end.

"I shall have the matter investigated. A wild man running loose IS dangerous."

But so quiet a man was Mr. Ward, that Dave's courage returned. Besides, a new theory had suggested itself. The wild man was evidently Mr. Ward's brother, a lunatic privately confined. Dave had heard of such things. Perhaps Mr. Ward wanted it kept quiet. That was why he had given him the twenty dollars.

"Say," Dave began, "now I come to think of it that wild man looked a lot like you—"

That was as far as Dave got, for at that moment he witnessed a transformation and found himself gazing into the same unspeakably ferocious blue eyes of the night before, at the same clutching talon-like hands, and at the same formidable bulk in the act of springing upon him. But this time Dave had no night-stick to throw, and he was caught by the biceps of both arms in a grip so terrific that it made him groan with pain. He saw the large white teeth exposed, for all the world as a dog's about to bite. Mr. Ward's beard brushed his face as the teeth went in for the grip on his throat. But the bite was not given. Instead, Dave felt the other's body stiffen as with an iron restraint, and then he was flung aside, without effort but with such force that only the wall stopped his momentum and dropped him gasping to the floor.

"What do you mean by coming here and trying to blackmail me?" Mr. Ward was snarling at him. "Here, give me back that money."

Dave passed the bill back without a word.

"I thought you came here with good intentions. I know you now. Let me see and hear no more of you, or I'll put you in prison where you belong. Do you understand?"

"Yes, sir," Dave gasped.

"Then go."

And Dave went, without further word, both his biceps aching intolerably from the bruise of that tremendous grip. As his hand rested on the door knob, he was stopped.

"You were lucky," Mr. Ward was saying, and Dave noted that his face and eyes were cruel and gloating and proud.

"You were lucky. Had I wanted, I could have torn your muscles out of your arms and thrown them in the waste basket there."

"Yes, sir," said Dave; and absolute conviction vibrated in his voice.

He opened the door and passed out. The secretary looked at him interrogatively.

"Gosh!" was all Dave vouchsafed, and with this utterance passed out of the offices and the story.

III

James G. Ward was forty years of age, a successful business man, and very unhappy. For forty years he had vainly tried to solve a problem that was really himself and that with increasing years became more and more a woeful affliction. In himself he was two men, and, chronologically speaking, these men were several thousand years or so apart. He had studied the question of dual personality probably more profoundly than any half dozen of the leading specialists in that intricate and mysterious psychological field. In himself he was a different case from any that had been recorded. Even the most fanciful flights of the fiction-writers had not quite hit upon him. He was not a Dr. Jekyll and Mr. Hyde, nor was he like the unfortunate young man in Kipling's "Greatest Story in the World." His two personalities were so mixed that they were practically aware of themselves and of each other all the time.

His other self he had located as a savage and a barbarian living under the primitive conditions of several thousand years before. But which self was he, and which was the other, he could never tell. For he was both selves, and both selves all the time. Very rarely indeed did it happen that one self did not know what the other was doing. Another thing was that he had no visions nor memories of the past in which that early self had lived. That early self lived in the present; but while it lived in the present, it was under the compulsion to live the way of life that must have been in that distant past.

In his childhood he had been a problem to his father and mother, and to the family doctors, though never had they come within a thousand miles of hitting upon the clue to his erratic, conduct. Thus, they could not understand his excessive somnolence in the forenoon, nor his excessive activity at night. When they found him wandering along the hallways at night, or climbing over giddy roofs, or running in the hills, they decided he was a somnambulist. In reality he was wide-eyed awake and merely under the nightroaming compulsion of his early self. Questioned by an obtuse medico, he once told the truth and suffered the ignominy of having the revelation contemptuously labeled and dismissed as "dreams."

The point was, that as twilight and evening came on he became wakeful. The four walls of a room were an irk and a restraint. He heard a thousand voices whispering to him through the darkness. The night called to him, for he was, for that period of the twenty-four hours, essentially a night-prowler. But nobody understood, and never again did he attempt to explain. They classified him as a sleep-walker and took precautions accordingly—precautions that very often were futile. As his childhood advanced, he grew more cunning, so that the major portion of all his nights were spent in the open at realizing his other self. As a result, he slept in the forenoons. Morning studies and schools were impossible, and it was discovered that only in the afternoons, under private teachers, could he be taught anything. Thus was his modern self educated and developed.

But a problem, as a child, he ever remained. He was known as a little demon, of insensate cruelty and viciousness. The family medicos privately adjudged him a mental monstrosity and degenerate. Such few boy companions as he had, hailed him as a wonder, though they were all afraid of him. He could outclimb, outswim, outrun, outdevil any of them; while none dared fight with him. He was too terribly strong, madly furious.

When nine years of age he ran away to the hills, where he flourished, night-prowling, for seven weeks before he was discovered and brought home. The marvel was how he had managed to subsist and keep in condition during that time. They did not know, and he never told them, of the rabbits he had killed, of the quail, young and old, he had captured and devoured, of the farmers' chicken-roosts he had raided, nor of the cave-lair he had made and carpeted with dry leaves and grasses and in which he had slept in warmth and comfort through the forenoons of many days.

At college he was notorious for his sleepiness and stupidity during the morning lectures and for his brilliance in the afternoon. By collateral reading and by borrowing the notebook of his fellow students he managed to scrape through the detestable morning courses, while his afternoon courses were triumphs. In football he proved a giant and a terror, and, in almost every form of track athletics, save for strange Berserker rages that were sometimes displayed, he could be depended upon to win. But his fellows were afraid to box with him, and he signalized his last wrestling bout by sinking his teeth into the shoulder of his opponent.

After college, his father, in despair, sent him among the cow-punchers of a Wyoming ranch. Three months later the doughty cowmen confessed he was too much for them and telegraphed his father to come and take the wild man away. Also, when the father arrived to take him away, the cowmen allowed that they would vastly prefer chumming with howling cannibals, gibbering lunatics, cavorting gorillas, grizzly bears, and man-eating tigers than with this particular Young college product with hair parted in the middle.

There was one exception to the lack of memory of the life of his early self, and that was language. By some quirk of atavism, a certain portion of that early self's language had come down to him as a racial memory. In moments of happiness, exaltation, or battle, he was prone to burst out in wild barbaric songs or chants. It was by this means that he located in time and space that strayed half of him who should have been dead and dust for thousands of years. He sang, once, and deliberately, several of the ancient chants in the presence of Professor Wertz, who gave courses in old Saxon and who was a philogist of repute and passion. At the first one, the professor pricked up his ears and demanded to know what mongrel tongue or hog-German it was. When the second chant was rendered, the professor was highly excited. James Ward then concluded the performance by giving a song that always irresistibly rushed to his lips when he was engaged in fierce struggling or fighting. Then it was that Professor Wertz proclaimed it no hog-German, but early German, or early Teuton, of a date that must far precede anything that had ever been discovered and handed down by the scholars. So early was it that it was beyond him; yet it was filled with haunting reminiscences of word-forms he knew and which his trained intuition told him were true and real. He demanded the source of the songs, and asked to borrow the precious book that contained them. Also, he demanded to know why young Ward had always posed as being profoundly ignorant of the German language. And Ward could neither explain his ignorance nor lend the book. Whereupon, after pleadings and entreaties that extended through weeks, Professor Wert took a dislike to the young man, believed him a liar, and classified him as a man of monstrous selfishness for not giving him a glimpse of this wonderful screed that was older than the oldest any philologist had ever known or dreamed.

But little good did it do this much-mixed young man to know that half of him was late American and the other half early Teuton. Nevertheless, the late American in him was no weakling, and he (if he were a he and had a shred of existence outside of these two) compelled an adjustment or compromise between his one self that was a nightprowling savage that kept his other self sleepy of mornings, and that other self that was cultured and refined and that wanted to be normal and live and love and prosecute business like other people. The afternoons and early evenings he gave to the one, the nights to the other; the forenoons and parts of the nights were devoted to sleep for the twain. But in the mornings he slept in bed like a civilized man. In the night time he slept like a wild animal, as he had slept Dave Slotter stepped on him in the woods.

Persuading his father to advance the capital, he went into business and keen and successful business he made of it, devoting his afternoons whole-souled to it, while his partner devoted the mornings. The early evenings he spent socially, but, as the hour grew to nine or ten, an irresistible restlessness overcame him and he disappeared from the haunts of men until the next afternoon. Friends and acquaintances thought that he spent much of his time in sport. And they were right, though they never would have dreamed of the nature of the sport, even if they had seen him running coyotes in night-chases over the hills of Mill Valley. Neither were the schooner captains believed when they reported seeing, on cold winter mornings, a man swimming in the tide-rips of Raccoon Straits or in the swift currents between Goat island and Angel Island miles from shore.

In the bungalow at Mill Valley he lived alone, save for Lee Sing, the Chinese cook and factotum, who knew much about the strangeness of his master, who was paid well for saying nothing, and who never did say anything. After the satisfaction of his nights, a morning's sleep, and a breakfast of Lee Sing's, James Ward crossed the bay to San Francisco on a midday ferryboat and went to the club and on to his office, as normal and conventional a man of business as could be found in the city. But as the evening lengthened, the night called to him. There came a quickening of all his perceptions and a restlessness. His hearing was suddenly acute; the myriad night-noises told him a luring and familiar story; and, if alone, he would begin to pace up and down the narrow room like any caged animal from the wild.

Once, he ventured to fall in love. He never permitted himself that diversion again. He was afraid. And for many a day the young lady, scared at least out of a portion of her young ladyhood, bore on her arms and shoulders and wrists divers black-and-blue bruises—tokens of caresses which he had bestowed in all fond gentleness but too late at night. There was the mistake. Had he ventured love-making in the afternoon, all would have been well, for it would have been as the quiet gentleman that he would have made love—but at night it was the uncouth, wife-stealing savage of the dark German forests. Out of his wisdom, he decided that afternoon love-making could be prosecuted successfully; but out of the same wisdom he was convinced that marriage as would prove a ghastly failure. He found it appalling to imagine being married and encountering his wife after dark.

So he had eschewed all love-making, regulated his dual life, cleaned up a million in business, fought shy of match-making mamas and bright-eyed and eager young ladies of various ages, met Lilian Gersdale and made it a rigid observance never to see her later than eight o'clock in the evening, run of nights after his coyotes, and slept in forest lairs—and through it all had kept his secret safe save Lee Sing... and now, Dave Slotter. It was the latter's discovery of both his selves that frightened him. In spite of the counter fright he had given the burglar, the latter might talk. And even if he did not, sooner or later he would be found out by some one else.

Thus it was that James Ward made a fresh and heroic effort to control the Teutonic barbarian that was half of him. So well did he make it a point to see Lilian in the afternoons, that the time came when she accepted him for better or worse, and when he prayed privily and fervently that it was not for worse. During this period no prize-fighter ever trained more harshly and faithfully for a contest than he trained to subdue the wild savage in him. Among other things, he strove to exhaust himself during the day, so that sleep would render him deaf to the call of the night. He took a vacation from the office and went on long hunting trips, following the deer through the most inaccessible and rugged country he could find—and always in the daytime. Night found him indoors and tired. At home he installed a score of exercise machines, and where other men might go through a particular movement ten times, he went hundreds. Also, as a compromise, he built a sleeping porch on the second story. Here he at least breathed the blessed night air. Double screens prevented him from escaping into the woods, and each night Lee Sing locked him in and each morning let him out.

The time came, in the month of August, when he engaged additional servants to assist Lee Sing and dared a house party in his Mill Valley bungalow. Lilian, her mother and brother, and half a dozen mutual friends, were the guests. For two days and nights all went well. And on the third night, playing bridge till eleven o'clock, he had reason to be proud of himself. His restlessness fully hid, but as luck would have it, Lilian Gersdale was his opponent on his right. She was a frail delicate flower of a woman, and in his night-mood her very frailty incensed him. Not that he loved her less, but that he felt almost irresistibly impelled to reach out and paw and maul her. Especially was this true when she was engaged in playing a winning hand against him.

He had one of the deer-hounds brought in and, when it seemed he must fly to pieces with the tension, a caressing hand laid on the animal brought him relief. These contacts with the hairy coat gave him instant easement and enabled him to play out the evening. Nor did anyone guess the while terrible struggle their host was making, the while he laughed so carelessly and played so keenly and deliberately.

When they separated for the night, he saw to it that he parted from Lilian in the presence or the others. Once on his sleeping porch and safely locked in, he doubled and tripled and even quadrupled his exercises until, exhausted, he lay down on the couch to woo sleep and to ponder two problems that especially troubled him. One was this matter of exercise. It was a paradox. The more he exercised in this excessive fashion, the stronger he became. While it was true that he thus quite tired out his night-running Teutonic self, it seemed that he was merely setting back the fatal day when his strength would be too much for him and overpower him, and then it would be a strength more terrible than he had yet known. The other problem was that of his marriage and of the stratagems he must employ in order to avoid his wife after dark. And thus, fruitlessly pondering, he fell asleep.

Now, where the huge grizzly bear came from that night was long a mystery, while the people of the Springs Brothers' Circus, showing at Sausalito, searched long and vainly for "Big Ben, the Biggest Grizzly in Captivity." But Big Ben escaped, and, out of the mazes of half a thousand bungalows and country estates, selected the grounds of James J. Ward for visitation. The self first Mr. Ward knew was when he found him on his feet, quivering and tense, a surge of battle in his breast and on his lips the old war-chant. From without came a wild baying and bellowing of the hounds. And sharp as a knife-thrust through the pandemonium came the agony of a stricken dog—his dog, he knew.

Not stopping for slippers, pajama-clad, he burst through the door Lee Sing had so carefully locked, and sped down the stairs and out into the night. As his naked feet struck the graveled driveway, he stopped abruptly, reached under the steps to a hiding-place he knew well, and pulled forth a huge knotty club—his old companion on many a mad night adventure on the hills. The frantic hullabaloo of the dogs was coming nearer, and, swinging the club, he sprang straight into the thickets to meet it.

The aroused household assembled on the wide veranda. Somebody turned on the electric lights, but they could see nothing but one another's frightened faces. Beyond the brightly illuminated driveway the trees formed a wall of impenetrable blackness. Yet somewhere in that blackness a terrible struggle was going on. There was an infernal outcry of animals, a great snarling and growling, the sound of blows being struck and a smashing and crashing of underbrush by heavy bodies.

The tide of battle swept out from among the trees and upon the driveway just beneath the onlookers. Then they saw. Mrs. Gersdale cried out and clung fainting to her son. Lilian, clutching the railing so spasmodically that a bruising hurt was left in her finger-ends for days, gazed horror-stricken at a yellow-haired, wild-eyed giant whom she recognized as the man who was to be her husband. He was swinging a great club, and fighting furiously and calmly with a shaggy monster that was bigger than any bear she had ever seen. One rip of the beast's claws had dragged away Ward's pajama-coat and streaked his flesh with blood.

While most of Lilian Gersdale's fright was for the man beloved, there was a large portion of it due to the man himself. Never had she dreamed so formidable and magnificent a savage lurked under the starched shirt and conventional garb of her betrothed. And never had she had any conception of how a man battled. Such a battle was certainly not modern; nor was she there beholding a modern man, though she did not know it. For this was not Mr. James J. Ward, the San Francisco business man, but one, unnamed and unknown, a crude, rude savage creature who, by some freak of chance, lived again after thrice a thousand years.

The hounds, ever maintaining their mad uproar, circled about the fight, or dashed in and out, distracting the bear. When the animal turned to meet such flanking assaults, the man leaped in and the club came down. Angered afresh by every such blow, the bear would rush, and the man, leaping and skipping, avoiding the dogs, went backwards or circled to one side or the other. Whereupon the dogs, taking advantage of the opening, would again spring in and draw the animal's wrath to them.

The end came suddenly. Whirling, the grizzly caught a hound with a wide sweeping cuff that sent the brute, its ribs caved in and its back broken, hurtling twenty feet. Then the human brute went mad. A foaming rage flecked the lips that parted with a wild inarticulate cry, as it sprang in, swung the club mightily in both hands, and brought it down full on the head of the uprearing grizzly. Not even the skull of a grizzly could withstand the crushing force of such a blow, and the animal went down to meet the worrying of the hounds. And through their scurrying leaped the man, squarely upon the body, where, in the white electric light, resting on his club, he chanted a triumph in an unknown tongue—a song so ancient that Professor Wertz would have given ten years of his life for it.

His guests rushed to possess him and acclaim him, but James Ward, suddenly looking out of the eyes of the early Teuton, saw the fair frail Twentieth Century girl he loved, and felt something snap in his brain. He staggered weakly toward her, dropped the club, and nearly fell. Something had gone wrong with him. Inside his brain was an intolerable agony. It seemed as if the soul of him were flying asunder. Following the excited gaze of the others, he glanced back and saw the carcass of the bear. The sight filled him with fear. He uttered a cry and would have fled, had they not restrained him and led him into the bungalow.

James J. Ward is still at the head of the firm of Ward, Knowles & Co. But he no longer lives in the country; nor does he run of nights after the coyotes under the moon. The early Teuton in him died the night of the Mill Valley fight with the bear. James J. Ward is now wholly James J. Ward, and he shares no part of his being with any vagabond anachronism from the younger world. And so wholly is James J. Ward modern, that he knows in all its bitter fullness the curse of civilized fear. He is now afraid of the dark, and night in the forest is to him a thing of abysmal terror. His city house is of the spick and span order, and he evinces a great interest in burglarproof devices. His home is a tangle of electric wires, and after bed-time a guest can scarcely breathe without setting off an alarm. Also, he had invented a combination keyless door-lock that travelers may carry in their vest pockets and apply immediately and successfully under all circumstances. But his wife does not deem him a coward. She knows better. And, like any hero, he is content to rest on his laurels. His bravery is never questioned by those friends who are aware of the Mill Valley episode.

THE BENEFIT OF THE DOUBT

CARTER WATSON, a current magazine under his arm, strolled slowly along, gazing about him curiously. Twenty years had elapsed since he had been on this particular street, and the changes were great and stupefying. This Western city of three hundred thousand souls had contained but thirty thousand, when, as a boy, he had been wont to ramble along its streets. In those days the street he was now on had been a quiet residence street in the respectable workingclass quarter. On this late afternoon he found that it had been submerged by a vast and vicious tenderloin. Chinese and Japanese shops and dens abounded, all confusedly intermingled with low white resorts and boozing dens. This quiet street of his youth had become the toughest quarter of the city.

He looked at his watch. It was half-past five. It was the slack time of the day in such a region, as he well knew, yet he was curious to see. In all his score of years of wandering and studying social conditions over the world, he had carried with him the memory of his old town as a sweet and wholesome place. The metamorphosis he now beheld was startling. He certainly must continue his stroll and glimpse the infamy to which his town had descended.

Another thing: Carter Watson had a keen social and civic consciousness. Independently wealthy, he had been loath to dissipate his energies in the pink teas and freak dinners of society, while actresses, race-horses, and kindred diversions had left him cold. He had the ethical bee in his bonnet and was a reformer of no mean pretension, though his work had been mainly in the line of contributions to the heavier reviews and quarterlies and to the publication over his name of brightly, cleverly written books on the working classes and the slum-dwellers. Among the twenty-seven to his credit occurred titles such as, "If Christ Came to New Orleans," "The Worked-out Worker," "Tenement Reform in Berlin," "The Rural Slums of England," "The people of the East Side," "Reform Versus Revolution," "The University Settlement as a Hot Bed of Radicalism" and "The Cave Man of Civilization."

But Carter Watson was neither morbid nor fanatic. He did not lose his head over the horrors he encountered, studied, and exposed. No hair brained enthusiasm branded him. His humor saved him, as did his wide experience and his conservative philosophic temperament. Nor did he have any patience with lightning change reform theories. As he saw it, society would grow better only through the painfully slow and arduously painful processes of evolution. There were no short cuts, no sudden regenerations. The betterment of mankind must be worked out in agony and misery just as all past social betterments had been worked out.

But on this late summer afternoon, Carter Watson was curious. As he moved along he paused before a gaudy drinking place. The sign above read, "The Vendome." There were two entrances. One evidently led to the bar. This he did not explore. The other was a narrow hallway. Passing through this he found himself in a huge room, filled with chair-encircled tables and quite deserted. In the dim light he made out a piano in the distance. Making a mental note that he would come back some time and study the class of persons that must sit and drink at those multitudinous tables, he proceeded to circumnavigate the room.

Now, at the rear, a short hallway led off to a small kitchen, and here, at a table, alone, sat Patsy Horan, proprietor of the Vendome, consuming a hasty supper ere the evening rush of business. Also, Patsy Horan was angry with the world. He had got out of the wrong side of bed that morning, and nothing had gone right all day. Had his barkeepers been asked, they would have described his mental condition as a grouch. But Carter Watson did not know this. As he passed the little hallway, Patsy Horan's sullen eyes lighted on the magazine he carried under his arm. Patsy did not know Carter Watson, nor did he know that what he carried under his arm was a magazine. Patsy, out of the depths of his grouch, decided that this stranger was one of those pests who marred and scarred the walls of his back rooms by tacking up or pasting up advertisements. The color on the front cover of the magazine convinced him that it was such an advertisement. Thus the trouble began. Knife and fork in hand, Patsy leaped for Carter Watson.

"Out wid yeh!" Patsy bellowed. "I know yer game!"

168

Carter Watson was startled. The man had come upon him like the eruption of a jack-in-the-box.

"A defacin' me walls," cried Patsy, at the same time emitting a string of vivid and vile, rather than virile, epithets of opprobrium.

"If I have given any offense I did not mean to—"

But that was as far as the visitor got. Patsy interrupted.

"Get out wid yeh; yeh talk too much wid yer mouth," quoted Patsy, emphasizing his remarks with flourishes of the knife and fork.

Carter Watson caught a quick vision of that eating-fork inserted uncomfortably between his ribs, knew that it would be rash to talk further with his mouth, and promptly turned to go. The sight of his meekly retreating back must have further enraged Patsy Horan, for that worthy, dropping the table implements, sprang upon him.

Patsy weighed one hundred and eighty pounds. So did Watson. In this they were equal. But Patsy was a rushing, rough-and-tumble saloon-fighter, while Watson was a boxer. In this the latter had the advantage, for Patsy came in wide open, swinging his right in a perilous sweep. All Watson had to do was to straight-left him and escape. But Watson had another advantage. His boxing, and his experience in the slums and ghettos of the world, had taught him restraint.

He pivoted on his feet, and, instead of striking, ducked the other's swinging blow and went into a clinch. But Patsy, charging like a bull, had the momentum of his rush, while Watson, whirling to meet him, had no momentum. As a result, the pair of them went down, with all their three hundred and sixty pounds of weight, in a long crashing fall, Watson underneath. He lay with his head touching the rear wall of the large room. The street was a hundred and fifty feet away, and he did some quick thinking. His first thought was to avoid trouble. He had no wish to get into the papers of this, his childhood town, where many of his relatives and family friends still lived.

So it was that he locked his arms around the man on top of him, held him close, and waited for the help to come that must come in response to the crash of the fall. The help came—that is, six men ran in from the bar and formed about in a semi-circle.

"Take him off, fellows," Watson said. "I haven't struck him, and I don't want any fight."

But the semi-circle remained silent. Watson held on and waited. Patsy, after various vain efforts to inflict damage, made an overture.

"Leggo o' me an' I'll get off o' yeh," said he.

Watson let go, but when Patsy scrambled to his feet he stood over his recumbent foe, ready to strike.

"Get up," Patsy commanded.

His voice was stern and implacable, like the voice of God calling to judgment, and Watson knew there was no mercy there.

"Stand back and I'll get up," he countered.

"If yer a gentleman, get up," quoth Patsy, his pale blue eyes aflame with wrath, his fist ready for a crushing blow.

At the same moment he drew his foot back to kick the other in the face. Watson blocked the kick with his crossed arms and sprang to his feet so quickly that he was in a clinch with his antagonist before the latter could strike. Holding him, Watson spoke to the onlookers:

"Take him away from me, fellows. You see I am not striking him. I don't want to fight. I want to get out of here."

The circle did not move nor speak. Its silence was ominous and sent a chill to Watson's heart.

Patsy made an effort to throw him, which culminated in his putting Patsy on his back. Tearing loose from him, Watson sprang to his feet and made for the door. But the circle of men was interposed a wall. He noticed the white, pasty faces, the kind that never see the sun, and knew that the men who barred his way were the nightprowlers and preying beasts of the city jungle. By them he was thrust back upon the pursuing, bull-rushing Patsy.

Again it was a clinch, in which, in momentary safety, Watson appealed to the gang. And again his words fell on deaf ears. Then it was that he knew of many similar knew fear. For he had known of many similar situations, in low dens like this, when solitary men were man-handled, their ribs and features caved in, themselves beaten and kicked to death. And he knew, further, that if he were to escape he must neither strike his assailant nor any of the men who opposed him.

Yet in him was righteous indignation. Under no circumstances could seven to one be fair. Also, he was angry, and there stirred in him the fighting beast that is in all men. But he remembered his wife and children, his unfinished book, the ten thousand rolling acres of the up-country ranch he loved so well. He even saw in flashing visions the blue of the sky, the golden sun pouring down on his flower-spangled meadows, the lazy cattle knee-deep in the brooks, and the flash of trout in the riffles. Life was good-too good for him to risk it for a moment's sway of the beast. In short, Carter Watson was cool and scared.

His opponent, locked by his masterly clinch, was striving to throw him. Again Watson put him on the floor, broke away, and was thrust back by the pasty-faced circle to duck Patsy's swinging right and effect another clinch. This happened many times. And Watson grew even cooler, while the baffled Patsy, unable to inflict punishment, raged wildly and more wildly. He took to batting with his head in the clinches. The first time, he landed his forehead flush on Watson's nose. After that, the latter, in the clinches, buried his face in Patsy's breast. But the enraged Patsy batted on, striking his own eye and nose and cheek on the top of the other's head. The more he was thus injured, the more and the harder did Patsy bat.

This one-sided contest continued for twelve or fifteen minutes. Watson never struck a blow, and strove only to escape. Sometimes, in the free moments, circling about among the tables as he tried to win the door, the pasty-faced men gripped his coat-tails and flung him back at the swinging right of the on-rushing Patsy. Time upon time, and times without end, he clinched and put Patsy on his back, each time first whirling him around and putting him down in the direction of the door and gaining toward that goal by the length of the fall.

In the end, hatless, disheveled, with streaming nose and one eye closed, Watson won to the sidewalk and into the arms of a policeman.

"Arrest that man," Watson panted.

"Hello, Patsy," said the policeman. "What's the mix-up?"

"Hello, Charley," was the answer. "This guy comes in—"

"Arrest that man, officer," Watson repeated.

"G'wan! Beat it!" said Patsy.

"Beat it!" added the policeman. "If you don't, I'll pull you in."

"Not unless you arrest that man. He has committed a violent and unprovoked assault on me."

"Is it so, Patsy?" was the officer's query.

"Nah. Lemme tell you, Charley, an' I got the witnesses to prove it, so help me God. I was settin' in me kitchen eatin' a bowl of soup, when this guy comes in an' gets gay wid me. I never seen him in me born days before. He was drunk—"

"Look at me, officer," protested the indignant sociologist. "Am I drunk?"

The officer looked at him with sullen, menacing eyes and nodded to Patsy to continue.

"This guy gets gay wid me. 'I'm Tim McGrath,' says he, 'an' I can do the like to you,' says he. 'Put up yer hands.' I smiles, an' wid that, biff biff, he lands me twice an' spills me soup. Look at me eye. I'm fair murdered."

"What are you going to do, officer?" Watson demanded.

172

"Go on, beat it," was the answer, "or I'll pull you sure."

The civic righteousness of Carter Watson flamed up.

"Mr. Officer, I protest—"

But at that moment the policeman grabbed his arm with a savage jerk that nearly overthrew him.

"Come on, you're pulled."

"Arrest him, too," Watson demanded.

"Nix on that play," was the reply.

"What did you assault him for, him a peacefully eatin' his soup?"

II

Carter Watson was genuinely angry. Not only had he been wantonly assaulted, badly battered, and arrested, but the morning papers without exception came out with lurid accounts of his drunken brawl with the proprietor of the notorious Vendome. Not one accurate or truthful line was published. Patsy Horan and his satellites described the battle in detail. The one incontestable thing was that Carter Watson had been drunk. Thrice he had been thrown out of the place and into the gutter, and thrice he had come back, breathing blood and fire and announcing that he was going to clean out the place. "EMINENT SOCIOLOGIST JAGGED AND JUGGED," was the first head-line he read, on the front page, accompanied by a large portrait of himself. Other headlines were: "CARTER WATSON ASPIRED TO CHAMPIONSHIP HONORS"; "CARTER WATSON GETS HIS"; "NOTED SOCIOLOGIST ATTEMPTS TO CLEAN OUT A TENDERLOIN CAFE"; and "CARTER WATSON KNOCKED OUT BY PATSY HORAN IN THREE ROUNDS."

At the police court, next morning, under bail, appeared Carter Watson to answer the complaint of the People Versus Carter Watson, for the latter's assault and battery on one Patsy Horan. But first, the Prosecuting Attorney, who was paid to prosecute all offenders against the People, drew him aside and talked with him privately.

"Why not let it drop!" said the Prosecuting Attorney. "I tell you what you do, Mr. Watson: Shake hands with Mr. Horan and make it up, and we'll drop the case right here. A word to the Judge, and the case against you will be dismissed."

"But I don't want it dismissed," was the answer. "Your office being what it is, you should be prosecuting me instead of asking me to make up with this—this fellow."

"Oh, I'll prosecute you all right," retorted the Prosecuting Attorney.

"Also you will have to prosecute this Patsy Horan," Watson advised; "for I shall now have him arrested for assault and battery."

"You'd better shake and make up," the Prosecuting Attorney repeated, and this time there was almost a threat in his voice.

The trials of both men were set for a week later, on the same morning, in Police Judge Witberg's court.

"You have no chance," Watson was told by an old friend of his boyhood, the retired manager of the biggest paper in the city. "Everybody knows you were beaten up by this man. His reputation is most unsavory. But it won't help you in the least. Both cases will be dismissed. This will be because you are you. Any ordinary man would be convicted."

"But I do not understand," objected the perplexed sociologist. "Without warning I was attacked by this man; and badly beaten. I did not strike a blow. I—"

"That has nothing to do with it," the other cut him off.

"Then what is there that has anything to do with it?"

"I'll tell you. You are now up against the local police and political machine. Who are you? You are not even a legal resident in this town. You live up in the country. You haven't a vote of your own here. Much less do you swing any votes. This dive proprietor swings a string of votes in his precincts—a mighty long string."

"Do you mean to tell me that this Judge Witberg will violate the sacredness of his office and oath by letting this brute off?" Watson demanded.

"Watch him," was the grim reply. "Oh, he'll do it nicely enough. He will give an extra-legal, extra-judicial decision, abounding in every word in the dictionary that stands for fairness and right."

"But there are the newspapers," Watson cried.

"They are not fighting the administration at present. They'll give it to you hard. You see what they have already done to you."

"Then these snips of boys on the police detail won't write the truth?"

"They will write something so near like the truth that the public will believe it. They write their stories under instruction, you know. They have their orders to twist and color, and there won't be much left of you when they get done. Better drop the whole thing right now. You are in bad."

"But the trials are set."

"Give the word and they'll drop them now. A man can't fight a machine unless he has a machine behind him."

III

But Carter Watson was stubborn. He was convinced that the machine would beat him, but all his days he had sought social experience, and this was certainly something new.

The morning of the trial the Prosecuting Attorney made another attempt to patch up the affair.

"If you feel that way, I should like to get a lawyer to prosecute the case," said Watson.

"No, you don't," said the Prosecuting Attorney. "I am paid by the People to prosecute, and prosecute I will. But let me tell you. You have no chance. We shall lump both cases into one, and you watch out."

Judge Witberg looked good to Watson. A fairly young man, short, comfortably stout, smooth-shaven and with an intelligent face, he seemed a very nice man indeed. This good impression was added to by the smiling lips and the wrinkles of laughter in the corners of his black eyes. Looking at him and studying him, Watson felt almost sure that his old friend's prognostication was wrong.

But Watson was soon to learn. Patsy Horan and two of his satellites testified to a most colossal aggregation of perjuries. Watson could not have believed it possible without having experienced it. They denied the existence of the other four men. And of the two that testified, one claimed to have been in the kitchen, a witness to Watson's unprovoked assault on Patsy, while the other, remaining in the bar, had witnessed Watson's second and third rushes into the place as he attempted to annihilate the unoffending Patsy. The vile language ascribed to Watson was so voluminously and unspeakably vile, that he felt they were injuring their own case. It was so impossible that he should utter such things. But when they described the brutal blows he had rained on poor Patsy's face, and the chair he demolished when he vainly attempted to kick Patsy, Watson waxed secretly hilarious and at the same time sad. The trial was a farce, but such lowness of life was depressing to contemplate when he considered the long upward climb humanity must make.

Watson could not recognize himself, nor could his worst enemy have recognized him, in the swashbuckling, rough-housing picture that was painted of him. But, as in all cases of complicated perjury, rifts and contradictions in the various stories appeared. The Judge somehow failed to notice them, while the Prosecuting Attorney and Patsy's attorney shied off from them gracefully. Watson had not bothered to get a lawyer for himself, and he was now glad that he had not.

Still, he retained a semblance of faith in Judge Witberg when he went himself on the stand and started to tell his story.

176

"I was strolling casually along the street, your Honor," Watson began, but was interrupted by the Judge.

"We are not here to consider your previous actions," bellowed Judge Witberg. "Who struck the first blow?"

"Your Honor," Watson pleaded, "I have no witnesses of the actual fray, and the truth of my story can only be brought out by telling the story fully—"

Again he was interrupted.

"We do not care to publish any magazines here," Judge Witberg roared, looking at him so fiercely and malevolently that Watson could scarcely bring himself to believe that this was same man he had studied a few minutes previously.

"Who struck the first blow?" Patsy's attorney asked.

The Prosecuting Attorney interposed, demanding to know which of the two cases lumped together was, and by what right Patsy's lawyer, at that stage of the proceedings, should take the witness. Patsy's attorney fought back. Judge Witberg interfered, professing no knowledge of any two cases being lumped together. All this had to be explained. Battle royal raged, terminating in both attorneys apologizing to the Court and to each other. And so it went, and to Watson it had the seeming of a group of pickpockets ruffling and bustling an honest man as they took his purse. The machine was working, that was all.

"Why did you enter this place of unsavory reputations?" was asked him.

"It has been my custom for many years, as a student of economics and sociology, to acquaint myself—"

But this was as far as Watson got.

"We want none of your ologies here," snarled Judge Witberg. "It is a plain question. Answer it plainly. Is it true or not true that you were drunk? That is the gist of the question."

When Watson attempted to tell how Patsy had injured his face in his attempts to bat with his head, Watson was openly scouted and flouted, and Judge Witberg again took him in hand.

"Are you aware of the solemnity of the oath you took to testify to nothing but the truth on this witness stand?" the Judge demanded. "This is a fairy story you are telling. It is not reasonable that a man would so injure himself, and continue to injure himself, by striking the soft and sensitive parts of his face against your head. You are a sensible man. It is unreasonable, is it not?"

"Men are unreasonable when they are angry," Watson answered meekly.

Then it was that Judge Witberg was deeply outraged and righteously wrathful.

"What right have you to say that?" he cried. "It is gratuitous. It has no bearing on the case. You are here as a witness, sir, of events that have transpired. The Court does not wish to hear any expressions of opinion from you at all."

"I but answered your question, your Honor," Watson protested humbly.

"You did nothing of the sort," was the next blast. "And let me warn you, sir, let me warn you, that you are laying yourself liable to contempt by such insolence. And I will have you know that we know how to observe the law and the rules of courtesy down here in this little courtroom. I am ashamed of you."

And, while the next punctilious legal wrangle between the attorneys interrupted his tale of what happened in the Vendome, Carter Watson, without bitterness, amused and at the same time sad, saw rise before him the machine, large and small, that dominated his country, the unpunished and shameless grafts of a thousand cities perpetrated by the spidery and vermin-like creatures of the machines. Here it was before him, a courtroom and a judge, bowed down in subservience by the machine to a dive-keeper who swung a string of votes. Petty and sordid as it was, it was one face of the many-faced machine that loomed colossally, in every city and state, in a thousand guises overshadowing the land.

A familiar phrase rang in his ears: "It is to laugh." At the height of the wrangle, he giggled, once, aloud, and earned a sullen frown from Judge Witberg. Worse, a myriad times, he decided, were these bullying lawyers and this bullying judge then the bucko mates in first quality hell-ships, who not only did their own bullying but protected themselves as well. These petty rapscallions, on the other hand, sought protection behind the majesty of the law. They struck, but no one was permitted to strike back, for behind them were the prison cells and the clubs of the stupid policemen—paid and professional fighters and beaters-up of men. Yet he was not bitter. The grossness and the sliminess of it was forgotten in the simple grotesqueness of it, and he had the saving sense of humor.

Nevertheless, hectored and heckled though he was, he managed in the end to give a simple, straightforward version of the affair, and, despite a belligerent cross-examination, his story was not shaken in any particular. Quite different it was from the perjuries that had shouted aloud from the perjuries of Patsy and his two witnesses.

Both Patsy's attorney and the Prosecuting Attorney rested their cases, letting everything go before the Court without argument. Watson protested against this, but was silenced when the Prosecuting Attorney told him that Public Prosecutor and knew his business.

"Patrick Horan has testified that he was in danger of his life and that he was compelled to defend himself," Judge Witberg's verdict began. "Mr. Watson has testified to the same thing. Each has sworn that the other struck the first blow; each has sworn that the other made an unprovoked assault on him. It is an axiom of the law that the defendant should be given the benefit of the doubt. A very reasonable doubt exists. Therefore, in the case of the People Versus Carter Watson the benefit of the doubt is given to said Carter Watson and he is herewith ordered discharged from custody. The same reasoning applies to the case of the People Versus Patrick Horan. He is given the benefit of the doubt and discharged from custody. My recommendation is that both defendants shake hands and make up."

In the afternoon papers the first headline that caught Watson's eye was: "CARTER WATSON ACQUITTED." In the second paper it was: "CARTER WATSON ESCAPES A FINE." But what capped everything was the one beginning: "CARTER WATSON A GOOD FELLOW." In the text he read how Judge Witberg had advised both fighters to shake hands, which they promptly did. Further, he read:

"'Let's have a nip on it,' said Patsy Horan.

"'Sure,' said Carter Watson.

"And, arm in arm, they ambled for the nearest saloon."

IV

Now, from the whole adventure, Watson carried away no bitterness. It was a social experience of a new order, and it led to the writing of another book, which he entitled, "POLICE COURT PROCEDURE: A Tentative Analysis."

One summer morning a year later, on his ranch, he left his horse and himself clambered on through a miniature canyon to inspect some rock ferns he had planted the previous winter. Emerging from the upper end of the canyon, he came out on one of his flower-spangled meadows, a delightful isolated spot, screened from the world by low hills and clumps of trees. And here he found a man, evidently on a stroll from the summer hotel down at the little town a mile away. They met face to face and the recognition was mutual. It was Judge Witberg. Also, it was a clear case of trespass, for Watson had trespass signs upon his boundaries, though he never enforced them.

Judge Witberg held out his hand, which Watson refused to see.

"Politics is a dirty trade, isn't it, Judge?" he remarked. "Oh, yes, I see your hand, but I don't care to take it. The papers said I shook hands with Patsy Horan after the trial. You know I did not, but let me tell you that I'd a thousand times rather shake hands with him and his vile following of curs, than with you."

180

Judge Witberg was painfully flustered, and as he hemmed and hawed and essayed to speak, Watson, looking at him, was struck by a sudden whim, and he determined on a grim and facetious antic.

"I should scarcely expect any animus from a man of your acquirements and knowledge of the world," the Judge was saying.

"Animus?" Watson replied. "Certainly not. I haven't such a thing in my nature. And to prove it, let me show you something curious, something you have never seen before." Casting about him, Watson picked up a rough stone the size of his fist. "See this. Watch me."

So saying, Carter Watson tapped himself a sharp blow on the cheek. The stone laid the flesh open to the bone and the blood spurted forth.

"The stone was too sharp," he announced to the astounded police judge, who thought he had gone mad.

"I must bruise it a trifle. There is nothing like being realistic in such matters."

Whereupon Carter Watson found a smooth stone and with it pounded his cheek nicely several times.

"Ah," he cooed. "That will turn beautifully green and black in a few hours. It will be most convincing."

"You are insane," Judge Witberg quavered.

"Don't use such vile language to me," said Watson. "You see my bruised and bleeding face? You did that, with that right hand of yours. You hit me twice—biff, biff. It is a brutal and unprovoked assault. I am in danger of my life. I must protect myself."

Judge Witberg backed away in alarm before the menacing fists of the other.

"If you strike me I'll have you arrested," Judge Witberg threatened.

"That is what I told Patsy," was the answer. "And do you know what he did when I told him that?"

"No."

"That!"

And at the same moment Watson's right fist landed flush on Judge Witberg's nose, putting that legal gentleman over on his back on the grass.

"Get up!" commanded Watson. "If you are a gentleman, get up—that's what Patsy told me, you know."

Judge Witberg declined to rise, and was dragged to his feet by the coat-collar, only to have one eye blacked and be put on his back again. After that it was a red Indian massacre. Judge Witberg was humanely and scientifically beaten up. His checks were boxed, his ears cuffed, and his face was rubbed in the turf. And all the time Watson exposited the way Patsy Horan had done it. Occasionally, and very carefully, the facetious sociologist administered a real bruising blow. Once, dragging the poor Judge to his feet, he deliberately bumped his own nose on the gentleman's head. The nose promptly bled.

"See that!" cried Watson, stepping back and deftly shedding his blood all down his own shirt front. "You did it. With your fist you did it. It is awful. I am fair murdered. I must again defend myself."

And once more Judge Witberg impacted his features on a fist and was sent to grass.

"I will have you arrested," he sobbed as he lay.

"That's what Patsy said."

"A brutal—sniff, sniff,—and unprovoked—sniff, sniff—assault."

"That's what Patsy said."

"I will surely have you arrested."

"Speaking slangily, not if I can beat you to it."

And with that, Carter Watson departed down the canyon, mounted his horse, and rode to town.

An hour later, as Judge Witberg limped up the grounds to his hotel, he was arrested by a village constable on a charge of assault and battery preferred by Carter Watson.

V

"Your Honor," Watson said next day to the village Justice, a well to do farmer and graduate, thirty years before, from a cow college, "since this Sol Witberg has seen fit to charge me with battery, following upon my charge of battery against him, I would suggest that both cases be lumped together. The testimony and the facts are the same in both cases."

To this the Justice agreed, and the double case proceeded. Watson, as prosecuting witness, first took the stand and told his story.

"I was picking flowers," he testified. "Picking flowers on my own land, never dreaming of danger. Suddenly this man rushed upon me from behind the trees. 'I am the Dodo,' he says, 'and I can do you to a frazzle. Put up your hands.' I smiled, but with that, biff, biff, he struck me, knocking me down and spilling my flowers. The language he used was frightful. It was an unprovoked and brutal assault. Look at my cheek. Look at my nose—I could not understand it. He must have been drunk. Before I recovered from my surprise he had administered this beating. I was in danger of my life and was compelled to defend himself. That is all, Your Honor, though I must say, in conclusion, that I cannot get over my perplexity. Why did he say he was the Dodo? Why did he so wantonly attack me?"

And thus was Sol Witberg given a liberal education in the art of perjury. Often, from his high seat, he had listened indulgently to police court perjuries in cooked-up cases; but for the first time perjury was directed against him, and he no longer sat above the court, with the bailiffs, the Policemen's clubs, and the prison cells behind him.

"Your Honor," he cried, "never have I heard such a pack of lies told by so bare-faced a liar—!"

Watson here sprang to his feet.

"Your Honor, I protest. It is for your Honor to decide truth or falsehood. The witness is on the stand to testify to actual events that have transpired. His personal opinion upon things in general, and upon me, has no bearing on the case whatever."

The Justice scratched his head and waxed phlegmatically indignant.

"The point is well taken," he decided. "I am surprised at you, Mr. Witberg, claiming to be a judge and skilled in the practice of the law, and yet being guilty of such unlawyerlike conduct. Your manner, sir, and your methods, remind me of a shyster. This is a simple case of assault and battery. We are here to determine who struck the first blow, and we are not interested in your estimates of Mr. Watson's personal character. Proceed with your story."

Sol Witberg would have bitten his bruised and swollen lip in chagrin, had it not hurt so much. But he contained himself and told a simple, straightforward, truthful story.

"Your Honor," Watson said, "I would suggest that you ask him what he was doing on my premises."

"A very good question. What were you doing, sir, on Mr. Watson's premises?"

"I did not know they were his premises."

"It was a trespass, your Honor," Watson cried. "The warnings are posted conspicuously."

"I saw no warnings," said Sol Witberg.

"I have seen them myself," snapped the Justice. "They are very conspicuous. And I would warn you, sir, that if you palter with the truth in such little matters you may darken your more important statements with suspicion. Why did you strike Mr. Watson?"

"Your Honor, as I have testified, I did not strike a blow."

The Justice looked at Carter Watson's bruised and swollen visage, and turned to glare at Sol Witberg.

"Look at that man's cheek!" he thundered. "If you did not strike a blow how comes it that he is so disfigured and injured?"

"As I testified—"

"Be careful," the Justice warned.

"I will be careful, sir. I will say nothing but the truth. He struck himself with a rock. He struck himself with two different rocks."

"Does it stand to reason that a man, any man not a lunatic, would so injure himself, and continue to injure himself, by striking the soft and sensitive parts of his face with a stone?" Carter Watson demanded

"It sounds like a fairy story," was the Justice's comment.

"Mr. Witberg, had you been drinking?"

"No, sir."

"Do you never drink?"

"On occasion."

The Justice meditated on this answer with an air of astute profundity.

Watson took advantage of the opportunity to wink at Sol Witberg, but that much-abused gentleman saw nothing humorous in the situation.

"A very peculiar case, a very peculiar case," the Justice announced, as he began his verdict. "The evidence of the two parties is flatly contradictory. There are no witnesses outside the two principals. Each claims the other committed the assault, and I have no legal way of determining the truth. But I have my private opinion, Mr. Witberg, and I would recommend that henceforth you keep off of Mr. Watson's premises and keep away from this section of the country—"

"This is an outrage!" Sol Witberg blurted out.

"Sit down, sir!" was the Justice's thundered command. "If you interrupt the Court in this manner again, I shall fine you for contempt. And I warn you I shall fine you heavily—you, a judge yourself, who should be conversant with the courtesy and dignity of courts. I shall now give my verdict:

"It is a rule of law that the defendant shall be given the benefit of the doubt. As I have said, and I repeat, there is no legal way for me to determine who struck the first blow. Therefore, and much to my regret,"—here he paused and glared at Sol Witberg—"in each of these cases I am compelled to give the defendant the benefit of the doubt. Gentlemen, you are both dismissed."

"Let us have a nip on it," Watson said to Witberg, as they left the courtroom; but that outraged person refused to lock arms and amble to the nearest saloon.

WINGED BLACKMAIL

PETER WINN lay back comfortably in a library chair, with closed eyes, deep in the cogitation of a scheme of campaign destined in the near future to make a certain coterie of hostile financiers sit up. The central idea had come to him the night before, and he was now reveling in the planning of the remoter, minor details. By obtaining control of a certain up-country bank, two general stores, and several logging camps, he could come into control of a certain dinky jerkwater line which shall here be nameless, but which, in his hands, would prove the key to a vastly larger situation involving more main-line mileage almost than there were spikes in the aforesaid dinky jerkwater. It was so simple that he had almost laughed aloud when it came to him. No wonder those astute and ancient enemies of his had passed it by.

The library door opened, and a slender, middle-aged man, weak-eyed and eye glassed, entered. In his hands was an envelope and an open letter. As Peter Winn's secretary it was his task to weed out, sort, and classify his employer's mail.

"This came in the morning post," he ventured apologetically and with the hint of a titter. "Of course it doesn't amount to anything, but I thought you would like to see it."

"Read it," Peter Winn commanded, without opening his eyes.

The secretary cleared his throat.

"It is dated July seventeenth, but is without address. Postmark San Francisco. It is also quite illiterate. The spelling is atrocious. Here it is:

"Mr. Peter Winn, SIR: I send you respectfully by express a pigeon worth good money. She's a loo-loo—"

"What is a loo-loo?" Peter Winn interrupted.

The secretary tittered.

"I'm sure I don't know, except that it must be a superlative of some sort. The letter continues:

"Please freight it with a couple of thousand-dollar bills and let it go. If you do I wont never annoy you no more. If you dont you will be sorry.

"That is all. It is unsigned. I thought it would amuse you."

"Has the pigeon come?" Peter Winn demanded.

"I'm sure I never thought to enquire."

"Then do so."

In five minutes the secretary was back.

"Yes, sir. It came this morning."

"Then bring it in."

The secretary was inclined to take the affair as a practical joke, but Peter Winn, after an examination of the pigeon, thought otherwise.

"Look at it," he said, stroking and handling it. "See the length of the body and that elongated neck. A proper carrier. I doubt if I've ever seen a finer specimen. Powerfully winged and muscled. As our unknown correspondent remarked, she is a loo-loo. It's a temptation to keep her."

The secretary tittered.

"Why not? Surely you will not let it go back to the writer of that letter."

Peter Winn shook his head.

"I'll answer. No man can threaten me, even anonymously or in foolery."

On a slip of paper he wrote the succinct message, "Go to hell," signed it, and placed it in the carrying apparatus with which the bird had been thoughtfully supplied.

"Now we'll let her loose. Where's my son? I'd like him to see the flight."

"He's down in the workshop. He slept there last night, and had his breakfast sent down this morning."

"He'll break his neck yet," Peter Winn remarked, half-fiercely, half-proudly, as he led the way to the veranda.

Standing at the head of the broad steps, he tossed the pretty creature outward and upward. She caught herself with a quick beat of wings, fluttered about undecidedly for a space, then rose in the air.

Again, high up, there seemed indecision; then, apparently getting her bearings, she headed east, over the oak-trees that dotted the park-like grounds.

"Beautiful, beautiful," Peter Winn murmured. "I almost wish I had her back."

But Peter Winn was a very busy man, with such large plans in his head and with so many reins in his hands that he quickly forgot the incident. Three nights later the left wing of his country house was blown up. It was not a heavy explosion, and nobody was hurt, though the wing itself was ruined. Most of the windows of the rest of the house were broken, and there was a deal of general damage. By the first ferry boat of the morning half a dozen San Francisco detectives arrived, and several hours later the secretary, in high excitement, erupted on Peter Winn.

"It's come!" the secretary gasped, the sweat beading his forehead and his eyes bulging behind their glasses.

"What has come?" Peter demanded. "It—the—the loo-loo bird."

Then the financier understood.

"Have you gone over the mail yet?"

"I was just going over it, sir."

"Then continue, and see if you can find another letter from our mysterious friend, the pigeon fancier."

The letter came to light. It read:

Mr. Peter Winn, HONORABLE SIR: Now dont be a fool. If youd came through, your shack would not have blew up—I beg to inform you respectfully, am sending same pigeon. Take good care of same, thank you. Put five one thousand dollar bills on her and let her go. Dont feed her. Dont try to follow bird. She is wise to the way now and makes better time. If you dont come through, watch out.

Peter Winn was genuinely angry. This time he indited no message for the pigeon to carry. Instead, he called in the detectives, and, under their advice, weighted the pigeon heavily with shot. Her previous flight having been eastward toward the bay, the fastest motor-boat in Tiburon was commissioned to take up the chase if it led out over the water.

But too much shot had been put on the carrier, and she was exhausted before the shore was reached. Then the mistake was made of putting too little shot on her, and she rose high in the air, got her bearings and started eastward across San Francisco Bay. She flew straight over Angel Island, and here the motor-boat lost her, for it had to go around the island.

That night, armed guards patrolled the grounds. But there was no explosion. Yet, in the early morning Peter Winn learned by telephone that his sister's home in Alameda had been burned to the ground.

Two days later the pigeon was back again, coming this time by freight in what had seemed a barrel of potatoes. Also came another letter:

Mr. Peter Winn, RESPECTABLE SIR: It was me that fixed yr sisters house. You have raised hell, aint you. Send ten thousand now. Going up all the time. Dont put any more handicap weights on that bird. You sure cant follow her, and its cruelty to animals.

Peter Winn was ready to acknowledge himself beaten. The detectives were powerless, and Peter did not know where next the man would strike— perhaps at the lives of those near and dear to him. He even telephoned to San Francisco for ten thousand dollars in bills of large denomination. But Peter had a son, Peter Winn, Junior, with the same firm-set jaw as his fathers, and the same knitted, brooding determination in his eyes. He was only twenty-six, but he was all man, a secret terror and delight to the financier, who alternated between pride in his son's aeroplane feats and fear for an untimely and terrible end.

"Hold on, father, don't send that money," said Peter Winn, Junior. "Number Eight is ready, and I know I've at last got that reefing down fine. It will work, and it will revolutionize flying. Speed—that's what's needed, and so are the large sustaining surfaces for getting started and for altitude. I've got them both. Once I'm up I reef down. There it is. The smaller the sustaining surface, the higher the speed. That was the law discovered by Langley. And I've applied it. I can rise when the air is calm and full of holes, and I can rise when its boiling, and by my control of my plane areas I can come pretty close to making any speed I want. Especially with that new Sangster-Endholm engine."

"You'll come pretty close to breaking your neck one of these days," was his father's encouraging remark.

"Dad, I'll tell you what I'll come pretty close to-ninety miles an hour—Yes, and a hundred. Now listen! I was going to make a trial tomorrow. But it won't take two hours to start today. I'll tackle it this afternoon. Keep that money. Give me the pigeon and I'll follow her to her loft where ever it is. Hold on, let me talk to the mechanics."

He called up the workshop, and in crisp, terse sentences gave his orders in a way that went to the older man's heart. Truly, his one son was a chip off the old block, and Peter Winn had no meek notions concerning the intrinsic value of said old block.

Timed to the minute, the young man, two hours later, was ready for the start. In a holster at his hip, for instant use, cocked and with the safety on, was a large-caliber automatic pistol. With a final inspection and overhauling he took his seat in the aeroplane. He started the engine, and with a wild burr of gas explosions the beautiful fabric darted down the launching ways and lifted into the air. Circling, as he rose, to the west, he wheeled about and jockeyed and maneuvered for the real start of the race.

This start depended on the pigeon. Peter Winn held it. Nor was it weighted with shot this time. Instead, half a yard of bright ribbon was firmly attached to its leg—this the more easily to enable its flight being followed. Peter Winn released it, and it arose easily enough despite the slight drag of the ribbon. There was no uncertainty about its movements. This was the third time it had made particular homing passage, and it knew the course.

At an altitude of several hundred feet it straightened out and went due east. The aeroplane swerved into a straight course from its last curve and followed. The race was on. Peter Winn, looking up, saw that the pigeon was outdistancing the machine. Then he saw something else. The aeroplane suddenly and instantly became smaller. It had reefed. Its high-speed plane-design was now revealed. Instead of the generous spread of surface with which it had taken the air, it was now a lean and hawklike monoplane balanced on long and exceedingly narrow wings.

When young Winn reefed down so suddenly, he received a surprise. It was his first trial of the new device, and while he was prepared for increased speed he was not prepared for such an astonishing increase. It was better than he dreamed, and, before he knew it, he was hard upon the pigeon. That little creature, frightened by this, the most monstrous hawk it had ever seen, immediately darted upward, after the manner of pigeons that strive always to rise above a hawk.

In great curves the monoplane followed upward, higher and higher into the blue. It was difficult, from underneath to see the pigeon, and young Winn dared not lose it from his sight. He even shook out his reefs in order to rise more quickly. Up, up they went, until the pigeon, true to its instinct, dropped and struck at what it thought to be the back of its pursuing enemy. Once was enough, for, evidently finding no life in the smooth cloth surface of the machine, it ceased soaring and straightened out on its eastward course.

A carrier pigeon on a passage can achieve a high rate of speed, and Winn reefed again. And again, to his satisfaction, he found that he was beating the pigeon. But this time he quickly shook out a portion of his reefed sustaining surface and slowed down in time. From then on he knew he had the chase safely in hand, and from then on a chant rose to his lips which he continued to sing at intervals, and unconsciously, for the rest of the passage. It was: "Going some; going some; what did I tell you!—going some."

Even so, it was not all plain sailing. The air is an unstable medium at best, and quite without warning, at an acute angle, he entered an aerial tide which he recognized as the gulf stream of wind that poured through the drafty-mouthed Golden Gate. His right wing caught it first—a sudden, sharp puff that lifted and tilted the monoplane and threatened to capsize it. But he rode with a sensitive "loose curb," and quickly, but not too quickly, he shifted the angles of his wing-tips, depressed the front horizontal rudder, and swung over the rear vertical rudder to meet the tilting thrust of the wind. As the machine came back to an even keel, and he knew that he was now wholly in the invisible stream, he readjusted the wing-tips, rapidly away from him during the several moments of his discomfiture.

The pigeon drove straight on for the Alameda County shore, and it was near this shore that Winn had another experience. He fell into an air-hole. He had fallen into air-holes before, in previous flights, but this was a far larger one than he had ever encountered. With his eyes strained on the ribbon attached to the pigeon, by that fluttering bit of color he marked his fall. Down he went, at the pit of his stomach that old sink sensation which he had known as a boy he first negotiated quick-starting elevators. But Winn, among other secrets of aviation, had learned that to go up it was sometimes necessary first to go down. The air had refused to hold him. Instead of struggling futilely and perilously against this lack of sustension, he yielded to it. With steady head and hand, he depressed the forward horizontal rudder—just recklessly enough and not a fraction more—and the monoplane dived head foremost and sharply down the void. It was falling with the keenness of a knife-blade. Every instant the speed accelerated frightfully. Thus he accumulated the momentum that would save him. But few instants were required, when, abruptly shifting the double horizontal rudders forward and astern, he shot upward on the tense and straining plane and out of the pit.

At an altitude of five hundred feet, the pigeon drove on over the town of Berkeley and lifted its flight to the Contra Costa hills. Young Winn noted the campus and buildings of the University of California—his university—as he rose after the pigeon.

Once more, on these Contra Costa hills, he early came to grief. The pigeon was now flying low, and where a grove of eucalyptus presented a solid front to the wind, the bird was suddenly sent fluttering wildly upward for a distance of a hundred feet. Winn knew what it meant. It had been caught in an air-surf that beat upward hundreds of feet where the fresh west wind smote the upstanding wall of the grove. He reefed hastily to the uttermost, and at the same time depressed the angle of his flight to meet that upward surge. Nevertheless, the monoplane was tossed fully three hundred feet before the danger was left astern.

Two or more ranges of hills the pigeon crossed, and then Winn saw it dropping down to a landing where a small cabin stood in a hillside clearing. He blessed that clearing. Not only was it good for alighting, but, on account of the steepness of the slope, it was just the thing for rising again into the air.

A man, reading a newspaper, had just started up at the sight of the returning pigeon, when he heard the burr of Winn's engine and saw the huge monoplane, with all surfaces set, drop down upon him, stop suddenly on an air-cushion manufactured on the spur of the moment by a shift of the horizontal rudders, glide a few yards, strike ground, and come to rest not a score of feet away from him. But when he saw a young man, calmly sitting in the machine and leveling a pistol at him, the man turned to run. Before he could make the corner of the cabin, a bullet through the leg brought him down in a sprawling fall.

"What do you want!" he demanded sullenly, as the other stood over him.

"I want to take you for a ride in my new machine," Winn answered. "Believe me, she is a loo-loo."

The man did not argue long, for this strange visitor had most convincing ways. Under Winn's instructions, covered all the time by the pistol, the man improvised a tourniquet and applied it to his wounded leg. Winn helped him to a seat in the machine, then went to the pigeon-loft and took possession of the bird with the ribbon still fast to its leg.

A very tractable prisoner, the man proved. Once up in the air, he sat close, in an ecstasy of fear. An adept at winged blackmail, he had no aptitude for wings himself, and when he gazed down at the flying land and water far beneath him, he did not feel moved to attack his captor, now defenseless, both hands occupied with flight.

Instead, the only way the man felt moved was to sit closer.

Peter Winn, Senior, scanning the heavens with powerful glasses, saw the monoplane leap into view and grow large over the rugged backbone of Angel Island. Several minutes later he cried out to the waiting detectives that the machine carried a passenger. Dropping swiftly and piling up an abrupt air-cushion, the monoplane landed.

"That reefing device is a winner!" young Winn cried, as he climbed out. "Did you see me at the start? I almost ran over the pigeon. Going some, dad! Going some! What did I tell you? Going some!"

"But who is that with you?" his father demanded.

The young man looked back at his prisoner and remembered.

"Why, that's the pigeon-fancier," he said. "I guess the officers can take care of him."

Peter Winn gripped his son's hand in grim silence, and fondled the pigeon which his son had passed to him. Again he fondled the pretty creature. Then he spoke.

"Exhibit A, for the People," he said.

BUNCHES OF KNUCKLES

ARRANGEMENTS quite extensive had been made for the celebration of Christmas on the yacht Samoset. Not having been in any civilized port for months, the stock of provisions boasted few delicacies; yet Minnie Duncan had managed to devise real feasts for cabin and forecastle.

"Listen, Boyd," she told her husband. "Here are the menus. For the cabin, raw bonita native style, turtle soup, omelette a la Samoset—"

"What the dickens?" Boyd Duncan interrupted.

"Well, if you must know, I found a tin of mushrooms and a package of egg-powder which had fallen down behind the locker, and there are other things as well that will go into it. But don't interrupt. Boiled yam, fried taro, alligator pear salad—there, you've got me all mixed, Then I found a last delectable half-pound of dried squid. There will be baked beans Mexican, if I can hammer it into Toyama's head; also, baked papaia with Marquesan honey, and, lastly, a wonderful pie the secret of which Toyama refuses to divulge."

"I wonder if it is possible to concoct a punch or a cocktail out of trade rum?" Duncan muttered gloomily.

"Oh! I forgot! Come with me."

His wife caught his hand and led him through the small connecting door to her tiny stateroom. Still holding his hand, she fished in the depths of a hat-locker and brought forth a pint bottle of champagne.

"The dinner is complete!" he cried.

"Wait."

She fished again, and was rewarded with a silver-mounted whisky flask. She held it to the light of a port-hole, and the liquor showed a quarter of the distance from the bottom.

"I've been saving it for weeks," she explained. "And there's enough for you and Captain Dettmar."

"Two mighty small drinks," Duncan complained.

"There would have been more, but I gave a drink to Lorenzo when he was sick."

Duncan growled, "Might have given him rum," facetiously.

"The nasty stuff! For a sick man? Don't be greedy, Boyd. And I'm glad there isn't any more, for Captain Dettmar's sake. Drinking always makes him irritable. And now for the men's dinner. Soda crackers, sweet cakes, candy—"

"Substantial, I must say."

"Do hush. Rice, and curry, yam, taro, bonita, of course, a big cake Toyama is making, young pig—"

"Oh, I say," he protested.

"It is all right, Boyd. We'll be in Attu-Attu in three days. Besides, it's my pig. That old chief what-ever-his-name distinctly presented it to me. You saw him yourself. And then two tins of bullamacow. That's their dinner. And now about the presents. Shall we wait until tomorrow, or give them this evening?"

"Christmas Eve, by all means," was the man's judgment. "We'll call all hands at eight bells; I'll give them a tot of rum all around, and then you give the presents. Come on up on deck. It's stifling down here. I hope Lorenzo has better luck with the dynamo; without the fans there won't be much sleeping to-night if we're driven below."

They passed through the small main-cabin, climbed a steep companion ladder, and emerged on deck. The sun was setting, and the promise was for a clear tropic night. The Samoset, with fore- and main-sail winged out on either side, was slipping a lazy four-knots through the smooth sea. Through the engine-room skylight came a sound of hammering. They strolled aft to where Captain Dettmar, one foot on the rail, was oiling the gear of the patent log. At the wheel stood a tall South Sea Islander, clad in white undershirt and scarlet hip-cloth.

Boyd Duncan was an original. At least that was the belief of his friends. Of comfortable fortune, with no need to do anything but take his comfort, he elected to travel about the world in outlandish and most uncomfortable ways. Incidentally, he had ideas about coral-reefs, disagreed profoundly with Darwin on that subject, had voiced his opinion in several monographs and one book, and was now back at his hobby, cruising the South Seas in a tiny, thirty-ton yacht and studying reef-formations.

His wife, Minnie Duncan, was also declared an original, inasmuch as she joyfully shared his vagabond wanderings. Among other things, in the six exciting years of their marriage she had climbed Chimborazo with him, made a three-thousand-mile winter journey with dogs and sleds in Alaska, ridden a horse from Canada to Mexico, cruised the Mediterranean in a ten-ton yawl, and canoed from Germany to the Black Sea across the heart of Europe. They were a royal pair of wanderlusters, he, big and broad-shouldered, she a small, brunette, and happy woman, whose one hundred and fifteen pounds were all grit and endurance, and withal, pleasing to look upon.

The Samoset had been a trading schooner, when Duncan bought her in San Francisco and made alterations. Her interior was wholly rebuilt, so that the hold became main-cabin and staterooms, while abaft amidships were installed engines, a dynamo, an ice machine, storage batteries, and, far in the stern, gasoline tanks. Necessarily, she carried a small crew. Boyd, Minnie, and Captain Dettmar were the only whites on board, though Lorenzo, the small and greasy engineer, laid a part claim to white, being a Portuguese half-caste. A Japanese served as cook, and a Chinese as cabin boy. Four white sailors had constituted the original crew for'ard, but one by one they had yielded to the charms of palm-waving South Sea isles and been replaced by islanders. Thus, one of the dusky sailors hailed from Easter Island, a second from the Carolines, a third from the Paumotus, while the fourth was a gigantic Samoan. At sea, Boyd Duncan, himself a navigator, stood a mate's watch with Captain Dettmar, and both of them took a wheel or lookout occasionally. On a pinch, Minnie herself could take a wheel, and it was on pinches that she proved herself more dependable at steering than did the native sailors.

At eight bells, all hands assembled at the wheel, and Boyd Duncan appeared with a black bottle and a mug. The rum he served out himself, half a mug of it to each man. They gulped the stuff down with many facial expressions of delight, followed by loud lip-smackings of approval, though the liquor was raw enough and corrosive enough to burn their mucous membranes. All drank except Lee Goom, the abstemious cabin boy. This rite accomplished, they waited for the next, the present-giving. Generously molded on Polynesian lines, huge-bodied and heavy-muscled, they were nevertheless like so many children, laughing merrily at little things, their eager black eyes flashing in the lantern light as their big bodies swayed to the heave and roll of the ship.

Calling each by name, Minnie gave the presents out, accompanying each presentation with some happy remark that added to the glee. There were trade watches, clasp knives, amazing assortments of fish-hooks in packages, plug tobacco, matches, and gorgeous strips of cotton for loincloths all around. That Boyd Duncan was liked by them was evidenced by the roars of laughter with which they greeted his slightest joking allusion.

Captain Dettmar, white-faced, smiling only when his employer chanced to glance at him, leaned against the wheel-box, looking on. Twice, he left the group and went below, remaining there but a minute each time. Later, in the main cabin, when Lorenzo, Lee Goom and Toyama received their presents, he disappeared into his stateroom twice again. For of all times, the devil that slumbered in Captain Dettmar's soul chose this particular time of good cheer to awaken. Perhaps it was not entirely the devil's fault, for Captain Dettmar, privily cherishing a quart of whisky for many weeks, had selected Christmas Eve for broaching it.

It was still early in the evening—two bells had just gone—when Duncan and his wife stood by the cabin companionway, gazing to windward and canvassing the possibility of spreading their beds on deck. A small, dark blot of cloud, slowly forming on the horizon, carried the threat of a rain-squall, and it was this they were discussing when Captain Dettmar, coming from aft and about to go below, glanced at them with sudden suspicion. He paused, his face working spasmodically. Then he spoke:

"You are talking about me."

His voice was hoarse, and there was an excited vibration in it. Minnie Duncan started, then glanced at her husband's immobile face, took the cue, and remained silent.

"I say you were talking about me," Captain Dettmar repeated, this time with almost a snarl.

He did not lurch nor betray the liquor on him in any way save by the convulsive working of his face.

"Minnie, you'd better go down," Duncan said gently. "Tell Lee Goom we'll sleep below. It won't be long before that squall is drenching things."

She took the hint and left, delaying just long enough to give one anxious glance at the dim faces of the two men.

Duncan puffed at his cigar and waited till his wife's voice, in talk with the cabin-boy, came up through the open skylight.

"Well?" Duncan demanded in a low voice, but sharply.

"I said you were talking about me. I say it again. Oh, I haven't been blind. Day after day I've seen the two of you talking about me. Why don't you come out and say it to my face! I know you know. And I know your mind's made up to discharge me at Attu-Attu."

"I am sorry you are making such a mess of everything," was Duncan's quiet reply.

But Captain Dettmar's mind was set on trouble.

"You know you are going to discharge me. You think you are too good to associate with the likes of me—you and your wife."

"Kindly keep her out of this," Duncan warned. "What do you want?"

"I want to know what you are going to do!"

"Discharge you, after this, at Attu-Attu."

"You intended to, all along."

"On the contrary. It is your present conduct that compels me."

"You can't give me that sort of talk."

"I can't retain a captain who calls me a liar."

Captain Dettmar for the moment was taken aback. His face and lips worked, but he could say nothing. Duncan coolly pulled at his cigar and glanced aft at the rising cloud of squall.

"Lee Goom brought the mail aboard at Tahiti," Captain Dettmar began.

"We were hove short then and leaving. You didn't look at your letters until we were outside, and then it was too late. That's why you didn't discharge me at Tahiti. Oh, I know. I saw the long envelope when Lee Goom came over the side. It was from the Governor of California, printed on the corner for any one to see. You'd been working behind my back. Some beachcomber in Honolulu had whispered to you, and you'd written to the Governor to find out. And that was his answer Lee Goom carried out to you. Why didn't you come to me like a man! No, you must play underhand with me, knowing that this billet was the one chance for me to get on my feet again. And as soon as you read the Governor's letter your mind was made up to get rid of me. I've seen it on your face ever since for all these months.. I've seen the two of you, polite as hell to me all the time, and getting away in corners and talking about me and that affair in 'Frisco."

"Are you done?" Duncan asked, his voice low, and tense. "Quite done?"

Captain Dettmar made no answer.

"Then I'll tell you a few things. It was precisely because of that affair in 'Frisco that I did not discharge you in Tahiti. God knows you gave me sufficient provocation. I thought that if ever a man needed a chance to rehabilitate himself, you were that man. Had there been no black mark against you, I would have discharged you when I learned how you were robbing me."

Captain Dettmar showed surprise, started to interrupt, then changed his mind.

"There was that matter of the deck-calking, the bronze rudder-irons, the overhauling of the engine, the new spinnaker boom, the new davits, and the repairs to the whale-boat. You OKd the shipyard bill. It was four thousand one hundred and twenty-two francs. By the regular shipyard charges it ought not to have been a centime over twenty-five hundred francs-"

"If you take the word of those alongshore sharks against mine—' the other began thickly.

"Save yourself the trouble of further lying," Duncan went on coldly. "I looked it up. I got Flaubin before the Governor himself, and the old rascal confessed to sixteen hundred overcharge. Said you'd stuck him up for it. Twelve hundred went to you, and his share was four hundred and the job. Don't interrupt. I've got his affidavit below. Then was when I would have put you ashore, except for the cloud you were under. You had to have this one chance or go clean to hell. I gave you the chance. And what have you got to say about it?"

"What did the Governor say?" Captain Dettmar demanded truculently.

"Which governor?"

"Of California. Did he lie to you like all the rest?"

"I'll tell you what he said. He said that you had been convicted on circumstantial evidence; that was why you had got life imprisonment instead of hanging; that you had always stoutly maintained your innocence; that you were the black sheep of the Maryland Dettmars; that they moved heaven and earth for your pardon; that your prison conduct was most exemplary; that he was prosecuting attorney at the time you were convicted; that after you had served seven years he yielded to your family's plea and pardoned you; and that in his own mind existed a doubt that you had killed McSweeny."

There was a pause, during which Duncan went on studying the rising squall, while Captain Dettmar's face worked terribly.

"Well, the Governor was wrong," he announced, with a short laugh. "I did kill McSweeny. I did get the watchman drunk that night. I beat

McSweeny to death in his bunk. I used the iron belaying pin that appeared in the evidence. He never had a chance. I beat him to a jelly. Do you want the details?"

Duncan looked at him in the curious way one looks at any monstrosity, but made no reply.

"Oh, I'm not afraid to tell you," Captain Dettmar blustered on. "There are no witnesses. Besides, I am a free man now. I am pardoned, and by God they can never put me back in that hole again. I broke McSweeny's jaw with the first blow. He was lying on his back asleep. He said, 'My God, Jim! My God!' It was funny to see his broken jaw wabble as he said it. Then I smashed him... I say, do you want the rest of the details?"

"Is that all you have to say?" was the answer.

"Isn't it enough?" Captain Dettmar retorted.

"It is enough."

"What are you going to do about it?"

"Put you ashore at Attu-Attu."

"And in the meantime?"

"In the meantime..." Duncan paused. An increase of weight in the wind rippled his hair. The stars overhead vanished, and the Samoset swung four points off her course in the careless steersman's hands. "In the meantime throw your halyards down on deck and look to your wheel. I'll call the men."

The next moment the squall burst upon them. Captain Dettmar, springing aft, lifted the coiled mainsail halyards from their pins and threw them, ready to run, on the deck. The three islanders swarmed from the tiny forecastle, two of them leaping to the halyards and holding by a single turn, while the third fastened down the engineroom, companion and swung the ventilators around. Below, Lee Goom and Toyama were lowering skylight covers and screwing up deadeyes. Duncan pulled shut the cover of the companion scuttle, and held on, waiting, the first drops of rain pelting his face, while the Samoset leaped violently ahead, at the same time heeling first to starboard then to port as the gusty pressures caught her winged-out sails.

All waited. But there was no need to lower away on the run. The power went out of the wind, and the tropic rain poured a deluge over everything. Then it was, the danger past, and as the Kanakas began to coil the halyards back on the pins, that Boyd Duncan went below.

"All right," he called in cheerily to his wife. "Only a puff."

"And Captain Dettmar?" she queried.

"Has been drinking, that is all. I shall get rid of him at Attu-Attu."

But before Duncan climbed into his bunk, he strapped around himself, against the skin and under his pajama coat, a heavy automatic pistol.

He fell asleep almost immediately, for his was the gift of perfect relaxation. He did things tensely, in the way savages do, but the instant the need passed he relaxed, mind and body. So it was that he slept, while the rain still poured on deck and the yacht plunged and rolled in the brief, sharp sea caused by the squall.

He awoke with a feeling of suffocation and heaviness. The electric fans had stopped, and the air was thick and stifling. Mentally cursing all Lorenzos and storage batteries, he heard his wife moving in the adjoining stateroom and pass out into the main cabin. Evidently heading for the fresher air on deck, he thought, and decided it was a good example to imitate. Putting on his slippers and tucking a pillow and a blanket under his arm, he followed her. As he was about to emerge from the companionway, the ship's clock in the cabin began to strike and he stopped to listen. Four bells sounded. It was two in the morning. From without came the creaking of the gaff-jaw against the mast. The Samoset rolled and righted on a sea, and in the light breeze her canvas gave forth a hollow thrum.

He was just putting his foot out on the damp deck when he heard his wife scream. It was a startled frightened scream that ended in a splash overside. He leaped out and ran aft. In the dim starlight he could make out her head and shoulders disappearing astern in the lazy wake.

"What was it?" Captain Dettmar, who was at the wheel, asked.

"Mrs. Duncan," was Duncan's reply, as he tore the life-buoy from its hook and flung it aft. "Jibe over to starboard and come up on the wind!" he commanded.

And then Boyd Duncan made a mistake. He dived overboard.

When he came up, he glimpsed the blue-light on the buoy, which had ignited automatically when it struck the water. He swam for it, and found Minnie had reached it first.

"Hello," he said. "Just trying to keep cool?"

"Oh, Boyd!" was her answer, and one wet hand reached out and touched his.

The blue light, through deterioration or damage, flickered out. As they lifted on the smooth crest of a wave, Duncan turned to look where the Samoset made a vague blur in the darkness. No lights showed, but there was noise of confusion. He could hear Captain Dettmar's shouting above the cries of the others.

"I must say he's taking his time," Duncan grumbled. "Why doesn't he jibe? There she goes now."

They could hear the rattle of the boom tackle blocks as the sail was eased across.

"That was the mainsail," he muttered. "Jibed to port when I told him starboard."

Again they lifted on a wave, and again and again, ere they could make out the distant green of the Samoset's starboard light. But instead of remaining stationary, in token that the yacht was coming toward them, it began moving across their field of vision. Duncan swore.

"What's the lubber holding over there for!" he demanded. "He's got his compass. He knows our bearing."

But the green light, which was all they could see, and which they could see only when they were on top of a wave, moved steadily away from them, withal it was working up to windward, and grew dim and dimmer. Duncan called out loudly and repeatedly, and each time, in the intervals, they could hear, very faintly, the voice of Captain Dettmar shouting orders.

"How can he hear me with such a racket?" Duncan complained.

"He's doing it so the crew won't hear you," was Minnie's answer.

There was something in the quiet way she said it that caught her husband's attention.

"What do you mean?"

"I mean that he is not trying to pick us up," she went on in the same composed voice. "He threw me overboard."

"You are not making a mistake?"

"How could I? I was at the main rigging, looking to see if any more rain threatened. He must have left the wheel and crept behind me. I was holding on to a stay with one hand. He gripped my hand free from behind and threw me over. It's too bad you didn't know, or else you would have staid aboard."

Duncan groaned, but said nothing for several minutes. The green light changed the direction of its course.

"She's gone about," he announced. "You are right. He's deliberately working around us and to windward. Up wind they can never hear me. But here goes."

He called at minute intervals for a long time. The green light disappeared, being replaced by the red, showing that the yacht had gone about again.

"Minnie," he said finally, "it pains me to tell you, but you married a fool. Only a fool would have gone overboard as I did."

"What chance have we of being picked up... by some other vessel, I mean?" she asked.

"About one in ten thousand, or ten thousand million. Not a steamer route nor trade route crosses this stretch of ocean. And there aren't any whalers knocking about the South Seas. There might be a stray trading schooner running across from Tutuwanga. But I happen to know that island is visited only once a year. A chance in a million is ours."

"And we'll play that chance," she rejoined stoutly.

"You ARE a joy!" His hand lifted hers to his lips. "And Aunt Elizabeth always wondered what I saw in you. Of course we'll play that chance. And we'll win it, too. To happen otherwise would be unthinkable. Here goes."

He slipped the heavy pistol from his belt and let it sink into the sea. The belt, however, he retained.

"Now you get inside the buoy and get some sleep. Duck under."

She ducked obediently, and came up inside the floating circle. He fastened the straps for her, then, with the pistol belt, buckled himself across one shoulder to the outside of the buoy.

"We're good for all day to-morrow," he said. "Thank God the water's warm. It won't be a hardship for the first twenty-hour hours, anyway. And if we're not picked up by nightfall, we've just got to hang on for another day, that's all."

For half an hour they maintained silence, Duncan, his head resting on the arm that was on the buoy, seemed asleep.

"Boyd?" Minnie said softly.

"Thought you were asleep," he growled.

"Boyd, if we don't come through this—"

"Stow that!" he broke in ungallantly. "Of course we're coming through. There is isn't a doubt of it. Somewhere on this ocean is a ship that's heading right for us. You wait and see. Just the same I wish my brain were equipped with wireless. Now I'm going to sleep, if you don't."

But for once, sleep baffled him. An hour later he heard Minnie stir and knew she was awake.

"Say, do you know what I've been thinking!" she asked.

"No; what?"

"That I'll wish you a Merry Christmas."

"By George, I never thought of it. Of course it's Christmas Day. We'll have many more of them, too. And do you know what I've been thinking? What a confounded shame we're done out of our Christmas dinner. Wait till I lay hands on Dettmar. I'll take it out of him. And it won't be with an iron belaying pin either, Just two bunches of naked knuckles, that's all."

Despite his facetiousness, Boyd Duncan had little hope. He knew well enough the meaning of one chance in a million, and was calmly certain that his wife and he had entered upon their last few living hours—hours that were inevitably bound to be black and terrible with tragedy.

The tropic sun rose in a cloudless sky. Nothing was to be seen. The Samoset was beyond the sea-rim. As the sun rose higher, Duncan ripped his pajama trousers in halves and fashioned them into two rude turbans. Soaked in sea-water they offset the heat-rays.

"When I think of that dinner, I'm really angry," he complained, as he noted an anxious expression threatening to set on his wife's face. "And I want you to be with me when I settle with Dettmar. I've always been opposed to women witnessing scenes of blood, but this is different. It will be a beating."

"I hope I don't break my knuckles on him," he added, after a pause.

Midday came and went, and they floated on, the center of a narrow sea-circle. A gentle breath of the dying trade-wind fanned them, and they rose and fell monotonously on the smooth swells of a perfect summer sea. Once, a gunie spied them, and for half an hour circled about them with majestic sweeps. And, once, a huge rayfish, measuring a score of feet across the tips, passed within a few yards.

By sunset, Minnie began to rave, softly, babblingly, like a child. Duncan's face grew haggard as he watched and listened, while in his mind he revolved plans of how best to end the hours of agony that were coming. And, so planning, as they rose on a larger swell than usual, he swept the circle of the sea with his eyes, and saw, what made him cry out.

"Minnie!" She did not answer, and he shouted her name again in her ear, with all the voice he could command. Her eyes opened, in them fluttered commingled consciousness and delirium. He slapped her hands and wrists till the sting of the blows roused her.

"There she is, the chance in a million!" he cried.

"A steamer at that, heading straight for us! By George, it's a cruiser! I have it!—the Annapolis, returning with those astronomers from Tutuwanga."

United States Consul Lingford was a fussy, elderly gentleman, and in the two years of his service at Attu-Attu had never encountered so unprecedented a case as that laid before him by Boyd Duncan. The latter, with his wife, had been landed there by the Annapolis, which had promptly gone on with its cargo of astronomers to Fiji.

"It was cold-blooded, deliberate attempt to murder," said Consul Lingford. "The law shall take its course. I don't know how precisely to deal with this Captain Dettmar, but if he comes to Attu-Attu, depend upon it he shall be dealt with, he—ah—shall be dealt with. In the meantime, I shall read up the law. And now, won't you and your good lady stop for lunch!"

As Duncan accepted the invitation, Minnie, who had been glancing out of the window at the harbor, suddenly leaned forward and touched her husband's arm. He followed her gaze, and saw the Samoset, flag at half mast, rounding up and dropping anchor scarcely a hundred yards away.

"There's my boat now," Duncan said to the Consul. "And there's the launch over the side, and Captain Dettmar dropping into it. If I don't miss my guess, he's coming to report our deaths to you."

The launch landed on the white beach, and leaving Lorenzo tinkering with the engine, Captain Dettmar strode across the beach and up the path to the Consulate.

"Let him make his report," Duncan said. "We'll just step into this next room and listen."

And through the partly open door, he and his wife heard Captain Dettmar, with tears in his voice, describe the loss of his owners.

"I jibed over and went back across the very spot," he concluded. "There was not a sign of them. I called and called, but there was never an answer. I tacked back and forth and wore for two solid hours, then hove to till daybreak, and cruised back and forth all day, two men at the mastheads. It is terrible. I am heartbroken. Mr. Duncan was a splendid man, and I shall never..."

But he never completed the sentence, for at that moment his splendid employer strode out upon him, leaving Minnie standing in the doorway. Captain Dettmar's white face blanched even whiter.

"I did my best to pick you up, sir," he began.

Boyd Duncan's answer was couched in terms of bunched knuckles, two bunches of them, that landed right and left on Captain Dettmar's face.

Captain Dettmar staggered backward, recovered, and rushed with swinging arms at his employer, only to be met with a blow squarely between the eyes. This time the Captain went down, bearing the typewriter under him as he crashed to the floor.

"This is not permissible," Consul Lingford spluttered. "I beg of you, I beg of you, to desist."

"I'll pay the damages to office furniture," Duncan answered, and at the same time landing more bunched knuckles on the eyes and nose of Dettmar.

Consul Lingford bobbed around in the turmoil like a wet hen, while his office furniture went to ruin. Once, he caught Duncan by the arm, but was flung back, gasping, half-across the room. Another time he appealed to Minnie.

"Mrs. Duncan, won't you, please, please, restrain your husband?"

But she, white-faced and trembling, resolutely shook her head and watched the fray with all her eyes.

"It is outrageous," Consul Lingford cried, dodging the hurtling bodies of the two men. "It is an affront to the Government, to the United States Government. Nor will it be overlooked, I warn you. Oh, do pray desist, Mr. Duncan. You will kill the man. I beg of you. I beg, I beg..."

But the crash of a tall vase filled with crimson hibiscus blossoms left him speechless.

The time came when Captain Dettmar could no longer get up. He got as far as hands and knees, struggled vainly to rise further, then collapsed. Duncan stirred the groaning wreck with his foot.

"He's all right," he announced. "I've only given him what he has given many a sailor and worse."

"Great heavens, sir!" Consul Lingford exploded, staring horror-stricken at the man whom he had invited to lunch.

Duncan giggled involuntarily, then controlled himself.

"I apologize, Mr. Lingford, I most heartily apologize. I fear I was slightly carried away by my feelings."

Consul Lingford gulped and sawed the air speechlessly with his arms.

"Slightly, sir? Slightly?" he managed to articulate.

"Boyd," Minnie called softly from the doorway.

He turned and looked.

"You ARE a joy," she said.

"And now, Mr. Lingford, I am done with him," Duncan said. "I turn over what is left to you and the law."

"That?" Consul Lingford queried, in accent of horror.

"That," Boyd Duncan replied, looking ruefully at his battered knuckles.

WAR

HE was a young man, not more than twenty-four or five, and he might have sat his horse with the careless grace of his youth had he not been so catlike and tense. His black eyes roved everywhere, catching the movements of twigs and branches where small birds hopped, questing ever onward through the changing vistas of trees and brush, and returning always to the clumps of undergrowth on either side. And as he watched, so did he listen, though he rode on in silence, save for the boom of heavy guns from far to the west. This had been sounding monotonously in his ears for hours, and only its cessation could have aroused his notice. For he had business closer to hand. Across his saddle-bow was balanced a carbine.

So tensely was he strung, that a bunch of quail, exploding into flight from under his horse's nose, startled him to such an extent that automatically, instantly, he had reined in and fetched the carbine halfway to his shoulder. He grinned sheepishly, recovered himself, and rode on. So tense was he, so bent upon the work he had to do, that the sweat stung his eyes unwiped, and unheeded rolled down his nose and spattered his saddle pommel. The band of his cavalryman's hat was fresh-stained with sweat. The roan horse under him was likewise wet. It was high noon of a breathless day of heat. Even the birds and squirrels did not dare the sun, but sheltered in shady hiding places among the trees.

Man and horse were littered with leaves and dusted with yellow pollen, for the open was ventured no more than was compulsory. They kept to the brush and trees, and invariably the man halted and peered out before crossing a dry glade or naked stretch of upland pasturage. He worked always to the north, though his way was devious, and it was from the north that he seemed most to apprehend that for which he was looking. He was no coward, but his courage was only that of the average civilized man, and he was looking to live, not die.

Up a small hillside he followed a cowpath through such dense scrub that he was forced to dismount and lead his horse. But when the path swung around to the west, he abandoned it and headed to the north again along the oak-covered top of the ridge.

The ridge ended in a steep descent-so steep that he zigzagged back and forth across the face of the slope, sliding and stumbling among the dead leaves and matted vines and keeping a watchful eye on the horse above that threatened to fall down upon him. The sweat ran from him, and the pollen-dust, settling pungently in mouth and nostrils, increased his thirst. Try as he would, nevertheless the descent was noisy, and frequently he stopped, panting in the dry heat and listening for any warning from beneath.

At the bottom he came out on a flat, so densely forested that he could not make out its extent. Here the character of the woods changed, and he was able to remount. Instead of the twisted hillside oaks, tall straight trees, big-trunked and prosperous, rose from the damp fat soil. Only here and there were thickets, easily avoided, while he encountered winding, park-like glades where the cattle had pastured in the days before war had run them off.

His progress was more rapid now, as he came down into the valley, and at the end of half an hour he halted at an ancient rail fence on the edge of a clearing. He did not like the openness of it, yet his path lay across to the fringe of trees that marked the banks of the stream. It was a mere quarter of a mile across that open, but the thought of venturing out in it was repugnant. A rifle, a score of them, a thousand, might lurk in that fringe by the stream.

Twice he essayed to start, and twice he paused. He was appalled by his own loneliness. The pulse of war that beat from the West suggested the companionship of battling thousands; here was naught but silence, and himself, and possible death-dealing bullets from a myriad ambushes. And yet his task was to find what he feared to find. He must on, and on, till somewhere, some time, he encountered another man, or other men, from the other side, scouting, as he was scouting, to make report, as he must make report, of having come in touch.

Changing his mind, he skirted inside the woods for a distance, and again peeped forth. This time, in the middle of the clearing, he saw a small farmhouse. There were no signs of life. No smoke curled from the chimney, not a barnyard fowl clucked and strutted. The kitchen door stood open, and he gazed so long and hard into the black aperture that it seemed almost that a farmer's wife must emerge at any moment.

He licked the pollen and dust from his dry lips, stiffened himself, mind and body, and rode out into the blazing sunshine. Nothing stirred. He went on past the house, and approached the wall of trees and bushes by the river's bank. One thought persisted maddeningly. It was of the crash into his body of a high-velocity bullet. It made him feel very fragile and defenseless, and he crouched lower in the saddle.

Tethering his horse in the edge of the wood, he continued a hundred yards on foot till he came to the stream. Twenty feet wide it was, without perceptible current, cool and inviting, and he was very thirsty. But he waited inside his screen of leafage, his eyes fixed on the screen on the opposite side. To make the wait endurable, he sat down, his carbine resting on his knees. The minutes passed, and slowly his tenseness relaxed. At last he decided there was no danger; but just as he prepared to part the bushes and bend down to the water, a movement among the opposite bushes caught his eye.

It might be a bird. But he waited. Again there was an agitation of the bushes, and then, so suddenly that it almost startled a cry from him, the bushes parted and a face peered out. It was a face covered with several weeks' growth of ginger-colored beard. The eyes were blue and wide apart, with laughter-wrinkles in the comers that showed despite the tired and anxious expression of the whole face.

All this he could see with microscopic clearness, for the distance was no more than twenty feet. And all this he saw in such brief time, that he saw it as he lifted his carbine to his shoulder. He glanced along the sights, and knew that he was gazing upon a man who was as good as dead. It was impossible to miss at such point blank range.

But he did not shoot. Slowly he lowered the carbine and watched. A hand, clutching a water-bottle, became visible and the ginger beard bent downward to fill the bottle. He could hear the gurgle of the water. Then arm and bottle and ginger beard disappeared behind the closing bushes. A long time he waited, when, with thirst unslaked, he crept back to his horse, rode slowly across the sun-washed clearing, and passed into the shelter of the woods beyond.

II

Another day, hot and breathless. A deserted farmhouse, large, with many outbuildings and an orchard, standing in a clearing. From the Woods, on a roan horse, carbine across pommel, rode the young man with the quick black eyes. He breathed with relief as he gained the house. That a fight had taken place here earlier in the season was evident. Clips and empty cartridges, tarnished with verdigris, lay on the ground, which, while wet, had been torn up by the hoofs of horses. Hard by the kitchen garden were graves, tagged and numbered. From the oak tree by the kitchen door, in tattered, weatherbeaten garments, hung the bodies of two men. The faces, shriveled and defaced, bore no likeness to the faces of men. The roan horse snorted beneath them, and the rider caressed and soothed it and tied it farther away.

Entering the house, he found the interior a wreck. He trod on empty cartridges as he walked from room to room to reconnoiter from the windows. Men had camped and slept everywhere, and on the floor of one room he came upon stains unmistakable where the wounded had been laid down.

Again outside, he led the horse around behind the barn and invaded the orchard. A dozen trees were burdened with ripe apples. He filled his pockets, eating while he picked. Then a thought came to him, and he glanced at the sun, calculating the time of his return to camp. He pulled off his shirt, tying the sleeves and making a bag. This he proceeded to fill with apples.

As he was about to mount his horse, the animal suddenly pricked up its ears. The man, too, listened, and heard, faintly, the thud of hoofs on soft earth. He crept to the corner of the barn and peered out. A dozen mounted men, strung out loosely, approaching from the opposite side of the clearing, were only a matter of a hundred yards or so away. They rode on to the house. Some dismounted, while others remained in the saddle as an earnest that their stay would be short. They seemed to be holding a council, for he could hear them talking excitedly in the detested tongue of the alien invader. The time passed, but they seemed unable to reach a decision. He put the carbine away in its boot, mounted, and waited impatiently, balancing the shirt of apples on the pommel.

He heard footsteps approaching, and drove his spurs so fiercely into the roan as to force a surprised groan from the animal as it leaped forward. At the corner of the barn he saw the intruder, a mere boy of nineteen or twenty for all of his uniform jump back to escape being run down. At the same moment the roan swerved and its rider caught a glimpse of the aroused men by the house. Some were springing from their horses, and he could see the rifles going to their shoulders. He passed the kitchen door and the dried corpses swinging in the shade, compelling his foes to run around the front of the house. A rifle cracked, and a second, but he was going fast, leaning forward, low in the saddle, one hand clutching the shirt of apples, the other guiding the horse.

The top bar of the fence was four feet high, but he knew his roan and leaped it at full career to the accompaniment of several scattered shots. Eight hundred yards straight away were the woods, and the roan was covering the distance with mighty strides. Every man was now firing. pumping their guns so rapidly that he no longer heard individual shots. A bullet went through his hat, but he was unaware, though he did know when another tore through the apples on the pommel. And he winced and ducked even lower when a third bullet, fired low, struck a stone between his horse's legs and ricochetted off through the air, buzzing and humming like some incredible insect.

The shots died down as the magazines were emptied, until, quickly, there was no more shooting. The young man was elated. Through that astonishing fusillade he had come unscathed. He glanced back. Yes, they had emptied their magazines. He could see several reloading. Others were running back behind the house for their horses. As he looked, two already mounted, came back into view around the corner, riding hard. And at the same moment, he saw the man with the unmistakable ginger beard kneel down on the ground, level his gun, and coolly take his time for the long shot.

The young man threw his spurs into the horse, crouched very low, and swerved in his flight in order to distract the other's aim. And still the shot did not come. With each jump of the horse, the woods sprang nearer. They were only two hundred yards away and still the shot was delayed.

And then he heard it, the last thing he was to hear, for he was dead ere he hit the ground in the long crashing fall from the saddle. And they, watching at the house, saw him fall, saw his body bounce when it struck the earth, and saw the burst of red-cheeked apples that rolled about him. They laughed at the unexpected eruption of apples, and clapped their hands in applause of the long shot by the man with the ginger beard.

UNDER THE DECK AWNINGS

"CAN any man—a gentleman, I mean—call a woman a pig?"

The little man flung this challenge forth to the whole group, then leaned back in his deck chair, sipping lemonade with an air commingled of certitude and watchful belligerence. Nobody made answer. They were used to the little man and his sudden passions and high elevations.

"I repeat, it was in my presence that he said a certain lady, whom none of you knows, was a pig. He did not say swine. He grossly said that she was a pig. And I hold that no man who is a man could possibly make such a remark about any woman."

Dr. Dawson puffed stolidly at his black pipe. Matthews, with knees hunched up and clasped by his arms, was absorbed in the flight of a gunie. Sweet, finishing his Scotch and soda, was questing about with his eyes for a deck steward.

"I ask you, Mr. Treloar, can any man call any woman a pig?"

Treloar, who happened to be sitting next to him, was startled by the abruptness of the attack, and wondered what grounds he had ever given the little man to believe that he could call a woman a pig.

"I should say," he began his hesitant answer, "that it—er—depends on the—er—the lady."

The little man was aghast.

"You mean...?" he quavered.

"That I have seen female humans who were as bad as pigs—and worse."

There was a long pained silence. The little man seemed withered by the coarse brutality of the reply. In his face was unutterable hurt and woe.

"You have told of a man who made a not nice remark and you have classified him," Treloar said in cold, even tones. "I shall now tell you about a woman—I beg your pardon—a lady, and when I have finished I shall ask you to classify her. Miss Caruthers I shall call her, principally for the reason that it is not her name. It was on a P. & O. boat, and it occurred neither more nor less than several years ago.

"Miss Caruthers was charming. No; that is not the word. She was amazing. She was a young woman, and a lady. Her father was a certain high official whose name, if I mentioned it, would be immediately recognized by all of you. She was with her mother and two maids at the time, going out to join the old gentleman wherever you like to wish in the East.

"She, and pardon me for repeating, was amazing. It is the one adequate word. Even the most minor adjectives applicable to her are bound to be sheer superlatives. There was nothing she could not do better than any woman and than most men. Sing, play—bah!—as some rhetorician once said of old Nap, competition fled from her. Swim! She could have made a fortune and a name as a public performer. She was one of those rare women who can strip off all the frills of dress, and in simple swimming suit be more satisfying beautiful. Dress! She was an artist.

"But her swimming. Physically, she was the perfect woman—you know what I mean, not in the gross, muscular way of acrobats, but in all the delicacy of line and fragility of frame and texture. And combined with this, strength. How she could do it was the marvel. You know the wonder of a woman's arm—the fore arm, I mean; the sweet fading away from rounded biceps and hint of muscle, down through small elbow and firm soft swell to the wrist, small, unthinkably small and round and strong. This was hers. And yet, to see her swimming the sharp quick English overhand stroke, and getting somewhere with it, too, was—well, I understand anatomy and athletics and such things, and yet it was a mystery to me how she could do it.

"She could stay under water for two minutes. I have timed her. No man on board, except Dennitson, could capture as many coins as she with a single dive. On the forward main-deck was a big canvas tank with six feet of sea-water. We used to toss small coins into it. I have seen her dive from the bridge deck—no mean feat in itself—into that six-feet of water, and fetch up no less than forty-seven coins, scattered willy-nilly over the whole bottom of the tank. Dennitson, a quiet young Englishman, never exceeded her in this, though he made it a point always to tie her score.

"She was a sea-woman, true. But she was a land-woman, a horsewoman—a—she was the universal woman. To see her, all softness of soft dress, surrounded by half a dozen eager men, languidly careless of them all or flashing brightness and wit on them and at them and through them, one would fancy she was good for nothing else in the world. At such moments I have compelled myself to remember her score of forty-seven coins from the bottom of the swimming tank. But that was she, the everlasting, wonder of a woman who did all things well.

"She fascinated every betrousered human around her. She had me—and I don't mind confessing it—she bad me to heel along with the rest. Young puppies and old gray dogs who ought to have known better—oh, they all came up and crawled around her skirts and whined and fawned when she whistled. They were all guilty, from young Ardmore, a pink cherub of nineteen outward bound for some clerkship in the Consular Service, to old Captain Bentley, grizzled and sea-worn, and as emotional, to look at, as a Chinese joss. There was a nice middle-aged chap, Perkins, I believe, who forgot his wife was on board until Miss Caruthers sent him to the right about and back where he belonged.

"Men were wax in her hands. She melted them, or softly molded them, or incinerated them, as she pleased. There wasn't a steward, even, grand and remote as she was, who, at her bidding, would have hesitated to souse the Old Man himself with a plate of soup. You have all seen such women—a sort of world's desire to all men. As a man-conqueror she was supreme. She was a whip-lash, a sting and a flame, an electric spark. Oh, believe me, at times there were flashes of will that scorched through her beauty and seduction and smote a victim into blank and shivering idiocy and fear.

"And don't fail to mark, in the light of what is to come, that she was a prideful woman. Pride of race, pride of caste, pride of sex, pride of power—she had it all, a pride strange and wilful and terrible.

"She ran the ship, she ran the voyage, she ran everything, and she ran Dennitson. That he had outdistanced the pack even the least wise of us admitted. That she liked him, and that this feeling was growing, there was not a doubt. I am certain that she looked on him with kinder eyes than she had ever looked with on man before. We still worshiped, and were always hanging about waiting to be whistled up, though we knew that Dennitson was laps and laps ahead of us. What might have happened we shall never know, for we came to Colombo and something else happened.

"You know Colombo, and how the native boys dive for coins in the shark-infested bay. Of course, it is only among the ground sharks and fish sharks that they venture. It is almost uncanny the way they know sharks and can sense the presence of a real killer—a tiger shark, for instance, or a gray nurse strayed up from Australian waters. Let such a shark appear, and, long before the passengers can guess, every mother's son of them is out of the water in a wild scramble for safety.

"It was after tiffin, and Miss Caruthers was holding her usual court under the deck-awnings. Old Captain Bentley had just been whistled up, and had granted her what he never granted before... nor since—permission for the boys to come up on the promenade deck. You see, Miss Caruthers was a swimmer, and she was interested. She took up a collection of all our small change, and herself tossed it overside, singly and in handfuls, arranging the terms of the contests, chiding a miss, giving extra rewards to clever wins, in short, managing the whole exhibition.

"She was especially keen on their jumping. You know, jumping feet-first from a height, it is very difficult to hold the body perpendicularly while in the air. The center of gravity of the male body is high, and the tendency is to overtopple. But the little beggars employed a method which she declared was new to her and which she desired to learn. Leaping from the davits of the boat-deck above, they plunged downward, their faces and shoulders bowed forward, looking at the water. And only at the last moment did they abruptly straighten up and enter the water erect and true.

"It was a pretty sight. Their diving was not so good, though there was one of them who was excellent at it, as he was in all the other stunts. Some white man must have taught him, for he made the proper swan dive and did it as beautifully as I have ever seen it. You know, headfirst into the water, from a great height, the problem is to enter the water at the perfect angle. Miss the angle and it means at the least a twisted back and injury for life. Also, it has meant death for many a bungler. But this boy could do it—seventy feet I know he cleared in one dive from the rigging—clenched hands on chest, head thrown back, sailing more like a bird, upward and out, and out and down, body flat on the air so that if it struck the surface in that position it would be split in half like a herring. But the moment before the water is reached, the head drops forward, the hands go out and lock the arms in an arch in advance of the head, and the body curves gracefully downward and enters the water just right.

"This the boy did, again and again, to the delight of all of us, but particularly of Miss Caruthers. He could not have been a moment over twelve or thirteen, yet he was by far the cleverest of the gang. He was the favorite of his crowd, and its leader. Though there were a number older than he, they acknowledged his chieftaincy. He was a beautiful boy, a lithe young god in breathing bronze, eyes wide apart, intelligent and daring, a bubble, a mote, a beautiful flash and sparkle of life. You have seen wonderful glorious creatures—animals, anything, a leopard, a horse-restless, eager, too much alive ever to be still, silken of muscle, each slightest movement a benediction of grace, every action wild, untrammeled, and over all spilling out that intense vitality, that sheen and luster of living light. The boy had it. Life poured out of him almost in an effulgence. His skin glowed with it. It burned in his eyes. I swear I could almost hear it crackle from him. Looking at him, it was as if a whiff of ozone came to one's nostrils—so fresh and young was he, so resplendent with health, so wildly wild.

"This was the boy. And it was he who gave the alarm in the midst of the sport. The boys made a dash of it for the gangway platform, swimming the fastest strokes they knew, pellmell, floundering and splashing, fright in their faces, clambering out with jumps and surges, any way to get out, lending one another a hand to safety, till all were strung along the gangway and peering down into the water.

222

"'What is the matter?' asked Miss Caruthers.

"'A shark, I fancy,' Captain Bentley answered. 'Lucky little beggars that he didn't get one of them.'

"'Are they afraid of sharks?' she asked.

"'Aren't you?' he asked back."

She shuddered, looked overside at the water, and made a move.

"'Not for the world would I venture where a shark might be,' she said, and shuddered again. 'They are horrible! Horrible!'

"The boys came up on the promenade deck, clustering close to the rail and worshiping Miss Caruthers who had flung them such a wealth of backsheesh. The performance being over, Captain Bentley motioned to them to clear out. But she stopped him.

"'One moment, please, Captain. I have always understood that the natives are not afraid of sharks.'

"She beckoned the boy of the swan dive nearer to her, and signed to him to dive over again. He shook his head, and along with all his crew behind him laughed as if it were a good joke.

"'Shark,' he volunteered, pointing to the water.

"'No,' she said. 'There is no shark.'

"But he nodded his head positively, and the boys behind him nodded with equal positiveness.

"'No, no, no,' she cried. And then to us, 'Who'll lend me a half-crown and a sovereign!'

"Immediately the half dozen of us were presenting her with crowns and sovereigns, and she accepted the two coins from young Ardmore.

"She held up the half-crown for the boys to see. But there was no eager rush to the rail preparatory to leaping. They stood there grinning sheepishly.

She offered the coin to each one individually, and each, as his turn came, rubbed his foot against his calf, shook his head, and grinned. Then she tossed the half-crown overboard. With wistful, regretful faces they watched its silver flight through the air, but not one moved to follow it.

"'Don't do it with the sovereign,' Dennitson said to her in a low voice.

"She took no notice, but held up the gold coin before the eyes of the boy of the swan dive.

"'Don't,' said Captain Bentley. 'I wouldn't throw a sick cat overside with a shark around.'

"But she laughed, bent on her purpose, and continued to dazzle the boy.

"'Don't tempt him,' Dennitson urged. 'It is a fortune to him, and he might go over after it.'

"'Wouldn't YOU?' she flared at him. 'If I threw it?'"

This last more softly.

Dennitson shook his head.

"'Your price is high,' she said. 'For how many sovereigns would you go?'

"'There are not enough coined to get me overside,' was his answer.

"She debated a moment, the boy forgotten in her tilt with Dennitson.

"'For me?' she said very softly.

"'To save your life—yes. But not otherwise.'

"She turned back to the boy. Again she held the coin before his eyes, dazzling him with the vastness of its value. Then she made as to toss it out, and, involuntarily, he made a half-movement toward the rail, but was checked by sharp cries of reproof from his companions. There was anger in their voices as well.

"'I know it is only fooling,' Dennitson said. 'Carry it as far as you like, but for heaven's sake don't throw it.'

"Whether it was that strange wilfulness of hers, or whether she doubted the boy could be persuaded, there is no telling. It was unexpected to all of us. Out from the shade of the awning the coin flashed golden in the blaze of sunshine and fell toward the sea in a glittering arch. Before a hand could stay him, the boy was over the rail and curving beautifully downward after the coin. Both were in the air at the same time. It was a pretty sight. The sovereign cut the water sharply, and at the very spot, almost at the same instant, with scarcely a splash, the boy entered.

"From the quicker-eyed black boys watching, came an exclamation. We were all at the railing. Don't tell me it is necessary for a shark to turn on its back. That one did not. In the clear water, from the height we were above it, we saw everything. The shark was a big brute, and with one drive he cut the boy squarely in half.

"There was a murmur or something from among us—who made it I did not know; it might have been I. And then there was silence. Miss Caruthers was the first to speak. Her face was deathly white.

"'I never dreamed,' she said, and laughed a short, hysterical laugh.

"All her pride was at work to give her control. She turned weakly toward Dennitson, and then, on from one to another of us. In her eyes was a terrible sickness, and her lips were trembling. We were brutes—oh, I know it, now that I look back upon it. But we did nothing.

"'Mr. Dennitson,' she said, 'Tom, won't you take me below!'

"He never changed the direction of his gaze, which was the bleakest I have ever seen in a man's face, nor did he move an eyelid. He took a cigarette from his case and lighted it. Captain Bentley made a nasty sound in his throat and spat overboard. That was all; that and the silence.

"She turned away and started to walk firmly down the deck. Twenty feet away, she swayed and thrust a hand against the wall to save herself. And so she went on, supporting herself against the cabins and walking very slowly." Treloar ceased. He turned his head and favored the little man with a look of cold inquiry.

"Well," he said finally. "Classify her."

The little man gulped and swallowed.

"I have nothing to say," he said. "I have nothing whatever to say."

TO KILL A MAN

THOUGH dim night-lights burned, she moved familiarly through the big rooms and wide halls, seeking vainly the half-finished book of verse she had mislaid and only now remembered. When she turned on the lights in the drawing-room, she disclosed herself clad in a sweeping negligee gown of soft rose-colored stuff, throat and shoulders smothered in lace. Her rings were still on her fingers, her massed yellow hair had not yet been taken down. She was delicately, gracefully beautiful, with slender, oval face, red lips, a faint color in the cheeks, and blue eyes of the chameleon sort that at will stare wide with the innocence of childhood, go hard and gray and brilliantly cold, or flame up in hot wilfulness and mastery.

She turned the lights off and passed out and down the hall toward the morning room. At the entrance she paused and listened. From farther on had come, not a noise, but an impression of movement. She could have sworn she had not heard anything, yet something had been different. The atmosphere of night quietude had been disturbed. She wondered what servant could be prowling about. Not the butler, who was notorious for retiring early save on special occasion. Nor could it be her maid, whom she had permitted to go that evening.

Passing on to the dining-room, she found the door closed. Why she opened it and went on in, she did not know, except for the feeling that the disturbing factor, whatever it might be, was there. The room was in darkness, and she felt her way to the button and pressed. As the blaze of light flashed on, she stepped back and cried out. It was a mere "Oh!" and it was not loud.

Facing her, alongside the button, flat against the wall, was a man. In his hand, pointed toward her, was a revolver. She noticed, even in the shock of seeing him, that the weapon was black and exceedingly long-barreled. She knew black and exceedingly long it for what it was, a Colt's. He was a medium-sized man, roughly clad, brown-eyed, and swarthy with sunburn. He seemed very cool. There was no wabble to the revolver and it was directed toward her stomach, not from an outstretched arm, but from the hip, against which the forearm rested.

"Oh," she said. "I beg your pardon. You startled me. What do you want?"

"I reckon I want to get out," he answered, with a humorous twitch to the lips. "I've kind of lost my way in this here shebang, and if you'll kindly show me the door I'll cause no trouble and sure vamoose."

"But what are you doing here?" she demanded, her voice touched with the sharpness of one used to authority.

"Plain robbing, Miss, that's all. I came snooping around to see what I could gather up. I thought you wan't to home, seein' as I saw you pull out with your old man in an auto. I reckon that must a ben your pa, and you're Miss Setliffe."

Mrs. Setliffe saw his mistake, appreciated the naive compliment, and decided not to undeceive him.

"How do you know I am Miss Setliffe?" she asked.

"This is old Setliffe's house, ain't it?"

She nodded.

"I didn't know he had a daughter, but I reckon you must be her. And now, if it ain't botherin' you too much, I'd sure be obliged if you'd show me the way out."

"But why should I? You are a robber, a burglar."

"If I wan't an ornery shorthorn at the business, I'd be accumulatin' them rings on your fingers instead of being polite," he retorted.

"I come to make a raise outa old Setliffe, and not to be robbing women-folks. If you get outa the way, I reckon I can find my own way out."

Mrs. Setliffe was a keen woman, and she felt that from such a man there was little to fear. That he was not a typical criminal, she was certain. From his speech she knew he was not of the cities, and she seemed to sense the wider, homelier air of large spaces.

228

"Suppose I screamed?" she queried curiously. "Suppose I made an outcry for help? You couldn't shoot me?... a woman?"

She noted the fleeting bafflement in his brown eyes. He answered slowly and thoughtfully, as if working out a difficult problem. "I reckon, then, I'd have to choke you and maul you some bad."

"A woman?"

"I'd sure have to," he answered, and she saw his mouth set grimly.

"You're only a soft woman, but you see, Miss, I can't afford to go to jail. No, Miss, I sure can't. There's a friend of mine waitin' for me out West. He's in a hole, and I've got to help him out." The mouth shaped even more grimly. "I guess I could choke you without hurting you much to speak of."

Her eyes took on a baby stare of innocent incredulity as she watched him.

"I never met a burglar before," she assured him, "and I can't begin to tell you how interested I am."

"I'm not a burglar, Miss. Not a real one," he hastened to add as she looked her amused unbelief. "It looks like it, me being here in your house. But it's the first time I ever tackled such a job. I needed the money bad. Besides, I kind of look on it like collecting what's coming to me."

"I don't understand," she smiled encouragingly. "You came here to rob, and to rob is to take what is not yours."

"Yes, and no, in this here particular case. But I reckon I'd better be going now."

He started for the door of the dining-room, but she interposed, and a very beautiful obstacle she made of herself. His left hand went out as if to grip her, then hesitated. He was patently awed by her soft womanhood.

"There!" she cried triumphantly. "I knew you wouldn't."

The man was embarrassed.

"I ain't never manhandled a woman yet," he explained, "and it don't come easy. But I sure will, if you set to screaming."

"Won't you stay a few minutes and talk?" she urged. "I'm so interested. I should like to hear you explain how burglary is collecting what is coming to you."

He looked at her admiringly.

"I always thought women-folks were scairt of robbers," he confessed. "But you don't seem none."

She laughed gaily.

"There are robbers and robbers, you know. I am not afraid of you, because I am confident you are not the sort of creature that would harm a woman. Come, talk with me a while. Nobody will disturb us. I am all alone. My—father caught the night train to New York. The servants are all asleep. I should like to give you something to eat—women always prepare midnight suppers for the burglars they catch, at least they do in the magazine stories. But I don't know where to find the food. Perhaps you will have something to drink?"

He hesitated, and did not reply; but she could see the admiration for her growing in his eyes.

"You're not afraid?" she queried. "I won't poison you, I promise. I'll drink with you to show you it is all right."

"You sure are a surprise package of all right," he declared, for the first time lowering the weapon and letting it hang at his side. "No one don't need to tell me ever again that women-folks in cities is afraid. You ain't much—just a little soft pretty thing. But you've sure got the spunk. And you're trustful on top of it. There ain't many women, or men either, who'd treat a man with a gun the way you're treating me."

She smiled her pleasure in the compliment, and her face, was very earnest as she said:

"That is because I like your appearance. You are too decent-looking a man to be a robber. You oughtn't to do such things. If you are in bad luck you should go to work. Come, put away that nasty revolver and let us talk it over. The thing for you to do is to work."

"Not in this burg," he commented bitterly. "I've walked two inches off the bottom of my legs trying to find a job. Honest, I was a fine large man once... before I started looking for a job."

The merry laughter with which she greeted his sally obviously pleased him, and she was quick to note and take advantage of it. She moved directly away from the door and toward the sideboard.

"Come, you must tell me all about it while I get that drink for you. What will it be? Whisky?"

"Yes, ma'am," he said, as he followed her, though he still carried the big revolver at his side, and though he glanced reluctantly at the unguarded open door.

She filled a glass for him at the sideboard.

"I promised to drink with you," she said hesitatingly. "But I don't like whisky. I... I prefer sherry."

She lifted the sherry bottle tentatively for his consent.

"Sure," he answered, with a nod. "Whisky's a man's drink. I never like to see women at it. Wine's more their stuff."

She raised her glass to his, her eyes meltingly sympathetic.

"Here's to finding you a good position—"

But she broke off at sight of the expression of surprised disgust on his face. The glass, barely touched, was removed from his wry lips.

"What is the matter!" she asked anxiously. "Don't you like it? Have I made a mistake?"

"It's sure funny whisky. Tastes like it got burned and smoked in the making."

231

"Oh! How silly of me! I gave you Scotch. Of course you are accustomed to rye. Let me change it."

She was almost solicitiously maternal, as she replaced the glass with another and sought and found the proper bottle.

"Better?" she asked.

"Yes, ma'am. No smoke in it. It's sure the real good stuff. I ain't had a drink in a week. Kind of slick, that; oily, you know; not made in a chemical factory."

"You are a drinking man?" It was half a question, half a challenge.

"No, ma'am, not to speak of. I HAVE rared up and ripsnorted at spells, but most unfrequent. But there is times when a good stiff jolt lands on the right spot kerchunk, and this is sure one of them. And now, thanking you for your kindness, ma'am, I'll just be a pulling along."

But Mrs. Setliffe did not want to lose her burglar. She was too poised a woman to possess much romance, but there was a thrill about the present situation that delighted her. Besides, she knew there was no danger. The man, despite his jaw and the steady brown eyes, was eminently tractable. Also, farther back in her consciousness glimmered the thought of an audience of admiring friends. It was too bad not to have that audience.

"You haven't explained how burglary, in your case, is merely collecting what is your own," she said. "Come, sit down, and tell me about it here at the table."

She maneuvered for her own seat, and placed him across the corner from her. His alertness had not deserted him, as she noted, and his eyes roved sharply about, returning always with smoldering admiration to hers, but never resting long. And she noted likewise that while she spoke he was intent on listening for other sounds than those of her voice. Nor had he relinquished the revolver, which lay at the corner of the table between them, the butt close to his right hand.

But he was in a new habitat which he did not know. This man from the West, cunning in woodcraft and plainscraft, with eyes and ears open, tense and suspicious, did not know that under the table, close to her foot, was the push button of an electric bell. He had never heard of such a contrivance, and his keenness and wariness went for naught.

"It's like this, Miss," he began, in response to her urging. "Old Setliffe done me up in a little deal once. It was raw, but it worked. Anything will work full and legal when it's got few hundred million behind it. I'm not squealin', and I ain't taking a slam at your pa. He don't know me from Adam, and I reckon he don't know he done me outa anything. He's too big, thinking and dealing in millions, to ever hear of a small potato like me. He's an operator. He's got all kinds of experts thinking and planning and working for him, some of them, I hear, getting more cash salary than the President of the United States. I'm only one of thousands that have been done up by your pa, that's all.

"You see, ma'am, I had a little hole in the ground—a dinky, hydraulic, one-horse outfit of a mine. And when the Setliffe crowd shook down Idaho, and reorganized the smelter trust, and roped in the rest of the landscape, and put through the big hydraulic scheme at Twin Pines, why I sure got squeezed. I never had a run for my money. I was scratched off the card before the first heat. And so, to-night, being broke and my friend needing me bad, I just dropped around to make a raise outa your pa. Seeing as I needed it, it kinda was coming to me."

"Granting all that you say is so," she said, "nevertheless it does not make house-breaking any the less house-breaking. You couldn't make such a defense in a court of law."

"I know that," he confessed meekly. "What's right ain't always legal. And that's why I am so uncomfortable a-settin' here and talking with you. Not that I ain't enjoying your company—I sure do enjoy it—but I just can't afford to be caught. I know what they'd do to me in this here city. There was a young fellow that got fifty years only last week for holding a man up on the street for two dollars and eighty-five cents. I read about it in the paper. When times is hard and they ain't no work, men get desperate. And then the other men who've got something to be robbed of get desperate, too, and they just sure soak it to the other fellows. If I got caught, I reckon I wouldn't get a mite less than ten years. That's why I'm hankering to be on my way."

"No; wait." She lifted a detaining hand, at the same time removing her foot from the bell, which she had been pressing intermittently. "You haven't told me your name yet."

He hesitated.

"Call me Dave."

"Then... Dave," she laughed with pretty confusion. "Something must be done for you. You are a young man, and you are just at the beginning of a bad start. If you begin by attempting to collect what you think is coming to you, later on you will be collecting what you are perfectly sure isn't coming to you. And you know what the end will be. Instead of this, we must find something honorable for you to do."

"I need the money, and I need it now," he replied doggedly. "It's not for myself, but for that friend I told you about. He's in a peck of trouble, and he's got to get his lift now or not at all."

"I can find you a position," she said quickly. "And—yes, the very thing!—I'll lend you the money you want to send to your friend. This you can pay back out of your salary."

"About three hundred would do," he said slowly. "Three hundred would pull him through. I'd work my fingers off for a year for that, and my keep, and a few cents to buy Bull Durham with."

"Ah! You smoke! I never thought of it."

Her hand went out over the revolver toward his hand, as she pointed to the tell-tale yellow stain on his fingers. At the same time her eyes measured the nearness of her own hand and of his to the weapon. She ached to grip it in one swift movement. She was sure she could do it, and yet she was not sure; and so it was that she refrained as she withdrew her hand.

"Won't you smoke?" she invited.

"I'm 'most dying to."

"Then do so. I don't mind. I really like it—cigarettes, I mean."

With his left band he dipped into his side pocket, brought out a loose wheat-straw paper and shifted it to his right hand close by the revolver. Again he dipped, transferring to the paper a pinch of brown, flaky tobacco. Then he proceeded, both hands just over the revolver, to roll the cigarette.

"From the way you hover close to that nasty weapon, you seem to be afraid of me," she challenged.

"Not exactly afraid of you, ma'am, but, under the circumstances, just a mite timid."

"But I've not been afraid of you."

"You've got nothing to lose."

"My life," she retorted.

"That's right," he acknowledged promptly, "and you ain't been scairt of me. Mebbe I am over anxious."

"I wouldn't cause you any harm."

Even as she spoke, her slipper felt for the bell and pressed it. At the same time her eyes were earnest with a plea of honesty.

"You are a judge of men. I know it. And of women. Surely, when I am trying to persuade you from a criminal life and to get you honest work to do....?"

He was immediately contrite.

"I sure beg your pardon, ma'am," he said. "I reckon my nervousness ain't complimentary."

As he spoke, he drew his right hand from the table, and after lighting the cigarette, dropped it by his side.

"Thank you for your confidence," she breathed softly, resolutely keeping her eyes from measuring the distance to the revolver, and keeping her foot pressed firmly on the bell.

"About that three hundred," he began. "I can telegraph it West to-night. And I'll agree to work a year for it and my keep."

"You will earn more than that. I can promise seventy-five dollars a month at the least. Do you know horses?"

His face lighted up and his eyes sparkled.

"Then go to work for me—or for my father, rather, though I engage all the servants. I need a second coachman—"

"And wear a uniform?" he interrupted sharply, the sneer of the free-born West in his voice and on his lips.

She smiled tolerantly.

"Evidently that won't do. Let me think. Yes. Can you break and handle colts?"

He nodded.

"We have a stock farm, and there's room for just such a man as you. Will you take it?"

"Will I, ma'am?" His voice was rich with gratitude and enthusiasm. "Show me to it. I'll dig right in to-morrow. And I can sure promise you one thing, ma'am. You'll never be sorry for lending Hughie Luke a hand in his trouble—"

"I thought you said to call you Dave," she chided forgivingly.

"I did, ma'am. I did. And I sure beg your pardon. It was just plain bluff. My real name is Hughie Luke. And if you'll give me the address of that stock farm of yours, and the railroad fare, I head for it first thing in the morning."

Throughout the conversation she had never relaxed her attempts on the bell. She had pressed it in every alarming way—three shorts and a long, two

236

and a long, and five. She had tried long series of shorts, and, once, she had held the button down for a solid three minutes. And she had been divided between objurgation of the stupid, heavy-sleeping butler and doubt if the bell were in order.

"I am so glad," she said; "so glad that you are willing. There won't be much to arrange. But you will first have to trust me while I go upstairs for my purse."

She saw the doubt flicker momentarily in his eyes, and added hastily, "But you see I am trusting you with the three hundred dollars."

"I believe you, ma'am," he came back gallantly. "Though I just can't help this nervousness."

"Shall I go and get it?"

But before she could receive consent, a slight muffled jar from the distance came to her ear. She knew it for the swing-door of the butler's pantry. But so slight was it—more a faint vibration than a sound—that she would not have heard had not her ears been keyed and listening for it. Yet the man had heard. He was startled in his composed way.

"What was that?" he demanded.

For answer, her left hand flashed out to the revolver and brought it back. She had had the start of him, and she needed it, for the next instant his hand leaped up from his side, clutching emptiness where the revolver had been.

"Sit down!" she commanded sharply, in a voice new to him. "Don't move. Keep your hands on the table."

She had taken a lesson from him. Instead of holding the heavy weapon extended, the butt of it and her forearm rested on the table, the muzzle pointed, not at his head, but his chest. And he, looking coolly and obeying her commands, knew there was no chance of the kick-up of the recoil producing a miss. Also, he saw that the revolver did not wabble, nor the hand shake, and he was thoroughly conversant with the size of hole the soft-nosed bullets could make. He had eyes, not for her, but for the hammer, which had risen under the pressure of her forefinger on the trigger.

"I reckon I'd best warn you that there trigger-pull is filed dreadful fine. Don't press too hard, or I'll have a hole in me the size of a walnut."

She slacked the hammer partly down.

"That's better," he commented. "You'd best put it down all the way. You see how easy it works. If you want to, a quick light pull will jiffy her up and back and make a pretty mess all over your nice floor."

A door opened behind him, and he heard somebody enter the room. But he did not turn his bead. He was looking at her, and he found it the face of another woman—hard, cold, pitiless yet brilliant in its beauty. The eyes, too, were hard, though blazing with a cold light.

"Thomas," she commanded, "go to the telephone and call the police. Why were you so long in answering?"

"I came as soon as I heard the bell, madam," was the answer.

The robber never took his eyes from hers, nor did she from his, but at mention of the bell she noticed that his eyes were puzzled for the moment.

"Beg your pardon," said the butler from behind, "but wouldn't it be better for me to get a weapon and arouse the servants?"

"No; ring for the police. I can hold this man. Go and do it—quickly."

The butler slippered out of the room, and the man and the woman sat on, gazing into each other's eyes. To her it was an experience keen with enjoyment, and in her mind was the gossip of her crowd, and she saw notes in the society weeklies of the beautiful young Mrs. Setliffe capturing an armed robber single-handed. It would create a sensation, she was sure.

"When you get that sentence you mentioned," she said coldly, "you will have time to meditate upon what a fool you have been, taking other persons' property and threatening women with revolvers. You will have time to learn your lesson thoroughly. Now tell the truth. You haven't any friend in trouble. All that you told me was lies."

He did not reply. Though his eyes were upon her, they seemed blank. In truth, for the instant she was veiled to him, and what he saw was the wide sunwashed spaces of the West, where men and women were bigger than the rotten denizens, as he had encountered them, of the thrice rotten cities of the East.

"Go on. Why don't you speak? Why don't you lie some more? Why don't you beg to be let off?"

"I might," he answered, licking his dry lips. "I might ask to be let off if..."

"If what?" she demanded peremptorily, as he paused.

"I was trying to think of a word you reminded me of. As I was saying, I might if you was a decent woman."

Her face paled.

"Be careful," she warned.

"You don't dast kill me," he sneered. "The world's a pretty low down place to have a thing like you prowling around in it, but it ain't so plumb low down, I reckon, as to let you put a hole in me. You're sure bad, but the trouble with you is that you're weak in your badness. It ain't much to kill a man, but you ain't got it in you. There's where you lose out."

"Be careful of what you say," she repeated. "Or else, I warn you, it will go hard with you. It can be seen to whether your sentence is light or heavy."

"Something's the matter with God," he remarked irrelevantly, "to be letting you around loose. It's clean beyond me what he's up to, playing such-like tricks on poor humanity. Now if I was God—"

His further opinion was interrupted by the entrance of the butler.

"Something is wrong with the telephone, madam," he announced. "The wires are crossed or something, because I can't get Central."

"Go and call one of the servants," she ordered. "Send him out for an officer, and then return here."

Again the pair was left alone.

"Will you kindly answer one question, ma'am?" the man said. "That servant fellow said something about a bell. I watched you like a cat, and you sure rung no bell."

"It was under the table, you poor fool. I pressed it with my foot."

"Thank you, ma'am. I reckoned I'd seen your kind before, and now I sure know I have. I spoke to you true and trusting, and all the time you was lying like hell to me."

She laughed mockingly.

"Go on. Say what you wish. It is very interesting."

"You made eyes at me, looking soft and kind, playing up all the time the fact that you wore skirts instead of pants—and all the time with your foot on the bell under the table. Well, there's some consolation. I'd sooner be poor Hughie Luke, doing his ten years, than be in your skin. Ma'am, hell is full of women like you."

There was silence for a space, in which the man, never taking his eyes from her, studying her, was making up his mind.

"Go on," she urged. "Say something."

"Yes, ma'am, I'll say something. I'll sure say something. Do you know what I'm going to do? I'm going to get right up from this chair and walk out that door. I'd take the gun from you, only you might turn foolish and let it go off. You can have the gun. It's a good one. As I was saying, I am going right out that door. And you ain't going to pull that gun off either. It takes guts to shoot a man, and you sure ain't got them. Now get ready and see if you can pull that trigger. I ain't going to harm you. I'm going out that door, and I'm starting."

Keeping his eyes fixed on her, he pushed back the chair and slowly stood erect. The hammer rose halfway. She watched it. So did he.

"Pull harder," he advised. "It ain't half up yet. Go on and pull it and kill a man. That's what I said, kill a man, spatter his brains out on the floor, or slap a hole into him the size of your fist. That's what killing a man means."

The hammer lowered jerkily but gently. The man turned his back and walked slowly to the door. She swung the revolver around so that it bore on his back. Twice again the hammer came up halfway and was reluctantly eased down.

At the door the man turned for a moment before passing on. A sneer was on his lips. He spoke to her in a low voice, almost drawling, but in it was the quintessence of all loathing, as he called her a name unspeakable and vile.

THE MEXICAN

NOBODY knew his history—they of the Junta least of all. He was their "little mystery," their "big patriot," and in his way he worked as hard for the coming Mexican Revolution as did they. They were tardy in recognizing this, for not one of the Junta liked him. The day he first drifted into their crowded, busy rooms, they all suspected him of being a spy—one of the bought tools of the Diaz secret service. Too many of the comrades were in civil an military prisons scattered over the United States, and others of them, in irons, were even then being taken across the border to be lined up against adobe walls and shot.

At the first sight the boy did not impress them favorably. Boy he was, not more than eighteen and not over large for his years. He announced that he was Felipe Rivera, and that it was his wish to work for the Revolution. That was all—not a wasted word, no further explanation. He stood waiting. There was no smile on his lips, no geniality in his eyes. Big dashing Paulino Vera felt an inward shudder. Here was something forbidding, terrible, inscrutable. There was something venomous and snakelike in the boy's black eyes. They burned like cold fire, as with a vast, concentrated bitterness. He flashed them from the faces of the conspirators to the typewriter which little Mrs. Sethby was industriously operating. His eyes rested on hers but an instant—she had chanced to look up—and she, too, sensed the nameless something that made her pause. She was compelled to read back in order to regain the swing of the letter she was writing.

Paulino Vera looked questioningly at Arrellano and Ramos, and questioningly they looked back and to each other. The indecision of doubt brooded in their eyes. This slender boy was the Unknown, vested with all the menace of the Unknown. He was unrecognizable, something quite beyond the ken of honest, ordinary revolutionists whose fiercest hatred for Diaz and his tyranny after all was only that of honest and ordinary patriots. Here was something else, they knew not what. But Vera, always the most impulsive, the quickest to act, stepped into the breach.

"Very well," he said coldly. "You say you want to work for the Revolution. Take off your coat. Hang it over there. I will show you, come—where are the buckets and cloths. The floor is dirty. You will begin by scrubbing it, and by scrubbing the floors of the other rooms. The spittoons need to be cleaned. Then there are the windows."

"Is it for the Revolution?" the boy asked.

"It is for the Revolution," Vera answered.

Rivera looked cold suspicion at all of them, then proceeded to take off his coat.

"It is well," he said.

And nothing more. Day after day he came to his work—sweeping, scrubbing, cleaning. He emptied the ashes from the stoves, brought up the coal and kindling, and lighted the fires before the most energetic one of them was at his desk.

"Can I sleep here?" he asked once.

Ah, ha! So that was it—the hand of Diaz showing through! To sleep in the rooms of the Junta meant access to their secrets, to the lists of names, to the addresses of comrades down on Mexican soil. The request was denied, and Rivera never spoke of it again. He slept they knew not where, and ate they knew not where nor how. Once, Arrellano offered him a couple of dollars. Rivera declined the money with a shake of the head. When Vera joined in and tried to press it upon him, he said:

"I am working for the Revolution."

It takes money to raise a modern revolution, and always the Junta was pressed. The members starved and toiled, and the longest day was none too long, and yet there were times when it appeared as if the Revolution stood or fell on no more than the matter of a few dollars. Once, the first time, when the rent of the house was two months behind and the landlord was threatening dispossession, it was Felipe Rivera, the scrub-boy in the poor, cheap clothes, worn and threadbare, who laid sixty dollars in gold on May

Sethby's desk. There were other times. Three hundred letters, clicked out on the busy typewriters (appeals for assistance, for sanctions from the organized labor groups, requests for square news deals to the editors of newspapers, protests against the high-handed treatment of revolutionists by the United States courts), lay unmailed, awaiting postage. Vera's watch had disappeared— the old-fashioned gold repeater that had been his father's. Likewise had gone the plain gold band from May Setbby's third finger. Things were desperate. Ramos and Arrellano pulled their long mustaches in despair. The letters must go off, and the Post Office allowed no credit to purchasers of stamps. Then it was that Rivera put on his hat and went out. When he came back he laid a thousand two-cent stamps on May Sethby's desk.

"I wonder if it is the cursed gold of Diaz?" said Vera to the comrades.

They elevated their brows and could not decide. And Felipe Rivera, the scrubber for the Revolution, continued, as occasion arose, to lay down gold and silver for the Junta's use.

And still they could not bring themselves to like him. They did not know him. His ways were not theirs. He gave no confidences. He repelled all probing. Youth that he was, they could never nerve themselves to dare to question him.

"A great and lonely spirit, perhaps, I do not know, I do not know," Arrellano said helplessly.

"He is not human," said Ramos.

"His soul has been seared," said May Sethby. "Light and laughter have been burned out of him. He is like one dead, and yet he is fearfully alive."

"He has been through hell," said Vera. "No man could look like that who has not been through hell—and he is only a boy."

Yet they could not like him. He never talked, never inquired, never suggested. He would stand listening, expressionless, a thing dead, save for his eyes, coldly burning, while their talk of the Revolution ran high and warm. From face to face and speaker to speaker his eyes would turn, boring like gimlets of incandescent ice, disconcerting and perturbing.

"He is no spy," Vera confided to May Sethby. "He is a patriot—mark me, the greatest patriot of us all. I know it, I feel it, here in my heart and head I feel it. But him I know not at all."

"He has a bad temper," said May Sethby.

"I know," said Vera, with a shudder. "He has looked at me with those eyes of his. They do not love; they threaten; they are savage as a wild tiger's. I know, if I should prove unfaithful to the Cause, that he would kill me. He has no heart. He is pitiless as steel, keen and cold as frost. He is like moonshine in a winter night when a man freezes to death on some lonely mountain top. I am not afraid of Diaz and all his killers; but this boy, of him am I afraid. I tell you true. I am afraid. He is the breath of death."

Yet Vera it was who persuaded the others to give the first trust to Rivera. The line of communication between Los Angeles and Lower California had broken down. Three of the comrades had dug their own graves and been shot into them. Two more were United States prisoners in Los Angeles. Juan Alvarado, the Federal commander, was a monster. All their plans did he checkmate. They could no longer gain access to the active revolutionists, and the incipient ones, in Lower California.

Young Rivera was given his instructions and dispatched south. When he returned, the line of communication was reestablished, and Juan Alvarado was dead. He had been found in bed, a knife hilt-deep in his breast. This had exceeded Rivera's instructions, but they of the Junta knew the times of his movements. They did not ask him. He said nothing. But they looked at one another and conjectured.

"I have told you," said Vera. "Diaz has more to fear from this youth than from any man. He is implacable. He is the hand of God."

The bad temper, mentioned by May Sethby, and sensed by them all, was evidenced by physical proofs. Now he appeared with a cut lip, a blackened cheek, or a swollen ear. It was patent that he brawled, somewhere in that outside world where he ate and slept, gained money, and moved in ways unknown to them. As the time passed, he had come to set type for the little revolutionary sheet they published weekly. There were occasions when he was unable to set type, when his knuckles were bruised and battered, when his thumbs were injured and helpless, when one arm or the other hung wearily at his side while his face was drawn with unspoken pain.

"A wastrel," said Arrellano.

"A frequenter of low places," said Ramos.

"But where does he get the money?" Vera demanded. "Only to-day, just now, have I learned that he paid the bill for white paper—one hundred and forty dollars."

"There are his absences," said May Sethby. "He never explains them."

"We should set a spy upon him," Ramos propounded.

"I should not care to be that spy," said Vera. "I fear you would never see me again, save to bury me. He has a terrible passion. Not even God would he permit to stand between him and the way of his passion."

"I feel like a child before him," Ramos confessed.

"To me he is power—he is the primitive, the wild wolf, the striking rattlesnake, the stinging centipede," said Arrellano.

"He is the Revolution incarnate," said Vera. "He is the flame and the spirit of it, the insatiable cry for vengeance that makes no cry but that slays noiselessly. He is a destroying angel in moving through the still watches of the night."

"I could weep over him," said May Sethby. "He knows nobody. He hates all people. Us he tolerates, for we are the way of his desire. He is alone.... lonely." Her voice broke in a half sob and there was dimness in her eyes.

Rivera's ways and times were truly mysterious. There were periods when they did not see him for a week at a time. Once, he was away a month. These occasions were always capped by his return, when, without advertisement or speech, he laid gold coins on May Sethby's desk. Again, for days and weeks, he spent all his time with the Junta. And yet again, for irregular periods, he would disappear through the heart of each day, from early morning until late afternoon. At such times he came early and remained late. Arrellano had found him at midnight, setting type with fresh swollen knuckles, or mayhap it was his lip, new-split, that still bled.

II

The time of the crisis approached. Whether or not the Revolution would be depended upon the Junta, and the Junta was hard-pressed. The need for money was greater than ever before, while money was harder to get. Patriots had given their last cent and now could give no more. Section gang laborers-fugitive peons from Mexico—were contributing half their scanty wages. But more than that was needed. The heart-breaking, conspiring, undermining toil of years approached fruition. The time was ripe. The Revolution hung on the balance. One shove more, one last heroic effort, and it would tremble across the scales to victory. They knew their Mexico. Once started, the Revolution would take care of itself. The whole Diaz machine would go down like a house of cards. The border was ready to rise. One Yankee, with a hundred I.W.W. men, waited the word to cross over the border and begin the conquest of Lower California. But he needed guns. And clear across to the Atlantic, the Junta in touch with them all and all of them needing guns, mere adventurers, soldiers of fortune, bandits, disgruntled American union men, socialists, anarchists, rough-necks, Mexican exiles, peons escaped from bondage, whipped miners from the bull-pens of Coeur d'Alene and Colorado who desired only the more vindictively to fight—all the flotsam and jetsam of wild spirits from the madly complicated modern world. And it was guns and ammunition, ammunition and guns—the unceasing and eternal cry.

Fling this heterogeneous, bankrupt, vindictive mass across the border, and the Revolution was on. The custom house, the northern ports of entry, would be captured. Diaz could not resist. He dared not throw the weight of his armies against them, for he must hold the south. And through the south the flame would spread despite. The people would rise. The defenses of city after city would crumple up. State after state would totter down. And at last, from every side, the victorious armies of the Revolution would close in on the City of Mexico itself, Diaz's last stronghold.

But the money. They had the men, impatient and urgent, who would use the guns. They knew the traders who would sell and deliver the guns. But to culture the Revolution thus far had exhausted the Junta. The last dollar had been spent, the last resource and the last starving patriot milked dry, and the great adventure still trembled on the scales. Guns and ammunition! The ragged battalions must be armed. But how? Ramos lamented his confiscated estates. Arrellano wailed the spendthriftness of his youth. May Sethby wondered if it would have been different had they of the Junta been more economical in the past.

"To think that the freedom of Mexico should stand or fall on a few paltry thousands of dollars," said Paulino Vera.

Despair was in all their faces. Jose Amarillo, their last hope, a recent convert, who had promised money, had been apprehended at his hacienda in Chihuahua and shot against his own stable wall. The news had just come through.

Rivera, on his knees, scrubbing, looked up, with suspended brush, his bare arms flecked with soapy, dirty water.

"Will five thousand do it?" he asked.

They looked their amazement. Vera nodded and swallowed. He could not speak, but he was on the instant invested with a vast faith.

"Order the guns," Rivera said, and thereupon was guilty of the longest flow of words they had ever heard him utter. "The time is short. In three weeks I shall bring you the five thousand. It is well. The weather will be warmer for those who fight. Also, it is the best I can do."

Vera fought his faith. It was incredible. Too many fond hopes had been shattered since he had begun to play the revolution game. He believed this threadbare scrubber of the Revolution, and yet he dared not believe.

"You are crazy," he said.

"In three weeks," said Rivera. "Order the guns."

He got up, rolled down his sleeves, and put on his coat.

"Order the guns," he said.

"I am going now."

III

After hurrying and scurrying, much telephoning and bad language, a night session was held in Kelly's office. Kelly was rushed with business; also, he was unlucky. He had brought Danny Ward out from New York, arranged the fight for him with Billy Carthey, the date was three weeks away, and for two days now, carefully concealed from the sporting writers, Carthey had been lying up, badly injured. There was no one to take his place. Kelly had been burning the wires East to every eligible lightweight, but they were tied up with dates and contracts. And now hope had revived, though faintly.

"You've got a hell of a nerve," Kelly addressed Rivera, after one look, as soon as they got together.

Hate that was malignant was in Rivera's eyes, but his face remained impassive.

"I can lick Ward," was all he said.

"How do you know? Ever see him fight?"

Rivera shook his head.

"He can beat you up with one hand and both eyes closed."

Rivera shrugged his shoulders.

"Haven't you got anything to say?" the fight promoter snarled.

"I can lick him."

"Who'd you ever fight, anyway!" Michael Kelly demanded. Michael was the promotor's brother, and ran the Yellowstone pool rooms where he made goodly sums on the fight game.

Rivera favored him with a bitter, unanswering stare.

The promoter's secretary, a distinctively sporty young man, sneered audibly.

"Well, you know Roberts," Kelly broke the hostile silence. "He ought to be here. I've sent for him. Sit down and wait, though from the looks of you, you haven't got a chance. I can't throw the public down with a bum fight. Ringside seats are selling at fifteen dollars, you know that."

When Roberts arrived, it was patent that he was mildly drunk. He was a tall, lean, slack-jointed individual, and his walk, like his talk, was a smooth and languid drawl.

Kelly went straight to the point.

"Look here, Roberts, you've been bragging you discovered this little Mexican. You know Carthey's broke his arm. Well, this little yellow streak has the gall to blow in to-day and say he'll take Carthey's place. What about it?"

"It's all right, Kelly," came the slow response. "He can put up a fight."

"I suppose you'll be sayin' next that he can lick Ward," Kelly snapped.

Roberts considered judicially.

"No, I won't say that. Ward's a top-notcher and a ring general. But he can't hashhouse Rivera in short order. I know Rivera. Nobody can get his goat. He ain't got a goat that I could ever discover. And he's a two-handed fighter. He can throw in the sleep-makers from any position."

"Never mind that. What kind of a show can he put up? You've been conditioning and training fighters all your life. I take off my hat to your judgment. Can he give the public a run for its money?"

"He sure can, and he'll worry Ward a mighty heap on top of it. You don't know that boy. I do. I discovered him. He ain't got a goat. He's a devil. He's a wizzy-wooz if anybody should ask you. He'll make Ward sit up with a show of local talent that'll make the rest of you sit up. I won't say he'll lick Ward, but he'll put up such a show that you'll all know he's a comer."

"All right." Kelly turned to his secretary. "Ring up Ward. I warned him to show up if I thought it worth while. He's right across at the Yellowstone, throwin' chests and doing the popular."

Kelly turned back to the conditioner. "Have a drink?"

Roberts sipped his highball and unburdened himself.

"Never told you how I discovered the little cuss. It was a couple of years ago he showed up out at the quarters. I was getting Prayne ready for his fight with Delaney. Prayne's wicked. He ain't got a tickle of mercy in his make-up. I chopped up his pardner's something cruel, and I couldn't find a willing boy that'd work with him. I'd noticed this little starved Mexican kid hanging around, and I was desperate. So I grabbed him, shoved on the gloves and put him in. He was tougher'n rawhide, but weak. And he didn't know the first letter in the alphabet of boxing. Prayne chopped him to ribbons. But he hung on for two sickening rounds, when he fainted. Starvation, that was all. Battered! You couldn't have recognized him. I gave him half a dollar and a square meal. You oughta seen him wolf it down. He hadn't had the end of a bite for a couple of days. That's the end of him, thinks I. But next day he showed up, stiff an' sore, ready for another half and a square meal. And he done better as time went by. Just a born fighter, and tough beyond belief. He hasn't a heart. He's a piece of ice. And he never talked eleven words in a string since I know him. He saws wood and does his work."

"I've seen 'm," the secretary said. "He's worked a lot for you."

"All the big little fellows has tried out on him," Roberts answered. "And he's learned from 'em. I've seen some of them he could lick. But his heart wasn't in it. I reckoned he never liked the game. He seemed to act that way."

"He's been fighting some before the little clubs the last few months," Kelly said.

"Sure. But I don't know what struck 'm. All of a sudden his heart got into it. He just went out like a streak and cleaned up all the little local fellows. Seemed to want the money, and he's won a bit, though his clothes don't look it. He's peculiar. Nobody knows his business. Nobody knows how he spends his time. Even when he's on the job, he plumb up and disappears most of each day soon as his work is done. Sometimes he just blows away for weeks at a time. But he don't take advice. There's a fortune in it for the fellow that gets the job of managin' him, only he won't consider it. And you watch him hold out for the cash money when you get down to terms."

It was at this stage that Danny Ward arrived. Quite a party it was. His manager and trainer were with him, and he breezed in like a gusty draught of geniality, good-nature, and all-conqueringness. Greetings flew about, a joke here, a retort there, a smile or a laugh for everybody. Yet it was his way, and only partly sincere. He was a good actor, and he had found geniality a most valuable asset in the game of getting on in the world. But down underneath he was the deliberate, cold-blooded fighter and business man. The rest was a mask. Those who knew him or trafficked with him said that when it came to brass tacks he was Danny-on-the-Spot. He was invariably present at all business discussions, and it was urged by some that his manager was a blind whose only function was to serve as Danny's mouth-piece.

Rivera's way was different. Indian blood, as well as Spanish, was in his veins, and he sat back in a corner, silent, immobile, only his black eyes passing from face to face and noting everything.

"So that's the guy," Danny said, running an appraising eye over his proposed antagonist. "How de do, old chap."

Rivera's eyes burned venomously, but he made no sign of acknowledgment. He disliked all Gringos, but this Gringo he hated with an immediacy that was unusual even in him.

"Gawd!" Danny protested facetiously to the promoter. "You ain't expectin' me to fight a deef mute." When the laughter subsided, he made another hit. "Los Angeles must be on the dink when this is the best you can scare up. What kindergarten did you get 'm from?"

"He's a good little boy, Danny, take it from me," Roberts defended. "Not as easy as he looks."

"And half the house is sold already," Kelly pleaded. "You'll have to take 'm on, Danny. It is the best we can do."

Danny ran another careless and unflattering glance over Rivera and sighed.

"I gotta be easy with 'm, I guess. If only he don't blow up."

Roberts snorted.

"You gotta be careful," Danny's manager warned. "No taking chances with a dub that's likely to sneak a lucky one across."

"Oh, I'll be careful all right, all right," Danny smiled. "I'll get in at the start an' nurse 'im along for the dear public's sake. What d' ye say to fifteen rounds, Kelly—an' then the hay for him?"

"That'll do," was the answer. "As long as you make it realistic."

"Then let's get down to biz." Danny paused and calculated. "Of course, sixty-five per cent of the gate receipts, same as with Carthey. But the split'll be different. Eighty will just about suit me." And to his manager, "That right?"

The manager nodded.

"Here, you, did you get that?" Kelly asked Rivera.

Rivera shook his head.

"Well, it is this way," Kelly exposited. "The purse'll be sixty-five per cent of the gate receipts. You're a dub, and an unknown. You and Danny split, twenty per cent goin' to you, an' eighty to Danny. That's fair, isn't it, Roberts?"

"Very fair, Rivera," Roberts agreed.

"You see, you ain't got a reputation yet."

"What will sixty-five per cent of the gate receipts be?" Rivera demanded.

"Oh, maybe five thousand, maybe as high as eight thousand," Danny broke in to explain. "Something like that. Your share'll come to something like a thousand or sixteen hundred. Pretty good for takin' a licking from a guy with my reputation. What d' ye say?"

Then Rivera took their breaths away. "Winner takes all," he said with finality.

A dead silence prevailed.

"It's like candy from a baby," Danny's manager proclaimed.

Danny shook his head.

"I've been in the game too long," he explained.

"I'm not casting reflections on the referee, or the present company. I'm not sayin' nothing about book-makers an' frame-ups that sometimes happen. But what I do say is that it's poor business for a fighter like me. I play safe. There's no tellin'. Mebbe I break my arm, eh? Or some guy slips me a bunch of dope?" He shook his head solemnly. "Win or lose, eighty is my split. What d' ye say, Mexican?"

Rivera shook his head.

Danny exploded. He was getting down to brass tacks now.

"Why, you dirty little greaser! I've a mind to knock your block off right now."

Roberts drawled his body to interposition between hostilities.

"Winner takes all," Rivera repeated sullenly.

"Why do you stand out that way?" Danny asked.

"I can lick you," was the straight answer.

Danny half started to take off his coat. But, as his manager knew, it was a grand stand play. The coat did not come off, and Danny allowed himself to be placated by the group. Everybody sympathized with him. Rivera stood alone.

"Look here, you little fool," Kelly took up the argument. "You're nobody. We know what you've been doing the last few months—putting away little local fighters. But Danny is class. His next fight after this will be for the championship. And you're unknown. Nobody ever heard of you out of Los Angeles."

"They will," Rivera answered with a shrug, "after this fight."

"You think for a second you can lick me?" Danny blurted in.

Rivera nodded.

"Oh, come; listen to reason," Kelly pleaded. "Think of the advertising."

"I want the money," was Rivera's answer.

"You couldn't win from me in a thousand years," Danny assured him.

"Then what are you holdin' out for?" Rivera countered. "If the money's that easy, why don't you go after it?"

"I will, so help me!" Danny cried with abrupt conviction. "I'll beat you to death in the ring, my boy—you monkeyin' with me this way. Make out the articles, Kelly. Winner take all. Play it up in the sportin' columns. Tell 'em it's a grudge fight. I'll show this fresh kid a few."

Kelly's secretary had begun to write, when Danny interrupted.

"Hold on!" He turned to Rivera.

"Weights?"

"Ringside," came the answer.

"Not on your life, Fresh Kid. If winner takes all, we weigh in at ten A.M."

"And winner takes all?" Rivera queried.

Danny nodded. That settled it. He would enter the ring in his full ripeness of strength.

"Weigh in at ten," Rivera said.

The secretary's pen went on scratching.

"It means five pounds," Roberts complained to Rivera.

"You've given too much away. You've thrown the fight right there.

Danny'll lick you sure. He'll be as strong as a bull. You're a fool. You ain't got the chance of a dewdrop in hell."

Rivera's answer was a calculated look of hatred. Even this Gringo he despised, and him had he found the whitest Gringo of them all.

IV

Barely noticed was Rivera as he entered the ring. Only a very slight and very scattering ripple of half-hearted hand-clapping greeted him. The house did not believe in him. He was the lamb led to slaughter at the hands of the great Danny. Besides, the house was disappointed. It had expected a rushing battle between Danny Ward and Billy Carthey, and here it must put up with this poor little tyro. Still further, it had manifested its disapproval of the change by betting two, and even three, to one on Danny. And where a betting audience's money is, there is its heart.

The Mexican boy sat down in his corner and waited. The slow minutes lagged by. Danny was making him wait. It was an old trick, but ever it worked on the young, new fighters. They grew frightened, sitting thus and facing their own apprehensions and a callous, tobacco-smoking audience. But for once the trick failed. Roberts was right. Rivera had no goat. He, who was more delicately coordinated, more finely nerved and strung than any of them, had no nerves of this sort. The atmosphere of foredoomed defeat in his own corner had no effect on him. His handlers were Gringos and strangers. Also they were scrubs—the dirty driftage of the fight game, without honor, without efficiency. And they were chilled, as well, with certitude that theirs was the losing corner.

"Now you gotta be careful," Spider Hagerty warned him. Spider was his chief second. "Make it last as long as you can—them's my instructions from Kelly. If you don't, the papers'll call it another bum fight and give the game a bigger black eye in Los Angeles."

All of which was not encouraging. But Rivera took no notice. He despised prize fighting. It was the hated game of the hated Gringo. He had taken up with it, as a chopping block for others in the training quarters, solely because he was starving. The fact that he was marvelously made for it had meant nothing. He hated it. Not until he had come in to the Junta, had he fought for money, and he had found the money easy. Not first among the sons of men had he been to find himself successful at a despised vocation.

He did not analyze. He merely knew that he must win this fight. There could be no other outcome. For behind him, nerving him to this belief, were profounder forces than any the crowded house dreamed. Danny Ward fought for money, and for the easy ways of life that money would bring. But the things Rivera fought for burned in his brain—blazing and terrible visions, that, with eyes wide open, sitting lonely in the corner of the ring and waiting for his tricky antagonist, he saw as clearly as he had lived them.

He saw the white-walled, water-power factories of Rio Blanco. He saw the six thousand workers, starved and wan, and the little children, seven and eight years of age, who toiled long shifts for ten cents a day. He saw the perambulating corpses, the ghastly death's heads of men who labored in the dye-rooms. He remembered that he had heard his father call the dye-rooms the "suicide-holes," where a year was death. He saw the little patio, and his mother cooking and moiling at crude housekeeping and finding time to caress and love him. And his father he saw, large, big-moustached and deep-chested, kindly above all men, who loved all men and whose heart was so large that there was love to overflowing still left for the mother and the little muchacho playing in the corner of the patio. In those days his name had not been Felipe Rivera. It had been Fernandez, his father's and mother's name. Him had they called Juan. Later, he had changed it himself, for he had found the name of Fernandez hated by prefects of police, jefes politicos, and rurales.

Big, hearty Joaquin Fernandez! A large place he occupied in Rivera's visions. He had not understood at the time, but looking back he could understand. He could see him setting type in the little printery, or scribbling endless hasty, nervous lines on the much-cluttered desk. And he could see the strange evenings, when workmen, coming secretly in the dark like men who did ill deeds, met with his father and talked long hours where he, the muchacho, lay not always asleep in the corner.

As from a remote distance he could hear Spider Hagerty saying to him: "No layin' down at the start. Them's instructions. Take a beatin' and earn your dough."

Ten minutes had passed, and he still sat in his corner. There were no signs of Danny, who was evidently playing the trick to the limit.

But more visions burned before the eye of Rivera's memory. The strike, or, rather, the lockout, because the workers of Rio Blanco had helped their striking brothers of Puebla. The hunger, the expeditions in the hills for berries, the roots and herbs that all ate and that twisted and pained the stomachs of all of them. And then, the nightmare; the waste of ground before the company's store; the thousands of starving workers; General Rosalio Martinez and the soldiers of Porfirio Diaz, and the death-spitting rifles that seemed never to cease spitting, while the workers' wrongs were washed and washed again in their own blood. And that night! He saw the flat cars, piled high with the bodies of the slain, consigned to Vera Cruz, food for the sharks of the bay. Again he crawled over the grisly heaps, seeking and finding, stripped and mangled, his father and his mother. His mother he especially remembered— only her face projecting, her body burdened by the weight of dozens of bodies. Again the rifles of the soldiers of Porfirio Diaz cracked, and again he dropped to the ground and slunk away like some hunted coyote of the hills.

To his ears came a great roar, as of the sea, and he saw Danny Ward, leading his retinue of trainers and seconds, coming down the center aisle. The house was in wild uproar for the popular hero who was bound to win. Everybody proclaimed him. Everybody was for him. Even Rivera's own seconds warmed to something akin to cheerfulness when Danny ducked jauntily through the ropes and entered the ring. His face continually spread to an unending succession of smiles, and when Danny smiled he smiled in every feature, even to the laughter-wrinkles of the corners of the eyes and into the depths of the eyes themselves. Never was there so genial a fighter. His face was a running advertisement of good feeling, of good fellowship. He knew everybody. He joked, and laughed, and greeted his friends through the ropes. Those farther away, unable to suppress their admiration, cried loudly: "Oh, you Danny!" It was a joyous ovation of affection that lasted a full five minutes.

Rivera was disregarded. For all that the audience noticed, he did not exist. Spider Lagerty's bloated face bent down close to his.

"No gettin' scared," the Spider warned.

"An' remember instructions. You gotta last. No layin' down. If you lay down, we got instructions to beat you up in the dressing rooms. Savve? You just gotta fight."

The house began to applaud. Danny was crossing the ring to him. Danny bent over, caught Rivera's right hand in both his own and shook it with impulsive heartiness. Danny's smile-wreathed face was close to his. The audience yelled its appreciation of Danny's display of sporting spirit. He was greeting his opponent with the fondness of a brother. Danny's lips moved, and the audience, interpreting the unheard words to be those of a kindly-natured sport, yelled again. Only Rivera heard the low words.

"You little Mexican rat," hissed from between Danny's gaily smiling lips, "I'll fetch the yellow outa you."

Rivera made no move. He did not rise. He merely hated with his eyes.

"Get up, you dog!" some man yelled through the ropes from behind.

The crowd began to hiss and boo him for his unsportsmanlike conduct, but he sat unmoved. Another great outburst of applause was Danny's as he walked back across the ring.

When Danny stripped, there was ohs! and ahs! of delight. His body was perfect, alive with easy suppleness and health and strength. The skin was white as a woman's, and as smooth. All grace, and resilience, and power resided therein. He had proved it in scores of battles. His photographs were in all the physical culture magazines.

A groan went up as Spider Hagerty peeled Rivera's sweater over his head. His body seemed leaner, because of the swarthiness of the skin. He had muscles, but they made no display like his opponent's. What the audience neglected to see was the deep chest. Nor could it guess the toughness of the fiber of the flesh, the instantaneousness of the cell explosions of the muscles, the fineness of the nerves that wired every part of him into a splendid fighting mechanism. All the audience saw was a brown-skinned boy of eighteen with what seemed the body of a boy. With Danny it was different. Danny was a man of twenty-four, and his body was a man's body. The contrast was still more striking as they stood together in the center of the ring receiving the referee's last instructions.

Rivera noticed Roberts sitting directly behind the newspaper men. He was drunker than usual, and his speech was correspondingly slower.

"Take it easy, Rivera," Roberts drawled.

"He can't kill you, remember that. He'll rush you at the go-off, but don't get rattled. You just and stall, and clinch. He can't hurt cover up, much. Just make believe to yourself that he's choppin' out on you at the trainin' quarters."

Rivera made no sign that he had heard.

"Sullen little devil," Roberts muttered to the man next to him. "He always was that way."

But Rivera forgot to look his usual hatred. A vision of countless rifles blinded his eyes. Every face in the audience, far as he could see, to the high dollar-seats, was transformed into a rifle. And he saw the long Mexican border arid and sun-washed and aching, and along it he saw the ragged bands that delayed only for the guns.

Back in his corner he waited, standing up. His seconds had crawled out through the ropes, taking the canvas stool with them. Diagonally across the squared ring, Danny faced him. The gong struck, and the battle was on. The audience howled its delight. Never had it seen a battle open more convincingly. The papers were right. It was a grudge fight. Three-quarters of the distance Danny covered in the rush to get together, his intention to eat up the Mexican lad plainly advertised. He assailed with not one blow, nor two, nor a dozen. He was a gyroscope of blows, a whirlwind of destruction. Rivera was nowhere. He was overwhelmed, buried beneath avalanches of punches delivered from every angle and position by a past master in the art. He was overborne, swept back against the ropes, separated by the referee, and swept back against the ropes again.

It was not a fight. It was a slaughter, a massacre. Any audience, save a prize fighting one, would have exhausted its emotions in that first minute. Danny was certainly showing what he could do—a splendid exhibition. Such was the certainty of the audience, as well as its excitement and favoritism, that it failed to take notice that the Mexican still stayed on his feet. It forgot Rivera. It rarely saw him, so closely was he enveloped in Danny's man-eating attack. A minute of this went by, and two minutes. Then, in a separation, it caught a clear glimpse of the Mexican. His lip was cut, his nose was bleeding. As he turned and staggered into a clinch, the welts of oozing blood, from his contacts with the ropes, showed in red bars across his back. But what the audience did not notice was that his chest was not heaving and that his eyes were coldly burning as ever. Too many aspiring champions, in the cruel welter of the training camps, had practiced this man-eating attack on him. He had learned to live through for a compensation of from half a dollar a go up to fifteen dollars a week—a hard school, and he was schooled hard.

Then happened the amazing thing. The whirling, blurring mix-up ceased suddenly. Rivera stood alone. Danny, the redoubtable Danny, lay on his back. His body quivered as consciousness strove to return to it. He had not staggered and sunk down, nor had he gone over in a long slumping fall. The right hook of Rivera had dropped him in midair with the abruptness of death. The referee shoved Rivera back with one hand, and stood over the fallen gladiator counting the seconds. It is the custom of prize-fighting audiences to cheer a clean knock-down blow. But this audience did not cheer. The thing had been too unexpected. It watched the toll of the seconds in tense silence, and through this silence the voice of Roberts rose exultantly:

"I told you he was a two-handed fighter!"

By the fifth second, Danny was rolling over on his face, and when seven was counted, he rested on one knee, ready to rise after the count of nine and before the count of ten. If his knee still touched the floor at "ten," he was considered "down," and also "out." The instant his knee left the floor, he was considered "up," and in that instant it was Rivera's right to try and put him down again. Rivera took no chances. The moment that knee left the floor he would strike again. He circled around, but the referee circled in between, and

Rivera knew that the seconds he counted were very slow. All Gringos were against him, even the referee.

At "nine" the referee gave Rivera a sharp thrust back. It was unfair, but it enabled Danny to rise, the smile back on his lips. Doubled partly over, with arms wrapped about face and abdomen, he cleverly stumbled into a clinch. By all the rules of the game the referee should have broken it, but he did not, and Danny clung on like a surf-battered barnacle and moment by moment recuperated. The last minute of the round was going fast. If he could live to the end, he would have a full minute in his corner to revive. And live to the end he did, smiling through all desperateness and extremity.

"The smile that won't come off!" somebody yelled, and the audience laughed loudly in its relief.

"The kick that Greaser's got is something God-awful," Danny gasped in his corner to his adviser while his handlers worked frantically over him.

The second and third rounds were tame. Danny, a tricky and consummate ring general, stalled and blocked and held on, devoting himself to recovering from that dazing first-round blow. In the fourth round he was himself again. Jarred and shaken, nevertheless his good condition had enabled him to regain his vigor. But he tried no man-eating tactics. The Mexican had proved a tartar. Instead, he brought to bear his best fighting powers. In tricks and skill and experience he was the master, and though he could land nothing vital, he proceeded scientifically to chop and wear down his opponent. He landed three blows to Rivera's one, but they were punishing blows only, and not deadly. It was the sum of many of them that constituted deadliness. He was respectful of this two-handed dub with the amazing short-arm kicks in both his fists.

In defense, Rivera developed a disconcerting straight-left. Again and again, attack after attack he straight-lefted away from him with accumulated damage to Danny's mouth and nose. But Danny was protean. That was why he was the coming champion. He could change from style to style of fighting at will. He now devoted himself to infighting. In this he was particularly wicked, and it enabled him to avoid the other's straight-left. Here he set the house wild repeatedly, capping it with a marvelous lockbreak and lift of an inside upper-cut that raised the Mexican in the air and dropped him to the mat. Rivera rested on one knee, making the most of the count, and in the soul of him he knew the referee was counting short seconds on him.

Again, in the seventh, Danny achieved the diabolical inside uppercut. He succeeded only in staggering Rivera, but, in the ensuing moment of defenseless helplessness, he smashed him with another blow through the ropes. Rivera's body bounced on the heads of the newspaper men below, and they boosted him back to the edge of the platform outside the ropes. Here he rested on one knee, while the referee raced off the seconds. Inside the ropes, through which he must duck to enter the ring, Danny waited for him. Nor did the referee intervene or thrust Danny back.

The house was beside itself with delight.

"Kill'm, Danny, kill'm!" was the cry.

Scores of voices took it up until it was like a war-chant of wolves.

Danny did his best, but Rivera, at the count of eight, instead of nine, came unexpectedly through the ropes and safely into a clinch. Now the referee worked, tearing him away so that he could be hit, giving Danny every advantage that an unfair referee can give.

But Rivera lived, and the daze cleared from his brain. It was all of a piece. They were the hated Gringos and they were all unfair. And in the worst of it visions continued to flash and sparkle in his brain—long lines of railroad track that simmered across the desert; rurales and American constables, prisons and calabooses; tramps at water tanks—all the squalid and painful panorama of his odyssey after Rio Blanca and the strike. And, resplendent and glorious, he saw the great, red Revolution sweeping across his land. The guns were there before him. Every hated face was a gun. It was for the guns he fought. He was the guns. He was the Revolution. He fought for all Mexico.

The audience began to grow incensed with Rivera. Why didn't he take the licking that was appointed him? Of course he was going to be licked, but why should he be so obstinate about it? Very few were interested in him, and they were the certain, definite percentage of a gambling crowd that plays long shots. Believing Danny to be the winner, nevertheless they had put their money on the Mexican at four to ten and one to three. More than a trifle was up on the point of how many rounds Rivera could last. Wild money had appeared at the ringside proclaiming that he could not last seven rounds, or even six. The winners of this, now that their cash risk was happily settled, had joined in cheering on the favorite.

Rivera refused to be licked. Through the eighth round his opponent strove vainly to repeat the uppercut. In the ninth, Rivera stunned the house again. In the midst of a clinch he broke the lock with a quick, lithe movement, and in the narrow space between their bodies his right lifted from the waist. Danny went to the floor and took the safety of the count. The crowd was appalled. He was being bested at his own game. His famous right-uppercut had been worked back on him. Rivera made no attempt to catch him as he arose at "nine." The referee was openly blocking that play, though he stood clear when the situation was reversed and it was Rivera who desired to rise.

Twice in the tenth, Rivera put through the right-uppercut, lifted from waist to opponent's chin. Danny grew desperate. The smile never left his face, but he went back to his man-eating rushes. Whirlwind as he would, he could not damage Rivera, while Rivera through the blur and whirl, dropped him to the mat three times in succession. Danny did not recuperate so quickly now, and by the eleventh round he was in a serious way. But from then till the fourteenth he put up the gamest exhibition of his career. He stalled and blocked, fought parsimoniously, and strove to gather strength. Also, he fought as foully as a successful fighter knows how. Every trick and device he employed, butting in the clinches with the seeming of accident, pinioning Rivera's glove between arm and body, heeling his glove on Rivera's mouth to clog his breathing. Often, in the clinches, through his cut and smiling lips he snarled insults unspeakable and vile in Rivera's ear. Everybody, from the referee to the house, was with Danny and was helping Danny. And they knew what he had in mind. Bested by this surprise-box of an unknown, he was pinning all on a single punch. He offered himself for punishment, fished, and feinted, and drew, for that one opening that would enable him to whip a blow through with all his strength and turn the tide. As another and greater fighter had done before him, he might do a right and left, to solar plexus and across the jaw. He could do it, for he was noted for the strength of punch that remained in his arms as long as he could keep his feet.

Rivera's seconds were not half-caring for him in the intervals between rounds. Their towels made a showing, but drove little air into his panting lungs. Spider Hagerty talked advice to him, but Rivera knew it was wrong advice. Everybody was against him. He was surrounded by treachery. In the fourteenth round he put Danny down again, and himself stood resting, hands dropped at side, while the referee counted. In the other corner Rivera had been noting suspicious whisperings. He saw Michael Kelly make his way to Roberts and bend and whisper. Rivera's ears were a cat's, desert-trained, and he caught snatches of what was said. He wanted to hear more, and when his opponent arose he maneuvered the fight into a clinch over against the ropes.

"Got to," he could hear Michael, while Roberts nodded. "Danny's got to win—I stand to lose a mint—I've got a ton of money covered—my own. If he lasts the fifteenth I'm bust—the boy'll mind you. Put something across."

And thereafter Rivera saw no more visions. They were trying to job him. Once again he dropped Danny and stood resting, his hands at his slide. Roberts stood up.

"That settled him," he said.

"Go to your corner."

He spoke with authority, as he had often spoken to Rivera at the training quarters. But Rivera looked hatred at him and waited for Danny to rise. Back in his corner in the minute interval, Kelly, the promoter, came and talked to Rivera.

"Throw it, damn you," he rasped in, a harsh low voice. "You gotta lay down, Rivera. Stick with me and I'll make your future. I'll let you lick Danny next time. But here's where you lay down."

Rivera showed with his eyes that he heard, but he made neither sign of assent nor dissent.

"Why don't you speak?" Kelly demanded angrily.

"You lose, anyway," Spider Hagerty supplemented. "The referee'll take it away from you. Listen to Kelly, and lay down."

"Lay down, kid," Kelly pleaded, "and I'll help you to the championship."

Rivera did not answer.

"I will, so help me, kid."

At the strike of the gong Rivera sensed something impending. The house did not. Whatever it was it was there inside the ring with him and very close. Danny's earlier surety seemed returned to him. The confidence of his advance frightened Rivera. Some trick was about to be worked. Danny rushed, but Rivera refused the encounter. He side-stepped away into safety. What the other wanted was a clinch. It was in some way necessary to the trick. Rivera backed and circled away, yet he knew, sooner or later, the clinch and the trick would come. Desperately he resolved to draw it. He made as if to effect the clinch with Danny's next rush. Instead, at the last instant, just as their bodies should have come together, Rivera darted nimbly back. And in the same instant Danny's corner raised a cry of foul. Rivera had fooled them. The referee paused irresolutely. The decision that trembled on his lips was never uttered, for a shrill, boy's voice from the gallery piped, "Raw work!"

Danny cursed Rivera openly, and forced him, while Rivera danced away. Also, Rivera made up his mind to strike no more blows at the body. In this he threw away half his chance of winning, but he knew if he was to win at all it was with the outfighting that remained to him. Given the least opportunity, they would lie a foul on him. Danny threw all caution to the winds. For two rounds he tore after and into the boy who dared not meet him at close quarters. Rivera was struck again and again; he took blows by the dozens to avoid the perilous clinch. During this supreme final rally of Danny's the audience rose to its feet and went mad. It did not understand. All it could see was that its favorite was winning, after all.

"Why don't you fight?" it demanded wrathfully of Rivera.

"You're yellow! You're yellow!" "Open up, you cur! Open up!" "Kill'm, Danny! Kill 'm!" "You sure got 'm! Kill 'm!"

In all the house, bar none, Rivera was the only cold man. By temperament and blood he was the hottest-passioned there; but he had gone through such vastly greater heats that this collective passion of ten thousand throats, rising surge on surge, was to his brain no more than the velvet cool of a summer twilight.

Into the seventeenth round Danny carried his rally. Rivera, under a heavy blow, drooped and sagged. His hands dropped helplessly as he reeled backward. Danny thought it was his chance. The boy was at, his mercy. Thus Rivera, feigning, caught him off his guard, lashing out a clean drive to the mouth. Danny went down. When he arose, Rivera felled him with a down-chop of the right on neck and jaw. Three times he repeated this. It was impossible for any referee to call these blows foul.

"Oh, Bill! Bill!" Kelly pleaded to the referee.

"I can't," that official lamented back. "He won't give me a chance."

Danny, battered and heroic, still kept coming up. Kelly and others near to the ring began to cry out to the police to stop it, though Danny's corner refused to throw in the towel. Rivera saw the fat police captain starting awkwardly to climb through the ropes, and was not sure what it meant. There were so many ways of cheating in this game of the Gringos. Danny, on his feet, tottered groggily and helplessly before him. The referee and the captain were both reaching for Rivera when he struck the last blow. There was no need to stop the fight, for Danny did not rise.

"Count!" Rivera cried hoarsely to the referee.

And when the count was finished, Danny's seconds gathered him up and carried him to his corner.

"Who wins?" Rivera demanded.

Reluctantly, the referee caught his gloved hand and held it aloft.

There were no congratulations for Rivera. He walked to his corner unattended, where his seconds had not yet placed his stool. He leaned backward on the ropes and looked his hatred at them, swept it on and about him till the whole ten thousand Gringos were included. His knees trembled under him, and he was sobbing from exhaustion. Before his eyes the hated faces swayed back and forth in the giddiness of nausea. Then he remembered they were the guns. The guns were his. The Revolution could go on.

About Author

John Griffith London (born **John Griffith Chaney**; January 12, 1876 – November 22, 1916) was an American novelist, journalist, and social activist. A pioneer in the world of commercial magazine fiction, he was one of the first writers to become a worldwide celebrity and earn a large fortune from writing. He was also an innovator in the genre that would later become known as science fiction.

His most famous works include The Call of the Wild and White Fang, both set in the Klondike Gold Rush, as well as the short stories "To Build a Fire", "An Odyssey of the North", and "Love of Life". He also wrote about the South Pacific in stories such as "The Pearls of Parlay", and "The Heathen".

London was part of the radical literary group "The Crowd" in San Francisco and a passionate advocate of unionization, workers' rights, socialism, and eugenics. He wrote several works dealing with these topics, such as his dystopian novel The Iron Heel, his non-fiction exposé The People of the Abyss, The War of the Classes, and Before Adam.

Family

Jack London's mother, Flora Wellman, was the fifth and youngest child of Pennsylvania Canal builder Marshall Wellman and his first wife, Eleanor Garrett Jones. Marshall Wellman was descended from Thomas Wellman, an early Puritan settler in the Massachusetts Bay Colony. Flora left Ohio and moved to the Pacific coast when her father remarried after her mother died. In San Francisco, Flora worked as a music teacher and spiritualist, claiming to channel the spirit of a Sauk chief, Black Hawk.

Biographer Clarice Stasz and others believe London's father was astrologer William Chaney. Flora Wellman was living with Chaney in San Francisco when she became pregnant. Whether Wellman and Chaney were legally married is unknown. Stasz notes that in his memoirs, Chaney refers to London's mother Flora Wellman as having been his "wife"; he also cites an advertisement in which Flora called herself "Florence Wellman Chaney".

According to Flora Wellman's account, as recorded in the San Francisco Chronicle of June 4, 1875, Chaney demanded that she have an abortion. When she refused, he disclaimed responsibility for the child. In desperation, she shot herself. She was not seriously wounded, but she was temporarily deranged. After giving birth, Flora turned the baby over for care to Virginia Prentiss, an African-American woman and former slave. She was a major maternal figure throughout London's life. Late in 1876, Flora Wellman married John London, a partially disabled Civil War veteran, and brought her baby John, later known as Jack, to live with the newly married couple. The family moved around the San Francisco Bay Area before settling in Oakland, where London completed public grade school.

In 1897, when he was 21 and a student at the University of California, Berkeley, London searched for and read the newspaper accounts of his mother's suicide attempt and the name of his biological father. He wrote to William Chaney, then living in Chicago. Chaney responded that he could not be London's father because he was impotent; he casually asserted that London's mother had relations with other men and averred that she had slandered him when she said he insisted on an abortion. Chaney concluded by saying that he was more to be pitied than London. London was devastated by his father's letter; in the months following, he quit school at Berkeley and went to the Klondike during the gold rush boom.

Early life

London was born near Third and Brannan Streets in San Francisco. The house burned down in the fire after the 1906 San Francisco earthquake; the California Historical Society placed a plaque at the site in 1953. Although the family was working class, it was not as impoverished as London's later accounts claimed. London was largely self-educated.

In 1885, London found and read Ouida's long Victorian novel Signa. He credited this as the seed of his literary success. In 1886, he went to the Oakland Public Library and found a sympathetic librarian, Ina Coolbrith, who encouraged his learning. (She later became California's first poet laureate and an important figure in the San Francisco literary community).

272

In 1889, London began working 12 to 18 hours a day at Hickmott's Cannery. Seeking a way out, he borrowed money from his foster mother Virginia Prentiss, bought the sloop Razzle-Dazzle from an oyster pirate named French Frank, and became an oyster pirate himself. In his memoir, John Barleycorn, he claims also to have stolen French Frank's mistress Mamie. After a few months, his sloop became damaged beyond repair. London hired on as a member of the California Fish Patrol.

In 1893, he signed on to the sealing schooner Sophie Sutherland, bound for the coast of Japan. When he returned, the country was in the grip of the panic of '93 and Oakland was swept by labor unrest. After grueling jobs in a jute mill and a street-railway power plant, London joined Coxey's Army and began his career as a tramp. In 1894, he spent 30 days for vagrancy in the Erie County Penitentiary at Buffalo, New York. In The Road, he wrote:

> Man-handling was merely one of the very minor unprintable horrors of the Erie County Pen. I say 'unprintable'; and in justice I must also say undescribable. They were unthinkable to me until I saw them, and I was no spring chicken in the ways of the world and the awful abysses of human degradation. It would take a deep plummet to reach bottom in the Erie County Pen, and I do but skim lightly and facetiously the surface of things as I there saw them.

—Jack London, The Road

After many experiences as a hobo and a sailor, he returned to Oakland and attended Oakland High School. He contributed a number of articles to the high school's magazine, The Aegis. His first published work was "Typhoon off the Coast of Japan", an account of his sailing experiences.

As a schoolboy, London often studied at Heinold's First and Last Chance Saloon, a port-side bar in Oakland. At 17, he confessed to the bar's owner, John Heinold, his desire to attend university and pursue a career as a writer. Heinold lent London tuition money to attend college.

London desperately wanted to attend the University of California, located in Berkeley. In 1896, after a summer of intense studying to pass certification exams, he was admitted. Financial circumstances forced him to leave in 1897 and he never graduated. No evidence has surfaced that he ever wrote for student publications while studying at Berkeley.

While at Berkeley, London continued to study and spend time at Heinold's saloon, where he was introduced to the sailors and adventurers who would influence his writing. In his autobiographical novel, John Barleycorn, London mentioned the pub's likeness seventeen times. Heinold's was the place where London met Alexander McLean, a captain known for his cruelty at sea. London based his protagonist Wolf Larsen, in the novel The Sea-Wolf, on McLean.

Heinold's First and Last Chance Saloon is now unofficially named Jack London's Rendezvous in his honor.

Gold rush and first success

On July 12, 1897, London (age 21) and his sister's husband Captain Shepard sailed to join the Klondike Gold Rush. This was the setting for some of his first successful stories. London's time in the harsh Klondike, however, was detrimental to his health. Like so many other men who were malnourished in the goldfields, London developed scurvy. His gums became swollen, leading to the loss of his four front teeth. A constant gnawing pain affected his hip and leg muscles, and his face was stricken with marks that always reminded him of the struggles he faced in the Klondike. Father William Judge, "The Saint of Dawson", had a facility in Dawson that provided shelter, food and any available medicine to London and others. His struggles there inspired London's short story, "To Build a Fire" (1902, revised in 1908), which many critics assess as his best.

His landlords in Dawson were mining engineers Marshall Latham Bond and Louis Whitford Bond, educated at Yale and Stanford, respectively. The brothers' father, Judge Hiram Bond, was a wealthy mining investor. The Bonds, especially Hiram, were active Republicans. Marshall Bond's diary mentions friendly sparring with London on political issues as a camp pastime.

London left Oakland with a social conscience and socialist leanings; he returned to become an activist for socialism. He concluded that his only hope of escaping the work "trap" was to get an education and "sell his brains". He saw his writing as a business, his ticket out of poverty, and, he hoped, a means of beating the wealthy at their own game. On returning to California in 1898, London began working to get published, a struggle described in his novel, Martin Eden (serialized in 1908, published in 1909). His first published story since high school was "To the Man On Trail", which has frequently been collected in anthologies. When The Overland Monthly offered him only five dollars for it—and was slow paying—London came close to abandoning his writing career. In his words, "literally and literarily I was saved" when The Black Cat accepted his story "A Thousand Deaths", and paid him $40—the "first money I ever received for a story".

London began his writing career just as new printing technologies enabled lower-cost production of magazines. This resulted in a boom in popular magazines aimed at a wide public audience and a strong market for short fiction. In 1900, he made $2,500 in writing, about $77,000 in today's currency. Among the works he sold to magazines was a short story known as either "Diable" (1902) or "Bâtard" (1904), two editions of the same basic story; London received $141.25 for this story on May 27, 1902. In the text, a cruel French Canadian brutalizes his dog, and the dog retaliates and kills the man. London told some of his critics that man's actions are the main cause of the behavior of their animals, and he would show this in another story, The Call of the Wild.

In early 1903, London sold The Call of the Wild to The Saturday Evening Post for $750, and the book rights to Macmillan for $2,000. Macmillan's promotional campaign propelled it to swift success.

While living at his rented villa on Lake Merritt in Oakland, California, London met poet George Sterling; in time they became best friends. In 1902, Sterling helped London find a home closer to his own in nearby Piedmont. In his letters London addressed Sterling as "Greek", owing to Sterling's aquiline nose and classical profile, and he signed them as "Wolf". London was later to depict Sterling as Russ Brissenden in his autobiographical novel Martin Eden (1910) and as Mark Hall in The Valley of the Moon (1913).

In later life London indulged his wide-ranging interests by accumulating a personal library of 15,000 volumes. He referred to his books as "the tools of my trade".

First marriage (1900–04)

London married Elizabeth "Bessie" Maddern on April 7, 1900, the same day The Son of the Wolf was published. Bess had been part of his circle of friends for a number of years. She was related to stage actresses Minnie Maddern Fiske and Emily Stevens. Stasz says, "Both acknowledged publicly that they were not marrying out of love, but from friendship and a belief that they would produce sturdy children." Kingman says, "they were comfortable together... Jack had made it clear to Bessie that he did not love her, but that he liked her enough to make a successful marriage."

London met Bessie through his friend at Oakland High School, Fred Jacobs; she was Fred's fiancée. Bessie, who tutored at Anderson's University Academy in Alameda California, tutored Jack in preparation for his entrance exams for the University of California at Berkeley in 1896. Jacobs was killed aboard the USAT Scandia in 1897, but Jack and Bessie continued their friendship, which included taking photos and developing the film together. This was the beginning of Jack's passion for photography.

During the marriage, London continued his friendship with Anna Strunsky, co-authoring The Kempton-Wace Letters, an epistolary novel contrasting two philosophies of love. Anna, writing "Dane Kempton's" letters, arguing for a romantic view of marriage, while London, writing "Herbert Wace's" letters, argued for a scientific view, based on Darwinism and eugenics. In the novel, his fictional character contrasted two women he had known.

London's pet name for Bess was "Mother-Girl" and Bess's for London was "Daddy-Boy". Their first child, Joan, was born on January 15, 1901, and their second, Bessie (later called Becky), on October 20, 1902. Both children were born in Piedmont, California. Here London wrote one of his most celebrated works, The Call of the Wild.

While London had pride in his children, the marriage was strained. Kingman says that by 1903 the couple were close to separation as they were "extremely incompatible". "Jack was still so kind and gentle with Bessie that when Cloudsley Johns was a house guest in February 1903 he didn't suspect a breakup of their marriage."

London reportedly complained to friends Joseph Noel and George Sterling:

> [Bessie] is devoted to purity. When I tell her morality is only evidence of low blood pressure, she hates me. She'd sell me and the children out for her damned purity. It's terrible. Every time I come back after being away from home for a night she won't let me be in the same room with her if she can help it.

Stasz writes that these were "code words for fear that was consorting with prostitutes and might bring home venereal disease."

On July 24, 1903, London told Bessie he was leaving and moved out. During 1904, London and Bess negotiated the terms of a divorce, and the decree was granted on November 11, 1904.

War correspondent (1904)

London accepted an assignment of the San Francisco Examiner to cover the Russo-Japanese War in early 1904, arriving in Yokohama on January 25, 1904. He was arrested by Japanese authorities in Shimonoseki, but released through the intervention of American ambassador Lloyd Griscom. After travelling to Korea, he was again arrested by Japanese authorities for straying too close to the border with Manchuria without official permission, and was sent back to Seoul. Released again, London was permitted to travel with the Imperial Japanese Army to the border, and to observe the Battle of the Yalu.

London asked William Randolph Hearst, the owner of the San Francisco Examiner, to be allowed to transfer to the Imperial Russian Army, where he felt that restrictions on his reporting and his movements would be less severe. However, before this could be arranged, he was arrested for a third time in four months, this time for assaulting his Japanese assistants, whom he accused of stealing the fodder for his horse. Released through the personal intervention of President Theodore Roosevelt, London departed the front in June 1904.

Bohemian Club

On August 18, 1904, London went with his close friend, the poet George Sterling, to "Summer High Jinks" at the Bohemian Grove. London was elected to honorary membership in the Bohemian Club and took part in many activities. Other noted members of the Bohemian Club during this time included Ambrose Bierce, Gelett Burgess, Allan Dunn, John Muir, Frank Norris, and Herman George Scheffauer.

Beginning in December 1914, London worked on The Acorn Planter, A California Forest Play, to be performed as one of the annual Grove Plays, but it was never selected. It was described as too difficult to set to music. London published The Acorn Planter in 1916.

Second marriage

After divorcing Maddern, London married Charmian Kittredge in 1905. London had been introduced to Kittredge in 1900 by her aunt Netta Eames, who was an editor at Overland Monthly magazine in San Francisco. The two met prior to his first marriage but became lovers years later after Jack and Bessie London visited Wake Robin, Netta Eames' Sonoma County resort, in 1903. London was injured when he fell from a buggy, and Netta arranged for Charmian to care for him. The two developed a friendship, as Charmian, Netta, her husband Roscoe, and London were politically aligned with socialist causes. At some point the relationship became romantic, and Jack divorced his wife to marry Charmian, who was five years his senior.

Biographer Russ Kingman called Charmian "Jack's soul-mate, always at his side, and a perfect match." Their time together included numerous trips, including a 1907 cruise on the yacht Snark to Hawaii and Australia. Many of London's stories are based on his visits to Hawaii, the last one for 10 months beginning in December 1915.

278

The couple also visited Goldfield, Nevada, in 1907, where they were guests of the Bond brothers, London's Dawson City landlords. The Bond brothers were working in Nevada as mining engineers.

London had contrasted the concepts of the "Mother Girl" and the "Mate Woman" in The Kempton-Wace Letters. His pet name for Bess had been "Mother-Girl;" his pet name for Charmian was "Mate-Woman."Charmian's aunt and foster mother, a disciple of Victoria Woodhull, had raised her without prudishness.Every biographer alludes to Charmian's uninhibited sexuality.

Joseph Noel calls the events from 1903 to 1905 "a domestic drama that would have intrigued the pen of an Ibsen.... London's had comedy relief in it and a sort of easy-going romance." In broad outline, London was restless in his first marriage, sought extramarital sexual affairs, and found, in Charmian Kittredge, not only a sexually active and adventurous partner, but his future life-companion. They attempted to have children; one child died at birth, and another pregnancy ended in a miscarriage.

In 1906, London published in Collier's magazine his eye-witness report of the San Francisco earthquake.

Beauty Ranch (1905–16)

In 1905, London purchased a 1,000 acres (4.0 km2) ranch in Glen Ellen, Sonoma County, California, on the eastern slope of Sonoma Mountain.He wrote: "Next to my wife, the ranch is the dearest thing in the world to me." He desperately wanted the ranch to become a successful business enterprise. Writing, always a commercial enterprise with London, now became even more a means to an end: "I write for no other purpose than to add to the beauty that now belongs to me. I write a book for no other reason than to add three or four hundred acres to my magnificent estate."

Stasz writes that London "had taken fully to heart the vision, expressed in his agrarian fiction, of the land as the closest earthly version of Eden ... he educated himself through the study of agricultural manuals and scientific tomes. He conceived of a system of ranching that today would be praised for its ecological wisdom." He was proud to own the first concrete silo in California, a circular piggery that he designed. He hoped to adapt the wisdom of Asian sustainable agriculture to the United States. He hired both Italian and Chinese stonemasons, whose distinctly different styles are obvious.

The ranch was an economic failure. Sympathetic observers such as Stasz treat his projects as potentially feasible, and ascribe their failure to bad luck or to being ahead of their time. Unsympathetic historians such as Kevin Starr suggest that he was a bad manager, distracted by other concerns and impaired by his alcoholism. Starr notes that London was absent from his ranch about six months a year between 1910 and 1916 and says, "He liked the show of managerial power, but not grinding attention to detail .... London's workers laughed at his efforts to play big-time rancher the operation a rich man's hobby."

London spent $80,000 ($2,280,000 in current value) to build a 15,000-square-foot (1,400 m2) stone mansion called Wolf House on the property. Just as the mansion was nearing completion, two weeks before the Londons planned to move in, it was destroyed by fire.

London's last visit to Hawaii, beginning in December 1915, lasted eight months. He met with Duke Kahanamoku, Prince Jonah Kūhiō Kalaniana'ole, Queen Lili'uokalani and many others, before returning to his ranch in July 1916. He was suffering from kidney failure, but he continued to work.

The ranch (abutting stone remnants of Wolf House) is now a National Historic Landmark and is protected in Jack London State Historic Park.

Animal activism

London witnessed animal cruelty in the training of circus animals, and his subsequent novels Jerry of the Islands and Michael, Brother of Jerry included a foreword entreating the public to become more informed about this practice. In 1918, the Massachusetts Society for the Prevention of Cruelty to Animals and the American Humane Education Society teamed up to create the Jack London Club, which sought to inform the public about cruelty to circus animals and encourage them to protest this establishment. Support from Club members led to a temporary cessation of trained animal acts at Ringling-Barnum and Bailey in 1925.

Death

London died November 22, 1916, in a sleeping porch in a cottage on his ranch. London had been a robust man but had suffered several serious illnesses, including scurvy in the Klondike. Additionally, during travels on the Snark, he and Charmian picked up unspecified tropical infections, and diseases, including yaws. At the time of his death, he suffered from dysentery, late-stage alcoholism, and uremia; he was in extreme pain and taking morphine.

London's ashes were buried on his property not far from the Wolf House. London's funeral took place on November 26, 1916, attended only by close friends, relatives, and workers of the property. In accordance with his wishes, he was cremated and buried next to some pioneer children, under a rock that belonged to the Wolf House. After Charmian's death in 1955, she was also cremated and then buried with her husband in the same spot that her husband chose. The grave is marked by a mossy boulder. The buildings and property were later preserved as Jack London State Historic Park, in Glen Ellen, California.

Suicide debate

Because he was using morphine, many older sources describe London's death as a suicide, and some still do. This conjecture appears to be a rumor, or speculation based on incidents in his fiction writings. His death certificate gives the cause as uremia, following acute renal colic.

The biographer Stasz writes, "Following London's death, for a number of reasons, a biographical myth developed in which he has been portrayed as an alcoholic womanizer who committed suicide. Recent scholarship based upon firsthand documents challenges this caricature." Most biographers, including Russ Kingman, now agree he died of uremia aggravated by an accidental morphine overdose.

London's fiction featured several suicides. In his autobiographical memoir John Barleycorn, he claims, as a youth, to have drunkenly stumbled overboard into the San Francisco Bay, "some maundering fancy of going out with the tide suddenly obsessed me". He said he drifted and nearly succeeded in drowning before sobering up and being rescued by fishermen. In the dénouement of The Little Lady of the Big House, the heroine, confronted by the pain of a mortal gunshot wound, undergoes a physician-assisted suicide by morphine. Also, in Martin Eden, the principal protagonist, who shares certain characteristics with London, drowns himself.

Plagiarism accusations

London was vulnerable to accusations of plagiarism, both because he was such a conspicuous, prolific, and successful writer and because of his methods of working. He wrote in a letter to Elwyn Hoffman, "expression, you see—with me—is far easier than invention." He purchased plots and novels from the young Sinclair Lewis and used incidents from newspaper clippings as writing material.

In July 1901, two pieces of fiction appeared within the same month: London's "Moon-Face", in the San Francisco Argonaut, and Frank Norris' "The Passing of Cock-eye Blacklock", in Century Magazine. Newspapers showed the similarities between the stories, which London said were "quite different in manner of treatment, patently the same in foundation and motive." London explained both writers based their stories on the same newspaper account. A year later, it was discovered that Charles Forrest McLean had published a fictional story also based on the same incident.

Egerton Ryerson Young claimed The Call of the Wild (1903) was taken from Young's book My Dogs in the Northland (1902). London acknowledged using it as a source and claimed to have written a letter to Young thanking him.

In 1906, the New York World published "deadly parallel" columns showing eighteen passages from London's short story "Love of Life" side by side with similar passages from a nonfiction article by Augustus Biddle and J. K. Macdonald, titled "Lost in the Land of the Midnight Sun". London noted the World did not accuse him of "plagiarism", but only of "identity of time and situation", to which he defiantly "pled guilty".

The most serious charge of plagiarism was based on London's "The Bishop's Vision", Chapter 7 of his novel The Iron Heel (1908). The chapter is nearly identical to an ironic essay that Frank Harris published in 1901, titled "The Bishop of London and Public Morality". Harris was incensed and suggested he should receive 1/60th of the royalties from The Iron Heel, the disputed material constituting about that fraction of the whole novel. London insisted he had clipped a reprint of the article, which had appeared in an American newspaper, and believed it to be a genuine speech delivered by the Bishop of London.

Views

Atheism

London was an atheist. He is quoted as saying, "I believe that when I am dead, I am dead. I believe that with my death I am just as much obliterated as the last mosquito you and I squashed."

Socialism

London wrote from a socialist viewpoint, which is evident in his novel The Iron Heel. Neither a theorist nor an intellectual socialist, London's socialism grew out of his life experience. As London explained in his essay, "How I Became a Socialist", his views were influenced by his experience with people at the bottom of the social pit. His optimism and individualism faded, and he vowed never to do more hard physical work than necessary. He wrote that his individualism was hammered out of him, and he was politically reborn. He often closed his letters "Yours for the Revolution."

London joined the Socialist Labor Party in April 1896. In the same year, the San Francisco Chronicle published a story about the twenty-year-old London's giving nightly speeches in Oakland's City Hall Park, an activity he was arrested for a year later. In 1901, he left the Socialist Labor Party and joined the new Socialist Party of America. He ran unsuccessfully as the high-profile Socialist candidate for mayor of Oakland in 1901 (receiving 245 votes) and 1905 (improving to 981 votes), toured the country lecturing on socialism in 1906, and published two collections of essays about socialism: The War of the Classes (1905) and Revolution, and other Essays (1906).

Stasz notes that "London regarded the Wobblies as a welcome addition to the Socialist cause, although he never joined them in going so far as to recommend sabotage." Stasz mentions a personal meeting between London and Big Bill Haywood in 1912.

In his late (1913) book The Cruise of the Snark, London writes about appeals to him for membership of the Snark's crew from office workers and other "toilers" who longed for escape from the cities, and of being cheated by workmen.

In his Glen Ellen ranch years, London felt some ambivalence toward socialism and complained about the "inefficient Italian labourers" in his employ. In 1916, he resigned from the Glen Ellen chapter of the Socialist Party, but stated emphatically he did so "because of its lack of fire and fight, and its loss of emphasis on the class struggle." In an unflattering portrait of London's ranch days, California cultural historian Kevin Starr refers to this period as "post-socialist" and says "... by 1911 ... London was more bored by the class struggle than he cared to admit."

Race

London shared common concerns among many European Americans in California about Asian immigration, described as "the yellow peril"; he used the latter term as the title of a 1904 essay. This theme was also the subject of a story he wrote in 1910 called "The Unparalleled Invasion". Presented as an historical essay set in the future, the story narrates events between 1976 and 1987, in which China, with an ever-increasing population, is taking over and colonizing its neighbors with the intention of taking over the entire Earth. The western nations respond with biological warfare and bombard China with dozens of the most infectious diseases. On his fears about China, he admits, "it must be taken into consideration that the above postulate is itself a product of Western race-egotism, urged by our belief in our own righteousness and fostered by a faith in ourselves which may be as erroneous as are most fond race fancies."

By contrast, many of London's short stories are notable for their empathetic portrayal of Mexican ("The Mexican"), Asian ("The Chinago"), and Hawaiian ("Koolau the Leper") characters. London's war correspondence from the Russo-Japanese War, as well as his unfinished novel Cherry, show he admired much about Japanese customs and capabilities. London's writings have been popular among the Japanese, who believe he portrayed them positively.

In "Koolau the Leper", London describes Koolau, who is a Hawaiian leper—and thus a very different sort of "superman" than Martin Eden—and who fights off an entire cavalry troop to elude capture, as "indomitable spiritually—a ... magnificent rebel". This character is based on Hawaiian leper Kaluaikoolau, who in 1893 revolted and resisted capture from forces of the Provisional Government of Hawaii in the Kalalau Valley.

An amateur boxer and avid boxing fan, London reported on the 1910 Johnson–Jeffries fight, in which the black boxer Jack Johnson vanquished Jim Jeffries, known as the "Great White Hope". In 1908, London had reported on an earlier fight of Johnson's, contrasting the black boxer's coolness and intellectual style, with the apelike appearance and fighting style of his Canadian opponent, Tommy Burns:

> [What won] on Saturday was bigness, coolness, quickness, cleverness, and vast physical superiority ... Because a white man wishes a white man to win, this should not prevent him from giving absolute credit to the best man, even when that best man was black. All hail to Johnson. ... superb. He was impregnable ... as inaccessible as Mont Blanc.

Those who defend London against charges of racism cite the letter he wrote to the Japanese-American Commercial Weekly in 1913:

> In reply to yours of August 16, 1913. First of all, I should say by stopping the stupid newspaper from always fomenting race prejudice. This of course, being impossible, I would say, next, by educating the people of Japan so that they will be too intelligently tolerant to respond to any call to race prejudice. And, finally, by realizing, in industry and

government, of socialism—which last word is merely a word that stands for the actual application of in the affairs of men of the theory of the Brotherhood of Man.

In the meantime the nations and races are only unruly boys who have not yet grown to the stature of men. So we must expect them to do unruly and boisterous things at times. And, just as boys grow up, so the races of mankind will grow up and laugh when they look back upon their childish quarrels.

In 1996, after the City of Whitehorse, Yukon, renamed a street in honor of London, protests over London's alleged racism forced the city to change the name of "Jack London Boulevard"[failed verification] back to "Two-mile Hill".

Eugenics

London supported eugenics, including forced sterilization of criminals or those deemed feeble minded. His novel Before Adam(1906–07) has been described as having pro-eugenic themes.

London wrote to Frederick H. Robinson of the periodical Medical Review of Reviews, stating, "I believe the future belongs to eugenics, and will be determined by the practice of eugenics."

Works

Short stories

Western writer and historian Dale L. Walker writes:

London's true métier was the short story ... London's true genius lay in the short form, 7,500 words and under, where the flood of images in his teeming brain and the innate power of his narrative gift were at once constrained and freed. His stories that run longer than the magic 7,500 generally—but certainly not always—could have benefited from self-editing.

London's "strength of utterance" is at its height in his stories, and they are painstakingly well-constructed. "To Build a Fire" is the best known of all his stories. Set in the harsh Klondike, it recounts the haphazard trek of a new arrival who has ignored an old-timer's warning about the risks of traveling alone. Falling through the ice into a creek in seventy-five-below weather, the unnamed man is keenly aware that survival depends on his untested skills at quickly building a fire to dry his clothes and warm his extremities. After publishing a tame version of this story—with a sunny outcome—in The Youth's Companion in 1902, London offered a second, more severe take on the man's predicament in The Century Magazine in 1908. Reading both provides an illustration of London's growth and maturation as a writer. As Labor (1994) observes: "To compare the two versions is itself an instructive lesson in what distinguished a great work of literary art from a good children's story."

Other stories from the Klondike period include: "All Gold Canyon", about a battle between a gold prospector and a claim jumper; "The Law of Life", about an aging American Indian man abandoned by his tribe and left to die; "Love of Life", about a trek by a prospector across the Canadian tundra; "To the Man on Trail," which tells the story of a prospector fleeing the Mounted Police in a sled race, and raises the question of the contrast between written law and morality; and "An Odyssey of the North," which raises questions of conditional morality, and paints a sympathetic portrait of a man of mixed White and Aleut ancestry.

London was a boxing fan and an avid amateur boxer. "A Piece of Steak" is a tale about a match between older and younger boxers. It contrasts the differing experiences of youth and age but also raises the social question of the treatment of aging workers. "The Mexican" combines boxing with a social theme, as a young Mexican endures an unfair fight and ethnic prejudice to earn money with which to aid the revolution.

Several of London's stories would today be classified as science fiction. "The Unparalleled Invasion" describes germ warfare against China; "Goliath" is about an irresistible energy weapon; "The Shadow and the Flash" is a tale about two brothers who take different routes to achieving invisibility; "A

Relic of the Pliocene" is a tall tale about an encounter of a modern-day man with a mammoth. "The Red One" is a late story from a period when London was intrigued by the theories of the psychiatrist and writer Jung. It tells of an island tribe held in thrall by an extraterrestrial object.

Some nineteen original collections of short stories were published during London's brief life or shortly after his death. There have been several posthumous anthologies drawn from this pool of stories. Many of these stories were located in the Klondike and the Pacific. A collection of Jack London's San Francisco Stories was published in October 2010 by Sydney Samizdat Press.

Novels

London's most famous novels are The Call of the Wild, White Fang, The Sea-Wolf, The Iron Heel, and Martin Eden.

In a letter dated December 27, 1901, London's Macmillan publisher George Platt Brett, Sr., said "he believed Jack's fiction represented 'the very best kind of work' done in America."

Critic Maxwell Geismar called The Call of the Wild "a beautiful prose poem"; editor Franklin Walker said that it "belongs on a shelf with Walden and Huckleberry Finn"; and novelist E.L. Doctorow called it "a mordant parable ... his masterpiece."

The historian Dale L. Walker commented:

> Jack London was an uncomfortable novelist, that form too long for his natural impatience and the quickness of his mind. His novels, even the best of them, are hugely flawed.

Some critics have said that his novels are episodic and resemble linked short stories. Dale L. Walker writes:

> The Star Rover, that magnificent experiment, is actually a series of short stories connected by a unifying device ... Smoke Bellew is a series of stories bound together in a novel-like form by their reappearing

protagonist, Kit Bellew; and John Barleycorn ... is a synoptic series of short episodes.

Ambrose Bierce said of The Sea-Wolf that "the great thing—and it is among the greatest of things—is that tremendous creation, Wolf Larsen ... the hewing out and setting up of such a figure is enough for a man to do in one lifetime. "However, he noted, "The love element, with its absurd suppressions, and impossible proprieties, is awful."

The Iron Heel is an example of a dystopian novel that anticipates and influenced George Orwell's Nineteen Eighty-Four. London's socialist politics are explicitly on display here. The Iron Heel meets the contemporary definition of soft science fiction. The Star Rover (1915) is also science fiction.

Apocrypha

Jack London Credo

London's literary executor, Irving Shepard, quoted a Jack London Credo in an introduction to a 1956 collection of London stories:

> I would rather be ashes than dust!
>
> I would rather that my spark should burn out in a brilliant blaze than it should be stifled by dry-rot.
>
> I would rather be a superb meteor, every atom of me in magnificent glow, than a sleepy and permanent planet.
>
> The function of man is to live, not to exist.
>
> I shall not waste my days in trying to prolong them.
>
> I shall use my time.

The biographer Stasz notes that the passage "has many marks of London's style" but the only line that could be safely attributed to London was the first. The words Shepard quoted were from a story in the San Francisco Bulletin, December 2, 1916, by journalist Ernest J. Hopkins, who visited the ranch just weeks before London's death. Stasz notes, "Even more so than today journalists' quotes were unreliable or even sheer inventions," and says no direct source in London's writings has been found. However, at least one line, according to Stasz, is authentic, being referenced by London and written in his own hand in the autograph book of Australian suffragette Vida Goldstein:

Dear Miss Goldstein:–

Seven years ago I wrote you that I'd rather be ashes than dust. I still subscribe to that sentiment.

Sincerely yours,

Jack London

Jan. 13, 1909

In his short story "By The Turtles of Tasman", a character, defending her "ne'er-do-well grasshopperish father" to her "antlike uncle", says: "... my father has been a king. He has lived .... Have you lived merely to live? Are you afraid to die? I'd rather sing one wild song and burst my heart with it, than live a thousand years watching my digestion and being afraid of the wet. When you are dust, my father will be ashes."

"The Scab"

A short diatribe on "The Scab" is often quoted within the U.S. labor movement and frequently attributed to London. It opens:

After God had finished the rattlesnake, the toad, and the vampire, he had some awful substance left with which he made a scab. A scab is a two-legged animal with a corkscrew soul, a water brain, a combination backbone of jelly and glue. Where others have hearts, he carries a tumor of rotten principles. When a scab comes down the street, men turn their backs and Angels weep in Heaven, and the Devil shuts the gates of hell to keep him out....

In 1913 and 1914, a number of newspapers printed the first three sentences with varying terms used instead of "scab", such as "knocker","stool pigeon"or "scandal monger"

This passage as given above was the subject of a 1974 Supreme Court case, Letter Carriers v. Austin, in which Justice Thurgood Marshall referred to it as "a well-known piece of trade union literature, generally attributed to author Jack London". A union newsletter had published a "list of scabs," which was granted to be factual and therefore not libelous, but then went on to quote the passage as the "definition of a scab". The case turned on the question of whether the "definition" was defamatory. The court ruled that "Jack London's... 'definition of a scab' is merely rhetorical hyperbole, a lusty and imaginative expression of the contempt felt by union members towards those who refuse to join", and as such was not libelous and was protected under the First Amendment.

Despite being frequently attributed to London, the passage does not appear at all in the extensive collection of his writings at Sonoma State University's website. However, in his book The War of the Classes he published a 1903 speech entitled "The Scab", which gave a much more balanced view of the topic:

> The laborer who gives more time or strength or skill for the same wage than another, or equal time or strength or skill for a less wage, is a scab. The generousness on his part is hurtful to his fellow-laborers, for it compels them to an equal generousness which is not to their liking, and which gives them less of food and shelter. But a word may be said for the scab. Just as his act makes his rivals compulsorily generous, so do they, by fortune of birth and training, make compulsory his act of generousness.
>
> [...]
>
> Nobody desires to scab, to give most for least. The ambition of every individual is quite the opposite, to give least for most; and, as a result, living in a tooth-and-nail society, battle royal is waged by the ambitious individuals. But in its most salient aspect, that of the struggle over the division of the joint product, it is no longer a battle between individuals, but between groups of individuals. Capital and labor apply

themselves to raw material, make something useful out of it, add to its value, and then proceed to quarrel over the division of the added value. Neither cares to give most for least. Each is intent on giving less than the other and on receiving more.

Legacy and honors

Mount London, also known as Boundary Peak 100, on the Alaska-British Columbia boundary, in the Boundary Ranges of the Coast Mountains of British Columbia, is named for him.

Jack London Square on the waterfront of Oakland, California was named for him.

He was honored by the United States Postal Service with a 25¢ Great Americans series postage stamp released on January 11, 1986.

Jack London Lake (Russian), a mountain lake located in the upper reaches of the Kolyma River in Yagodninsky district of Magadan Oblast.

Fictional portrayals of London include Michael O'Shea in the 1943 film Jack London, Jeff East in the 1980 film Klondike Fever, Aaron Ashmore in the Murdoch Mysteries episode "Murdoch of the Klondike" from 2012, and Johnny Simmons in the 2014 miniseries Klondike. (Source: Wikipedia)

NOTABLE WORKS

NOVELS

The Cruise of the Dazzler (1902)

A Daughter of the Snows (1902)

The Call of the Wild (1903)

The Kempton-Wace Letters (1903) (published anonymously, co-authored with Anna Strunsky)

The Sea-Wolf (1904)

The Game (1905)

White Fang (1906)

Before Adam (1907)

The Iron Heel (1908)

Martin Eden (1909)

Burning Daylight (1910)

Adventure (1911)

The Scarlet Plague (1912)

A Son of the Sun (1912)

The Abysmal Brute (1913)

The Valley of the Moon (1913)

The Mutiny of the Elsinore (1914)

The Star Rover (1915) (published in England as The Jacket)

The Little Lady of the Big House (1916)

Jerry of the Islands (1917)

Michael, Brother of Jerry (1917)

Hearts of Three (1920) (novelization of a script by Charles Goddard)

The Assassination Bureau, Ltd (1963) (left half-finished, completed by Robert L. Fish)

SHORT STORIES

"An Old Soldier's Story" (1894)

"Who Believes in Ghosts!" (1895)

"And 'FRISCO Kid Came Back" (1895)

"Night's Swim In Yeddo Bay" (1895)

"One More Unfortunate" (1895)

"Sakaicho, Hona Asi And Hakadaki" (1895)

"A Klondike Christmas" (1897)

"Mahatma's Little Joke" (1897)

"O Haru" (1897)

"Plague Ship" (1897)

"The Strange Experience Of A Misogynist" (1897)

"Two Gold Bricks" (1897)

"The Devil's Dice Box" (1898)

"A Dream Image" (1898)

"The Test: A Clondyke Wooing" (1898)

"To the Man on Trail" (1898)

"In a Far Country" (1899)

"The King of Mazy May" (1899)

"The End Of The Chapter" (1899)

"The Grilling Of Loren Ellery" (1899)

"The Handsome Cabin Boy" (1899)

"In The Time Of Prince Charley" (1899)

"Old Baldy" (1899)

"The Men of Forty Mile" (1899)

"Pluck and Pertinacity" (1899)

"The Rejuvenation of Major Rathbone" (1899)

"The White Silence" (1899)

"A Thousand Deaths" (1899)

"Wisdom of the Trail" (1899)

"An Odyssey of the North" (1900)

"The Son of the Wolf" (1900)

"Even unto Death" (1900)

"The Man with the Gash" (1900)

"A Lesson in Heraldry" (1900)

"A Northland Miracle" (1900)

"Proper "GIRLIE"" (1900)

"Thanksgiving on Slav Creek" (1900)

"Their Alcove" (1900)

"Housekeeping in the Klondike" (1900)

"Dutch Courage" (1900)

"Where the Trail Forks" (1900)

"Hyperborean Brew" (1901)

"A Relic of the Pliocene" (1901)

"The Lost Poacher" (1901)

"The God of His Fathers" (1901)

""FRISCO Kid's" Story" (1901)

"The Law of Life" (1901)

"The Minions of Midas" (1901)

"In the Forests of the North" (1902)

"The "Fuzziness" of Hoockla-Heen" (1902)

"The Story of Keesh" (1902)

"Keesh, Son of Keesh" (1902)

"Nam-Bok, the Unveracious" (1902)

"Li Wan the Fair" (1902)

"Lost Face"

"Master of Mystery" (1902)

"The Sunlanders" (1902)

"The Death of Ligoun" (1902)

"Moon-Face" (1902)

"Diable—A Dog" (1902), renamed Bâtard in 1904

"To Build a Fire" (1902, revised 1908)

"The League of the Old Men" (1902)

"The Dominant Primordial Beast" (1903)

"The One Thousand Dozen" (1903)

"The Marriage of Lit-lit" (1903)

"The Shadow and the Flash" (1903)

"The Leopard Man's Story" (1903)

"Negore the Coward" (1904)

"All Gold Cañon" (1905)

"Love of Life" (1905)

"The Sun-Dog Trail" (1905)

"The Apostate" (1906)

"Up the Slide" (1906)

"Planchette" (1906)

"Brown Wolf" (1906)

"Make Westing" (1907)

"Chased by the Trail" (1907)

"Trust" (1908)

"A Curious Fragment" (1908)

"Aloha Oe" (1908)

"That Spot" (1908)

"The Enemy of All the World" (1908)

"The House of Mapuhi" (1909)

"Good-by, Jack" (1909)

"Samuel" (1909)

"South of the Slot" (1909)

"The Chinago" (1909)

"The Dream of Debs" (1909)

"The Madness of John Harned" (1909)

"The Seed of McCoy" (1909)

"A Piece of Steak" (1909)

"Mauki" (1909)

"The Whale Tooth" (1909)

"Goliath" (1910)

"The Unparalleled Invasion" (1910)

"Told in the Drooling Ward" (1910)

"When the World was Young" (1910)

"The Terrible Solomons" (1910)

"The Inevitable White Man" (1910)

"The Heathen" (1910)

"Yah! Yah! Yah!" (1910)

"By the Turtles of Tasman" (1911)

"The Mexican" (1911)

"War" (1911)

"The Unmasking of the Cad" (1911)

"The Scarlet Plague" (1912)

"The Captain of the Susan Drew" (1912)

"The Sea-Farmer" (1912)

"The Feathers of the Sun" (1912)

"The Prodigal Father" (1912)

"Samuel" (1913)

"The Sea-Gangsters" (1913)

"The Strength of the Strong" (1914)

"Told in the Drooling Ward" (1914)

"The Hussy" (1916)

"Like Argus of the Ancient Times" (1917)

"Jerry of the Islands" (1917)

"The Red One" (1918)

"Shin-Bones" (1918)

"The Bones of Kahekili" (1919)

SHORT STORY COLLECTIONS

Son of the Wolf (1900)

Chris Farrington, Able Seaman (1901)

The God of His Fathers & Other Stories (1901)

Children of the Frost (1902)

The Faith of Men and Other Stories (1904)

Tales of the Fish Patrol (1906)

Moon-Face and Other Stories (1906)

Love of Life and Other Stories (1907)

Lost Face (1910)

South Sea Tales (1911)

When God Laughs and Other Stories (1911)

The House of Pride & Other Tales of Hawaii (1912)

Smoke Bellew (1912)

A Son of the Sun (1912)

The Night Born (1913)

The Strength of the Strong (1914)

The Turtles of Tasman (1916)

The Human Drift (1917)

The Red One (1918)

On the Makaloa Mat (1919)

Dutch Courage and Other Stories (1922)

AUTOBIOGRAPHICAL MEMOIRS

The Road (1907)

The Cruise of the Snark (1911)

John Barleycorn (1913)

NON-FICTION AND ESSAYS

Through the Rapids on the Way to the Klondike (1899)

From Dawson to the Sea (1899)

What Communities Lose by the Competitive System (1900)

The Impossibility of War (1900)

Phenomena of Literary Evolution (1900)

A Letter to Houghton Mifflin Co. (1900)

Husky, Wolf Dog of the North (1900)

Editorial Crimes — A Protest (1901)

Again the Literary Aspirant (1902)

The People of the Abyss (1903)

How I Became a Socialist (1903)

The War of the Classes (1905)

The Story of an Eyewitness (1906)

A Letter to Woman's Home Companion (1906)

Revolution, and other Essays (1910)

Mexico's Army and Ours (1914)

Lawgivers (1914)

Our Adventures in Tampico (1914)

Stalking the Pestilence (1914)

The Red Game of War (1914)

The Trouble Makers of Mexico (1914)

With Funston's Men (1914)

POETRY

Of Man of the Future (1915)

Oh You Everybody's Girl (19)

On the Face of the Earth You are the One (1915)

Rainbows End (1914)

Republican Rallying Song (1916)

Sonnet (1901)

The Gift of God (1905)

The Klondyker's Dream (1914)

The Lover's Liturgy (1913)

The Mammon Worshippers (1911)

The Republican Battle-Hymn (1905)

The Return of Ulysses (1915)

The Sea Sprite and the Shooting Star (1916)

The Socialist's Dream (1912)

The Song of the Flames (1903)

The Way of War (1906)

The Worker and the Tramp (1911)

Tick! Tick! Tick! (1915)

Too Late (1912)

Weasel Thieves (1913)

When All the World Shouted my Name (1905)

Where the Rainbow Fell (1902)

Your Kiss (1914)

PLAYS

Theft (1910)

Daughters of the Rich: A One Act Play (1915)

The Acorn Planter: A California Forest Play (1916)